Praise for Sarah McCarty

"McCarty is a sparse, minimalistic writer, with a great ear for dialogue. She's a passionate observer of history, and manages to deftly and accurately weave her spicy stories through with important facts and issues of the epoch she invokes. She's also good at capturing that intangible magnetism surrounding dangerous, rugged men...I'm hooked."

—*USATODAY.com*

"If you like your historicals packed with emotion, excitement and heat, you can never go wrong with a book by Sarah McCarty."

—*Romance Junkies*

"It's so great to see that Ms. McCarty is able to truly take these eight men and give them such vastly different stories and vastly different heroines, all of whom allow us to see different aspects of what life was really like for Western Frontier women, be it good, horrific, or simply unfortunate."

—*Romance Books Forum*

"Sarah McCarty's series is an exciting blend of raw masculinity, spunky, feisty heroines and the wild living in the Old West...with spicy, hot love scenes. Ms. McCarty gave us small peeks into each member of the Hell's Eight and I'm looking forward to reading the other men's stories."

—*Erotica Romance Writers*

"What really sets McCarty's stories apart from simple erotica is the complexity of her characters and conflicts... definitely spicy, but a great love story, too."

—*RT Book Reviews*

"Readers who enjoy erotic romance but haven't found an author who can combine it with a historical setting may discover a new auto-buy author...I have."

—*All About Romance*

...ry's men of Hell's Eight

**Read more about the daring heroes of Hell's Eight
in these titles**

SARAH McCARTY

Ace's Wild

HQN™

ISBN-13: 978-0-373-77830-0

Ace's Wild

Recycling programs
for this product may
not exist in your area.

Copyright © 2015 by Sarah McCarty

This edition published by arrangement with Harlequin Books S.A.

For questions and comments about the quality of this book,
please contact us at CustomerService@Harlequin.com.

® and TM are trademarks of Harlequin Enterprises Limited or its
corporate affiliates. Trademarks indicated with ® are registered in the
United States Patent and Trademark Office, the Canadian Intellectual
Property Office and in other countries.

www.HQNBooks.com

Printed in U.S.A.

For Mark. A man who I trust to lead me in the darkness, to hold me in the light, and who never makes me regret taking that leap of faith into his arms. May you all be blessed to find someone just like him.

CHAPTER ONE

Simple, Texas
November, 1860

SHE WAS GOING to hell, for sure. Petunia Wayfield stepped off the rough board walkway into the dirt street, barely missing a pile of excrement left by some animal. Dust rose in a puff around her skirts. It'd been a long spell since the last rain. If this drought kept up another month, Christmas was going to be a dusty affair. Shielding her eyes against the late-morning sun, Petunia chided her morals. Here she was, fresh out of a sermon on the seven deadly sins, and she was about to commit two of the worst: the sins of gluttony and—she paused before stepping back up onto the opposite walk—lust. And she blamed it all on Maddie Miller's cinnamon rolls. Because if Petunia had never smelled the delicious aroma of those baked goods wafting out from beneath the pink-and-white awning that decorated the front of Maddie's bakery, she never would have stepped through the door the very moment that Ace Parker had stepped out. Would never have smashed her face into his chest; would never have associated the temptation of cinnamon rolls with the scent of hot, masculine man. At least that's what she told herself. Because it was what any rational, practical woman would tell herself. Even if it was a lie.

With a sigh, Petunia continued on toward the bakery. It wasn't like she needed that cinnamon roll. At almost thirty, she didn't need the soft, warm, delicious, yeasty bun filled with fragrant cinnamon and topped with a melted sugar glaze to add to her womanly shape, but she wanted it. She also didn't need a six-foot-plus tall, broad-shouldered, lean-hipped, no-better-than-he-needed-to-be-maybe-worse-than-some, smart-mouthed gambler like Ace. But, she admitted resignedly as she opened the bakery door and the little bell jingled announcing her presence, Petunia wanted him, too. With the same shameless, mouthwatering, crave-it-no-matter-what lust that had her slipping out on a sermon early to satiate her need for decadence.

On some level Petunia had always felt that she was just one reckless decision from slipping into dissolution. Which was a sad thing for the only daughter of the pillar of Benton, Massachusetts, society to be admitting. Her father liked to blame her wayward tendencies on the flaw in his upbringing after her mother's early demise. She preferred to call those tendencies *progressive thinking*. It was a point they'd never agreed upon and which had sent her West on her own without her father's financial support. And the expected outcome of that venture was yet another bone of contention. He expected her to fail at establishing her business in California while she expected to succeed. She just needed her luck back.

She swore she'd never had such a run of bad luck as she'd had since leaving Benton. First, the stagecoach had broken down in Simple. Which wouldn't have been so bad except the one-night stay at that supposed boardinghouse on the edge of town had resulted in her being robbed of all her money except the few coins she'd sewn into her petticoat… Only the love life of the local school-marm had saved her from ruin, or worse yet, having to send a letter home to her father asking for help. That was an absolute last resort. Petunia Wayfield was not a woman that failed.

The aroma of sweet dough and cinnamon surrounded her in a blissful hug as she pushed the door closed. Petunia closed her eyes and breathed deeply, drawing the comfort in. This was what she needed, the occasional sensual indulgence, not an ongoing challenge like Ace Parker.

Liar, the little voice inside whispered.

She took another breath, fighting the truth. For the first time in her life, she actually wanted, genuinely wanted, a man. But it couldn't be some nice steady man of business. Oh, no. True to the contrariness of a nature her father bemoaned as misplaced in a woman, she had to lust after a man who was completely wrong for her. A man whose way of life mocked her beliefs. A man for whom, if she did succumb, she'd be nothing more than a toy. Everything inside rejected the notion. She was no man's toy. She was a modern woman, an independent woman, a woman who intended to have the vote one day. She was not any man's plaything.

"It does my baker's heart good to see you step through that door and take in that first breath like you've just found heaven." Maddie Miller interrupted her thoughts with her usual sweet cheerfulness.

Petunia opened her eyes and smiled at Maddie standing behind the counter, a big white apron covering her green dress, flour dusting her freckled cheek and stray curls of red hair escaping her bun. The one thing Petunia prided herself on was not being silly.

"Probably because I just did." A board squeaked as she stepped up to the low counter. Your cinnamon buns are my one weakness, I'm afraid."

Again that whisper of *liar*.

As if she heard the silent rebuke, Maddie paused, a tray of just risen rolls in her hand.

"I don't know why people think weaknesses are bad."

Because only the strong survived. Petunia bit her tongue on the comment.

"If a body is never weak, how would they ever know what they needed?" Maddie asked, swapping the trays and putting the hot, unfrosted rolls on the counter beside a bowl of frosting before closing the oven door.

For that Petunia didn't have an answer. "That's a good point." Darn it.

Maddie just smiled and dropped the cloth she'd been using to carry the hot pan beside it. Resting her hands on her hips she stretched her back and gave Petunia a knowing glance. "Besides, there are some weaknesses that are just plain enjoyable."

And that fast Petunia felt laid open and vulnerable. "Not in my experience."

"Maybe you don't have enough experience."

There was a time when Petunia had thought Maddie a bit, well, simplistic, but soon she'd seen the real woman. The woman who'd started her own business from nothing but scratch and need, a woman who'd won the heart of the notorious Caden Miller. A woman who'd refused her husband until he respected her independence. Looking at the petite redhead on the other side of the counter, Petunia found it hard to believe someone so soft-looking could be so determined, but it was just another reminder of how one shouldn't judge by appearances. Maddie could be a very focused woman. And right now she was uncomfortably focused on Petunia.

"Have you seen Ace this afternoon?" Maddie asked with a nonchalance Petunia couldn't imitate.

"No. Should I have?"

"I heard he had words with Brian Winter at the saloon last night."

Petunia handed Maddie the bowl of frosting. "Why would that concern me?"

Maddie rolled her eyes and took it. "I have no idea. Outside of the fact you're unhappy with Brian and the way he treats his son."

Petunia licked the sweet glaze off her finger. Brian Winter was a brute to the helpless. But Ace Parker was far from helpless. "If Brian was at the saloon, it was to gamble. It only stands to reason any fighting that went on had to do with cards or money or both."

"Uh-huh."

She ignored the skepticism. "Mr. Parker is not the civic-minded sort."

"You like to believe that."

"Because it's true."

Maddie didn't argue the point. "He can't be all bad. He's the region assayer."

"For reasons of his own, I'm sure."

Maddie looked up from the frosting she was stirring. "It's a respectable job."

"He probably won it in a poker game."

The wood spoon thumped against the side of the crockery bowl. Maddie switched the subject. "How was the reverend's sermon this morning? He sounded all riled up, even from over here."

He had been, for sure. "He was enthusiastic and as motivating as ever."

"About what today?"

Petunia smiled slightly. "The sin of turning the other cheek."

"That's a sin?" Maddie asked, pouring glaze over the fresh batch of rolls. Petunia was a bit ahead of the church crowd, but soon the shop would be packed with a line out the door.

"He had a new take on it."

"Oh?"

Petunia felt certain the sermon was aimed at her endeavors to help the children and less fortunate of Simple and the lack of interest of the townsfolk. "It's his opinion that people around here have gotten too used to turning a blind eye, even when they should be paying attention."

Maddie smiled and set the glaze aside. "A theory near and dear to your heart."

Petunia nodded. "You should have attended. He was quite animated."

Maddie's expression closed right up as she started moving the rolls to the display plates. As curious as Maddie always was about the reverend's sermons, as far as Petunia could tell, the woman had never set foot inside the church.

"You should come on in one Sunday."

Maddie became overly busy getting a roll just so on the display plate. After a few seconds she looked up, a not so engaging smile on her face.

"Well, if I did that, who would cook the cinnamon rolls for the congregation when the sermonizing is over?"

She was clearly flustered at the idea of going to church. For the life of her, Petunia didn't know why.

There was no one more kind and considerate than Maddie. It was a mystery, and mysteries were Petunia's downfall. She poked a little more.

"I'm sure the reverend would love to see you at service more than he'd rather see a cinnamon roll."

Maddie shook her head. "I don't know about that. The man is particularly fond of his pastries. Missing one might just throw him off his sermon."

Maddie's resistance just increased Petunia's curiosity. "Wouldn't hurt to try."

The pink gingham curtain behind the counter hissed slightly as it slid open. Caden Miller, Maddie's husband, stepped from behind the cloth barrier and slipped his arm protectively around his wife's waist. There was all the love any woman could want in that embrace, but there was steel in his blue eyes as he looked at Petunia, reminding her he was one of the legendary Hell's Eight. Men known for their bravery and loyalty. Caden, in particular, for his unpredictable nature. The tiny shop suddenly seemed that much smaller.

"There's no purer angel walking this earth than my Maddie, with or without church." Dropping a kiss on the top of Maddie's head, he challenged Petunia to continue her prodding.

Petunia was not a fool. "Good morning, Caden."

A nod of his head acknowledged her greeting. "If you don't believe me," he continued, taking the cinnamon bun out of Maddie's hand, "all you've got to do is taste her baked goods." The little paper napkin beneath wrinkled as he set it on the counter and pushed it toward Petunia.

A lock of hair fell across his forehead. Maddie turned and brushed it back, her fingers lingering on his cheek. Caden's expression softened as he turned his head and

kissed her palm. Petunia felt a pang of envy and more
than a little superfluous. "They are the height of my
Sundays."

Maddie turned to her and smiled in her easy, open
way. "Between you and Caden my head is going to swell
so much, I'll have a hard time getting through the door."

"No problem, Maddie mine." Caden stole a pastry for
himself. "I know where you store the hat pins. If things
need popping I'll be right on it."

Maddie shook her head and laughed. "Thanks."

"It's my husbandly duty to make sure you stay—"
his gaze lowered to Maddie's ample curves "—all in
proportion."

"Caden!"

All Maddie's protest inspired was a chuckle from her
husband and an offer to share his roll. Petunia's blush
faded as Maddie laughed again and took a bite. It was
good to see a man who knew how to be a man and cared
about his wife. And there was one thing everyone knew
about Caden. Caden loved Maddie with everything in
him, which surprisingly seemed to be a whole heck of
a lot. Surprising because if you asked half the town's
populace, they'd tell you stories, all of them designed to
convince you that Caden Miller didn't have a heart. But
he did, and she was plump and sweet with red hair and
green eyes and a talent for baking.

The scent of the cinnamon roll on the counter beck-
oned. There had been a time when Petunia would have
said it was better than any man's arms, but watching
Maddie relax into Caden's embrace, seeing how natural
they were together, Petunia was beginning to have those
doubts that said maybe the course she'd set for herself

and the beliefs she held to so strongly were not *all* that a woman needed.

Petunia passed her money across the counter, took the roll and ignored that pang of envy that she didn't have time for. "Thank you."

She had an important meeting in two days, and she couldn't afford any distractions. There were things in this town that people didn't want to see that she insisted they would. Too many children in her school were neglected, hungry or abused while others were just left out of an education entirely simply because their mothers were forced to work above stairs in the saloon. It was unacceptable. It had to change. Every child deserved to be safe and educated and before she left this town she was determined some changes would be made, no matter how unpopular her determination made her with most, including Caden. The man was a bit overprotective. Maddie's quiet support of her cause did not put her in danger. With a smile she made her excuses. "I'm going to scoot before the reverend gets here and lectures me about slipping out on church early."

Caden grinned. "Are you worried about eternal damnation?"

She reached for the door, her mouth watering, impatience nibbling at her the way she wanted to nibble on the roll. "Not this week."

Maddie chuckled. "You have a nice day, Petunia."

Petunia glanced back, the door half-open, the little bell's jangle just a ting of sound. Caden stood behind Maddie, his arm still around her waist. He looked like hell waiting for a place to land, all squared shoulders and contained aggression. Maddie, on the other hand, looked…at peace. The hand resting on Caden's was re-

laxed. Her fingers stroked across his darker skin. Such
a small gesture, but it had such a profound effect. Caden
visibly relaxed. Petunia smiled. Maddie was a woman
who knew her power and wielded it wisely. Yet she
wouldn't step inside a church she clearly longed to visit.
It made no sense. If Petunia had more time she'd definitely be exploring that wrinkle. But time she didn't have.
As soon as she saved enough for her ticket, she'd be on
her way to starting her own dream.

"Thank you, Maddie. You both have one, too."

The "Will do" came from Caden.

Outside, she stopped and took that long-awaited,
much-anticipated first bite. The pastry melted in her
mouth. She closed her eyes and just appreciated the moment, letting the pleasure roll through her.

"You know, if you wore that exact same expression on
your face at the next dance, you might spend more time
on the floor dancing than on the side talking."

Petunia didn't have to open her eyes to know who
was goading her. Ace Parker. The thorn in her side,
her personal Achilles' heel, Caden and Maddie's best
friend. She'd never understand how two productive people could appreciate a man of such low character. Opening her eyes, she found herself looking straight into the
shadowed intensity of his. A frisson of awareness shot
through her, hooking deep and drawing invisible wires
tight. Damn the man. He even had beautiful eyes. She
wanted to knock the black cowboy hat off his head so she
could see the sky-blue irises flecked with those mesmer-
izing shards of icy gray. Eyes that saw too much. Eyes
that made her want to… To push. Shove. Fight. His mouth
quirked at the corner. She couldn't look away.

They made her want to surrender. Damn him.

It was easy to see how Ace won so many poker games. There was an uncanny calm about the man. A subdued power that drew a person to trust where they probably shouldn't. But she wasn't a wrangler halfway through a bottle of cheap whiskey. She was a strong woman of intellect. Taking a slow breath, she gave him a small smile of her own, keeping it casual as if her breasts weren't tingling and her lungs weren't struggling to remember how to get her next breath.

"Of course a man of your predilections wouldn't understand that it might be my preference to not carry on on the dance floor."

"I understand, as a woman, you might be well on the shelf, but you're not dead. You've got time to turn things around."

He wasn't the first to imply she needed to find a man, marry and devote herself to raising children. Petunia swallowed the bit of cinnamon roll and forced that smile to stay in place. It was hard. Very hard when she wanted nothing more than to touch his cheek, feel that slight stubble against her fingertips. He probably hadn't even been to bed yet. "I'll keep that in mind between my other endeavors."

Ace leaned against the doorjamb, that quirk becoming a grin, but whereas hers felt tight, his looked easy. The aggravating man seemed to find humor in everything, especially in the matters close to her heart.

"Would that be the endeavor that involves taking children from the whorehouse, putting them in your house and trying to make them respectable?"

She tucked her roll into the napkin and straightened. There'd be no enjoying it while he was picking at her. "That would be the one."

"And you think the citizens of this town are going to go along with that? Having those children of lust in their school with their properly raised and primly conceived children?"

It was probably a flaw in her defense that she did enjoy his way with words. "I don't plan on giving them much choice."

He sighed. "You just can't shove reform down people's throats."

"When the alternative is leaving innocents neglected, uneducated and unloved, to grow up to be a bane on our society far into the future, I can force whatever I want."

His left eyebrow crooked up. "You think you've got that much muscle?"

"I think with Christmas coming up, and the spirit of charity that goes with it, I have a good chance of making a start."

"And you're just going to take that inch?"

She nodded. "And stretch it into a mile."

His right eyebrow joined the left. "And you don't expect resentment?"

"Oh, I expect resentment." She was already experiencing some. Her roll was getting cold.

"But you plan on getting past it?"

She nodded again. "I plan on getting past it."

Ace shook his head and straightened, opening the door for Caden, who was bringing chairs out to the porch. "You know, no matter how many good deeds you do, they are never going to elect you mayor."

She gritted her teeth. "The town already has a mayor."

"Which you don't think much of."

He had to be observant to know that.

The mayor was a lazy man, and lazy men tended to

stay the heck out of her way. So she was content with him in that office. "I'm hoping he'll be supportive."

If only by his disinterest.

Maddie spoke up from where she was wiping down the counter. "It *is* a good cause."

Ace looked over at her. "It may be, but going about it this way is just going to make enemies."

"Why?" Petunia stepped back as Caden set the chair in front of the door to hold it open. "Why should helping children make any enemies?"

Caden looked up from where he was bracing the chair. "Because those children have fathers who prefer that they stay hidden."

"If those children have fathers," she snapped, "then those fathers should be taking care of them."

Ace shrugged. "They are, in their way."

"It's better than nothing," Caden offered, folding his arms across his chest.

"Not by much."

Petunia could see the first of the congregation leaving the church. If she didn't get moving, she'd be forced to be civil to people who'd be taking veiled stabs at her. Her plan really wasn't popular. "No living thing should suffer needlessly because others are too lazy or too worried about how it looks to help them. Society is only as strong as its weakest link."

Ace swore. She flinched, even as every nerve ending snapped to attention. His eyes narrowed, and as if on cue her breath caught. Darn it! Why *this* with this man? It was so…inconvenient.

Caden looked between the two of them and just sighed. "You know if you two spent a little less time fighting and a little bit more talking, you'd probably find out you're on the same side of most of your discussions."

She lifted her chin. "I highly doubt I have anything in common with Mr. Parker."

From the tug Ace gave his hat, he wasn't any too pleased with the observation, either. "Yeah. You'd have to shove a broomstick up my ass to get me to be that uptight."

"Ace!" Maddie reprimanded from within the store.

Petunia just raised her brow. Did he think his crudeness would shock her? "We could probably arrange that."

"You and what posse?"

"I imagine we could assemble a few of your disgruntled companions to make it happen."

Ace made a sound. She couldn't tell if he was choking on outrage or laughter. Before she could ask, Caden interrupted.

"Never seen two cats fight as much as you two do. At least not without a hell of a good reason."

Ace was entirely too quick to say, "I've got a reason."

And she was entirely too curious to know what it was. Before she could open her mouth to retort, Maddie came around the counter. "Please. We like you both."

Caden didn't move, but the air suddenly seemed thicker. "What my wife is trying to say, Ace, is that no one cares about your reason. As my wife's friend, Petunia is always a welcome guest in my home." His voice lowered just a fraction. "And always under my protection."

Ace pulled up straight. Shoulders squared as subtle tension entered his stance. His "The hell you say" was low and threatening.

Maddie stopped dead. The catch in Petunia's breathing became permanent. Caden wasn't even ruffled. "You heard me."

If Caden had spoken to her in that tone, Petunia would be running. Ace didn't even bat an eye. Caden waved his hand. Maddie went back behind the counter.

"This is none of your business, Caden."

"So take me to court."

"That's not fair, Caden," Maddie called. "You know Judge Bracen is holding a grudge against Ace."

"Another one of your satisfied customers?" Petunia asked with a lift of her brows.

Ace shrugged. "He's not pleased I didn't declare that fool's gold of his genuine."

"Cost him a pretty penny on that land deal."

"I'm sorry to hear that," Petunia interrupted, wanting this to end before it got more combative. She might not want to like Ace, but she did like Caden and Maddie, and Maddie was sympathetic to her cause. Caden she wasn't so sure of. Out of the corner of her eye she could see the set of Ace's shoulders. Along her nerve endings she felt the weight of his stare, and that breathless trembling started anew. It was definitely time to go.

"Thank you for the cinnamon roll, Maddie." She forced herself to take a nibble. The soft pastry sat like lead in her mouth. Tension skimmed along her nerves. "It's delicious as always." She nodded to Caden. Ace she ignored.

He naturally couldn't let that pass. "Not even going to say goodbye?" he asked as she turned.

Nope. Not a goodbye. Not a glance. Not anything that would feed her weakness. Lifting her skirts with her free hand, she stepped off the walk, ignoring the inner prompting that wanted to know if he watched her, if he was smiling, if there was approval in his eyes. She forced herself to continue toward home and not give him the satisfaction of looking back. It was the hardest thing she'd done in a long, long time.

ACE WATCHED PETUNIA stroll down the street in that purposeful way of hers and shook his head. Seems he'd been watching Petunia since the day she'd stepped off the stage all pale blond elegance and temptation. She wasn't the sort of woman a man like him would approach. Buttoned-up women were notoriously boring in and out of bed, but there was a reckless side to Petunia that no amount of blue serge could conceal. One that, once fed by the fire of conviction, could take her where angels feared to tread. Like right up into Simon Laramie's face when he'd protested her effort to feed his hungry kids. Laramie outweighed her by a hundred pounds, but she'd stood there like size didn't matter and taken him to town. A man had to admire that much gumption. Protect it. Preserve it… Nurture it. Shit. He wanted to punch a wall. He wanted to follow her, pick her up, toss her over his shoulder, swat her on that delicately rounded ass and carry her off to his bed with her gasp still ringing in his ear. He wanted her in his arms. His bed. His home. With a silent curse, Ace cut that line of thinking short. Again.

That was the dangerous side of Petunia Wayfield. She made him want things he'd long ago given up hoping for. A wife. Family. Men like him didn't have those things. But it didn't mean they couldn't protect the one who fed that faintest of hopes. About a month ago, he'd accepted Petunia was that one for him. There was something within her that drew him. Fascinated him. Enthralled him to the point that lately, all he could think about was her lying bound in his bed, that sweet pale flesh wearing his mark, her femininity sweetly displayed. His blood heated even as he ground his teeth. The woman was like a bad case of poison ivy, a constant irritation.

"Why do you tease her so?" Maddie asked when Petunia was out of earshot.

For no reason fit for Sunday discussion. "The woman has too much starch in her bloomers."

"So you irritate her just to get a reaction," Maddie stated, coming up beside him and shaking out her cleaning cloth.

He smiled, watching Petunia step up onto the opposite walk, for a moment catching the hint of ankle beneath her layers of skirt and petticoats. His cock, semihard, threatened to become an embarrassment. He pulled his gaze away. "She does have a short fuse."

"It seems to me the only reason you want to take the starch out of her bloomers," Caden remarked, taking a seat in the chair he'd just settled against the door, "is because you want to be getting in them."

Ace snorted. "The woman's an old maid."

Maddie huffed and put her hands on her hips. The cloth fluttered against her side. "She's intelligent, passionate and she cares about the same things you do. You could do worse."

Petunia couldn't.

"The only reason that woman's ever been in a saloon is to try and shut it down. She probably thinks it's hell on a good day."

Maddie snorted. "You're always rooting for the underdog, just like her."

"Not that anyone notices."

Caden stretched his legs out. "That's because you

don't want them to notice." Ignoring Ace's glare, Caden caught Maddie's hand and pulled her into his side. The ease with which she relaxed into Caden's embrace sent another pang through Ace.

"And why is that?" Maddie asked, shoving the cloth in her apron pocket.

Ace leaned over and tugged her hair, goading Caden with the casual familiarity. "Maybe because I'm not an upstanding pillar of the community."

Caden growled under his breath and knocked his hand away.

Maddie sighed and caught Caden's hand in hers, all the while shaking her head at Ace. "I know you, remember?"

It was Ace's turn to shake his head. The last thing he needed was Maddie speculating on his comings and goings and ways to put an end to them. He liked his life in town. He liked the adventure. He liked the challenge. He liked the occasional fight, and he loved the card games. It alleviated the boredom of working at the assayer's office. The job was a useful tool for sorting out bad news coming to town, but not much else. Once in a while he did stick his nose into business that wasn't strictly his, but unlike Petunia, he didn't make his life's work out of it.

"This town's got enough do-gooders," he told Maddie. "One more isn't needed."

Maddie looked at him calmly. Almost expectantly. "Petunia's going to need help."

"You might as well get that look out of your eye, Maddie. Whatever Petunia's got going, it's not my problem."

"It will be."

He didn't like the knowing glance or the implication behind it. The woman saw too much. "No, it won't."

"I wouldn't be so sure about that," Caden interrupted. "This latest project of hers isn't going to go over well. There are some prominent citizens in this town who'd be mighty upset to see a couple of those children brought forward into polite society."

"Then they shouldn't have created them," Ace retorted.

"I don't think that was the plan."

"It's still the result. Not like you can mistake who their fathers are."

Damn, now he was sounding just like Petunia.

"It would have been better for those children if their mother had just left town with them."

"And leave their meal ticket?" Ace shook his head. "No way in hell. As long as those kids exist, Hester has leverage."

"But they don't exist. They're not allowed out of that awful house," Maddie added. "And that little girl, she's almost eight now…"

Maddie's voice broke. Caden rubbed her arm. The one thing Maddie knew all about was how a little girl growing up in a whorehouse lived on the edge of trouble. It made him burn to think about the life Maddie had been forced to live before coming to Hell's Eight. Petunia was right about one thing. No child deserved that.

Pressing her hand briefly over Caden's, Maddie took a step back, straightened her hair and then her skirt. Ace said nothing, letting her gather her composure, regretting it as soon as she did, because she turned those soulful green eyes on him again and declared, "You need to help Hester."

"I do?"

"Yes."

"Why?"

"Because you're wrong about her."

Ace sighed. It didn't really matter whether he was right or wrong about Hester. When it came to the kids, Petunia and Maddie were right. The situation was getting bad. Hester needed to take those kids and leave town. Or Dougall, their father, was going to have to claim them, but they couldn't be left to be as they were living in the whorehouse. He thought of the little girl, pretty face, pretty hair, but still a little girl and tempting to some. Unprotected except by her mother and a couple of the nicer whores, but their ability to guard her was limited. And if it was decided she needed to earn her keep, then earn her keep she would.

"It's a mess, and Petunia's meddling is going to make it blow up before anything can be done."

"She means well," Caden interjected.

"She always means well." Ace growled as the aggravation swelled within him. "She meant well when she decided every child at school should have a decent lunch."

"She was right," Maddie chimed in. "They should."

"Except that those families that couldn't afford it now live with the mockery of others, and Simon Laramie is gunning for her ass because the whole world now knows that he can't feed his own kids."

"It's not her fault he chose to make a public spectacle of it."

Simon was new to the area, and he wasn't established, and the drought hadn't helped. He wasn't the only one feeling the pinch or the weather. But he was the most vocal about being made a public charity case.

"His pride was on the line."

"His children were hungry," Maddie countered.

"She could have gone about it differently."

"Be fair, Ace," Caden interjected. "You know Laramie is about as stiff-necked an ass as there is. He'd rather see those kids starve to death than admit he needed help."

"Well, that little mess of Petunia's took a bit to clear up." And he'd been the one who'd had to do it. He rubbed the knuckles of his right hand, experiencing again that satisfying moment when it'd connected with Laramie's mouth. Petunia might be a pain in the ass but she wasn't—as Laramie put it—a bitch.

"But now he's your enemy and not hers," Maddie said as if that were the way it should be.

"Oh, he's her enemy, too. Make no mistake about that."

"But he'll have to go through you to get to her."

"Shit, Ace, you might as well call Petunia Hell's Eight and get it over with."

"That will never happen."

The look Caden shot him was almost as pitying as Maddie's. "Uh-huh."

Their knowing expressions were almost as annoying as Petunia's tendency to gather enemies in her wake. The longer Petunia stayed in town, the more her problems were going to become his, because Caden was right, he couldn't leave her to whomever. She might be a pain in the ass, but in an odd way she'd become *his* pain in the ass. That being the case, she needed to get on that stagecoach. For both their sakes.

Down the street at the church, people were beginning to meander free of their socializing. Petunia disappeared into the schoolhouse. "Somebody's got to rein that woman in."

"I vote for you."

It was his turn to say, "Uh-huh."

"It's not like she's going to be around much longer," Maddie argued. "Just as soon as she gets the money for a coach ticket, she's moving on."

"She's been saving for that ticket for a long time," Caden interjected.

Yeah, she had. And she still wasn't gone. Mighty suspicious that. "You *sure* she's planning on moving on?"

Maddie suddenly became all business, straightening her apron and smoothing her hair. "Looks like customers are heading this way. Time to get busy."

The back of Ace's neck tingled. Maddie was not the fussing type. Especially when it came to business. She was up to something. He looked at Caden. Caden shrugged and looked at his wife.

"Out with it, Maddie."

She sighed and dropped the pretense. "It's not that Petunia doesn't plan on leaving—"

Ace got that sinking feeling in his gut. "But?"

Maddie shrugged. "But there were things that she felt needed doing first."

"Things?" Ace asked. "What things?" What the hell had Petunia gotten herself into now?

"You remember Penelope?"

"Clyde Peyton's widow?"

"Yes. She broke her leg."

"Yeah, I remember. Doc set it. Said it healed fine."

"She couldn't work while it was broken."

"And?" There was always an "and" with Petunia.

"She couldn't feed her kids because Michael Orvis wouldn't extend her credit at the mercantile."

Ace sighed. "Don't tell me."

"Petunia used her savings to pay off what she could of the bill, so Mr. Orvis would give Penny more credit."

"So you're saying, she's nowhere near the price of her ticket."

Ace didn't know if he was relieved or annoyed.

"You could just buy it for her," Caden pointed out.

"If I thought I could get her to take it, I would." That was a lie. He had a lust/hate relationship with Petunia's presence in town. More lust than hate. More want than was sensible.

"So what are we going to do?" Maddie asked.

"Why do we have to do anything?" Ace asked. "Can't we just let her suffer the consequences of her actions, for once?"

Maddie looked horrified at the very thought. "She has no idea of the potential repercussions. She's used to Eastern ways." She turned to Caden. "Do something."

"Don't put me in this," Caden said.

Maddie glanced down the street where her Sunday customers were meandering their way. "Please?"

Caden rocked back in the chair as she hurried back into the bakery. The bell above the door jangled a protest. "You heard the little woman."

Ace bit down hard on his back molars, reaching for patience. "I'm tired of cleaning up Petunia's messes. I'm not her father. I'm not her brother. I'm not her husband."

"But you want her," Caden said, putting it right out there.

"There's nothing about the woman to want. She wears her hair scraped back so tight her eyebrows meet her ears. And if her corset were laced any tighter, she'd die of suffocation."

Caden laughed and waved to the folk approaching.

"You ought to be grateful for that. More wind means more words."

"I don't need more words from that woman."

"Yes, you do, just sweeter ones."

"You could dump a bucket of sugar on that woman, and she wouldn't be sweet enough."

Maddie fussed with the tray of buns and called out, "I think the right man could sweeten her up."

"Eavesdropping isn't an attractive trait," Ace snapped at her.

"But a useful one."

Ace shook his head at Caden. "She isn't even ashamed of it."

"Why should she be?" Caden asked with a fond look at his wife. "It gets her what she wants to know."

"You should be setting a better example."

Caden snorted. "Since when have any of us worried about what others thought?"

Since never.

Maddie stopped sorting the rolls and looked straight at him. "In that case, Ace Parker, you could stop saving her and just start courting her."

For the first time in a long time, Ace flinched. "I'm a gambler and a brawler."

"You're a good man with a good heart, but you run too much."

He didn't need Maddie weaving rainbows around the impossible. "Let it go, Maddie."

"Letting it go doesn't change the truth. You want her." She came back to the porch, licking frosting off her fingers. "She wants you. You have many things in common, including a passion for doing the right thing. The only difference between you is she's open about it."

"Gambling is not the right thing."

Maddie huffed. "Gambling bores you."

"The hell it does."

Caden touched Maddie's shoulder. "Let it go, Maddie mine."

She slammed her hands on her hips and jerked her chin at Ace. "So he can continue doing what he doesn't like doing? So he can continue to be unhappy?"

"A man's got a right to be unhappy if he wants to be."

"But it's silly when everything he wants is just an arm's reach away. He's just too afraid to grab it."

The hell he was. Frustration and anger prodded. Frustration because customers were gathering, and he couldn't say what he wanted. Anger because Maddie didn't know what the hell she was talking about. The last thing any woman needed was for him to give in to the needs that drove him. Especially a prim and proper woman like Petunia. Just the thought of touching her the way she needed had his blood heating dangerously.

On a tight "I'll see you later," Ace turned on his heel and strode down the street, absently nodding in response to greetings, his mind consumed with the thought of pinning Petunia's wrists to the bed, of kissing her so deeply her thoughts became transparent, her body pliant, her will his… He clenched his hands into fists, fighting back the desire. "Fuck."

Behind him he heard Caden say, "That was too much, Maddie."

And from Maddie, an uncharacteristic "I'm not sure it was enough."

CHAPTER TWO

THE SMALL ONE-ROOM schoolhouse was quiet in the minutes before the day started, but soon Petunia would walk out the sturdy wooden door and ring the bell, and the excitement would start. Twenty children from the ages of five to thirteen would push through the doorway, sit at their desks and look at her with expressions ranging from boredom to anticipation. Educating growing minds was a hard job, a taxing job and one Petunia loved. But as soon as she saved the money for her ticket, she was going to hop on the stage and continue on to San Francisco to take advantage of the newly wealthy's desire to compete socially with East Coast established society. If she were careful, she could take that desire to "do them one better" and use it to open a school that would fund her dream to truly educate all.

Just thinking about leaving brought Ace to mind. And bringing Ace to mind just revived the familiar combination of ache and anger. Just who did that man think he was to take apart her way of life as if there was something wrong with it? He, who was in the middle of every fight, every scheme, every betting game that took place in this town.

And in the middle of every type of aid, too, the little voice of fairness inside whispered.

Damn it! Petunia erased the word she'd just misspelled

on the chalkboard and started over. Just once she wanted to catch Ace doing something so wrong, so evil, that this irrational attraction she had for him would die an ignoble death. But every time she'd seen him fight, he'd been defending someone, and while she didn't approve of gambling, he didn't do it recklessly. He did drink more than she approved of, but when he was drunk, he never harmed anyone. He just got more quiet from what she could tell, more mysterious.

She sighed as she set the chalk down and dusted off her hands. The one thing she didn't need was for Ace to become any more mysterious. He already had too much appeal for her.

As was her habit, she went behind her desk and set up her papers in the order of what her lesson was going to be for the day. She started simply and then worked up to the more complicated for the older students. She was going to be losing Analisa soon. Unfortunately, her mother wanted her home to help with her siblings and the work around their small farm. Analisa had a bright mind and a desire to learn. She'd asked Petunia for help, to convince her parents to let her stay in school. Unfortunately, no matter how much Petunia tried, she couldn't convince her parents of the importance of continuing their daughter's education. As long as Analisa could read, write and count, the adults in her life seemed satisfied.

Petunia shook her head and set her math book to the side. They just couldn't see the brand-new world out there waiting for them and the possibilities that existed. They just wanted to stay in this little town, in this little world, in this little spot and ignore it all. She shook her head. She would never understand it.

Outside the door, she could hear the students playing in the small school yard. She always gave them this time. They seemed to have so little time to just enjoy being young.

Sighing, Petunia placed the creative writing instructional on the top of the second pile. She might only have these children's minds for the period of time it took her to earn the money for her stage ticket. But in that time, she intended to plant the seeds of curiosity and just maybe, in one of them, that seed would grow, and they would see something of the world besides this tiny town. At least that was her hope.

From the yard came the regrettably familiar sound of a singsong chant. Frowning, she went back to the window. She wasn't surprised to see a slight boy with shaggy hair and threadbare clothing cornered by a bigger boy. Every school yard had its victims and its bullies. And here the bully was Buster, and the victim was Terrance Winter, probably because he had the look of a child whose family didn't care, and in a town this small, neglect was like throwing a red rag in a chicken pen. They all started pecking.

Petunia opened the heavy door in time to hear, "Fatty lip, fatty lip, Terry isn't worth a shit."

Gritting her teeth, she reached up and rang the bell. Hard. All sound stopped. One by one, the children trickled to line up in front of the short steps. All except Terry and his tormentor.

"Buster Hayworth," she snapped. "Line up, please."

A murmur rippled through the line of children. Some kids ooh'd, others giggled. Buster came reluctantly around the corner, the shock of blond hair on his forehead standing up straight as it always did, the expression on his face angelic. She'd learned on the first day when he stuck a frog in her desk drawer not to fall for the false sincerity in his big blue eyes.

"You'll be staying after class tomorrow. I'd appreciate it if you informed your parents of that."

"But, Miss Wayfield, I was only—"

She cut off the protest with a wave of her hand. "You were only trying to make someone else's life miserable within *my* earshot, in *my* school. You know that's not allowed."

He opened his mouth. She cut him off again.

"I don't want to hear it. You will inform your parents tonight that you will be staying after school tomorrow. No excuses."

His eyes got bigger. "My dad will blister my butt."

Something she felt needed to be done. "Well, then, maybe the double punishment will make you think the next time before you decide to be mean-spirited to one of your own."

Buster scowled. "He's not one of mine."

"He's a student in this class. That makes him part of your school family. You should be helping him, not hurting him. The world would be a better place if everyone did that."

He looked at her askance, hands in his pockets. "You don't know much about the world, do you, Miss Petunia?"

She looked back at him. "I know a lot about it. I just don't accept that what is must always be."

He shook his head, gave her one last wheedling smile. She pointed to the line unmoved. He went.

"Now, all of you sit down and get out your slates and start practicing your alphabet until I get there. You older kids help the younger ones, and Buster—" she stopped him at the door "—I want to see your letters improve. They were very sloppy last Friday."

After the last child wandered in, Petunia sighed and went in search of Terrance.

She found him standing by the back steps, hands still in his pockets and his head still down. He was so young to have so much life beaten out of him. Petunia approached him slowly. Reaching the steps, she tucked her skirts under her and sat down so she wouldn't tower over him. She'd always found it was easier to do that when she was dealing with children.

He still didn't look at her. She was afraid she knew why. Putting her finger under his chin, she lifted his face and barely suppressed a gasp. His lower lip was split open and swollen, and his eye was black-and-blue. The bruise spread down his cheek and followed his jawline to his chin. The kind of mark only a man's fist could make.

She didn't need to ask who'd done this. But the severity of the beating... It was a wonder Terrance's father hadn't killed him.

She touched his cheek delicately. Why did it have to be her student most interested in learning whose world made it so impossible for him to succeed? "What happened?"

He shrugged. "You know."

"Pretend I don't. Tell me."

"Pa got into a game last night."

Standing, she took his hand and walked toward the well. "I take it he wasn't successful."

He shook his head. "No, he lost everything."

She took a clean handkerchief out of her pocket when they reached the well, a sick feeling in the pit of her stomach. "Everything?"

"Everything."

Petunia had never seen such hopelessness in a face of any age. Dipping her handkerchief into the bucket of cool water she'd drawn earlier, she pressed it to his eye. He winced and blinked at her with the other. His hazel eyes didn't have the artifice of Buster's, but they had the appeal of sincerity.

"I'm sorry, Terrance."

He nodded and swallowed hard. "I might be leaving."

Petunia was probably the only one who understood how devastating that revelation was to a boy more suited to scholar than farmer.

"But we haven't even finished the story of Ulysses."

It was a stupid thing to say.

He looked at her with a bit of hope. "Maybe you can tell it to me real fast."

"Maybe." She dipped the cloth again and applied it to his lip. Again the wince. "Or maybe we can just do something about the situation."

Terrance shook his head. "Nothing to be done. Dad lost the mortgage money to that gambler, Ace."

And had come home to take out his frustration on his son. "I see."

"Everybody knows what's Ace Parker's stays Ace Parker's."

"Do you think he cheated?"

He looked horrified. "Ace? No."

She did not understand how the boy could idolize the man who'd just taken everything from him.

His gaze slid from hers. "My pa might have, though. He was pretty beat up when he came in."

Gambling room justice. Petunia shook her head. Only a man could understand it. It was nothing to put a family out on the street. But let a man cheat at cards, and all damnation broke loose.

"I see," she said again. "Well, Terrance, I'm glad you came to school today."

"I wanted to hear Ulysses."

She'd begun reading them *Ulysses Tales*, a little bit at a time, changing the language so the kids could comprehend the greater message, making it fun and entertaining.

"I'm glad you came, even though it was hard, and you must be hurting."

"I've had worse."

Yes, he had but if she had her way, there wouldn't be any more. Terrance was a prime example of why the type of boarding school she wanted to establish needed building. "And maybe after school today we can see if something can be done about your problem."

He shook his head and stepped back. "Pa is who he is."

Yes, he was. "But you love him."

A boy should love his father. But more important, a man should be worthy of that love.

Ducking his head, Terrance shrugged his shoulders. "I used to. He didn't used to always be this mad. Just since Ma's been gone."

She'd never been able to find out if Terrance's mother had left or passed on.

"Sometimes life can be hard, but tomorrow can be much better."

He didn't even look at her on that one. She guessed she couldn't blame him. For a child his age, life had to seem pretty darn impossible. Wringing out the handkerchief, she came to a decision.

"I'll tell you what, Terrance. I can't make any promises, but after school today, I'll go talk to Mr. Parker."

Hope sprang into Terrance's eyes. She felt a pang at feeding it to him. To him, the schoolteacher was all powerful. And at the end of the day, she was going to have to be. Or learn to live with the guilt.

"You will? Thank you."

She shook her head at him. "It's not going to be that easy. As you said, Ace Parker isn't one for letting things go."

"But neither are you."

He had a point there.

"You're right, and I'm going to do my best to see if we can come up with some compromise that will fix your problem. All right?"

He nodded.

"Now do you want to go inside and practice your letters with everybody else, or do you want to be excused for the day?"

He grabbed up his books and headed to the door. She guessed that was an answer. She followed more slowly. For an eight-year-old boy, Terrance had a serious dedication to learning that if she had her way, would not be snuffed out. Not by his father, not by life and certainly not by a gambler with a possessive streak. Ace didn't need the strip of land Terrance's father pretended to farm. But Terrance did. Which meant just one thing. Ace was going to have to give it up.

PETUNIA STOOD OUTSIDE the saloon and straightened the dark blue jacket of her most favorite suit, wishing the day wasn't so unseasonably hot. Wishing she could just look the other way like so many people did. Wishing there was a way to keep her promise to Terrance without actually having to speak to Ace. Wishing she'd been able to run into him somewhere in town today rather than having to track him down in his lair. She stared at the saloon doors and bit her lip.

If wishes were horses, beggars would ride.

The only other time she'd been in a saloon had been in the company of several suffragettes, and even that protest had been timed to occur during the hours of nonoperation. And it'd ended with her spending twenty minutes in jail before her father had fetched her out.

Truth be told, she'd been rather disappointed with the "grand adventure." Outside of one picture featuring a scantily clad woman, the saloon had been bland and smelly and not at all the gaudily exciting place she'd expected to see. This building was probably the same. Bland and smelly and sparsely populated with the same people she saw on the street every day. So why was she standing here hesitating?

A movement down the street caught her attention. Terrance. He stood on the sidewalk watching her, hands clenched at his sides. His posture set to run. Clearly, he expected her to chicken out.

Well, he had another think coming. She was a Wayfield. The family motto, longer than most, spoke to noble attributes. But quitting wasn't one of them. With a lift of her chin and small wave to Terrance, she stepped through the swinging doors.

Her initial thought as the gloom of the place surrounded her was this wasn't so bad. On her first breath, she started to change her mind. The stench of stale sweat and sour beer hung thick in the still air. By the time her eyes adjusted in the dim light, she was ready to back right out. This was not her world. There was no optimism here. Just apathy reflected in the way a blonde woman dressed in a loosely tied wrapper sat at the long bar and picked at a plate of food. The thud of slamming wood made her jump.

"You lost, ma'am?"

She turned to the barkeep. She couldn't remember his name, but she'd seen him around town. He had a rather distinctive appearance with that greased back black hair and large waxed mustache.

"No."

"Maybe she's looking for a job," the woman at the bar said. "A person can't hold body and soul together on what this town pays a schoolmarm."

The woman was attractive in a blowsy sort of way, but not welcoming. Petunia straightened her shoulders and lifted her chin a notch.

"I'm not looking for a job."

The woman met her gaze squarely, and took a bite of egg. "A bit of excitement, then?"

Petunia took another step into the room. A drunk she hadn't noticed at the table to the left eyed her from hat to boot.

"I'd take a turn on her."

She arched her brow at him. "You would do better to lay off the drink and indulge in a bath, rather than to speculate on a fornication that I doubt you'd be able to perform anyway."

"What the hell does that mean?" he said looking at her askance, or maybe he was just trying to focus.

The woman at the bar laughed and sat up straighter. The wrapper slipped open exposing an amazing amount of white flesh. "I think you've just been accused of not being able to get it up, Jimmy."

Jimmy huffed. "Hell, there hasn't been a day since

I've been born that I haven't been able to get it up. Hell,
I'll prove it." He stood up, knocking the table back
and shoved his suspenders off his shoulders. When he
reached for his belt Petunia decided it was time for her
to take charge before the man bared all in an effort to
prove something she couldn't care less about. But just
to be safe, she stepped out of his reach.

"I do apologize for interrupting your afternoon, but
I'm looking for Ace Parker."

"Hey, Acey!" A woman leaning over the railing at the
top of the stairs screeched. "You've got company waiting downstairs."

The woman looked as tired and as worn as the blonde
woman at the bar. But her lung capacity assured Petunia
that Ace knew he had a guest. Folding her hands in front
of her, she waited. Patiently. For three minutes. But the
longer she stood there feeling everyone's eyes upon her,
the more she became excruciatingly aware of the tendrils
of hair she tucked behind her ear trying to come loose,
the tightness of her bun, the difficulty of keeping a smile
on her face and the utter lack of response on Ace's part.

The blonde at the bar waved a forkful of egg at her.
"Doesn't look like he's coming."

She raised her eyebrow. "Does he often ignore company?"

The bartender kept wiping glasses. The blonde popped
the bite of egg into her mouth.

"Ace pretty much does what he likes, and it doesn't
look like he wants to do you."

The edges of Petunia's temper started to fray right
along with her patience.

The drunk from the table by the door shuffled over.

Thankfully, he still had his pants on. "I can keep you busy, honey."

She put her gloved hand over her mouth and nose as he got closer. He reeked of alcohol and other things she didn't care to identify.

"Could you please call him again?" she asked the lady at the top of the stairs.

"Ace! The lady doesn't fancy cooling her heels waiting for you any longer."

Still no response. The woman leaned over the rail, her breasts all but spilling free as she shrugged. "Sorry, honey, doesn't look like it's your lucky day."

"No, it's definitely not." Sighing, she gathered up her skirts. "But sometimes you just have to make your own luck."

When her foot landed on the first stair, the woman at the bar gasped.

"Honey, you don't want to be doing that."

Petunia spared her a glance. "No, I'm sure I don't." But she kept climbing.

"Ace, you'd better get out here," the woman at the railing yelled when she reached the halfway point. Whether it was repetition that inspired it or that half octave increase in the woman's pitch, this time there was a response.

"Stop your caterwauling, Bess. I'm not expecting anyone."

Petunia reached the landing. Bess blocked her way. This close Petunia could see she was older than she'd thought, maybe in her midthirties, but still pretty in an overdone sort of way.

"Excuse me, please." The *please* was a courtesy. One way or another, she was getting down that hall.

Instead of moving, Bess caught her arm. "Whatever you're doing, it's not worth your reputation. If you don't leave now, no decent man will touch you."

The genuine concern in the woman's gaze kept Petunia from rolling her eyes. "I'm twenty-nine years old and well and clearly on the shelf. If a decent man was going to touch me, he likely would have done it sometime in the previous thirteen years."

Bess took her measure, sighed and shook her head. "I hope you know what you're doing."

Stepping around Bess, she nodded. "Oh, I know what I'm doing." To herself she muttered, "It's the results that are in question."

Bess caught her arm again, drawing her up short. "He's had a lot to drink."

"Is that good or bad?"

"Honestly? It could go either way."

Petunia set her shoulders. "Well, if it can go either way, then it might just as well go mine."

The woman sighed. "It's the third door down."

"Thank you."

Determination kept her feet moving. When she reached Ace's room, the door was ajar. She knocked.

"Go the hell away, Bess."

Petunia pushed the door open. Ace was lying on his stomach on the bed in a decadent sprawl, his muscled back, broad shoulders, and lean hips and strong legs were dark against the white sheets.

"I'm not Bess but if I were, I'd take offense at the language you just used."

Ace went very still. His fingers tightened on the pillow. On a "What the fuck?" he rolled over, grabbing the sheet and pulling it over his lap. His front was just as mouthwatering as his back. The light sprinkling of hair across his chest made her fingers tingle to follow it down over that hard ladder of muscle across his stomach. To follow it beneath the sheet to see where it ended…

"I repeat. Language."

"I'll talk any way I want." He shook the hair out of his eyes. "What the hell are you doing here?"

"I needed to talk to you."

"You can't be up here."

She rather enjoyed his discomfort. "Apparently, I can."

"Turn around."

She did, listening as he got out of bed and yanked on his pants. "Of all the idiotic things you've done, Pet."

"My name is Petunia, and to you, Miss Wayfield."

"Since you're standing in my room, on the upper floor of a saloon, in what technically is a brothel, I'll call you any goddamn thing I want."

"I'd appreciate it if you cleaned up your language."

"I'd have appreciated it if you'd let me sleep."

"May I turn around now?"

"Yes."

She was disappointed to see him shrugging into his shirt.

"We have business to discuss."

"We have business? The most we've ever exchanged is a few insults over a cinnamon bun. And I didn't even buy you that."

"Nonetheless, we do."

He finished buttoning his shirt. "You need to get the hell out of here."

"I need to talk to you."

Grabbing his hat, Ace crossed the room and grabbed her elbow. Her pulse leaped. Tingles raced up her arm and over her shoulder, sending goose bumps across her chest. Beneath her jacket, her nipples tightened. What was it about this man that affected her so?

"I'll thank you to let me go."

He pushed her toward the door. "I'll thank you to get the hell out of my room."

"I did try to speak to you down in the lobby."

"That's not a lobby, it's a saloon." He shoved her through the door. "Do you know what you've done to your reputation?"

"You realize I don't care?" The dryness of her tone got her a look. "I am, as you pointed out, completely on the shelf."

"I don't realize anything except a reputation is a hard thing to replace."

"I have no intention of rebuilding it. I've done nothing wrong."

"You're in a brothel."

"It's the middle of the day."

"It's a brothel!" He shoved her down the hallway. Bess was standing where Petunia had left her. Ace shot her a glare. "What the hell were you thinking, Bess? Letting her up here."

"What did you expect me to do?" Bess snapped back.

"Trip her and knock her down, throw a punch."

"She wasn't looking for me."

"Son of a bitch," he muttered under his breath. "Fucking women."

Petunia wanted to shout back "Fucking men" but no matter how liberated she was, she hadn't gotten to the point where she could say words like that.

Ace hustled her down the stairs. Her skirt caught on her heel, tripping her. He hauled her up. "Keep moving."

"It would be easier if you slowed down."

"I'm getting you the hell out of here before some-body sees you with me and starts thinking we need to get married."

"I have no intention of getting married."

He grunted. "Probably a lot of men grateful for that fact."

She planted her feet. "Did you just insult me?"

He yanked her forward. "I haven't begun yet."

"Should have taken me, honey." Jimmy lurched to-ward them. "Seems like he's not in any too hurry to have you."

Ace swore. Petunia looked over her shoulder at the drunk and smiled sweetly. "I insisted on clean sheets."

He hauled her along to the back of the saloon. "I hope nobody saw you come in here."

"I imagine everyone on the street watched me come in here."

"Son of a bitch."

"I don't know what you're worried about. Even if they march you down the aisle with a shotgun at your back, I'll never say *I do*."

This time he was the one to jerk them to a halt. "Why the hell not?"

"Because my standards for a husband are a bit higher."

Pushing her through the back door and into the alley, he snarled. "I bet."

Letting go of her arm, he faced her. He was still standing too close for Petunia to catch a decent breath. And with his shirt flapping open like that, he was still too much temptation for her mind to focus the way she needed it to. She wanted to run her fingers through the dusting of hair on his chest to see if it was soft or wiry.

She also had an incredible urge to bite his right pectoral. To leave her mark on him.

Clenching her fists at her sides, Petunia reached for focus. It stayed just out of reach. The circular scar just to the left of Ace's breastbone was far more tempting. She wondered how he'd gotten it. She wondered how it'd feel. Were the edges soft or rough? Was his skin warm to the touch or cool? How would he taste?

With a growled curse, Ace yanked his shirt closed. "So what was so important that you had to come storming into my bedroom?"

"I did not storm."

He sighed. "I'll rephrase. What was so important you had to wake me from a good sleep and put us both in peril of a shotgun wedding?"

She wanted to stomp her foot. "Will you stop harping on a wedding?"

The muscles in his jaws bunched. His tone when he spoke was more even. "What was so damn important?"

"You were at a card game last night with the father of one of my students."

"I was in a game last night with a lot of fathers of a lot of kids."

"Terrance's father is Brian Winter."

"Ah, that one."

"What does *ah* mean?"

"He drinks too much, has too many tales and bets more than he can afford."

"That's why I'm here. I want you to give him back what you won."

He blinked. "You want me to do what?"

"I want you to give him back what you won."

"Why in hell would I do that?"

"Because he lost more than he can afford to."

"Not my problem."

"He took out his frustration on his son. And without a home the Winters will have to leave…"

Ace's expression didn't change.

"Terrance is a good student with an inquisitive mind. He deserves a chance to grow up to be a man who can use that mind."

"Nobody ever said life was fair."

Now she wanted to growl. "Life might not be fair, but people can be."

"And you think it's fair to ask me to give back my winnings?"

"Yes."

"You do realize this is how I make the majority of my living?"

"Yes, I realize you make money this way, a lot of it. Enough that you can afford to give him back his."

Ace leaned back against the building and folded his arms across his chest. It was a position that spoke of confidence and power. Her knees went weak.

"What's in it for me?"

"The knowledge that you bought a little boy some time."

"You think because I give this money back, Brian won't go back to that table again?"

"Giving the money back isn't enough."

"Not enough?"

She shook her head. "You can't gamble with him anymore."

Another of those slow blinks. "I can't?"

"No."

"Honey, I'm a grown man and so is he, and your nose, cute as it is, is sticking where it doesn't belong."

That was too much. Very calmly, very precisely she said, "This morning, Terrance, *my* student, came into *my* classroom with a black eye and a split lip asking for *my* help because he's being put out of his home. That being the case, I'm here to appeal to whatever shred of decency that still exists in your body to give that horrible man back his money so that little boy will have a home tomorrow."

Ace pushed his hat back and rubbed his forehead. In the late-afternoon light, she could see the paleness of his skin, the tightness of his expression. He was hungover.

He sighed. "That's a hell of a lot of words to throw at a man before coffee."

She looked at him. "I've got more."

"Save them."

"Then just say you'll do it, and I'll let you go get your cup of coffee."

"That's a fool's mission."

"You're Hell's Eight and a Texas Ranger. There has to be honor in you somewhere."

"That's a common myth." Taking off his hat, he ran his hand through his hair again before asking, "He beat the boy?"

"He beats Terrance every time you take his money."

His hands dropped to his sides. "I don't *take* his money. He loses it."

"That's splitting hairs."

"Not in my book."

"Fine, I'll rephrase. Every time he loses at your table, he takes it out on his son. His eight-year-old son," she added for emphasis.

"Fuck."

She really needed to learn to use that word. It conveyed so much with so little. "I'll thank you not to use that language around me."

This time the look she got wasn't so sympathetic. She didn't push, just waited. After a minute he said, "I'll do it on one condition."

She knew better than to say "anything." "What's your condition?"

"I want a kiss."

"A kiss?"

Pushing off the wall, he took a step closer. She took one back.

"Just a kiss."

The wall brushed her shoulder. She melted against it, her gaze hopelessly dropping to his lips. *Just.*

The word with all its implications lingered in her mind. Just the feel of his breath on her skin. Just the touch of his lips to hers. Just that slight pressure. That gentle parting. Just that hot claiming…

Ace reached out, and she flinched. He smiled, a devil's smile that promised so much as his finger grazed her temple in a featherlight caress. In a rough drawl, he murmured, "Don't."

Such a soft, seductive order. A shiver snaked down her spine. When she would have leaned away, he shook his head and issued another. "Stay."

She did for no other reason than he was the one who issued it. He increased the pressure ever so slightly— just enough—drawing his fingertips down her cheek and along her jaw, finding the sensitive skin of her neck. She gasped as sensation gathered. Goose bumps sprang up. His nostrils flared. She didn't move and, for an instant, neither did he. They just stood there in the alley with the warmth of the sun heating the air between them. "What do you say, schoolmarm? Do we have a deal?"

"I think you want a lot."

He shrugged. "You're asking a lot."

Placing her hand on his chest, savoring the flex of hard muscles and the soft hiss of his indrawn breath, Petunia stood on tiptoe, intending to kiss his cheek. He shook his head and smiled, and that finger, that oh, so tantalizing finger, traveled to the corner of her lip, teasing the delicate skin there, coaxing forth another airy gasp and more goose bumps.

"I want a real kiss."

The raspy tone melted into the heat of his touch, melted into her. Her gaze dropped to the sculpted beauty of his mouth. That mouth with those full lips she'd always fantasized about sliding over hers, parting hers. Oh, yes, a real kiss... She wanted that, too.

With a subtle pressure, he tipped her face up. She didn't resist. Why would she?

"Like you mean it," he added.

That jerked her gaze to his, and she caught something in his expression that challenged everything feminine in her. Doubt. He didn't think she'd do it, she realized. He probably thought she was too prim, too proper, too much on the shelf to kiss a man. He probably assumed she didn't even know how. He probably thought he was scaring her. With a shake of her head, she leaned back and smiled.

He had another think coming. Ace Parker was one heck of an inspiration.

CHAPTER THREE

HE WAS TOO old and too experienced to shudder at the touch of a woman's hand, any woman's hand, but when Petunia's settled as light as thistledown against his chest, Ace did just that. Desire started deep in his gut and climbed upward right along with her fingers, rolling like thunder through his resistance, making a mockery of the dare he'd laid before them. This wasn't a game. This was real. And he didn't want it. Not the desire. Not the weakness. Not her.

But it didn't matter what he didn't want as her skirts swished about his ankles, and her weight leaned against him in sweet enticement. He wanted *her*, had since the first moment he'd seen her step off the stagecoach two months ago, self-contained, graceful, elegant. A lady. The one thing he could never have.

"You're going to have to bend down."

The soft whisper joined the thunder, adding to the volume. Her hands slid up his chest, tucking behind his neck. Lightning flashed on the edges of his control. She tugged. He didn't go. That wasn't who he was, how he'd allow it to be between them.

Sliding his hand down the delicate line of her back, he demanded, "Why?"

He wanted it put into words, to hear it from her lips.

She blinked up at him, confusion and desire deepening the blue of her eyes. "For that kiss you wanted."

Who did she think she was kidding? This wasn't about any goddamn deal. This was about the attraction that neither of them wanted. This was about them. As natural as his next breath one hand settled into the hollow of her back. The other, her shoulder. She was tall. She fit his embrace as if she were made for it. Fit his hands as if she were made for them. His voice rasped from his throat, more growl than seduction. "Ask me nicely."

He felt the tremor that shook her head to toe, but it wasn't fear that had her pupils dilating and her tongue sliding over her lower lip in soft pink enticement. His cock thickened painfully within the restriction of his pants.

"Please…" She cleared her throat. He adjusted his stance. "Please, lean down."

Knives couldn't cut more cleanly than that simple compliance. The barrier he kept between them tore free in the aftermath. His fingers slipped down her arm, chaining the delicacy of her wrist between his fingers while he urged her closer. The soft plea whispered like a siren's song in his head, bringing forth the side of him he kept hidden. She watched him carefully as he brought her hand down between them. He liked her eyes on him. Her world narrowed to him. Her other hand naturally followed the first.

"That's it," he whispered as her fingers spread over his heart. "Feel me. Feel what I want."

"A kiss."

"Yes." Yes, he wanted a kiss. A kiss was a beginning to so much more.

A kiss could be everything. He leaned down, but not

so far she didn't have to stretch that delectable body up the length of his. Her hands against his chest kept him from feeling the fullness of her breasts, but he could imagine how they'd feel in his hands, hard-tipped and delicate just like her. Her hand slipped down into his. Curling his fingers around hers, he pressed it to his chest, struggling with the want to press her closer, the utter need to drag her hands overhead, to pin her with his hands and body, to kiss her until the walls she'd built so well came tumbling down, and there was just him and her and the truth between them. Until she gave him what he needed.

Surrender.

Ace gritted his teeth, loosening his grip, controlling the wild impulse, forcing himself back to even breaths, to what was.

Pet was a good woman, not a whore. She was going to kiss him to pay a debt that wasn't even hers because she thought it was the only way to save a boy. Fuck. He was a bastard. He took a step back. She went with him, following as naturally as he could desire. His good intentions took a hit. Before he could regroup, her lips touched his, and that fast, all thoughts of right or wrong drowned under a wave of lust so strong, it stole his breath. Her lips parted, catching it, linking them in a moment fraught with danger. With promise.

Why? he asked silently. *Why this woman? Why now?*

The answer came in her soft moan as her lips nibbled at his. Because she wanted him. And lust didn't need any more explanation than the proximity of two compatible bodies. Or so he told himself as her lips moved gently against his, untutored but determined, always so determined, this woman. Tilting her lance against the windmills, needing to make a difference, too naive to realize that no matter what she did, nothing ever really changed. Except this. This kiss changed everything. And she didn't even know what she was inviting.

It was a fleeting pressure, surprisingly soft, surprisingly sweet. A kiss just like he'd asked for. But not what he wanted. And damn, if this was all he was ever going to have, he was going to have it the way he wanted. Cupping Pet's skull in his hand, Ace forestalled her escape with the slight pressure of his fingers against the back of her neck. He expected struggle, but she didn't move, just stood there looking expectantly at him. Her eyes were heavy lidded and ripe with the question within. The perfect picture of a woman enthralled. Everything inside him perked. It was a struggle to find his voice.

"The deal was a real kiss, a kiss like you meant it."

She blinked. "That's how I kiss when I mean it."

She couldn't be that green. Not at her age with her bold manner. "No one kisses like that when they mean it."

She blinked at him again, and he realized that maybe she really was that naive. Maybe that pressure-on-pressure kiss was, to her, boldness itself. If that was the case, it was a damn shame. Pet was a woman of passion, and no woman of passion should go through life thinking that casual contact constituted lust, certainly not any woman that kissed him. If Pet was going to walk away from him today and tell someone tomorrow that she got Ace Parker to do what she wanted by kissing him, it was going to be a goddamn kiss that both of them remembered fondly.

"I've seen your *serious*, my Pet, and that wasn't it."

"My name is Petunia."

How the hell she managed to stick that aristocratic nose in the air while in his embrace, he had no idea, but she managed it. It ticked him off more than her *My name is Peturnia, and to you, Miss Wayfield* amused him.

"I prefer Pet."

Licking her lips, she stepped to the side, away from the wall. "You make me sound like a dog."

"Oh, you're much more valuable than a dog."

Her "Gee, thanks" made him smile. As did the little wiggle she did for freedom. He let her smooth her skirts and tug on that tight jacket that made the most of her curves before spreading his fingers across her nape and tickling the sensitive skin. She shivered. He did it again. No shiver this time, but the sharp intake of breath was even more satisfying. It said she was still aware of him.

He took a step forward, and she took a step back in a now-familiar dance. He turned slightly, angling in with his body so that the wall was behind her again. The image of her standing there, arms pinned above her head, helpless in his arms while he ravished her mouth, wouldn't leave his mind.

Once again her hand pressed against his chest. But this time in denial. Raising an eyebrow at her, he pointed out the obvious.

"If you want me to give up my winnings to a man who doesn't deserve it, I'm going to want more than that quick peck."

"You're not giving it up for a man. You're giving it up for a boy."

"It's a hell of a lot of money. You're a fool if you think I'm giving it back for a kiss my grandmother might give me."

Her nails bit slightly through the fabric of his shirt in irritation. His cock throbbed. He wanted her.

"I'm not a fool," she growled.

No, she wasn't. She was just doing what she could because she didn't think anybody else cared, and maybe they didn't. It was easy to forget about the people that lived on the edge, he knew. He'd been forgotten about most of his life. But the one thing good about living on edges is that it made a body tough.

"Did you ever think that growing up as he is might work for Terrance as an adult?"

The shake of her head was immediate. "He's a scholar not a fighter."

"You said he was eight."

"Some things you can just tell."

Ace sighed. "And you want to save him."

She didn't even try to deny it. "He's a bright child, too bright for such a future."

A do-gooder to the core. "You can't control everything."

"No, but I can give him this chance."

He backed her up another step, controlling her movement with his body and his fingers on the back of her neck. And she went, as soft and as sweet as if she knew what he needed. He tucked the information away, even though he knew he shouldn't. This was one woman with whom he couldn't play his games, a good woman. Too good for him, which was why he had no business taking that last step that brought her back up against the wall. But he took it anyway.

"What are you doing?"

He smiled at the question. "Taking my kiss."

When she opened her mouth to protest, he shook his head. "Trust me, you don't want to say it."

"You don't even know what it is!"

He liked the fire indignation put in her eyes. He liked to bring the fire out in her. Liked to know he could make her burn when others only left her cold.

Pressing his lips against her forehead, he said quietly, "I know. Now, come here."

She did. Spreading his legs so she was trapped between them, he leaned down until his chest pressed against hers, and he could feel the tips of her breasts poking into his shirt. Those nipples could have been hard because the air was cooling, or they could be hard because she found him as attractive as he found her. Ace leaned in a little farther, testing his resolve, teasing his desire. She didn't back up, couldn't back up, and that only tempted him more. She was imprisoned between his body and the wall, helpless, and that little catch in her breath as he bent his head, his shadow blocking the sun from her eyes, just brought all of his lust to the fore. His cock hardened to the point of pain; his heart picked up its beat.

When his mouth was a hair's breadth from hers, he murmured, "This time kiss me like you know what you're doing."

He wasn't at all surprised with the immediate "I know how to kiss." His Pet was a fighter. Smiling into her eyes, he gave her something to hold on to.

"Prove it."

DEAR HEAVENS, HE wanted her to prove it. Staring up into Ace's light blue eyes, searching for sanity, Petunia only found more temptation than an on-the-shelf woman should be forced to confront. Honest to goodness curl-her-toes and burn-her-reputation-in-perdition temptation. And it was harder to resist than any sermon preached. Because it felt so good. Surrounded by Ace's arms, his scent, his heat, she found it amazingly easy to imagine succumbing to her baser instincts, to wallow in the sheer pleasure of his weight against her, to tempt him the way Eve had tempted Adam. Except she wanted to offer Ace so much more than an apple. And she wanted him to take it. All of it. Everything she could give. The fact that he would wasn't the scary thing it should have been.

She was sure she wasn't the first woman that Ace had wanted. His conquests littered the town. But he might just be the only man who'd ever truly wanted her. Not to prove a point. Not to gain access to her family's power or money, but because she was a woman he found attractive. Her fingers curled into his chest. The immediate hitch in his breathing padded her confidence. Inside, she started smiling. He really did want her.

Prove it.

For the skip of a heartbeat, she didn't know if she could. She was a spinster. A suffragette. A scholar. What did she know of kissing the socks off a man? As if sensing her panic—which was silly since she hadn't given any outward sign of her distress—Ace nudged her thigh with his knee.

"Want me to bend down?"

His voice, deeper than normal, rasped like velvet over her senses. And she wanted more. Tempting Ace Parker was madness, it was foolishness, it was reckless, but she'd already given herself an excuse. She'd made a deal, and no Wayfield ever reneged on a deal. And all she had to do to hold up her end was to kiss him like she meant it, and suddenly that didn't seem so very hard. There was so much she could imagine doing with this man. He might be a reprobate, he might be a gambler, but he was the only man in her recollection who could make her feel like a schoolgirl and forget her morally correct upbringing. He was, quite frankly, her one chance to feel what other women felt so easily. To give what other women found so easy to give. To be who she always thought she could be.

That did not mean, however, that she was ready to just roll over. When he tried to pull closer, she shook her head. She shouldn't have found the cock of his eyebrow endearing, but she did.

"What?"

"We had a deal. This is my kiss."

His fingers relaxed infinitesimally on her neck. Highlighting just how subtle his control had been. "So it is."

She fitted her mouth to his, rubbing gently until she found that perfect spot that sent tingles shooting inward, wishing she knew more than she did, wanting to make this a kiss he remembered, wanting against reason to be memorable.

Again that soothing touch on her neck. His mouth opened against hers, guiding her, she realized.

"Thank you," she whispered.

Ace took her gratitude and upped it with the lightest touch of his tongue. Those tingles burst into streaks of lightning. She returned the caress, and he moaned. She did it again, and again, experimenting with going deeper, wider, turning her head so her tongue could touch his. It wasn't enough.

"More," he whispered, slipping his thigh between hers.

Yes, she wanted more. She'd noticed Ace the first day she'd walked into town, and he'd made sure she could never give up that infatuation, teasing and taunting her, irritating her with his very existence. And now it was her turn to tease him. His lips were full, fuller than she expected, softer than she expected but so good. Giving in to the wildness throbbing inside, she nibbled and bit at his mouth, demanding something he needed to give.

He groaned deep in his throat. She stood higher on her toes, pulling him down, dragging herself up, rubbing her breasts against his chest, trying to get closer, but she couldn't. There was no way she could get close enough. The kiss was good, but it wasn't good enough, and she didn't know what to do. She dug her nails into the back of his neck in silent demand. Again she got that look that asked for the words. She blushed at the thought. But what choice did she have? This was her one chance, and she wasn't done with it yet.

She had to struggle to find her voice and when she did, it was a breathy thread of sound that took the command out of her order. "Fix it."

He didn't seem to have the same trouble. His voice was deep and even and seductive in its calm. "You know our deal."

This time it was her turn to growl but not with passion. "Not that." Nipping his lip, she snapped, "This."

Catching her chin in his hand, he held her still, his mouth just inches from hers. She couldn't breathe, couldn't look away. God, she wanted him.

"Do you want my mouth, Pet?"

She nodded.

With a little jiggle of her chin, he snapped her gaze to his. "Not good enough. Do you want my mouth?"

Why did he have to be so demanding?

She nodded again, hoping it would suffice, not willing to give him everything, not understanding how he could resist the fire she could feel burning just beyond her reach. She could only imagine how good it would feel while he had to know.

His fingers rubbed against her nape; his thumb crept over her cheek, catching the corner of her mouth, pressing gently, forcing her lips to part naturally around it. She touched it with her tongue. His pupils dilated and his nostrils flared, but he didn't give ground.

"If you want it, my Pet, you're going to have to ask for it."

"Kiss me."

She'd thought he'd kiss her then, but though his eyes narrowed, all he did was hold her still and give another order, "Ask nicely."

She wanted to stomp his toe. "Just kiss me."

A tap on her cheek made her look up again. There was desire in the hard lines of his face and the softness of his mouth, but in his eyes…in his eyes was the will of a man who expected to be obeyed. A shiver she didn't understand went down her spine. Between her legs, moisture gathered.

"Say it right," he ordered.

He wanted her to beg. She wasn't a begging woman, but the word slipped past her control, filling the silence between them with an import she didn't understand. "Please."

It was enough. With a curse that sounded like the sweetest music to her impatient ear, he stepped in, his hands sliding down her back, pulling her into his body, thigh to thigh, hip to hip, breast to chest, mouth-to-mouth. Oh, God, mouth-to-mouth. Wrapping her arms around his neck, she pulled him closer still. Another growl, and his mouth smoothed across hers. Against her groin, his erection pressed. Thick, hard and foreign. A shock at first followed by a soothing burst of pleasure. She had the urge to spread her thighs, to grind against him, but she couldn't move, and even that was good. So good, and she was so hungry. The hot, wet touch of his tongue along the seam of her lips had her jumping again.

"Open."

This order growled against her mouth didn't annoy her at all. She opened, willingly, eagerly, joyfully, her heart pounding so loudly in her ears, it blocked out the world, and there was only him. Ace took advantage of her surrender, full, wonderful, glorious advantage, claiming her mouth in a single thrust of his tongue. She opened wider; he teased further. His breath became hers; his moan hers and hers his, she realized. It was a blending; it was a mating; it was a... She couldn't find the word but the feeling. Oh, the feeling! It surged forward out of the most primitive part of her in an exultant burst of joy. Free at last; she was free. And just in that moment when she would have given that moment a name, Ace fisted his hand on her bun and pulled her mouth from his, leaving her aching as he stepped back.

For a second, Petunia couldn't comprehend what had happened. The only things that kept her from tumbling were the wall at her back and his hand on her arm. She felt bereft and abandoned. Lost.

"You've got your deal."

A slap to the face couldn't have been more shocking than his withdrawal. The afternoon sun had sunk behind the buildings, and she felt the chill of the shadows sink into her bones, even as he took that second step away. For him, it had been nothing more than a kiss, probably one of thousands, but for her it had been a moment that shook her world in ways that was going to take days to figure out. She licked her lips, tasting him. Her breasts felt swollen and tender, and when she looked down, her nipples were evident through her clothes. She brought her hands up, only realizing the mistake of that when he laughed.

Jerking out of his grip, she felt her bun give and her hair fall around her shoulders. Petunia didn't need to look into Ace's face to know he'd only been amusing himself. He was who he was, and she was a fool.

"Bastard."

He had the gall to smile. "I assure you, my parents were married."

She hated that he could be so reasonable when she was fumbling just to get her tongue around words.

"Our bargain's done?" she asked, yanking her jacket down and untangling her reticule from her wrist, pretending that her nipples weren't still tingling, that her breath still wasn't raspy, that her voice wasn't a shadow of its former conviction.

Ace picked his hat up off the doorknob and settled it on his head as he nodded, studying her in a way that made her want to… She didn't know what it made her want to do but whatever it was, it wasn't what she was used to, and she didn't want to explore it while he watched.

"You'll give back the money?"

"I'll handle it."

She reached behind her for the door. She wanted away. He stopped her before she got her hand on the knob.

"Not that way."

Her first instinct was to tell him to go to hell. Her second was to swear. He was right. She couldn't go through the saloon. She didn't want to go down the alley, either, but she didn't have much of a option. He took her arm as she hesitated.

"You go that way, you won't get home before dark."

That was the truth. This late the streets started to get wild, and schoolmarm or not, a woman alone was easy prey for the miners and cowhands who flooded the town when they got a bit of gold dust in their pocket.

"Come."

"Does everything you say have to come out an order?"

"Yes."

Twisting her hair back up into a bun as she skipped to keep up, she muttered, "I don't like it."

"You'll get used to it."

She didn't think so.

He steered her down the alley to two buildings over and opened a door. It was the mercantile; she should have thought of that herself.

He said, "Go through here."

Part of her hoped there was some gallantry trapped somewhere inside him because he didn't leave her to find her own way home, but more of her wanted to believe he was a reprobate that she could dismiss as a mistake. Her "Thank you" came out choked. His "You're welcome" was just as tight.

That tightness in his voice could be because the moment had affected him just as much as it had her, but she didn't fool herself into believing it was the truth. She might be an old maid who didn't get kissed often, but if the stories were to be believed, he was a man who spent a lot of his time in other women's beds. And what he did there was something that was whispered about and speculated on, but she never understood why his bed sport created so many blushes and twitters among the loose women of town until now. The man was a warlock. She wasn't going to be just another conquest to him.

"Thank you for the kiss."

His eyebrow rose. She smiled, not giving him any option but to respond in kind.

"You're welcome."

It was time to go. She didn't want to. Hugging her arms to her chest, she asked one last time, more to delay rather than because she doubted his word. Ace was many things, but she'd never heard he wasn't a man of his word.

With her hand on the doorknob she asked, "You'll give Brian back his money?"

She couldn't see his eyes between the shadows of his hat and the creeping of dusk, but there was no mistaking the promise in his voice.

He tipped his hat. "I'll handle it."

CHAPTER FOUR

THE NEXT MORNING, Ace ate breakfast, ignored the shocked looks from the women not used to seeing him up before 3:00 p.m., settled his hat on his head and walked out of the saloon. Before the doors stopped swinging behind him, his best friend and fellow ranger, Luke Bellen, pushed off the wall and fell into step beside him, his dark gray duster flapping around his legs. He'd clearly been waiting for him.

"Morning."

Ace looked over. "You're up early."

Luke shrugged. "More like late. I haven't been to bed yet."

"Was she any good?"

Luke smiled. "Good enough."

As they stepped off the walk, the wind kicked up, blowing fine brown dust on everything.

"Figures," Luke said, looking down at the particles clinging to his shiny black boots. "I just got these cleaned."

"They're boots," Ace pointed out. "They spend all day in the dirt. They're not supposed to be pretty."

Luke glanced at Ace's scuffed, well-worn brown footwear and shook his head. "If you're going to stick with this gambling thing, you need to pay more attention to your wardrobe."

Ace shrugged. Gambling was an outlet. It gave him a rush of excitement. It kept his mind from dwelling on other things. It was a bit of competition when things got dull, a chance to beat the odds. He liked to beat the odds. "I haven't made up my mind if I'm sticking with it."

"Still, if you're going to play the role, you ought to look the part."

"I look just fine."

"You look pissed."

"Really?" He reached in his pocket for his makings. "What makes you say that?"

"You've got your hat pulled down low."

Pausing, he shook some tobacco onto a paper. "I could be blocking the dust," he said, licking the paper to help seal it up.

Luke held out his hand for the makings when he was done. "Or you could be pissed."

Ace stepped up on the walk on the far side of the street. "Looks like I'm going to have to break that habit."

Luke shrugged and shook tobacco onto a paper. "Most can't tell. Unfortunately for you, I've known you since we were infants sharing a crib."

Striking a sulfur on a boot heel, Ace shielded his smoke from the wind. Holding the cigarette in his mouth, he muttered around it, "Only reason we had to share a crib was because your mama couldn't stand your squalling."

"I didn't like being alone."

"You don't remember."

"I can guess."

Ace shook out the match. Luke's mother had been the delicate type, never standing up for herself, not even against her son. Which had led to Luke always getting what he wanted, by hook or crook. A habit he carried into adulthood.

He took a slow drag on the cigarette. The acrid smoke burned his nostrils. "So why you tagging along with me today?"

"'Cause you look like you're heading for trouble."

"What makes you think that?"

"The fact that you only smoke when you're contemplating murder."

"That's not the only time." He also liked a cigarette after sex.

"Well, it's a well-known fact the teacher's got a burr up her butt about Terrance Winter. Add that to the fact that rumor has it Miss Wayfield went into the saloon looking for you yesterday and then you come out of the alley with your lips all kiss bitten."

"You've been spying on me."

"I prefer to think of it as keeping busy."

Luke had been *keeping busy* a lot lately. Ace touched his still tender lower lip, remembering that moment when Pet had lost control and bitten him. He cocked an eyebrow at his friend. "Kiss bitten?"

Luke shrugged again.

Ace shook his head. "I swear the words that come out of your mouth could tarnish that killer reputation of yours."

"It's the poet in me."

"Uh-huh."

Luke didn't tell anyone he penned dime novels to sell back East about the life of the wild men in the Wild West. It'd started out as a dare between him and one of his ladies and developed into a passion. Not one Luke flaunted, but a passion nonetheless and one that kept growing.

Easterners had insatiable appetites for the excitement of the West. Hell, if most of them came here, they'd shit their pants the first day out, but reading it in their parlor at night, Ace guessed it was a safe bit of adventure.

"When you going to write something more serious than those dime novels?" he asked Luke.

"When you going to settle down and be who you ought to be rather than hiding?" Luke countered.

"I'm not hiding. I'm an assayer, or haven't you heard the latest?"

"That takes up an hour a day. The rest of the time you practice being a wastrel."

"I'm not wasting. I make good money gambling."

"I know there's a cost. Isn't that what the teacher was riding you about?"

"That woman has way too much time on her hands."

"I don't think it's a matter of time. It's a matter of passion."

Yeah, Pet had a lot of passion.

"I'd turn it my way if she'd look at me," Luke mused.

Ace didn't believe the innocence in that statement for a minute. Any more than he expected Luke to believe the calm distance in his "Have you tried?"

Luke shook his head. "Nah. No point. That lady treats me like the fence post in a corral. Handy when needed but otherwise not worth the attention. Mind telling me where we're going?"

Ace waved to the end of town. "I'm going to the livery."

"And after that?"

"For a ride."

"Would this ride entail a trip by the Winters' place?"

"Might."

Luke took a drag on his cigarette. "Going to have one of your infamous chats with him?"

"Might be."

"You know your chat's not going to do any good, don't you? That man's just soaked in gambling the way other men are soaked in gin."

"He drinks that, too."

"Not whiskey?"

"He drinks anything."

"He hit the boy again?"

Ace nodded. It wasn't the first time he and Luke had talked about that situation.

"Are you going to kill him?"

"Might."

Luke shot him a look. "That would be murder."

"Not if he takes a shot at me first."

"You plan on being that provoking?"

Ace shrugged. He didn't really know what he was going to do yet. "If the lay of the land demands it."

They reached the livery. Ace nodded to the stable hand and went to the stall that contained his sorrel.

"Crusher is getting fat hanging around here," Luke observed going to the next stall over, which contained his big roan.

Ace shook his head. "Not like Buddy's wasting away."

"I take him out every day."

"I take out Crusher, too, but it's not the same as riding trail."

They were all getting soft. Ace shook his head. Respectable. Fuck that.

"No, it's not." Luke patted Buddy's neck before he reached for the saddle. "Do you miss it?"

"What?"

"The old days," Luke said, tossing the saddle on Buddy's back, "when all we did was ride from one bad place to the next, one bad fight to the next."

Ace shook his head and eased the saddle back on Crusher before cinching it up. "That got old."

"Yeah, it did." For a moment they were both silent as old memories—old battles—rose to haunt them.

Luke broke the silence first like he always did. Ace often wondered if it wasn't being alone Luke hated as much as quiet. Holding his smoke in his mouth as he tied the rifle scabbard onto the saddle, he asked, "Can you believe Caine, Shadow, Tracker, hell, even Sam, settled down into business?" He dropped the stirrup down and patted Buddy's flank. "They're almost darn right respectable."

There was that word again. Ace smiled ruefully, checked his own weapons and led Crusher out of the livery. Yeah, they were. They'd achieved something none of them ever thought they would when they'd stood side by side as boys in the aftermath of the Mexican Army's attack, hands blistered from digging graves for their loved ones and made a promise to follow Caine Allen on the path of revenge. They'd almost starved that first year, all their promises vanishing with them, but they'd found Tia, and she'd healed them body and soul. Over time, they'd settled those debts, become Texas Rangers. And now, respectable.

Ace stubbed out his smoke on the sole of his boot once outside, shaking his head as Luke winced. "I'm making up for the rest of you."

"Uh-huh." Luke leaned over and ground his out in the dirt before dusting his fingers off on the saddle blanket.

"So what are we planning on doing if Winter meets us at the door with a shotgun?"

"Whatever the hell we want."

Luke smiled that easy smile he trotted out when he was contemplating mayhem. "More fodder for my next book."

Ace shook his head at the nonsense. Luke had a penchant for nice clothes and pretty words, but there was no one else Ace would want more by his side in a fight. Luke might dress fancy, but he fought like a cornered badger, with no quit and no mercy.

"What do you think would happen if people actually knew you lived what you wrote in those damn novels?" Ace asked.

Luke shuddered. "We'd be drowning in the frills and bows of all those prim Eastern women who'd want a piece of the real thing."

"What's with the *we*? You can keep all those fancy Eastern women for yourself."

"Oh, hell, no!"

Ace couldn't help but smile. Luke did like his women wild.

He waved toward the fancy vest and coat Luke was never without. "You're dressed for it."

"Clothes don't make the man. And under all this I'm the same no-account desperado I've always been." He swung up on Buddy and picked up the reins. "No lady can handle that."

That was the truth. Ace couldn't imagine anything worse for Luke than being tied up with something all prim and proper.

He wheeled Crusher around to the north. "Then you

best not be saying that too loud. You know fate has a sense of humor."

Luke shuddered again and kneed Buddy into step beside him. "Even fate wouldn't be that cruel."

They passed Pet's little house next to the school. There was no class on Friday. She was probably inside planning a lesson. Or sleeping. The thought of her all sleep warm and ready made him hard. Fuck.

Shaking his head he muttered, "Don't bet on it."

THE WINTERS' PLACE was little more than an overgrown mud wasp's nest, consisting of sawed sticks and logs packed together with dirt to make a home. From somewhere around back came the irregular sound of an ax hitting wood.

Luke pulled up and spat. "You'd have to take a step up to make this a hovel. No wonder Terrance is never clean."

Ace looked around with the same disgust. "It would be hard to wash this filth off."

And it wasn't the filth of the surroundings that Ace was talking about. It was the utter lack of self-respect the home reflected. Brian Winter didn't think much of himself or much of his prospects. "Might explain why he was at the gambling table every night looking for a miracle."

"And every morning taking out his disappointment on his son. This place isn't fit for a hog to live in," Luke said, kicking a nail-studded board out of his way before he dismounted. "Whatever we do, we can't be leaving the boy in this."

"It's not our responsibility." The words sounded hollow when he looked around. It shouldn't have taken Pet coming to town to bring this to his attention. He might have been walled up in that saloon too long.

Luke spat. "It's got to be someone's."

"He's almost the age we were when we were on our own." It wasn't the challenge Luke took it as.

"You forget we almost starved to death till Tia took us in hand?"

He didn't forget much, least of all the hunger, the pain of knowing his parents were dead and that he had nowhere after the massacre to go except with the other boys of Hell's Eight. Then there had been Tia. Tia, who'd taken on the role of mother, guide, disciplinarian. She'd saved their souls, shaped their anger, given them a purpose.

"We had each other."

"He's got no one."

Terrance had better than one. He had Pet.

Ace made the call. "He's got us now."

Luke nodded. "Amen."

They cleared around the little hovel, and they could see Terrance in the back splitting wood. The ax was bigger than the boy. *Too small, too skinny.* Those were the words that jumped into Ace's head. Hell, even his shirt draping off his thin shoulders made Ace feel guilty.

"He's going to cut off a foot," Luke muttered.

There was something in that boy's swing that told Ace there was more to him than the disappointment that life was handing him. "I don't think so."

Just then, Terrance looked up. The only word Ace could think of to describe his expression was *terrified*.

Luke must have seen it, too. "We're not going to hurt you, boy."

Terrance didn't put the ax down. Ace turned to Luke. "Must be your sour face that he's reacting to."

"Ha-ha." His gaze was locked on the bruise on Terrance's face. It was hard to look at. Harder to believe a man would do that to his own son.

"You shouldn't be here," Terrance said, glancing anxiously at the house.

"Or maybe his father's," Luke muttered before calling out, "Miss Wayfield sent us."

He only looked more terrified. "She didn't say nothing about you coming here." The kid looked at the house again. It wasn't hard to imagine why.

"Is your father home, son?" Ace asked, trying to think how one talked to a kid. Shit. He wasn't sure he ever had.

Terrance nodded.

Ace wanted to spit. "Is he still drunk or is he awake enough to move?"

From the fact that there weren't any fresh bruises on the kid, Ace was guessing that his father was probably still sleeping off last night's bottle.

Shifting the ax in his hand, Terrance gestured to the measly woodpile. "I've got to finish my chores."

"That didn't answer the man's question," Luke said.

"I've got my answer." Ace nodded to the woodpile. "You finish your chores, and we'll go talk with your pa."

"If we can wake him up," Luke muttered, disgust in his voice as he looked around again.

"It would be better if you didn't."

Ace dismounted and stood beside the boy. "Better if I didn't have to come out here at all, but neither one of us is getting what we want in that."

"Why did you come here?" the boy asked, resentment in his eyes.

"I lost a bet."

Terrance blinked. "You never lose."

"I know. It's not an experience I'm enjoying."

A shout came from the house. Terrance jumped and dropped the ax.

Ace put his hand on his shoulder. All he felt was bone. The potential of muscle too undernourished to grow pissed him off. Luke was right; they had only been a year or two older than this boy when they were set loose on the world, and they'd been heading for wreck and ruin until they found Tia, who'd stepped out of her own grief to put a rein on theirs. Who'd fed them and cared for them and made them slow down and learn. A widow dealing with her own loss who'd given them a home. They owed it to Tia to help Terrance.

"No matter what happens, you stay out here, you hear me? You don't go in the house."

"You won't hurt my pa?"

Ace couldn't promise him that. "I just need to talk to him."

"About what?"

He squeezed the boy's shoulder, gentling his grip immediately when he felt the fragility. He should be a sturdy kid at this age. He had the build of a boy who was going to be a big man, but he was far too thin.

"He's got something I want."

"What?"

"Just stay here and finish your chores."

"I got to bring water to the house next."

"Don't."

"But…"

Ace looked over to Luke. "Keep him here."

"Will do." Luke took off his coat and neatly draped it over his saddle, before smiling at Terrance. "I'll help you with your chores while we wait."

Ace headed for the house. From behind he heard Terrance say, "You'd better go with him," followed by Luke's "Why?"

"My pa can be mean."

"Ace can be meaner," Luke retorted.

Ace smiled and tugged his hat brim down just a bit. That was the truth. As Winter was about to find out.

The inside of the house wasn't much better than the outside. No, it was worse—the stench of dirt and molding sod fermented with the reek of vomit, drunkenness and stale cigarette butts.

Ace stood just inside the door. As his eyes adjusted to the gloom, he could see Winter sprawled on the only bed in the room. To one side of the door was a pallet of blankets on the floor. Christ, he treated the kid like a dog.

"Where the fuck you been, Terrance?" the man called, before moaning, "Where's my goddamn water?"

Winter fumbled blindly around the bed. Ace stepped forward and picked up the whiskey bottle Winter was searching for, and poured the contents over the man's head.

"What the fuck!"

Winter came flying out of the bed, arms flailing, shirttails flapping, stumbling as he got to his feet, clearly still drunk.

"Who the hell are you?"

Ace grabbed the bucket from the floor, threw the last of the water in his face. "Sober up. We need to talk."

Brian dragged his hands down his face, recognition dawning in his eyes. "I don't have a goddamn thing to talk about with you."

"You owe me money."

"I'll get it."

Ace made a point of looking around as Winter sat

back down on the bed and grabbed the dirty sheets and rubbed them across his face. It didn't help. The two day's growth of beard on his face caught the rough fabric leaving threads attached. Christ, he was a mess. How did the man sink this low?

"I told you I'd get you the money."

"Uh-huh." Ace took a seat at his table. The chair rocked under his weight. He caught himself before he could tip over.

"Leg's loose," Brian said.

"So I see." He nodded at Brian. "If you don't stop reaching under that mattress for that shotgun, I'm going to put a bullet in your shoulder."

Brian froze, his eyes going to the gun still in Ace's holster. "I heard you were fast."

"And I heard you were stupid. You keep reaching for that gun and we'll both know no one was lying."

"You got no right to be in my home."

"Nope. I don't, but I'm here anyway."

A cunning expression crossed his face. "You must want something."

"I told you, we need to talk."

Brian got up. The stench and sight of him made Ace's stomach heave. Luke was right. They weren't leaving the boy here.

Brian picked up the battered metal coffeepot by the well-tended fire. Terrance's work, no doubt. He shook the empty pot. "Where the hell is that lazy boy with the water for my coffee? Terrance!" he hollered.

"Terrance isn't coming." It felt good saying that.

Brian turned. The sweat stains on his faded red long johns stood out even in the dim light. "What the hell do you mean he's not coming?"

"He's helping Luke."

"With what?"

"Doesn't matter." Ace shoved the adjacent chair over with his foot. It caught on the uneven floor and fell over. "Sit your ass down."

Brian picked up the chair, still staring at the door. "I want my coffee."

"What you want is whiskey. You're not getting either until we're done, so the faster you sit, the faster you can get on with your life."

"What the hell do you want? Spit it out."

"Terrance."

The truth lay between them.

Without batting an eyelid, Brian asked, "For what?"

"It's none of your business."

"So that's how it is." Again that cunning expression slid over his face. "The boy will cost you."

With a push of his foot, Ace tipped the other man's chair over backward. When the swearing stopped he said, "You make another insinuation like that and I'll gut you. You hear me?"

Brian got up. Ace grazed the butt of his revolver with his fingertips.

"I hear you." Brian grunted, righting the chair. "Still going to cost you, though."

Ace wanted to drive his crooked teeth down his throat. "I figured."

"What's the boy worth to you?" Winter asked as he sat down again.

Ace just wanted this over with. "I'll cancel your gambling debt from last night."

A shrewd look entered Brian's eyes. "That's not enough."

You won't hurt my pa? Fuck, it never paid to be the good guy.

"What debts do you owe around town?"

Brian named a number that made Ace blink. Fortunately, most of those debts were to him or people who owed him, so it wasn't going to take much out of pocket to even Brian's score.

"How about I settle all your debts? Including the ones to me and in turn I take the boy?"

"All of them?"

"Yeah."

"Well, that will be a help but a man needs a stake to start over, and a man needs help to run a place like this."

Greedy bastard. "Plus two hundred."

Brian's eyes widened. "You got the money?"

"You'll get it."

"You're not getting the boy until I get the money."

Oh, that wasn't going to play. "I'm taking the boy when I leave here."

"I'm just supposed to go on your word?"

"Either you take my word, or I take your life."

Brian blinked. Ace waited for his booze-soaked mind to absorb that.

"Make up your mind. I don't have much time."

"You in a hurry for something?"

"I'm always in a hurry for something." He just never knew what it was that he was searching for, but he always had that nagging feeling that it was coming. That something good his mom had always promised him was waiting just around the next corner, the something good that always turned into something bad. "Do we have a deal?"

He didn't particularly care whether Brian agreed or

not. When he left here Terrance was going with him, but it would be cleaner if the ties were severed.

Brian held out his hand. "It's a deal."

It'd be a cold day in hell before Ace shook the hand of a man who'd sell his son. Especially for the reasons Winter implied. Just thinking about how easily he'd done it pissed Ace off. Until on a "What the hell" Ace punched Winter in the face, knocking him over backward. The man went down hard. When he didn't get up, Ace prodded his still form with his boot. He didn't move. Winter was out cold. Leaving him lying on the floor, Ace stood and strolled out of the hovel masking his anger and disgust. Worthless bastard. Not worth one bit of the concern in Terrance's expression.

With a slight nod of his head, he answered the question in Luke's eyes. With Terrance he was a bit more vocal. "Your pa and I had a talk."

Terrance nodded. His fists clenched.

"He's not feeling good right now."

"He isn't?" It was a credit to the optimism children held that the boy thought his father must be sick. "He needs his water for his coffee. He doesn't feel good until he has that."

"I'm going to go to town and get Doc."

"I'll stay with him."

Ace caught his arm. When the boy looked up, Ace bit back the harsh truth that nothing was going to help the man. He was so steeped in his greed and his booze that his morals were all off.

"You're going to come with me."

"Where to?"

"Miss Wayfield's."

"The schoolmarm?" He looked horrified.

Ace couldn't blame him. He couldn't think of a much worse fate for an eight-year-old boy than to be stuck with a schoolteacher. But then again, he couldn't think of a much worse fate than for a schoolteacher to be stuck with an eight-year-old boy. He smiled to himself. "Yep, she'll know what to do with you."

The boy took a step backward out of his reach. "Why does she have to do anything with me?"

Luke came up behind him, stopping his retreat. "Because you're eight, because you can't take care of yourself, but mostly because people care about you."

"I can take care of myself."

"Just saying it doesn't make it true, son."

"I can!"

Luke shot him a warning glance. "We know you can but remember Ace telling you he lost that bet?"

The boy nodded.

"Well, he lost it to Miss Wayfield."

The boy blinked. "Miss Wayfield gambles?"

With every breath she takes, Ace thought. The woman had a daring side that nobody but him seemed to see.

"She worries about you, boy. She sent me out here to check on you and your dad and she said if I found things were not looking good, that your dad needed help…"

Luke rolled his eyes at the tale. Ace glared at him over the boy's head.

"That I was to bring you back to town."

"What am I going to do in town?"

"Well," Luke said, "if you are as hungry as I am, have a steak dinner."

Ace could practically see the saliva flooding the kid's mouth, see the hunger in his eyes, but then Terrance shook his head, and his face took on a stubborn expression.

"I don't have any money."

"You don't need any money. I lost the bet, remember?"

"What was the bet?"

"The bet doesn't matter. What matters was the penalty."

"And what was that?"

"Steak dinners all around," Luke chimed in.

"For me, too?"

Especially for him but keeping the boy's pride in mind, he nodded. "For you, too, kid."

"And my dad said it's all right?"

"Yup."

"I don't know if I should go."

"He told me to take you." It wasn't exactly a lie.

"And you'll send the doctor?"

Ace heard the kid's stomach growl. He had to admire the boy's sense of honor. As hungry as he was and as much as he wanted that steak dinner, he wasn't leaving until he was sure his dad was all right.

"I'll send the doctor." The boy seemed satisfied. "Do you have anything you need to get? Anything special you need?"

The kid licked his lips, looked at Ace then at Luke then at Ace then back at Luke again. "I do have something."

"What?"

"It's real special."

Ace was out of patience. "Then fetch it."

Luke glared at Ace. "If it's in the house, tell me where it is and I'll get it."

"It isn't in the house."

They followed Terrance over to the corner of a fallen-down shack behind the house. The boy hesitated, looking around carefully before reaching in and pulling out a box poked through with holes. Very carefully he lifted the lid. Ace expected him to pull out marbles or pretty-colored rocks, the normal boy things. Instead, he pulled out a baby rabbit.

"This is Lancelot."

Luke choked. "Mighty big name for such a little critter."

Terrance nodded and stroked the rabbit, which looked completely relaxed. "It's from one of the stories Miss Wayfield told us. He didn't have a home."

Tucking the bunny in his shirt, he squared off against Ace and Luke. From the expression on his face, he was ready to take them both on if they made a comment. The boy held the bunny through his shirt. "He needs me."

Ace didn't have anything to say to that.

"He does!"

"Well, that's that, then." Ace wasn't going to fight a kid over a rabbit. "Is there anything else?"

Terrance shook his head.

"Then let's get a move on. I've got a game waiting."

They headed back to the horses. The boy didn't look at the house again, but he tensed as they passed it as if expecting his father to come out and take away that steak dinner.

Ace put his hand on his shoulder and squeezed gently. Terrance didn't look up after the initial tensing, and he stayed tense under his hand. Ace didn't know what Pet was going to do with the boy but whatever she did, it had to be better than this.

"It will be all right, son."

Terrance looked at him, disbelief clearly in his gaze.

Ace resisted the urge to squeeze his shoulder again. "I know it doesn't seem like it, but you'll see."

"Nothing like a steak dinner to change a man's perspective," Luke added.

At the thought of dinner, the boy perked right up again. Luke mounted Buddy. Ace gave Terrance a boost up behind.

"Watch that rabbit now. You don't want to crush him."

Terrance nodded. Good Christ. Was this what he'd come to? Babysitting a kid and a bunny? Ace shook his head and swung up on Crusher.

"Then let's get going."

The sooner the kid and the bunny were Pet's problem, the happier he'd be.

CHAPTER FIVE

"YOU CAN'T BE SERIOUS," Petunia demanded of Ace as she watched Terrance through the window of the restaurant. He was sitting at a table looking like heaven had just been placed before him in the form of a huge steak. Beside him, Luisa hovered. From her frequent hand gestures, Petunia assumed she was encouraging him to eat. Luisa was the quintessential mother, though she had no children of her own. From her come-get-a-hug manner to her soft brown eyes shining from a plump face touched with wrinkles from a lifetime of smiles, she made a body feel welcome. From the relaxed set of his shoulders, Terrance was not exempt from her charm.

"You said take care of it. It's taken care of," Ace said with aggravating calm.

"I can't take care of a child!"

Ace, damn him, just looked at her that way he had that made her feel transparent and vulnerable, like one too many buttons had slipped loose on her blouse.

"You take care of several all day."

"As a means to an end! You know I'm just saving up for a ticket out of here."

That got her a smile that made her palm itch to smack it off his face.

"It'd be a shame if everyone else knew that."

Somewhere in their heads they had to know this, but

traditional beliefs held that women loved children, and the townsfolk of Simple were assuming that Petunia had found her place here. That being the case, they seemed happy to pretend she hadn't ever declared this job was only temporary. She curled her fingers into a fist, suppressing the impulse to smack him. "You know they'll advertise for someone else if they know for sure I'm leaving."

"Yes, I do."

"They'll fire me if they find someone."

"Yes."

He had her over a barrel. She needed a different approach. Playing a long shot, she met his gaze and said softly, "It would hurt me."

Nothing in his expression changed. "What makes you think I give a shit about that?"

She didn't, but she was gambling. The only thing she knew about gambling was if she was going to do it, she had to be all in. So she bluffed.

"Because you're not a cruel man."

Something flickered across his face. "You don't know me at all."

No, she didn't, beyond the fact that he drove her senses crazy, and she always wanted to touch him or nibble on him or do all kinds of things she couldn't even put a name to when she was in his company. She knew very little about him except that he had one respectable job, one unrespectable one and lived a dissolute life.

"You're not going to say anything to them?"

"No, I'm not."

She didn't like the way he said that. "Because you're a good man under all that bluster?"

"Hell, no!"

"Then why not?"

His smile held all the confidence she was faking. "Because you're not going to make me."

"I can't take care of that child."

"Someone has to."

She tried again. "What is he going to do when I leave?"

"He needs a place to stay *tonight*."

In other words, one step at a time.

"We don't have the boarding school set up yet. Terrance can't stay there."

He shrugged. "That's not my problem. You told me to handle it. I did."

"I asked you to give Brian Winter his money back!"

"Giving him his money back wouldn't have been the end, and I would have to go back there tomorrow doing the same thing. You've harped on my lazy nature enough over the past couple months to know doing the same thing over and over isn't my cup of tea."

"You don't even drink tea."

He smiled that cat-and-mouse smile that made her pulse jump and her palm itch. "Actually, I do... sometimes."

She could feel the walls closing in and her dream slipping away again.

"It's almost Christmas," he added as if she needed another stab to the heart. "You want the boy to live to see it?"

"Now, that's not fair."

"You didn't see what I saw at the Winters' place."

"Was it really that bad?"

"The boy is lucky his situation caught your eye." A

grimace and a shake of his head. "And the rest of us need to be shamed it didn't catch ours."

She blinked. "Why, Mr. Parker, are you saying there's a place for a busybody do-gooder in this world?"

There was a pause and a nod and then, "I'm saying you've earned yours."

The quirk of his lips, neither smile nor frown, was irritating in all it didn't say. Almost as irritating as the way he leaned against the porch rail, arms folded across his chest, as if he owned that space. And the way he looked at her, as if he owned her, too, just made her bristle. She wasn't just any man's plaything.

"So what are you going to do, Pet? Are you going to take the boy or am I going to have to add tattletale to my list of sins?"

Pfft. Who, except her, would even notice that sin on his long list?

"I'm thinking."

"Not much to think about."

No, there wasn't. Tattling about her plans to leave wouldn't hurt Ace's reputation but for her, his tattling would be catastrophic. She was a month away from having enough money for her ticket. Taking in the boy could very well cost that money and some time—it would be too dangerous to travel come winter—but on the other hand, she'd have longer to save and the end result would be more money in her pocket come spring. But if Ace spread his tale, she'd lose her job. She had no doubt Ace would take care of her and arrange it so she'd still be able to take care of Terrance and anyone else who needed it, but she wouldn't have an independent income. She wouldn't make it to California.

Which meant a slight change in her plans. She needed

to open the school. She felt the twinge of guilt for the kids she'd be leaving behind, especially Terrance, but he'd have a safe place to live, and if she could find somebody to run it with a good heart, then it would make a difference. There was a whole lot she needed to do in the next month, but she was a woman that worked well under pressure, and it wasn't the first time she'd faced these kinds of deadlines.

"I have yet to secure the Haylens' old place for the school." The Haylens' house was on the edge of town. It was a bit ramshackled, but it was huge with six bedrooms and a good-size yard. With elbow grease and determination, it would be perfect.

"I'll take care of that."

"You think you can sway Tyson to sell?" She'd been trying for a month to no avail. Every time she approached the irritating man, the price went up. And it hadn't exactly started at reasonable.

He just looked at her. "I said I'd handle it."

And that was that as far as he was concerned. So be it. Petunia folded her own arms across her chest. "Fine. Then under the condition you get the Haylen place for us tomorrow, Terrance can sleep on my sofa tonight."

"I'm sure he's slept on worse."

Which just brought them back to the questions that had been plaguing her since Ace and Luke had ridden back into town with Terrance in tow.

"Did Brian really just let you walk in and take his son?" She knew Brian was a wastrel, but she didn't believe he was that much of a wastrel. If nothing else, Terrance had value as a worker that made his father's life easier.

"Not exactly, but in the end we came to an agreement."

Petunia dropped her gaze to Ace's hands, the ones he had tucked under his arms. She didn't know what possessed her. It was against all propriety, but she reached out and caught his right pinky in her fingers. His hand was warm, but the palm surprisingly calloused for a man who gambled. He hadn't always been a gambler or an assayer, she reminded herself. According to legend, Hell's Eight was a lot of things. A group of almost mythical warriors. Fierce. Relentless.

She tugged. The only thing that moved was his left eyebrow.

"You wanting something?"

"I want to see your hand."

"Why, going to slip a ring on it?"

She huffed. "I'm not that kind of woman, and you're not that kind of man."

The smile he gave her was genuine. "You've got that half right."

She tugged again. This time he let her win. She was surprised to see the knuckles unscarred.

"Satisfied?" he asked, tucking his hand back under his arm and shifting his position.

"Hardly."

She noticed the butt of the revolver on his left hip had a little less shine. It was then she remembered he was left-handed.

"Can I see the other hand?"

"Why?"

"I'm contrary that way."

"I'll give you that. You're contrary."

He didn't make any move to show her his hand. She didn't push it.

Rubbing her fingertips on her thigh she said, "I'm going to take it from that that those knuckles are bruised."

"Assume all you want."

"Did you hurt him?"

That got his attention. "Worried about his sorry ass?"

"No, I'm more hoping you beat him into the ground. He's a brute and a bully, and it's about time somebody gave him what he really deserved."

"Well, I wouldn't go that far, but he's nursing a headache for sure."

It soothed a bit of her anger to know that. "Is he going to come after Terrance?"

"At some point I imagine he will remember he's a father, but I don't think it'll be in the near future."

"How does Terrance feel about that?"

"I don't think he feels anything. He seems to live for the right now."

For some reason she felt the need to defend Terrance. "He's a boy."

"Uh-huh"

The wind blew a hair across her face. She brushed it out of her eyes. It fell back down, tickling her temple. "You don't like children?"

"I don't have anything against them. I don't have anything for them beyond I don't intend to have any ever."

"Why not?"

"Do you really think I'd make a good father?"

Surprisingly, she did. He might have a wastrel profession but he also had a reputation for fighting for the underdog. He'd be a strong and protective father. And while breath filled his lungs, his children would never want.

Half turning, he pushed the hair that was tickling off her temple. "That hard an answer to come up with?"

"I was actually thinking you'd make a very good father. But heaven help your daughters."

His brow snapped down, and that hand that had just touched her so tenderly curled into a fist. She had the oddest impression that he was hurt. "You think I'd hurt my girls?"

One would think she'd have the sense to be afraid, but she wasn't. "I think they'd grow up in danger of becoming old maids waiting for a suitor brave enough to come courting."

"Damn straight." His expression traveled from wary to speculative in the space of a breath. "Have you been spending a lot of time thinking on me?"

She didn't like to admit the truth. She also refused to lie. "Some. There's not much to do in this town besides look at the local color, and you are colorful."

"Do you always give a direct answer?"

"I try to be honest."

"When it suits you?"

She sighed. Life would be so much easier if she could lie. "Even when it doesn't."

"Why? Lying's easier."

It was her turn to shrug. "People taking the easy way all the time is one of the reasons children like Terrance don't get a chance, why women get black eyes from the men they love and why men sometimes have to be what they don't want to be just to survive."

"The last doesn't make sense."

"Sure it does. Not every man's temperament is suited to a warrior's life."

Ace huffed. "Any man worth his salt knows how to fight."

"I know, and it's easier to say that rather than to accept differences."

Ace stared at her for the longest time. "You are one strange woman, Petunia Wayfield."

She kept her wince internal. "So I've been told."

"By people that don't appreciate it, I bet."

"Nope," she agreed, "no more than you do."

"Oh?" His fingers skimmed the side of her cheek. "I appreciate this."

This? This, her face? This, her position? Or this, the all of her?

"It's just not for me."

It just came tripping right off her tongue. "Why not?"

And his response came easily off his. "Because under all that spit and fire you're a sweet, gentle woman who needs a man to hold her place." Cupping her chin, he tipped her gaze to his. "It just can't be me."

With that he turned on his heel and walked away, leaving her sputtering for a comeback.

He was halfway to the saloon before, finally, she found her voice again. "What makes you think I'd want you?"

There was no way he could have heard that muttered utterance. No way at all, but his laugh when it drifted back, still flicked her nerves. The man was impossible. Fine looking, but impossible. Taking a moment to admire the breadth of his shoulders and the narrowness of his hips and, Lord help her, the space in between, she watched until he stepped inside the saloon. The faint sound of greeting followed by a lilt of feminine laughter drifted in his wake. Anger pricked her pride before it dug a wedge deeper. She hated the thought of another woman touching Ace. She hated the thought that he thought she was good and sweet and treated both qualities as if they were something bad.

Rubbing her forehead, she sighed. She'd been hating a lot of things lately. More than usual the past few years. The way Ace saw her was just one more item tacked on to a long list. Truth was, she was frustrated and tired. If she could just get out to California where the rules were so much more liberal, where money made the person, not the gender, it would all be well.

More feminine laughter drifted out along with the faint murmur of Ace's voice. Petunia would give anything to know what he was saying. She'd give anything to have the courage to march into that saloon and demand that he explain himself. Oh, hell, she rubbed her hands up and down her arm. Who was she kidding? She wanted an opportunity to prove him wrong about her, that she was more than enough woman for him and that being good didn't make you useless, and being sweet didn't mean you weren't passionate. She was so tired of that silliness. She'd seen it so often, it'd smothered her for so long, it just made her teeth grind when somebody applied it to her. Anybody could be sweet when the moment called for it. Anybody could be kind. Anybody could be good. No one thing was the sum total of a person.

Slowly and deliberately she turned her back on the saloon. Through the restaurant window she saw Terrance was almost done with his dinner. Flicking her skirt straight and smoothing her hair, Petunia headed across the street to Luisa's. Putting off the inevitable wasn't going to make it go away. There was only one other patron in the restaurant, and he didn't even give her the time of day when she stepped through the door. He was just shoveling his food into his mouth as fast as he could,

some of it catching on his beard. No doubt he was eager
to get over to the saloon for some cards and women.

She shuddered. She wouldn't want to be the one re-
ceiving his attentions tonight. Honestly, she didn't know
how those women above stairs did it. Which just went
to prove how much society needed to change. Women
shouldn't have to sell their bodies to survive. They ought
to be able to make a living wage. They ought to be able
to have some recourse to get out of a bad marriage and
not be penniless and shunned. They ought to be able to
keep their children. They ought to be able to vote, and
they truly, truly ought to be able to have some standing
under the law.

The anger in her thoughts must have showed on her
face because as soon as she stopped beside the table,
Terrance looked up at her, and his eyes went wide and
he swallowed hard, his fork frozen halfway between
the plate and his mouth. Luisa, seated beside Terrance,
looked at her curiously. Petunia took a breath and forced
a smile.

"Hello, Terrance."

He nodded. Luisa handed him his napkin. He took it
and wiped his mouth and his hands. Someone at some
time had taught him basic manners. And he was trotting
them out for her, the only thanks he could offer. Wrapped
in a red velvet ribbon of hope.

"Hello, Miss Wayfield."

In many ways they were alike. Struggling to be who
they were in a world that wanted to call them something
else. She could help him with that. Her smile began to
feel more natural. "That sure looks like a delicious supper."

"The best ever."

Luisa smiled and ruffled his hair at the compliment. "He has the honey tongue, this one."

His steak was half-eaten. Petunia would have been hard-pressed to eat a quarter of it. Looking at the thinness of his arms and the bones poking out his shoulders against his shirt, she figured he would probably eat that plate and more if his stomach would hold it. Terrance had the appearance of boy long starved for many things.

A part of her wished she could stay in Simple and fix everything, but she couldn't. She knew that. It wasn't practical. Neither the laws nor the community would back her. No, she had to keep her focus. Her future was in California. In California she was going to own her own business, own her own life and she was going to make a difference. But she could get things started for Terrance. It might delay her departure a little bit… She glanced at his bruised eye. He was her student. She owed him that. Forcing a smile, she said brightly, "My goodness, Terrance. That's a man's appetite you have there!"

"It's good." Luisa smiled at Terrance. "He has a good appetite. He will eat that steak all gone and then dessert."

"You're going to have dessert, too?" Where was he going to put it all?

Terrance nodded enthusiastically. "Apple pie," he said as though they were talking about the best of nirvana which, to a boy without a mother to bake for him, she supposed apple pie might qualify.

"I make a good apple pie," Luisa said proudly.

"That she does," Petunia agreed. "I've had it a time or two myself."

She couldn't help but run her hands over her hips. She had to stop going to Maddie's bakery and coming here to Luisa's restaurant, but the truth was if left to her own devices, eating was minimal because she didn't like to cook, and her efforts were marginally edible at best, but she loved to eat, and part of her salary as a teacher was two free meals a day at any of the town's three restaurants. So basically, she paid for coffee in the morning because she didn't care for breakfast, and then ate well the rest of the day.

Terrance took another bite of potato, chewed, swallowed and then frowned. "Mr. Parker says I'm going to be staying with you tonight."

"That's right."

A little of the fear left his face. "And then I'll go home tomorrow?"

Her smile came more naturally. If Ace was going to put the pressure on her, she'd throw some back on him.

"Mr. Parker said your father had to work on some… Had some things to deal with…some business to handle before…" Oh, gosh, she wasn't good at lying.

The expression on Terrance's face said he knew what she was trying to say, but she forced herself through to the finish because, well, because he was a little boy, and the truth that his father was a wastrel wasn't something a woman threw in a little boy's face. Not if she could leave him some illusions.

Clearing her throat, she started over. "Your father has some things to work on before you can go home, but tonight you're going to stay with me at my house and then tomorrow we found this special place where you'll stay. It's sort of like a hotel for children."

His eyes lit up. "I've never stayed at a hotel. Pa says they're real fancy."

"Well, this hotel might not be that fancy but…"

"Does it have a bed?"

She blinked. The question took her aback. "A very nice bed with clean sheets and a blanket and a soft pillow."

Luisa blinked rapidly and patted his back. "And a nice quilt."

Petunia looked at her. She didn't know if they had quilts.

"I'm going to give you one that belonged to my son. A welcome present."

Luisa's son had died in his teens.

"It is a good quilt. Many happy memories inside, many happy dreams."

"A quilt with happy dreams?" Terrance asked skeptically.

Luisa tilted her head back and looked down her nose sternly. It was a very effective look. "You doubt my word?"

"No." He cut into his steak before asking, "Where's your son now?"

"He died."

With the innocence of youth, Terrance persisted, "How?"

Luisa wiped her eyes. "He went swimming in the spring when the water was angry."

"He drowned?"

She nodded.

Terrance had the grace to look sad, to feel bad. He poked his potatoes with his fork. "I suppose you miss him."

Luisa looked at him. "I miss him very much, but I thank God for every day I had with him, and I know when my time comes, I will see him in heaven again."

"You think he went to heaven?"

"I think all boys go to heaven. All children go to heaven."

"My pa says Ma's in heaven." He clearly wanted confirmation.

"I'm sure she is."

He poked his food again and looked up from under his lashes. He had very thick lashes for a boy, but his cheeks were too angular and too sharp and his chin too pointed to look angelic. He was all angles, all sadness and doubt, which only made Petunia want to give him hope. "I hope so."

"I didn't know your mother but I can see her in you."

"If you never met her," he scoffed, "how can you see her?"

It was Luisa who answered. "Because I've seen your father but there are parts of you that look nothing like him, so it has to be your mother showing. I'm told she was a very smart, sweet woman, and I'm sure like my Marcos, she sits in heaven watching over you."

He poked the food harder and muttered, "She hasn't done a very good job."

"What makes you say that?" Petunia asked, hoping for a clue, something to grab a hold of on this boy who was so withdrawn into himself. Whose only outlet was learning.

Again it was Luisa who answered. "Because she sent you Mr. Parker and Miss Wayfield."

He didn't glance up. "She could have sent them sooner."

Luisa grimaced. "Maybe time is different up there, or maybe she had to wait her turn, but she sent them. On this you should focus."

"I really don't have to go back?"

The question was directed at Petunia. If she hadn't told Ace she'd take Terrance before, she would have in that moment. "No, you don't have to go back."

He cut a piece of meat aggressively. And again. And again, and again until it lay in his plate in bites almost too small to chew.

"My father won't like that. He likes to have me around."

"I'm sure he does."

"He'll come for me."

She figured as much. "If he does, then we'll talk to him and see what happens."

"My pa isn't big on talking."

She smiled and ruffled his hair. "Well, we're safe, then, because I can talk enough for four people."

"That's what Mr. Parker said. Said you got a mouth enough for three women."

"Did he now?" Within earshot of a child, no less. Petunia would be having a word with him about that.

"He didn't say it in a bad way. He likes you."

Out of the mouths of babes. Her fantasies garnered hope.

Luisa's husband, Antonio, came out of the kitchen, wiping his hands on his apron. He was a big man, overweight in a way that spoke of contentment. *Robust* maybe was a better description. He had dark eyes, slight bags beneath; five o'clock shadow showed on his cheeks, but he had a smile that always lit up anyone's day. He put his arm around Luisa's shoulders.

"The women, they are treating you right?" he asked Terrance.

Terrance cringed into himself, pulling in his shoulders tight, clearly nervous around the big man. His nod was barely discernible.

"Good. Good." Antonio asked, "If you are done with this meal, I have for you a dessert I made special."

That got the boy to look up. "I was going to have apple pie."

"You can have apple pie," Antonio chuckled, "but this, this dessert I made just for you."

Terrance blinked. "Never met a man who cooked before."

"You like to eat?"

He nodded.

"Then you must learn to cook. It's not good for a man to be dependent on a woman for everything. It is also good for a man to be able to treat his wife now and then."

Terrance just stared at him, clearly not knowing what to think of that. Antonio smiled and took his plate. The look of loss on Terrance's face spoke volumes. Antonio waved it away with another chuckle.

"Do not worry. We will pack this up in a nice basket and send it home with you. You can finish it later but now, now it is time for dessert. After a good meal the tongue needs a joy."

He turned and went back into the kitchen. When he came back out, he was carrying two plates. One was the apple pie, whipped cream on top. The other was a clear bowl, and through it you could see layers of cake and jelly and berries.

"This is a treat my mother used to make on special days when we were celebrating." He set the plates down in front of Terrance. "It is very good."

Terrance hesitantly touched the whipped cream on top of the pie with his finger. "What are we celebrating?"

Antonio rested his hands on his stomach. "New

friendships, good food and new beginnings. All good things.

"Go ahead," Antonio said, handing him his fork, "*Mangia*. Eat. I would not serve you something bad."

Terrance touched his finger to his tongue. His eyes went wide, and he grabbed his fork. Clearly he'd never had whipped cream before. Antonio laughed at the boy's enthusiasm, but Petunia just shook her head. How could a boy not know the taste of whipped cream? It had been a staple in her house.

As if reading her thoughts, Luisa whispered, "Things come to us in their own time, but when they come, we celebrate."

It was simple philosophy. One that was hard for Petunia to wrap her mind around.

"I believe in planning."

"And when the plans go wrong?"

She shrugged.

When Terrance slowed down, Luisa took the bowl from him and the pie.

At his protest she said, "This, too, we will wrap. There is no need to eat it all at once. You will give yourself a stomachache."

Petunia was afraid that was already ahead.

"Can I take the carrots, too?" he asked.

"Of course." Luisa handed the plates to Antonio, who took them back into the kitchen. "Lancelot must eat big and grow, too. Do not give him any of the dessert, though. Such things are not good for bunnies."

"Lancelot?" Petunia asked, too afraid she already knew the answer.

Terrance tucked his chin and looked up at her, every muscle telegraphing stubborn. Wiping his hands and face

with his napkin, he stood. When he stepped away from
the table, Petunia saw the box on the seat beside him.
Almost defiantly, he opened the lid. From the cozy hay
lined inside, a little brown baby rabbit wiggled his nose
at her. Just as carefully, Terrance closed the lid and met
her gaze squarely. "He's my friend. I take care of him."

"I'm sure a very good friend." She didn't know what
else to say.

His shoulders squared. "He goes where I go."

It was the first time Petunia had known Terrance to
stand up for anything. "I'm not sure we'll have room in
the house for him."

"If he fits in the chair, he can fit in the house."

There was no refuting that logic, but everything in
her rebelled at the thought of an animal in her house.

"I'm sure he'd be happier outside. He'd be able to go
to the bathroom when he wanted to and eat grass."

Terrance spread his legs and clenched his fists. The
rabbit clearly mattered to him. "He goes on paper in the
house."

Petunia had been prepared for the boy's tears at leaving his home. She'd been prepared to give a long explanation of how Terrance's life was going to change. She
hadn't prepared for the contingency of a rabbit boarder
and its belligerent owner.

Luisa's words so recently spoken came back to haunt
her.

And when the plans go wrong?

Apparently, she took on a bunny boarder.

Terrance relaxed when she smiled and ruffled his hair.
"Well, if he's that nice a guest, there won't be any problem having him in the house."

Luisa nodded. Light flashed off the threads of gray in

her rich black hair "I always have scraps leftover. I will send them along for him to eat every day."

"Yes, he will need good food to grow into his name," Antonio added as he came back with the basket of leftovers, not even blinking at the conversation. Had everyone known about Lancelot but her? There was no sense fighting what couldn't be helped. She took the basket from Antonio. "Good, but now I think it's time we get him home. He's going to be tired now that his belly's full."

Luisa stopped them. "Wait. I must fetch the quilt."

Petunia had forgotten about the quilt. She passed the basket to Terrance. He hugged it tightly.

A few minutes later, Luisa returned with a blue-and-white folded quilt in her arms. She rubbed it softly with her fingertips, before thrusting it at Petunia.

"This is for the boy. For his dreams."

As soon as Petunia took the offering, Antonio put his arm around his wife and pulled her into his side. Luisa wiped at her eyes with her apron. Antonio brushed her hair with his lips and murmured, "It is good, *carina*. This is good."

"Say thank-you," Petunia told Terrance quietly.

He did, hugging Lancelot's box and his basket of food. She clutched the quilt and suddenly wondered if she really knew what she was getting into. This simple rescue of a small boy was gaining momentum faster than she could contain. She wanted the town involved, but seeing the emotion in Luisa's eyes, the torment in Antonio's, the hope in Terrance's, she just didn't know... Taking a breath, she reminded herself she was just the bridge. Once she had someone hired to manage the school, and the proper people convinced the boarding school was their pet project, she could be on her way. She just had to get through tonight. That was all. Just tonight.

CHAPTER SIX

ACE SECURED TYSON HAYLEN's house in two days. She didn't know how he did it and didn't ask. She was just grateful for the space. A rambunctious child and a happy bunny were a lot to fit in her small, two-room house. She'd been confident her search for someone to run the school would have been equally as successful, but it hadn't happened the way Petunia had planned. She'd given herself three days to find a house mistress for the Providence, as she'd named the school. The first day she'd gotten one applicant. An elderly woman too frail to even climb the front stairs without help. Day two she got three more applicants. One woman with the smell of gin on her breath, another who could only watch the children between noon and dark but couldn't stay the night, and the third was a man whose motives she completely did not trust.

On day three, no one showed up at all, and the reality that this might just not work out was slowly eating at her confidence. As she sat in the kitchen after school ended at three o'clock, making a snack for Terrance, she was beginning to wonder if she was going to have to send to one of the bigger towns, San Antonio or such, to find someone who would care for the house. If she had to do that it was going to set her back another month or

even two, and she really couldn't afford that. The passes
closed in the winter.

The knock at the door was loud. Before she could get
out of her chair, it came again hard and fast. Someone
wanted in. The hairs on the back of her neck rose and
her stomach dropped.

"Stay here," she told Terrance. He looked at her, his
hand on Lancelot in his lap, and nodded. She eyed the
gun Ace had left her by the back door. Guns made her
nervous.

Maybe it was Brian.

Grabbing the gun, she shook her head. If it were Brian
Winter, he wouldn't knock. He'd burst in all righteous indignation and with the aggression of a drunken boor. She
set the gun back against the wall. Straightening her skirts
and smoothing her hair, she walked sedately through the
house. Terrance didn't need to live in any more fear than
necessary. Peeking out the stained-glass side windows
she could just make out the distorted yet unmistakable
shape of a skirt. Her visitor was a woman. She opened
the front door.

The sight that greeted her was just as brash as the
knock. A garishly blowsy woman stood there clutching the hands of two children. The boy was around Terrance's age, his hair slicked back from his hostile face.
Water still dripped from his hair, dampening the shoulders of his freshly ironed, well-worn shirt. At some point
it had probably been blue but now was kind of a washed-
out gray. His pants hung loose on him, but were still
too short.

The little girl was maybe a couple years younger. Her
blond hair was pulled back tight and clearly ringlets had
been forced into what was normally straight hair. Both

children were well scrubbed. Both looked as scared as all get-out.

Petunia looked up from the children to take in the woman with them. She was a sight to behold. It was hard to tell her age; there was so much powder on her face. Her blue eyes were heavily lined in black kohl. Her hair was swept up into a messy arrangement, and her generous breasts all but spilled out of her loose top.

That might have been shame that flashed across her face as Pet asked, "May I help you?" but if it was, it was gone so fast it left no lingering impression. Before she could double-check, the woman's expression became just as brash as the knock and the outfit.

"I'm right sorry I didn't have time to dress proper for this." She pushed the children in the door. Before Petunia could protest, she followed behind them, a cloud of perfume swirling along. Petunia choked and waved her hand in front of her face.

Hustling the children into the adjoining parlor, the woman explained as calmly as if she were making sense, "I need my last payment, and if I don't show up tonight I won't get it, and there won't be time after we get settled in here for me to change." With a wave of her hand she indicated her outfit. It didn't take a genius to figure out where she worked. "So this will just have to do."

As explanations went, it didn't cover much. "Do?"

The woman motioned the children into a chair. "Sit," she ordered, before turning back to face her. "My name's Hester."

"Hester?" Pet knew she sounded like a parrot, but she just couldn't quite figure out what a soiled dove from the saloon was doing in her living room with two children

in tow. She looked on the porch. There weren't any suit-
cases. "Were you looking to place your children here?"

The woman snapped straight so fast her hair crackled, and dust from the starch floated in the sunbeams.
"If I haven't abandoned my children before this, I'd not
be starting now, just when things are going my way."

She said that as if that made sense. Petunia took a deep
breath, counted to five and slowly released it. "I'm sorry.
Could you tell me, please, what you are doing here?"

Hester reached into her bodice and pulled out a piece
of paper. As she unfolded it, Petunia recognized her flyer.
The one that she'd put up at the store.

"I came for the job."

Oh, dear. Petunia almost said that out loud, but caught
herself. She closed the door quietly and joined them in
the parlor. "I don't think you understand the position."

"You're looking for somebody that can watch after
children."

"Yes"

"Well, I'm a mother of two, and I was the oldest of
twelve growing up. One thing I know is children."

"Yes, but the other requirements of the position are
somebody who's—" how did she put this delicately?
"—got the background that will inspire confidence in
the good citizens funding this home."

"You mean someone who's not a whore."

Well, that was one way to do it. "To be indelicate, yes."

Hester snorted. "Well, I wasn't always a whore. There
was a time back when I had these two, when I was a wife
and mother and as respectable as you can get."

Looking at her now, Petunia found that hard to believe.

"But then their pa ran off to find gold and stopped sending money back," Hester continued.

"I see." It was a common enough story.

"I followed him out here hoping to catch up with him, but turns out he'd done divorced me."

"How can he divorce you without your permission?"

"That's what I asked. Apparently, it doesn't take much. A lie here. Some gold dust there…" She shrugged.

Pet felt a stirring of sympathy.

"And he married up with some pretty little thing, got a second family and isn't at all interested in this one anymore."

Petunia glanced at the children, and that stirring of sympathy deepened. There was something vaguely familiar about both. Something she couldn't quite put her finger on…

"So I took my maiden name back, Mansfield, and did what I had to do to feed my kids."

It was another common story. There were questions in regard to recourse Petunia would have asked anyone else, but Hester struck her as a woman who would have exhausted all avenues.

"I've been a whore going on three years. I was a respectable woman for thirty before that, and I aim to go back to it."

"I see." She didn't know what else to say. And since Hester's feet were firmly planted, she didn't see any other option other than to conduct an interview. Smoothing her skirts, she sat on the faded wingback chair near the archway. "Well, what are your qualifications?"

Hester looked around the shabby, dusty interior. "Number one, I'm a heck of a lot better housekeeper than this."

Petunia had an immediate urge to pick up a rag and dust. As if reading her mind, Hester started straightening the pile of papers in the corner.

"The house requires work," Petunia admitted.

"I'm not afraid of hard work."

No, Hester didn't look like she was. She wasn't a particularly tall woman or a particularly broad woman. There was just something very…solid about her. Something more substantial than her bountiful bosom, and if she'd had any other background than the one she had, Petunia might have pursued the application further, but she was having a hard enough time getting the good people of this community to crack their wallets open to take care of the less fortunate. The squawk that would arise if she put Hester in charge… She shook her head. All the sweet talk in the world wouldn't squash that.

"I'm sorry. It's just not possible."

Hester looked up. "Anything's possible." Dropping the advertisement neatly onto the table, she folded her arms across her chest. "I understand you got stranded here yourself."

"I did."

"And by the grace of God, you were able to get a teaching position."

"Yes."

"And if you hadn't been able to, what would you have done?"

She didn't want to say, *Telegraphed my father*, so she settled for, "I'm not sure."

"I can tell you right now what you would have done. Whatever it took, 'cause that's the only option women have. I found that married or not, that's just how it is."

The logic played right into the reality of a woman's plight Petunia wanted to change.

"If it were up to me, I might consider giving you a try, but my first responsibility has got to be toward these children and to making sure they have a roof over their heads."

"Rumor is the only child you have right now is Terrance Winter."

"Yes, he is staying here." Hearing his name, Terrance appeared in the doorway holding Lancelot.

"Well, this here is my son, Phillip, and my daughter, Brenda. They're good kids. I keep up with their schooling in the mornings before I go to bed. They know their manners."

Their manners were evident from the way they sat, quietly and respectful.

"We don't have much right now, but we know right from wrong."

Petunia sighed. Hester wasn't going to make this easy. "If you know right from wrong, then you know how small this community is."

Hester nodded and more starch drifted free. Caught in the late-day sun that drifted in the room. "Not to mention small-minded."

How could she argue with that? "Terrance, would you please take Brenda and Phillip into the kitchen and give them some cookies and milk?"

Terrance nodded. Brenda went eagerly, fascinated by Lancelot. Phillip went with a bit more drag in his step.

"Make them welcome, Terrance," she added.

Terrance nodded. Hester jerked her chin at Phillip when he paused in the doorway. "Go on now."

As soon as they were in the kitchen, Hester rubbed

her hands together. It was the first sign of nervousness Petunia had seen her display. "I appreciate you having the rest of this talk in private. Living as we do, there's no way they can't know how things are."

It was Petunia's turn to sigh. "I wish I could help you. I truly do."

Hester set her hands on her hips. Her breasts bounced, and for a moment Petunia worried they'd spill free.

"If you're worried about certain people, prominent people, in this community squawking, I guarantee you they won't."

Interesting. "What makes you think they won't?"

"Because I'll make sure of it."

That was a useful talent to have. "You can do that?"

"I have one or two pieces of leverage."

The look she gave the door was significant, and that sense of familiarity about the children nagged at Petunia again. "Why do your children look familiar?"

Hester didn't even hesitate. "You've probably met their father."

"Who's their father?"

"Dougall MacFarlane."

Petunia couldn't suppress a gasp. "The mayor?"

"Yeah, the town's big man. As you can imagine, we were quite the embarrassment showing up here. He'd prefer you'd run us out of Simple on a rail rather than give me this job."

"So why don't you go?"

"Well, when I had the money, I kept thinking he'd come around. You know, at least take care of his kids but that new wife of his, she didn't want any part of it. Then I ran out of money, and he told me since I didn't go when he gave me the money the first time, he wouldn't help again, and he'd make life difficult for me." She made to smooth her hair and then obviously remembered its starched state. Her hand dropped to her side. "He's keeping his word," she added ruefully.

"Why didn't you go?"

Hester shrugged in that way of hers. "Nothing to go back to. My parents are dead. His parents don't live in that town, and where we come from it's so small there's no jobs to be had, no money to be had. But I thought if we were here. Well…" She shrugged and shook her head. "Well, I thought he'd take care of his kids at least."

"And you can't make him?"

"There are no laws saying he has to."

"So he just pretends you don't exist?"

She nodded. "Apparently, his plan when he came out West was to get rich and get rid of the past, all of it."

"And he can't."

"No, but he won't take this job from me. I'll make sure of that. I don't have much," she said, "but this new wife being pregnant and him looking to be cozying up to the governor for that seat he wants to have up there in the capitol give me advantage. He can't afford right now the noise I could make revealing who I am."

"So why don't you make enough noise so he gives you the money?"

"Two reasons. One, he might have me killed. He's that ambitious, and two, my kids deserve to know what it feels like to be respectable. I don't want him, but I want respectable back. This job is the new start I've been looking for."

The woman had thought of everything. Petunia couldn't help but admire that practicality mixed with determination and purpose.

She came to a decision. "If you can get MacFarlane to support you, then I'll give you a try."

Because the reality was, she didn't have much of a choice, either.

Hester's smile thinned. "He'll give it."

Petunia was beginning to believe it. There was something about Hester that just made you believe whatever she said would happen, would. And with the kind of leverage—all right, blackmail—Hester could bring to bear, Petunia might be able to get a bit more support for her cause.

Hester looked to the kitchen. "I've got to get to work."

"The children can stay here tonight if you'd like."

"You got room?"

"I've got room. No real beds yet, but room I have."

Hester nodded. "They can make do on pallets. They're better off here than over there."

Petunia couldn't argue with that. "Have they eaten supper?"

She shook her head. "Not yet."

"Is there anything in particular they like?"

"They'll eat whatever's put in front of them. They're not picky. They're good children."

With Hester as a mother, Petunia just bet they were. Maybe a bit resentful, maybe a little wild, maybe a little angry because of their father, but they were obedient, and she didn't think they went against Hester often.

"I'll be back when my shift is over."

"And what time is that?"

"About two."

"You sure you don't want me to keep them until morning?"

Hester shook her head. "Phillip will fret if he doesn't

see me at two." With a resigned shrug that said more than words, she explained, "He's protective of me since his dad left."

Petunia just bet. "He sounds like a good boy."

"He is, just growing up too fast."

Walking over to a small dish by the front door, Petunia grabbed the spare key. Turning, she held it out.

"I'll see you at two, then."

"I've got the job?"

Petunia nodded. It was probably the best and worst decision she'd ever made, but this seemed the week for such things.

Hester smiled so big, her makeup cracked. "You won't regret it."

"I'm not planning on it."

IT WASN'T A key in the lock that woke Petunia. It was the raspy squeal of the downstairs kitchen window being opened. Petunia froze beneath the blankets, her breath caught in her lungs. Someone was breaking into the house. Sliding out of bed, she reached for the shotgun. It wasn't by the bed. With all the chaos of the extra children in the house and refereeing the inevitable disagreements, she'd forgotten it in the kitchen. Darn it.

There was nothing to do but go downstairs. Thank goodness her door was at the top of the stairs, well between the children and any threat. Opening her door slowly, very slowly so as not to have it squeak a warning to whomever was coming inside, she tiptoed into the hall. At the top of the stairs, she felt eyes upon her. Her heart leaped into her throat, but it was Phillip and Terrance at the door to their room. She put her finger to her lips and waved them back inside. They moved as one, exactly a half inch toward the inside of the door. She pointed again and then made a motion like closing the door.

She didn't know who was breaking in; hopefully, it was just a cowboy looking for some food. But if it was anything more serious, she wanted as many locked doors as possible between the threat and the children. They reluctantly obeyed.

At the top of the stairs was a small cast-iron lamp. She picked it up. As weapons went it wasn't much, but it was certainly better than nothing. And the heft gave her a bit of confidence. She looked back. The doors were closed. No more excuses.

Her breath sounded harsh to her ears as she eased her way down the stairs, treading carefully, trying to remember which stair it was that had the creak. Fourth from the bottom, she finally remembered, which wasn't much help because she was so panicked she couldn't remember where she was on the stairs. She didn't even know what time it was. All she knew was it was dark and from the heaviness of the air against her skin, it felt like morning.

Thoughts raced through her mind. Would Hester climb through the window if she lost her key? She didn't think so, but what did she know of Hester? She knew nothing about the woman except that she was bold as brass. Maybe she would climb through the window. Maybe it was just Hester. Maybe her heart was thundering in her chest for nothing, and maybe two minutes from now she'd be at the stove boiling water, getting ready to share a cup of tea with the woman.

The hairs on the back of her neck rose in warning. Tingles spread across her skin. Somehow, she didn't think it was Hester.

"All right, Lord," she half prayed, half said under her breath, "it's just you and me on this one."

It was her habit to talk to God when she was in these situations. She liked to believe that He backed her in all her endeavors. She was on the side of good, but there was always a chance on any given day that God was preoccupied elsewhere. Hopefully, this wouldn't be that day. She had three little responsibilities upstairs. It was her job to keep them safe.

She debated screaming but the house was on the edge of the town. No one would hear and again, whoever was in the house, because he had to be in the house by now, might assume she didn't know he was there. A scream would take away her only advantage.

She felt the slightest of gives on the next stair. The squeaky stair. She quickly pulled her foot back, but not fast enough. It made a slight soft little groan, so soft a sound she wasn't sure it even carried past her. Gripping the railing with a shaking hand, she tried to steady her breath. That was close, too close.

"Terrance," a man's voice called, the words slurring together. "Where are you, boy? I've come to get you."

Brian. Brian Winter was in her house, and from the sound of things, he'd been drinking. It was too easy to recall the size of the man. The weight of the lamp in her hand that had been so soothing just minutes before became pathetically inadequate. She tightened her grip on it nevertheless. There was no chance Brian would leave without his son. There was nothing to do but to confront him, but she wasn't going to do it on the stairs. She didn't want him anywhere near the children.

From the noise, he was near the kitchen. Petunia forced her feet to the bottom of the stairs. A crash from the hall, probably the little key table, alerted her Brian was close. Too close.

Her first thought was that if he passed by her, she could slip behind him into the parlor and then get to the kitchen to the gun. She knew where it was. Right there beside the back door leaning against the wall. Why tonight of all nights had she forgotten the gun?

He was almost to the door. She could hear him. Smell him.

Please, Lord.

Holding her breath, she inched a little farther into the shadows. Too far. Her hip bumped the table on the landing, and the glass hurricane lamp on top of it teetered. She grabbed for it, only to send it sailing. The crash echoed through the house.

Shadows shifted as Brian whirled around. "Who's there?"

There was no choice. She was going to have to confront him. Petunia took another breath, trying to make her voice as calm as possible.

"I believe that should be my question."

Hopefully, he was too drunk to hear the quiver of fear laced through every word.

There was a snort that could have been disgust or victory.

"That you, teacher?"

"Who else would you expect to be greeting you at this hour of the night in my home?"

"I might be expecting my goddamn kid." Another shift in the shadows. He was coming toward her. "The one you took away."

"I didn't take anybody away." She inched along the

wall toward the kitchen. "Mr. Parker brought Terrance to my care."

She didn't feel a bit guilty throwing Ace out there. That was one man that could take care of himself.

"Bullshit. He wouldn't have done anything, if you hadn't pushed the issue."

For a drunk, he was amazingly logical. Damn it.

"It doesn't really matter, does it, who brought him to me?" She stubbed her finger against the molding of the parlor arch. "The fact is he needed bringing."

"The hell he did. He's my kid, and you have no goddamn right to take him."

As far as she could tell, he wasn't moving. "The right of it isn't in dispute."

She didn't know what good stalling would do, but until a better idea came along, she was going with it.

"I've been talking with a lawyer over there in the saloon, and he says you can't take my kid."

Her heartbeat thundered in her ears. She was close. So close. "Are you sure he was an attorney?"

"He knows more than you do."

She didn't want to argue with him. She backed into the room. He didn't follow.

"I'm going to get my kid now."

The heck he was. "No, Mr. Winter, you're not."

He was following now. His silhouette filled the doorway, pushing out the light. His hands were balled into fists. For a horrifying moment she had the cowardly thought that if she just let him have Terrance, he'd go.

He snarled, "Fucking bitch."

She hefted the lamp and pulled herself up straight. If he persisted in trying to take his anger out on Terrance, he was going to find out just how much of a bitch she could be.

"You need to go. Now."

"I'm not going anywhere without my son."

She made a last ditch grasp at reason. "Your son is sleeping, unless your boorish behavior woke him up. You can come by in the morning, and we'll discuss this."

"There is no discussion to be had." He surged into the room. "I'm taking my kid."

The force of his anger drove her back like a blow. The folds of her sleeping gown wrapped around her legs. The sofa hit the backs of her legs. She was trapped, and he kept on coming. Dear God, where was the gun?

"I've got a gun," she bluffed.

"No, you don't."

Was she that bad a liar? "Do you want to take another step and find out?"

He took another step. "Even if you did, you wouldn't pull the trigger."

She could feel sweat breaking out on her back, taste the fear in her mouth. If she had the gun right now she'd be pulling the trigger if only because she was shaking so badly. The only other time she'd ever had to confront a man, there had been others around. But this, this was different. There was just her and him and three vulnerable children trapped in the sinister cloak of darkness.

He lunged. She ducked to the side. His hand caught her nightgown. There was a jerk at her shoulder and the fabric ripped. She stumbled but miraculously was free. She spun around, shadows spinning with her. Bracing her feet, she spotted the deeper black of his bulk coming at her. She threw the lamp and screamed. She heard a shout from upstairs.

"Stay back, children!" she yelled as Brian grabbed at her again. *Dear God, stay back.* She dived for the door. He caught her gown again, and she screamed again, pointless noise that somehow gave her strength. The material tore more. Two shadows shot past her.

"Pa, stop!"

Oh, God, that was Terrance. "Run, Terrance, run!"

He didn't run. There was another shadow, more swearing from Brian, the sound of a fist connecting with flesh. A young voice swore in the most foul of language.

"Fucking bastard."

Then the awful thud of something hitting the floor.

Another cry broke through the dark. Deeper and more guttural. It had to be from Brian. The boys were fighting him.

Springing to her feet, Petunia sprinted for the kitchen and the gun, tripping over the table and her torn gown. She needed to get the gun. It was their only hope. Grabbing it from beside the back door, she ran back, hearing the sounds of violence, willing herself faster, fearing for the kids, fearing for them all.

Suddenly, there was a crash. The front door slammed against the wall.

"You son of a bitch." This time it was a woman's voice.

Glass smashed and then an agonized howl.

"Touch my son, will you?" There was a soft hiss and then a burst of light. Another scream from Brian.

"Get used to it, you bastard. There're going to be a lot of flames where you're going."

Petunia rushed back into the living room to see Brian jumping about, in horror, his arm on fire.

"Oh, my God!" Petunia grabbed for the throw on the settee.

"Let him burn," Hester snarled.

Petunia glared at her, covering the flames creeping up Brian's back. "He'll take the whole damn house with him!"

Terrance already had the other blanket off the chair. Hester snatched it from him. Brian swung at her when she would have thrown it over his arm. "I'll kill you."

The stench of burned wool, hair and kerosene filled the room.

"Hold still, you ass."

He didn't hold still. Instead, he just kept screaming, "I'll kill you. I'll kill you."

Petunia threw her weight on him, smothering the last of the flames as she did. "Not today you won't."

Hester joined in. Brian collapsed to the floor. Terrance followed, crying, "Pa!"

Petunia couldn't tell if it was fear or love in his voice.

Brian started to get to his feet. Hester kicked out, catching him in the chin. He dropped like a felled ox.

Dusting off her hands, Hester looked over at Petunia. "Just another reason you need me around here."

Petunia leaned against the wall and pulled the remnants of her gown closed. Dear heavens, what a mess. "Why is that?"

"I know how to fight dirty."

She swallowed hard and nodded. "So I see."

Brian still wasn't moving. Terrance was sitting beside him stroking his hair, whispering things she couldn't hear.

"What are we going to do with him?"

"Throw him out with the garbage." Hester lit one of the few remaining lamps, and looked down at Brian before giving him a poke with her foot. "He's a bit big for us to be tossing." Turning, she called, "Phil!" Phillip looked up from where he sat. "Run over to the saloon and fetch Mr. Parker."

Petunia groaned. Anyone but him. "Why do we need him?"

"Because he'll know what to do."

"Everyone knows what to do. Call the sheriff and be done with it."

Hester shook her head, staring at the mess. "Ace's not going to be pleased to see this."

"I'm not too pleased myself." If word got out, the scandal and speculation would shut her down.

"Ace will handle it."

"Why would he even bother?"

Hester shot her a pitying look. "'Cause everyone knows, he's got you marked as his. And no one messes with what belongs to that man."

CHAPTER SEVEN

IT DIDN'T TAKE Ace long to arrive. Petunia expected him to blow through the door like a thunderstorm unleashed. Instead, he strode into the house more like the calm before the storm rather than the storm itself. As if coming to the rescue of two women and three children was an everyday occurrence. And maybe it was. Violence was a part of his life, not hers.

With one glance he took in the broken door, the broken glass and her shaking hands as she stood at the top of the stairs after checking on Brenda. She got to the landing in time to see him absorb the spectacle of Brian cowering next to the fireplace, Terrance sitting at his side, tears dripping down his cheeks and Hester standing over both, a shotgun pointing at Brian's privates.

He tipped his hat. "Evening, Hester."

"Evening, Ace."

He looked at Brian. "I told you what would happen if you interfered, Winter."

Petunia entered the room just in time to hear the man mutter, "I just came by to get my boy."

"At two o'clock in the morning?"

"Man's got a right to see his son."

"Not at two o'clock in the morning and not after I told you to steer clear."

Terrance touched his father's shoulder. "Pa, please."

Brian shrugged him off. "Get away."

Petunia had had enough. "Terrance, I need you to show Phillip how to make us all some coffee."

Terrance reluctantly stood and looked at his father.

Ace backed her order with one of his own. "Go."

Terrance bolted from the room. One look at Ace's eyes and Petunia wanted to bolt, too. She'd been wrong about Ace's calm. The man was furious.

And no one messes with what belongs to that man.

Ordinarily, she'd have protested that claim, but right now having him in the house was a comfort.

Ace rolled up his sleeves and squatted beside Brian. "You can put away the gun, Hester. I've got this."

"I think I'll hold on to it."

"Suit yourself."

"Easy for you to say," Brian snarled. "You're not the one facing a nervous woman at the trigger."

"If Hester was the nervous type, you'd be downright holey." Ace lifted the charred remnant of Brian's sleeve.

"Fucking bitch set me afire."

"You touched my son," Hester retorted.

"He's burned," Petunia pointed out because she didn't know what else to say.

"He's damn lucky he's not chewing on his balls," Hester shot back.

"Hester! The children can hear."

The shake in Ace's shoulders could have been a laugh. She couldn't see his face well enough to tell. She didn't see anything to laugh about here. Scandal in the first week of the school's operation could jeopardize everything.

"In case you're too drunk to notice, you've had a lucky escape," Ace said, standing. "Now, are you going to get your butt up off that floor or am I going to let Hester feed you your balls for breakfast?"

Winter rolled to his feet, cradling his arm. "I got a right to see my son."

Ace grabbed the back of his shirt. "You don't have any rights I don't choose to give you."

"You're not the sheriff."

"I'm better than the sheriff. I'm the law."

"What are you going to do with him?" Petunia asked.

He looked at her under the brim of his hat. "Do you care?"

Oddly enough, she did. "Yes."

"He's a drunk and a wastrel."

"He's still a human being."

Grabbing Brian by the back of the collar, Ace shoved him toward the door. "A piss-poor excuse for one."

"Amen," Hester agreed, lowering the shotgun.

Another shove had Brian bouncing off the opposite wall.

"Be careful!" Petunia snapped.

Ace paused, for once genuine surprise on his face. "You worried I'm going to break him?"

"No. We just plastered that wall."

Ace gave him another shove. Brian started to snivel. "If he dents it, he'll fix it."

Petunia checked the wall before following them to the front door. "I don't want him around here."

"I'll handle it."

Petunia stopped him when he opened the door with a cold deadly resolve. There was something in that "I'll handle it" that gave her pause.

"What are you going to do with him?"

"Something he's not going to forget."

"You're not going to kill him?"

He looked at her. "You asked me to handle it. That's what I'm doing."

"But…"

With another look he cut her off. "You don't get a but. You don't get a say. You just get to have the scum out of your house."

She couldn't be a party to murder.

Another shove and Brian was out the door. "You run and I'll put a bullet in your ass," Ace growled.

Petunia went to close the door. Ace stopped her, catching her chin in his hand, tipping her gaze to his. "When I get back, we're going to talk."

"About what?"

"Where the hell was the gun?"

"Um…"

"I told you to keep it with you at all costs."

A fission of fear went through her. Or excitement. The man had her so addled she couldn't tell the difference anymore.

"I won't forget again."

His eyes were very dark as he nodded. "I know."

On that ominous note, he left. She closed the door slowly, leaning her head against it as she turned the key. How on earth had life gotten so complicated?

"Locking the door isn't going to change anything," Hester said.

"It might buy me some time."

"Did you see his face? That is one pissed-off man."

Petunia turned around. Hester stood in the doorway to the parlor, the shotgun cradled in her arms.

"He has no right to threaten me."

Hester laughed and leaned the gun against the wall.

"You've got a lot to learn about men, honey, if you think that makes any difference."

"Well, if he comes back—"

Hester shook her head. "Oh, he'll be back."

"If he comes back," Petunia repeated, "then we will sit down and talk about it."

Hester folded her arms across her chest. "You don't know Ace Parker very well, do you?"

"And you do?"

"Better than you, apparently."

"And what does that mean?" It suddenly occurred to Petunia that working at the saloon, Hester had plenty of opportunities to know Ace intimately. The thought disturbed her more than it should.

"Don't get your bloomers in a twist," Hester said. "I don't know him biblically. I'm not to his taste."

"And what exactly would Mr. Parker's taste be?"

Hester looked her over from head to toe. "You're not his usual type but I'd say—"

"Is my pa going to be all right?" Terrance interrupted.

Of all the lousy timing! Petunia bit her tongue and forced a smile. "He's fine. Mr. Parker's taking care of him."

"Is he going to go to jail?"

"That wouldn't be the worst place for him," Hester said gently. "Might be he could dry out, get a few good meals under his belt, find some common sense even."

"They feed them there?"

Petunia nodded. "They feed them there."

"I can visit him?"

Hester looked at Petunia. Petunia shook her head. It didn't make sense, but some of the worst people had the best ones caring about them.

"I'll take you myself."

"How long will he be in jail?"

She wanted to hug him so badly. Kneeling before him, Petunia settled for brushing his hair off his forehead. "Not long at all, I'm sure. Just long enough for him to rest up and see some sense."

Terrance nodded. "He doesn't think right when he drinks."

No child should know that about a parent. Petunia wanted to smack Brian all over again.

"You were very brave tonight."

"I couldn't let him hurt you."

"I appreciate that, and I appreciate you don't want him hurt, either." Biting her lip, Petunia struggled with the right thing to say. "Sometimes our parents put us in difficult positions without meaning to."

"It didn't used to always be this way."

"I know he must have been a good man at some time." He said, "You do?"

She smiled as Hester stepped past, going up to comfort her own children. Petunia did hug Terrance then. "He has you for a son. That much good doesn't come from bad."

He suffered the embrace. "Dad said my ma loved him."

"I'm sure she did." At some point.

"He was real sad when she died."

Which might explain Brian's drinking.

Taking him by the hand, she led him to the kitchen. "Well, I'm sure if Mr. Parker talks to him, it will have some effect."

"Do you really think so?" he asked, taking his seat.

She poured him a glass of water. Her hands were still

shaking, she realized, as the glass rattled when she set it on the wood. It was so hard to remember that Brian was this boy's father, and no matter what the man did the boy loved him and was going to defend him.

She took a seat adjacent to Terrance. "Mr. Parker has the look of a man who routinely works miracles."

He didn't touch the water. "Do you think he can fix my pa?"

"I hope so, but right now we both need some sleep. I've got to teach school in the morning, and you've got division to master."

"Can I take some cookies with me?"

After everything else that had happened, what could it hurt? "Just two, though. Any more and you won't be able to sleep."

"I can sleep."

She smiled and repeated, "Just two."

He took his cookies and left the room. Only when she heard that fourth stair creak did she fold her hands and drop her head to her forearms and cry.

AN HOUR LATER there was a knock at the front door. Hester looked up from where she sat across the table.

"I guess we know who that is."

Petunia was afraid she did, too.

"I assume that it's time for me to go to bed."

A shiver snaked down Petunia's spine. "There's no need."

Hester shook her head and pushed to her feet. "I'll be up in my room if you need me."

If all she'd done was go to bed, it would have been fine. But along the way to her room, she just had to stop at the front door and open it. Darn it.

"Evening again, Ace."

"Evening, Hester."

Petunia wished she could see his face.

"I want you to know I appreciate what you did for us," Hester said.

"It was my pleasure."

That sounded entirely too genuine.

With a wave of her hand, Hester indicated the hall behind her. "Petunia's in the kitchen."

Ace took off his hat. The small part of Petunia that'd hoped he'd leave this until tomorrow died. A man didn't take off his hat unless he was serious.

With a look over her shoulder that could have meant anything, Hester said, "I'm off to bed."

In the next heartbeat there was nothing between Petunia and Ace except an empty hallway. He looked as fresh as he had that afternoon. While she knew she had dark circles under her eyes, her hair was coming out of its braid and her clothes were rumpled. And her hands were still shaking. It really wasn't fair. She had the urge to kick him again.

He collected the gun from where it was propped against the wall of the landing. "Why is the gun on the landing," he asked, entering the kitchen and leaning the rifle against the wall beside the door, "and not here?"

"Hester put it there."

"That's not what I told you to do."

"I don't like guns."

He eyed her for a moment. It was hard to stand still under that stare.

"Hester's a little rough around the edges, but she's gold through and through, and she can handle the job. You should hire her."

"I already have."

He set his hat on the counter. "Townsfolk aren't going to like it."

"The townsfolk can go to hell."

He cocked his eyebrow at her. "You've taken to swearing."

"Tonight I feel the need."

She expected a smile, not…concern?

"Invite me in for a cup of coffee."

"You're already in."

"Humor me."

He didn't really give her much choice. Not just because he'd ordered it, but because he was already moving down the small hallway toward the front door. Was he coming or going? She followed behind, licking her suddenly dry lips as she noticed the breadth of his shoulders, the thickness of his thighs, the tightness of his butt. She was halfway down the hall before she remembered the gun.

She didn't need to say more than "Oh, shoot" for him to know what she was thinking.

"Leave it. I'm here."

A woman could do a lot of things to feel awkward. Show up at the right party in the wrong dress, say the wrong thing at the wrong moment, fall in love with the wrong man, but none of those things could make Petunia feel as silly as that heart-clutching moment when Ace stepped out the door. It closed behind him with a soft click. Sillier still while she waited on this side and him on the other, anticipating a knock that might not come. But when it came, so did her smile. When she opened it, he was standing there, hat in hand, looking for all the world like a suitor.

"Evening."

Maybe it was the stress of the evening. Maybe it was her own sense of the absurd, but her smile softened, felt more natural. Seeped inside. Stepping back, she waved him in. "Good evening."

He stepped inside. The foyer suddenly seemed too small. Her mouth too dry.

"Would you care for coffee?"

His lips quirked. "That I would."

She closed the door behind him and followed him—again—down the hall. There was something so wrong about that, but at the same time right.

He set his hat on the spindle of one of the kitchen chairs as if he'd done it a hundred times before. As if he had a right to do it here. As if he was staking a claim. Running his hand through his straight brown hair, he pulled out a chair kitty-corner to the other and sat down. Leaning back in his chair, he put his feet up and stretched his legs out. He looked entirely too comfortable like that. Too…male.

She grabbed a towel and picked up the cooling coffeepot. "You know," she pointed out drily, "it wouldn't hurt you to get it yourself."

His smile was pure, confident male.

"If I were you I wouldn't push it."

"Are you threatening me?"

"Threats aren't my way."

She put the pot carefully down on a hot burner and took a steadying breath. It wasn't the first time she'd had a man threaten her, but it was the first time that a threat made her feel like rich, creamy butter in a too-hot crock. There wasn't anything particularly sexual about the way Ace was sitting back in that chair staring at

her the way he did with those eyes that bored right into
her, but there was something in his energy that made
her knees weak, the area between her thighs ache and
her nipples pull tight. His gaze dropped to the front of
her nightgown. She quickly folded her arms over the betraying sight but it was too late, and they both knew it.
She had to say something.

"I'll get the cups."

He stopped her with a quiet "Turn around, Pet."

She didn't want to, but again she had no choice. Not
only because she owed him, but because it was an order.
And Ace had issued it. And for some reason, that made
a difference. She turned. Lamplight softened most people's expressions, but it did nothing to dampen the tension in Ace's. He was staring at her with that intentness
she'd only seen once before when a menagerie had come
through town. Behind the bars of a small cage, this mag-
nificent tiger had paced. Back and forth, back and forth.
Tail twitching, lethal and menacing, his energy had pro-
jected beyond the cage. He'd had that same look that Ace
was wearing now. Back then bars had separated them.
Her stomach had twisted. There was nothing separat-
ing her from Ace.

"I'm not even sure why you're angry."

"You're not?"

She took a cup off the shelf and handed it to him. He
took it with that same unnatural calm.

"No. It's not my fault the man broke into my house."

"No, I can't blame you for that. It was predictable,
though. Hence my telling to keep that gun at hand."

"We had a lot going on today. I just forgot."

His eyes flashed. "And damn near got yourself killed.

If Hester hadn't arrived when she had, you would have
been dead."

"I was holding my own."

He looked at her with complete disgust. "You were?
In whose opinion?"

"Mine." She slammed her cup on the table. "And since
you weren't here to assess, you'll have to go by that."

Ace snorted. "You may be tall for a woman, but you're
still a woman, and that means you're no match for a man
in a hand-to-hand fight."

"I wasn't planning on fighting with him hand to
hand."

"What were you planning on using?"

The shotgun. Which had been in the kitchen. She
sighed and pushed her hair off her face. It wasn't that she
didn't get his point. She just wasn't willing to concede
that her forgetting the gun gave him any rights.

The corner of his mouth lifted at the quick acknowl-
edgment of his point. "I'll take your silence for understanding."

"Take it however you want."

The water on the stove began to heat. The pot crackled
with tension as it expanded. The tension in the room was
no less volatile. Petunia took the sugar from the counter
and put it on the table. His fingers wrapped around her
wrist.

"Let me go."

"Make me."

Her free hand doubled up into a fist. She was so mad
at Brian, at life, at circumstances, she actually swung.
Ace caught her fist as easily as if she had just waved it in
front of him. The speed of his reflexes made her blink.
A subtle excitement started deep in her gut, springing

up to her breasts and down between her legs, and that place that had been dormant for so long heated to a slow ache. Lust, she knew it was lust, completely and inappropriately occurring at a time when she needed her anger. Rational thought didn't help with the spread; neither did the way his eyes met hers. He wanted her, too.

She couldn't let that sway her. "I'm not yours to boss around."

He didn't even hesitate. "You're whatever I decide you're going to be."

Everything inside her screamed denial, but that stronger pulse of awareness kept her honest because, right now, right here, in this moment it was true. So true that rather than deny it, she just lifted her chin and dared him to prove it.

His right hand relaxed its grip, and his thumb stroked along her pulse. She knew he felt that instant leap of response. He was too experienced a man not to know the signs of a woman's interest.

"You want me."

She nodded. "There'd be no point in denying it after that kiss."

"There was no point in denying it after the first time we met."

"Just because I want you doesn't mean I'm going to do anything about it."

He shook his head. "Little girl, that's a fool's belief."

"I'm not a girl."

He stood. His cock pressed against his denims. Thick and hard. Tempting. Her fingers curled over the need to stroke that hard ridge.

"This is a real bad time to be reminding me of that."

It was a warning she couldn't seem to heed. She held

her ground when he stood, abandoning reason for the anticipation of whatever it was he was going to do next. She didn't know what it was but whatever it was, she wanted it. From the depths of her soul she wanted it.

"I know."

His response was short and sweet. "Run, Pet."

Hers was just as succinct. Placing her hands on his chest, she lifted her too-heavy lids and met his gaze. "No."

"Fuck."

He took that step in. The one that brought his chest pressing against her breasts, his hips against hers. His foot slid between hers. The inside of his knee bumped hers, spreading her legs wider. Throwing her off balance, he took another step forward. She had to take one back or topple. He took another and another, forcing her back as he raised her hands up. When her hips hit the counter, he brought her hands down behind, pressing her palms to the cool wood as he arched her backward.

She had a good idea of how she looked, her thin nightgown pulled taut across her breasts, her back and neck arched. Standing there like an offering. She shivered from head to toe.

In the shadows, his blue eyes appeared darker, his lips fuller; his breath came shorter. His gaze touched her face, her throat, her breasts. Her nipples hardened as if the stroke of his attention were the stroke of his fingers.

His foot hit the inside of hers.

"Spread your legs."

It was the most scandalous thing that anybody had ever said to her. It was also the most erotic. Of their own volition, her feet separated. He stepped between.

His groin pressed intimately against her, and she felt for
the first time in her life a man's hardness where it belonged. It was a shock, a revelation and a promise. One
she wanted him to keep. He leaned over, his body pressing on hers. She had a choice. Hold her ground or col-
lapse. The twitch of his lips told her what he expected.
She locked her elbows and raised her chin up, matching
him challenge for challenge.

"If you think to intimidate me," she told him, "you
can just quit right now. But if you're going to kiss me,
then make it worth my while."

She felt his start from his chest to his toes. Good. Let
him dismiss her now.

"I'm a woman not a girl, Ace. You're not going to
scare me with displays of passion. I might be a virgin,
but I'm not innocent to the ways of the world. And quite
frankly, it's been a hell of a night that started with a man
bullying me, but I promise you, it's not going to end with
another doing the same."

"Son of a bitch."

She wasn't sure if it was a curse or a prayer, it was
said so softly.

"You are hell on a man's good intentions, Petunia
Wayfield."

"Who said I wanted your intentions, good or otherwise?"

His fingertips skimmed from her cheek down her neck
to her breasts, blazing a path, finding the peak of her left
nipple, pinching it gently.

"These do."

She caught her breath as the sensation streaked south-
ward. Fire caught in lightning, burning away so much
of her defenses. She expected him to let go. He didn't.

He pinched harder, watching her eyes, looking for...she didn't know what. The pressure increased; so did the tension and the pleasure. He pinched harder still. His fingers rubbed lightly and there came that point where she could sense that pain waiting just beyond. Her breath caught, and his lips perked up in a smile.

But not the smile she expected. He didn't look victorious. He looked sad, and the next second he took her over that plateau in a quick press that straddled the line from pleasure to pain and just as quickly took her back, leaving her stumbling mentally as his hand cradled her breast. Tenderness, where before he'd been rough, pleasure soothing, where before there'd been pain.

"That's why it's not wise to tease, my Pet."

He made it sound like more than a nickname.

"I'm not one of your pretty little boys from back East who follow the rules, and I'm not your needy gentleman out here looking for a good woman to grace their bed. When I take a woman I take her body and soul, until she's mine to do with as I will. I take her past any limits either of us think we have."

She could see it in her mind. Feel it in her body. Her pussy clenched, and her breath caught.

"But you bring them back," she whispered.

He shook his head, and his fingers once again closed around her nipple, tightening, twisting, promising. "Not always."

The kettle on the stove rattled as the water boiled. He stepped back, leaving her there expectant and bereft. It took her a good three seconds to gather her wits and stand up straight. Her left nipple throbbed, so did her pussy. Her mind raced.

Ace walked over to the door and grabbed the gun. Coming back, he shoved it in her hands.

"Don't let me catch you without this by your side again."

It was an order. She nodded and not just because it was common sense. For a long while he stared at her, not saying a word, just wrestling with something inside. Something that had emotions chasing across his face— desire, determination, regret and then desire again. With a sigh, he tucked her hair behind her ear.

"And don't let me catch you with your defenses down again."

"Why?" The challenge just slipped out.

"Because you won't like the consequences."

She wasn't so sure. For an endless minute, tension arced between them. Ace was the one to break it, grabbing his hat and heading out the back door. As it closed silently behind him, her whole body quivered on a heavy sigh. That tension she didn't understand and couldn't control rippled through her. Closing her eyes, she forced herself to relax her white-knuckle grip on the gun.

She didn't need to see to picture him leaving her, walking with that long, confident stride of his, leaving her behind as if this were only his decision to make.

When I take a woman I take her body and soul, until she's mine to do with as I will.

Licking her lips, she remembered that moment when he'd taken her to the point of tolerance and then beyond. The shock, the pleasure, the bliss. Ace had been in control of her, of himself. Of them. And she'd never felt more alive.

...you won't like the consequences.

The kettle rattled again as the coffee boiled. Cupping her breast in her hand, she looked out the window, her own determination settling deep. They'd see about that.

CHAPTER EIGHT

ACE STROLLED INTO the saloon, his temper as frayed as the edges of his oldest pair of denims. The stench hit him first. It wasn't something he normally noticed, but apparently tonight everything was out to annoy him. The saloon was pretty much empty except for a couple of passed-out derelicts. By four in the morning, people either found their bed or someone else's to sleep in. Only a few diehards took advantage of Jenkins's open-all-night-whenever-he-felt-like-it hours. Ace went straight to the bar.

Jenkins greeted him with a jerk of his chin. "Bit late to be about, isn't it, Ace?"

"Bit late to not be sleeping, isn't it?"

"You've got me there. What will you have?"

Ace flipped a coin onto the counter. "Just give me a whiskey."

Jenkins put a glass down and reached behind the bar. "Glass or bottle?"

"Bottle."

"That bad a night?"

He took the bottle. "Getting awful nosy in your old age, aren't you, Jenkins?"

Jenkins backed up a step. "Just making conversation, Ace."

"Did I ask for conversation?" He pulled the cork. The

acrid scent of the liquor wafted up to him. "All I remember asking for is whiskey."

"So you did, and I'll be leaving you to it."

"Thank you."

Taking his cloth, Jenkins went to the other end of the bar and started wiping it down.

The retreat soothed a bit of Ace's aggression. His fingers closed around the glass. It was warm and hard like Pet's nipple. He stroked his fingers up across the smooth surface wanting the sensation to replace memory.

Snorting, he poured whiskey into the glass. As if that was ever going to happen. Pet had the sweetest breasts, small and firm, topped with surprisingly big nipples. Their shape was burned into his flesh, her response into his memory.

Fuck. He tossed back the glass. Instead of the memory fading, it grew, pounding at him, demanding he go back and get more. Shit. He did love to play with a woman's breasts. Loved to tease them past the point of bearing to the edge of pain. And then he loved to push them over, catching them softly on the other side, loved to see the wonder and trust in their eyes. Like he'd seen in Pet's.

Damn, that woman was something. All fire and passion. When he'd pinched her nipple, he'd expected her to retreat but instead she'd actually leaned in, a subtle surrender she wasn't even aware of, a potent temptation to the demons inside him. He'd almost given in to that temptation when she bent back across the counter, her breasts raised for his pleasure, her head arched back. Whether she knew it or not, she'd submitted to him right then, and everything in him wanted to take her up on the challenge to show her that he was man enough to tame that spirit in her, to hold her safe.

He imagined his hand gliding over her cheek to her neck, gathering up her hair, wrapping the silken strands in his fist, holding tight as he arched her back. Hearing that little catch in her breath when he bent her to the edge of her endurance before he leaned down and nibbled at her lips, nipped at her neck and bit at her breasts, stimulating them until he heard that next gasp that said she was ready for more, so much more.

His cock, which still hadn't subsided fully from their earlier encounter, hardened again, pressing painfully against the seam of his pants. He shifted his position, easing the tension as he swore under his breath.

Pouring another glass, he tossed the whiskey back, welcoming the distraction of the burn. He focused on it, on the fumes that burned his nostrils, wanting to burn the scent of her from his memory.

Petunia was a good woman, all bravado on the outside but as delicate in nature as she was in build. Way too delicate for him. He tended to more robust women. Women that could handle what he had to offer. Petunia... He shook his head imagining her with her hands tied above her head, stripped bare, her body posed just so waiting for that first kiss of the flogger or maybe the brush of his hand. He shook his head. Petunia wasn't made for that. She was made for the contained attentions of an educated man, a refined man, one that wouldn't ask too much of her too often. Not a hell-bent desperado like himself, not a man with his proclivities. While she might be curious now, she'd never survive his bed, not with her spirit intact.

And he liked that spirit. It was rare and brave and caring. Not many people still tilted at windmills. He poured another whiskey. Before he could set the bottle back down on the counter, a plump white hand slid into his line of vision. The fingers wrapped around his glass. Following the vision came the smell of cheap perfume and heavy powder, drenching him. He knew that scent.

A husky voice whispered in his ear, "Hello, Ace."

He looked over his shoulder. "Hi, Rose."

Rose smiled her tired, pretty, slightly crooked smile. This late in the evening her makeup was a little bit smeared and had settled into the fine lines around her eyes. Her hair fell sloppily around her face. She tossed back the shot with the enthusiasm of a man, another outward sign of her hard life. Clearing her throat, she put the glass down.

"You're here awfully late."

"So it would appear."

He refilled the glass. When she reached for it again, he slammed his hand down on hers. Not hard enough to hurt but hard enough to excite. His fingers closed over hers, exerting a subtle pressure. He felt the shiver that snaked up her arm and felt the tension enter her muscles when he didn't let go.

"You need to ask before reaching for what's mine, Rose. We talked about that before."

Her smile was knowing, teasing, an invitation. "So we did."

Inside him the lust rose, wavered and refocused. He couldn't have Pet, but he could have this.

"We also discussed," he told her looking into her reddened blue eyes, "what was going to happen next time you forgot."

Another shiver, but again not of fear. She stepped in bringing her large plump breasts against his shoulder.

She was a sturdy woman. The corset she wore empha-
sized the generous curves above and below her waist.

"So we did."

She had pale skin that marked so beautifully.

"You got a customer?" he asked her.

She shook her head. Bits of powder fell free. "I'm
free."

Against his will, thoughts of Petunia's soft blond hair
that caught the sun and fluctuated between shades of almost white to amber intruded. Clean and sweet-smelling,
he'd kill to feel it slide over his chest, his stomach, his
cock. He tossed the shot down and turned the glass upside down over the neck of the bottle.

He grabbed up both as he stood. "Not anymore you
aren't."

She turned, and he smacked her ass hard enough to
leave a sting. Rose might be getting a little long in the
tooth but she liked what he did, and he didn't have to feel
guilty or worry at the end he'd gone too far. She could
take whatever he handed out.

"Let's get on upstairs," he told her.

She smiled at him over her shoulder and put a little
extra swing to her hips. But she didn't wait. She went
ahead. He shook his head. Her own demons must be
riding her hard tonight. She knew what that impudence
would provoke. Grabbing her hand, he stopped her at the
bottom of the stairs. With a tug he put her behind him.
But he didn't let go of her hand.

"It's been a long time," he told her.

She nodded. But didn't speak.

"At least you remembered something." He didn't like
a lot of chatter while he worked.

He led the way up the stairs, smiling at her relief at the

shift of power. They'd played together enough to know that that shift had to happen for that evening to be enjoyed. People thought whores were victims, and maybe they were in some respects, but when it came to controlling the play behind the bedroom door, most times it was the woman that was in charge while the man was at the mercy of his desires. He discovered early on that Rose wasn't a woman that relished control or at the very least, she was a woman that enjoyed a break from that control.

Her heels clicked on the well-worn stairs behind him as she followed.

"Anybody ever tell you you're a bit of a bastard, Ace?" she asked.

"A time or two."

Petunia, just a few days ago.

"Did it ever bother you?" she asked.

He looked back over his shoulder. "Not particularly. Why?"

When he got to the top of the stairs, he turned, changing his grip on her hand to help her over that last rickety one. Jenkins had to replace that board soon or somebody was going to get hurt.

Rose shook her head. "Because you seem too decent sometimes to be such a bastard all the time."

He smiled. "Well, I like to keep them guessing." He stopped at door four. "Same room?"

She nodded. He went in. She immediately went over to the cedar chest and took out fresh sheets. Another advantage to being a steady customer was Rose knew what he liked. The ease with which she prepared for her customers made her a favorite when the mood came over him. She was appreciative, uncomplicated and maybe yeah, a little bit in love with him but not enough that it was a problem.

She dumped the old sheets out in the hall and finished smoothing the bed. He took off his hat and set it on the chair.

"You done?"

She nodded and straightened. With a crook of his finger, he motioned her over. She stood in front of him, the tension under her skin exciting the dominance in him. He loved that moment right before a woman surrendered everything. When she knew she might be letting herself in for more than she could handle but she did it anyway, because it was exciting, because she wanted to be fulfilled, because it was her nature.

"Undress me."

She did with far too much competence.

"Slower."

She immediately obeyed. Skillfully unbuttoning buttons and pushing aside fabric. She stopped when she got to his gun belt.

Stroking her hair, he smiled. "Good girl."

He took it off and set it on the bed. He was particular about his guns. With another crook of his finger, he summoned her again. On the first step, he shook his head. She'd been good. She deserved a reward. He knew what excited her. With a flick of his finger he motioned to the floor. Her breath caught, and her bottom lip slipped between her teeth. She crawled the rest of the way, a flush rising on her skin. Humiliation didn't excite him, but it wasn't all about him, and Rose might be a whore, but she was also a friend. And she mattered.

"Now my pants."

It should have been far more stimulating than it was

to have Rosie on her knees before him working buttons free, but there was always something inherently dissatisfying about these encounters. Something missing, and the search for it sometimes drove him further than he wanted to go. But tonight it was even more dissatisfying than normal.

He sat down and held out his leg giving her easy access to his boots. She straddled it the way she knew he liked, giving him a good view of her buttocks. They were broad and ample, well suited to cushioning a man's thrusts or taking a spank. Shit, they'd always been very pleasing, but now they were just too much. Pet's face flashed into his mind. *Damn it.* He didn't need to be thinking about her now, especially now. He knew from experience, once a man let the forbidden lodge in his head, it could take over, weaken him, and Petunia Wayfield was definitely forbidden fruit.

The first boot hit the floor with a soft thud. Rose lowered his leg slowly, letting it slip down easy, before straddling his other leg. He put his foot against her ass, feeling the soft white skin shift under the thin robe as she wiggled off his second boot. Picking up his boots she placed them neatly by the bed before opening the chest again and returning with a cloth-wrapped package. Flipping the canvas back, she asked, "What are you in the mood for tonight?"

He couldn't get the image of Pet out of his mind. Dangerous territory that. He closed his eyes. Other images seeped through the break in control. Memories chased their heels. He knew what was coming. Faces scowling down at him. Fists connecting with his flesh. Fighting and losing. Hearing his mother scream. His father's shout. Needing to get to them. Failing. Always failing.

Walking over the bodies, smelling the stench of blood and death, hoping against hope. Fighting the last memory that always wanted center stage, bringing the curtain down before he turned that corner, stepped up onto the porch, saw what he wouldn't see…

Opening his eyes he picked up the restraints and flogger—Rose's favorites—and he smiled at the excitement in her eyes. Sometimes it was best to keep things simple. "To forget."

"So what do you want that necessitated me coming on down here before the break of dawn?" Hester asked, bursting into the kitchen with her usual energy.

"It's hardly the break of dawn." Petunia had gone to bed at the break of dawn.

"Close enough."

Petunia got up from the table and fetched another cup and placed it at the seat across from hers. Hester immediately pulled the cup over.

"Going to be one of those conversations, eh?"

It took every inch of fabric to keep Hester's breasts covered as she leaned in to grab the coffeepot. Petunia felt a stab of envy. Hester could have done without half her bosom and still been considered buxom, whereas she…

Petunia looked down at her own modest blessings and mentally rolled her eyes. Whereas she could use two cotton balls and all but double hers. In her youth she'd padded her corsets, but it'd never looked right, and she'd eventually given up, settling for more worthwhile pursuits than faking a cleavage she was never going to have. She'd learned to embrace the power of her mind and stopped worrying about trying to find a way to look busy at dances when she was never asked to dance and started spending more and more time in books and ideas. When that had gotten boring, she'd started putting those ideas into action. With her father's money and protection it had been an easy path to follow. But now, fifteen years later, she was back to feeling like the awkward wallflower at the dance. And it was all Ace's fault, damn it.

With a grimace, she admitted, "I'm afraid so."

With a crook of her finger Hester plunked down in the opposite seat. "Then pass me the cream and sugar."

There was something infinitely likable about Hester's straightforward approach to problems. "It's a delicate subject."

Hester tensed. A little of the cream slopped as she poured it into the coffee. The clay jug rattled as she set it back on the table.

"You're not thinking of firing me, are you? Because I've got to tell you, woman," she went on before Petunia could respond. "Seems to me you need someone like me around here. If a ladylike little prissy little thing had been here last night when Brian crept in? Well, she'd have just screamed and dropped down on the floor in a dead faint, and where would you be now? Raped or dead or Lord knows what. And Lord knows what that man would have gone on to do to those kids in the state he was in. That Brian when he gets drinking is trouble. Sober he's just lazy but drunk he's mean as a bull with a thorn stuck under his tail."

She paused to take a breath. Petunia held up her hand. "I'm not firing you!"

Hester sat back in her chair and just stared. "You're not?"

"Good grief, no. Not with the way you swing a statue. That's a hard qualification to come by."

For a second Hester just blinked. And then another. Petunia got a sinking feeling in her stomach. "You're not going to cry, are you?"

She hadn't meant to sound so horrified. But Hester was…Hester. Feisty. Indomitable. And if Hester started crying, Petunia would lose her resolve.

Hester shook her head. "No."

"Good. Because then I would, too."

Picking up her cup, Hester took a sip, looking at Petunia over the rim. "There's going to be some that say you are wrong for hiring me."

"Won't be the first time somebody's told me I'm wrong."

"That still won't make it right."

Petunia took a sip herself, savoring the taste of the rich fragrant beverage before swallowing. She did love her coffee. "Changed your mind about wanting the job?"

"Heck, no."

"Then let me worry about the objectors."

"All right. Then why don't you tell me what you do want me worrying about."

"It's not exactly a worry."

Hester snorted indelicately. "Maybe not for me."

The words wouldn't come.

"Any chance it has something to do with Ace?"

"A mighty big one."

"Well, that man's been grist for the mill since he hit town. You might consider him a well-chewed subject."

"Lovely."

Hester hummed in her throat. "He is that."

The zing that went through Petunia at the thought of Hester with Ace took her by surprise.

"You didn't think you're the only one lusting after that man, did you?"

"No."

"But you want to be."

"Not necessarily."

That was a lie. She didn't want Ace touching anyone else until she figured out what it was about the man that made him so different. Other men had always just been too weak in their approach, too pliant in their manner, too hesitant in their touch. Too something.

But with Ace, everything fell into place, her desire, her will. The man looked at her with that air of expectation, and everything in her centered. He crooked his finger, and she wanted to run into his arms. He bent, and she wanted to rise up on her toes.

If she was Chinese she would say he was the yang to her yin. If she was her mother, she'd simply say he was the griddle to her batter. He did make her sizzle. And she was a woman who in nearly thirty years, had never even reached lukewarm. She wasn't willing to go another thirty years before finding out where that sizzle ended. The question was where to start?

"Are you going to sit there staring at that coffee cup all day or you going to ask me whatever it is you want to ask me?" Hester asked.

"Have you taken to reading minds?"

"You're poker face is a bit rusty."

"Wonderful."

"The boys will be up soon enough. You might want to get to it."

"I'm working up to it." Petunia sighed. "Some things don't just come tripping off the tongue, you know."

Hester leaned back in her chair and sipped her coffee. Cream only. Pet suppressed a shudder. She took hers with milk and a liberal dose of honey.

"You want to know about Ace."

It wasn't a question. "I suppose being able to read people is very helpful in your profession."

"In my former profession, you mean."

It was reasonable that Hester was going to be touchy about that definition for a spell. "Yes, your former profession."

Hester took a sip of her coffee. "Knowing people does save time and trust me, when you're working that job you want your customers in and out as fast as possible."

Pet choked on the pun, intended or not. Hester just smiled.

"So what did our Mr. Parker want to discuss with you last night?"

"He wasn't happy that I left the gun behind."

Hester raised her brows. "He wasn't happy that you didn't have the gun with you or was it more like he was unhappy that you disobeyed his order?"

That was too close to the mark. Petunia looked up only to find Hester staring back at her.

"How do you know that?" Again the suspicion that Hester and Ace had shared more than a friendship perked.

"I haven't missed the way the man looks at you or the way you look at him. You're like two starving dogs staring at the same bone."

Petunia could have wished for a less colorful analogy, but it was appropriate.

Damn it.

The only way she was going to find a cure for this malady was to step into the fire, singe her wings, experience whatever it was her soul said she needed and get it over with.

"Oh, go on and ask me," Hester urged, popping the lid off the muffin tin and pulling one out.

Petunia bit her lip. The words tingled on her tongue. She could stare down executives and men of power. Plant her feet in the face of an enraged man but she couldn't ask the simple question.

Hester popped the top off the muffin and nibbled on the edge. And still Petunia couldn't get the words off her tongue.

"You're enjoying this, aren't you?"

Hester rolled her eyes. "You Goody Two-shoes, you always get stuck when it gets down to the nitty-gritty."

"What do you think I want to ask?"

Hester took another bite and chewed slowly, smiling. As she swallowed, Petunia realized there was something innately sensual about the woman that more than made up for her lack of conventional beauty.

"You want to know what he's like in bed."

Petunia choked on her sip of coffee. When the coughing fit stopped, Hester was still sitting there looking at her, a small smile gracing her face. She broke off another piece of her muffin, put it to her lips.

"Well? Isn't that what you want to know?"

Petunia nodded, using the next cough to cover for the fact embarrassment was winning over curiosity.

This time it was Hester who got up. She took the pitcher that was beside the sink and poured water into a clean cup and brought it over.

"Here, wash that down."

"I'll be okay," she managed to choke out.

Hester shook her head. "I don't want you having any excuses not to have this discussion."

She did manage to choke out a "why" before she took a sip of water.

"Because I like Ace, and I'm thinking you're not too bad yourself."

"You implied I'm not what he wants."

Hester waved dismissively with her hand. "Just because men get ideas doesn't mean they're right, and I've got a feeling about you."

Silly how so vague a statement could create such hope. "You do?"

She nodded. "You're a strong woman. Above and beyond everything else, Ace needs a strong woman. The ones he takes up with, they give him what he needs for the moment, but they can't give him what he needs long-term. A strong man with a weak woman, that's just poison."

"I thought he wasn't the settling kind."

"That's what he keeps telling everybody."

"You don't believe that?"

Hester shrugged. "I think no man is the settling kind until he meets the right woman."

It wasn't the first time she'd heard that. "Maybe I'm not a settling woman."

"We're not talking about settling, we're talking about making love."

Petunia hated the flush that flooded her face. She hated it more when Hester laughed.

"That is what we're talking about, isn't it?"

"Yes."

"And I take it you don't have any experience."

Petunia shook her head.

"Lord bless you, woman. You've got to be what? Staring hard at thirty?"

She nodded.

"You're a fine-looking woman. There had to be men who wanted to be with you."

"None of them made me want to give up my independence."

"Or your virginity," Hester hazarded.

Petunia wasn't used to such plain speaking, but getting to the point had its advantages.

"So what is he like?"

"Well. First off, 'cause you seem the jealous type and I don't want any knives in me before this is over, I've never been with Ace."

Petunia was inordinately glad to hear that. "But you know others that have been?"

"Oh, yes. He has his regulars."

Jealousy, futile but powerful bit into her voice.

"Regulars for what?"

"Ace…" Hester shook her head. "He's a good man, but a forceful man in bed. He demands everything from a woman. Her complete submission to anything he wants."

Inside Petunia that heat flickered. She remembered his kiss, the way he'd grabbed her hair, remembered last night on the counter when he'd bent her to his will.

"That's not a bad thing."

Hester just smiled a knowing smile. "I knew I had a feeling about you and no, for some, it's not a bad thing."

Some? "What aren't you telling me?"

"Nothing you won't find out soon enough."

"That's not fair."

"It's as fair as muffins and an early morning wake-up will get you."

It was ridiculous to feel so disappointed.

"But Ace wants to be with you," Hester continued. "How far he wants to go with you, how much he wants to show of himself to you, that's between you and him. It's not my place to get between a man and his woman."

"I'm not his woman."

Yet.

"Well, let me put this in a way that I think matters. If you want to know why he makes your heart flutter when you look at him, why you can't breathe when he gets close, you're going to have to chase him, because that man thinks you're too delicate to take his love."

"I'm not delicate."

"I'm not the one you have to convince."

"How would you suggest I go about doing that?"

Hester polished off the last bite of muffin and washed it down with the last coffee before yawning. "You're a clever woman. You've been studying the man for months. Figure it out."

Figure it out. Another project on her plate. Petunia looked out the window. All that looked back was the vague outline of her reflection. No help there.

"And now—" Hester stood "—I'm going to go up-stairs and get a few more hours of sleep. Something you should do, too. Turning that man's mind is not as easy as turning his head."

The man was stubborn. Petunia pushed her cup of coffee aside. "Right behind you."

Picking up the lamp, she followed Hester walking out through the dark hall, feeling the approach of the day and the simmer of excitement. By the time they reached the landing she knew what she wanted and what she was going to do. Now, all she needed was a plan.

CHAPTER NINE

PETUNIA STARTED OUT her plan with flirtation. Not her best skill, but Ace's lack of response gave her ample time to perfect it. From flirtation she moved on to seduction and now, three days later, she was pulling out the big guns. She was up to aggravation. Just let him try and ignore what she was going to do next.

If the rumor of the school board offering her a Christmas bonus was true, she'd be on a stage to California in three weeks, moving on to her dream, leaving behind the only man she'd ever been attracted to. Two little rickety louvered doors stood in front of her. They didn't keep out bugs, pest or pestilence but they might as well be bars for as much success as she was having pushing through them.

Petunia took another breath and slowly relaxed her shoulders and then her arms and lastly her hands. She could do this. She would do this. Just let Ace Parker brush her aside this time.

She prepared to push through the louvered doors. It felt like every eye in town was on her as she headed for the saloon. God help Ace. If this cost her her job, he was just going to have to buy her a ticket because this was all his fault. If any other woman had rubbed against him or made suggestive comments in his ear like she'd been doing this past week, she had no doubt he'd have been all over them. It was just her he resisted. Damn it.

She hit the doors. It was a bit more force than she intended. They slammed open and in the wake of the ensuing bang, every eye in the house, bleary or alert, focused on her. Stopping just inside the door, she scanned the room.

"Can I help you, miss?" Jenkins asked from behind the bar.

"You could tell me where Ace Parker is."

Jenkins pointed to the far left corner of the room.

She turned and there he was, sitting at a table with three men. A woman perched on the arm of his chair. She had to go. His chair scraped across the floor as he pushed it back. She got to his side just as he stood. How had she forgotten how tall he was? Cricking her neck back, she smiled up at him.

"Good evening, Mr. Parker."

Her tone couldn't be more innocent.

His couldn't be more dry. "Evening, Miss Wayfield. What brings you into this highly improper environment at this time of the evening?"

She didn't prevaricate and didn't lower her voice. "You."

The shock of that pronouncement had more chairs scraping and heads turning.

If she'd thought to shock Ace, though, she had another think coming. He just stood there matching her nonchalance for nonchalance. The blonde at his side scooted a little closer. Petunia disliked her on sight.

"I've been trying to get your attention."

"He's a busy man," the blonde interrupted, slipping an arm around his waist.

"And the last I checked, highly articulate," Petunia snapped. "Now, if you don't mind, no one has addressed you."

The blonde snapped back, "And no one invited you in here."

Petunia rolled her eyes. "It's a public place. No invitation needed."

"She's got you there, Rose," Jenkins called over.

To Ace, Petunia asked, "Seriously?"

"It's not her brains I'm interested in."

Rose spun around. "Are you saying I'm dumb?"

"I'm saying you're pretty," Ace inserted smoothly, removing Rosie's arm from his waist before sitting back down. Like a limpet, Rosie reattached herself to his side and smiled.

Rosie smiled. Petunia wanted to smack her with her reticule for being so silly. Instead, she ignored her.

"I've been trying to get your attention for days," Petunia said to Ace.

"Have you?"

"Yes."

"I hadn't noticed."

"That would make you the only one in town."

"Maybe I wasn't interested."

The way he said that so cold and final made her stomach sink. Until she looked into his eyes. There was only one word to describe what she saw in his eyes. Hunger.

"Well, for once, Mr. Parker, this isn't going to be all about you and what you want."

He cocked an eyebrow at her. "You don't say?"

Now she wanted to smack him. The blonde stroked his arm. And Rose. She definitely wanted to smack Rose.

"I do."

"And who put you in charge?"

She was excruciatingly aware of all their listeners. She couldn't falter now.

"It's not so much a case of someone putting me in charge as it is someone not taking charge."

His eyes narrowed. "Be careful, Pet."

"I'm always careful."

"Aw, hell." The man across the table from Ace huffed. "Looks like you got better things to play with than cards, gambler." He folded his hands and dropped the cards on the table. "I fold."

The other two men at the table looked at her and him and did the same.

She smiled. "Thank you. I appreciate your consideration."

"I sure as shit don't."

"Like the pretty lady said, Ace, it's not all about what you want." The men started dividing up the money.

Sidling up to the table, she braced her hand on the back of the chair, and leaning in, Petunia asked him, "Do you know what you want, Ace?"

His eyes dropped, and she knew the exact moment he noticed her gaping blouse. "Son of a bitch!"

Quick as lightning, he grabbed her arm. "Excuse us, Rose. Gentlemen."

Impatience snapped around them as he was forced to wait while Rose untangled herself. Petunia smiled. It served him right. She was still smiling as he popped her off balance and marched her toward the door. She had to scurry to keep up. They hit the louvered doors with such force they bounced back and caught her on the shoulder.

He didn't even turn his head when she cried out, just kept on walking.

"Where are we going?"

No answer. A quick glance showed her house ahead.
Behind, an audience. She wanted his attention, not the
whole town's.

She tugged at his arm. "People are looking."

All her tugging did was hurt her wrist.

"Let them look."

The steel in his tone gave her pause. "I just wanted
your attention."

"And now you've got it."

A belated sense of caution nipped at her frustration.
"Ace…"

"Don't."

"But…"

"Don't beg, don't plead, don't aggravate. Just shut up."

She shut up. Until they got to Providence. Then she
tried to put her foot down. Afternoon or not, it still wasn't
proper that he go into her house. He didn't seem to care
as he dragged her through the gate and, tossing open the
front door, he hauled her in. She caught it and closed it
behind them. Prying eyes were everywhere.

"This isn't proper," she gasped.

A muscle in his jaw flexed. "I'll make a note."

Without hesitation, he pulled her over to the straight-
back chair sitting by the little potbelly stove.

She started to get a very unromantic feeling. "What
are you doing?"

"What your pappy should have done to you long ago."
In one smooth move, he sat and yanked her off balance.
Another tug had her lying over his lap. She braced her
hands on the seat and pushed up. He put his elbow in
the middle of her back and held her down. He was the
stronger, so she stayed down. It was that simple. That

infuriating. That arousing. She kicked her feet. All she'd wanted was a kiss.

The first tug of her skirt sent a frisson of fear through her. The second added a swirl of dark excitement. The third added a cool draft and a shocking realization that he was lifting her skirts.

"No! What are you doing?" She reached back trying to stop him, but before she could get another syllable out, they were above her head and she knew, just knew, Ace was staring at her ass hidden by nothing but her thin bloomers. The swirl of dark excitement wrapped around her horror, muting it. His hand fell, and she jumped, legs jerking, breath catching, expecting pain but feeling instead the weight and heat of his touch. A threat, a promise. He wouldn't...

"Don't," she gasped. The sound reached her before the sting. The realization came third. He'd spanked her. On her ass. In the living room of her own house.

"How dare you?" She wriggled, flopping about like a fish out of water. "Let me up this minute!"

Another slap, on the other cheek, this time harder, the sting sharper. "You, Pet, don't give me orders."

Gritting her teeth she all but growled, "And you don't spank me."

His hands moved over her ass in a subtle soothing—or was it a warning? None of this was going as she planned. "Oh, trust me. This is the only thought running through my head right now that you want me playing out."

She struggled harder. "Damn you, let me up!"

The next spank came harder burning over the top of the first. "Don't curse."

The sting lingered, like the graze of his fingers, and beneath the indignity something bigger bloomed. Something dark and tempting that called out to everything feminine within her. It shamed her. It aroused her. It scared her. She put everything she had into the next bid for freedom. The ensuing spank stole her breath.

"Hold still."

Her "No" broke on a sob. Her confusion rode the heat as it pooled between her legs. What was he doing to her?

The next slap took her breath but the afterburn went straight to her pussy. He didn't have to say it.

You don't give me orders.

Oh, God. How could something so decadent feel so good?

"I don't want this." It was a lie.

"I do." That was a truth.

"Ace!"

His forearm stayed firmly planted in the hollow of her spine. Her hands stayed firmly planted on the rung of the chair. It was a battle of wills, and she wasn't giving in.

"You might as well just settle down and enjoy this. You've earned it."

"No."

"Suit yourself."

His palm slid over her butt in a skimming caress, almost contemplative in the nature. Goose bumps sprang across her skin, and the nerve endings under the sensitized skin stretched and lifted in a silent plea. Was she crazy? Was he?

A series of light spanks warmed her skin, not pain, not pleasure but a prelude her body recognized and her mind rejected. The spanking built gradually, leveling, surging, falling, stinging, burning, punishing, pleasuring. Keeping her off balance. Centering her attention. The sound of the slaps filled the room in an erotic cadence. Sensation filled her body in the same rhythmic bursts, and the moment consumed her mind. Anybody looking through the window could see, but she didn't care anymore. She needed to know, to understand, what was happening. She tried to resist as he soothed her well-warmed ass with a soft caress. But with a simple brush of his hand from her ass to her knee, he stole the impetus and turned the last of her rebellion into curiosity because never in her life had she felt such fiery pleasure. It streaked up her body, raced in goose bumps along her flesh and snatched her very breath from her lungs. There was nothing civilized about this. It was raw, primitive and perfect. Every spank a statement. Every caress a possession. She needed more.

He shifted in the chair. Before she could catch her balance, he was back at it, delivering another series of light, stinging slaps at the back of her thigh and while she was squirming from that, another pass of his hand down her leg, his nails dragging lightly across the goose bumps, inspiring more. Her pussy reacted. Desire flooded out reason. She wasn't a little girl to be spanked. She was a woman, and even though it made no sense, she'd never felt more than one right now. His hand grazed up the inside of her thigh, sliding over the cotton of her pantaloons, higher and higher in a deliberate tease. With a moan she let go of the chair and collapsed across his thighs, legs spread in breathless, shivering capitulation.

She wanted this.

ACE PAUSED WHEN Petunia went still across his lap. Resting his palm on the firm flesh of her buttocks, he could feel the heat of her flesh through her bloomers. There was expectancy to the way she lay across his lap, he recognized. An anticipation that matched that in him. The only difference was she was waiting for something she didn't recognize.

Him. She was waiting for him.

Tantalizingly, temptingly, the knowledge lured him. Petunia wasn't his usual type. She wasn't sturdy, she wasn't strong, she wasn't world-weary, but there was something about the woman that drew him in ways that shredded his good intentions and made mincemeat of the vow he made many years ago to never tarnish innocence. He might cheat a time or two at cards with men who deserved it, but there were also those times he'd thrown a hand or two to keep some farmer from losing everything in a reckless moment. In the end, he figured it balanced out.

He wasn't all bad, he wasn't all good but he was far from a do-gooder, and Pet was nothing but one. Like Quixote in the novels, she was always tipping her optimism at some windmill, playing hands that any good gambler would drop and making them work on nothing but sheer determination. She called him a gambler but she was the one who truly gambled, risking everything on a determined hope.

Her hips shifted on his, flexed ever so subtly, teasing him. "Ace…"

The shy whisper brought him back to the here and now. And, looking at the lush flare of her upturned ass, the here and now was a very seductive place. He dug his fingers into the firm flesh just enough to cause indents, just enough to bring that expectancy back to her. The problem was he loved all that passion simmering in Pet, wanted to contain it, direct it, eliminate the scattered force and make her… He sighed and admitted, his.

Every morning he got up and he looked in the mirror

and checked what he saw reflected back. Making sure normal still covered the darkness. Lately it had been getting harder and harder to look at the man staring back and not see the cracks in the facade. Ever since Petunia had arrived in town, he'd been getting careless, reckless, even. Needing. Wanting. But Petunia in her innocence and hope was the one thing he couldn't have. He could try to be normal; Lord knows he faked it a few times in the past, even managed it, for a day or two sometimes a month, but he had only to look at them now. Her skirts pulled up over her head, the only thing between his hand and her ass was the material of her pantaloons, the next spank twitching in his muscles, to know that that subterfuge wasn't possible between them. It didn't matter what he wanted; it didn't matter what his cock wanted; it didn't matter what the devil on his shoulder screamed. She was who she was. He was who he was and never the two could join.

Except for now, temptation whispered. He had now. He could know this small piece of her and let her taste this small piece of him. He could be the memory that every man in the future tried to replace. The thought put a tight smile on his lips. *Fuck, yeah. Let them try to replace this.*

He brought his hand down just a little harder this time, aiming for fresh flesh. Bringing back Pet's focus, centering her attention where he wanted it, on him.

"You've been begging for this for a long time, my pet."

She squirmed as he expected her to. Moaned as he wanted her to. He wanted that fight; he wanted that challenge. He wanted her to throw everything she had at him and then he wanted to catch it and mold it until everything she threw at him was her and everything he caught was her until everything he was, was her.

She squirmed and squealed against his thighs as he released the need, cried when he rained the smacks up and down her thighs, moaned when he ghosted the inside, but it was her desperate, "Please" that reached him.

He swore under his breath as she collapsed over his thighs, her torso jerking with her breaths. He'd lost control. The knowledge swamped him. He never lost control. A man couldn't play the games he did and lose control. And with Pet of all people. That was unforgivable. He wanted her balanced between pleasure and pain, aching and wanting. He didn't want her anywhere else. He never wanted her afraid of him.

Resting his palm on her ass, he rubbed soothingly, gentling her with quiet touches, giving her time to relax. He was the stronger one. The dominant. The one she had to be able to trust. His fingers slipped between her legs. The muslin was wet with her excitement. Deep inside him his demons stirred. *Yes.*

Before he could block it, possessiveness surged through him. This was what he wanted; this was what he longed for; this was his woman; this was his. He couldn't stop himself from turning her over, lifting her up, pulling her flushed face closer to his, staring into her wide eyes, breathing deep of her scent as he took in that initial reaction to his cock pushing against her pussy. The acceptance. The excitement. The utter need.

"This is why," he whispered against her lips as he rocked beneath her, "you need to stay away from me."

Her hands cupped his face. Her mouth bit at his as she pulled him closer. "This is why I won't."

The truth so simple, so impossible, hung between them.

His mouth opened over hers. He wanted her instant response. What he got was her resistance and even that was right. He nibbled at her lips.

"Open."

She shook her head and smiled. He brought his hand up to her chin, gripping tightly so she couldn't escape. Squeezing gently until her stubbornness gave, and her mouth parted. She tasted as sweet as she had the other day, but she also tasted hot and wild as a part of her she hadn't even recognized, that he hadn't allowed himself to believe existed, stepped into the world for the first time. She tasted like pure, beautiful lust. His cock throbbed between them, aching and hard. Desire rode his resolve just as hard.

In another time and place, she'd been his, and in another time and place she would be his, but in this time, in this world, all they could have was this moment. This kiss. Her fingers dug into his chest, eight points of pressure through his shirt, another bond. He ran his tongue over the inside of her lips lightly, teasingly, bringing passion past what she thought she should be, bringing out who she was.

She didn't sit as straight in his lap. He twisted slightly, letting her fall against him slightly, a soft, nearly imperceptible surrender. He took it for what it was, awareness.

"Yes," he muttered against her lips, "just like that. Give yourself to me."

"I don't want to," she whispered back.

"Liar."

He kissed her harder, pushing those words back into her mouth with his tongue, nibbling at her resistance with his lips, molding her into compliance with the soft drag of his nails down her spine. She gasped when his fingers grazed the hollow, smiled when with the slightest of pressure he seduced the last of her resistance and tempted her curiosity. She wanted to know where this between them could lead. Fuck. So did he.

He took another kiss, pressing harder, pushing stronger, driving her faster than he knew she would comfortably go, but he only had the now, and he wanted all he could cram into it because as soon as this meekness vanished, she was going to be pissed as hell.

"Kiss me back," he ordered.

"Make me," she ordered right back.

Oh, she was a wild one. Fisting his hand in her hair, he pulled her head back, staring down into those eyes. They were always full of determination and passion, but it was different now. She was focused on him.

"Do you need me to?" He'd give her that excuse if she needed it.

She stared at him for a minute as she processed the question before shaking her head. To his shock, the fingers digging into his chest opened flat, and her palm slid up over his shoulders, and her fingertips were against his nape and he felt those nails dig in the way he liked, pulling him down into her soft embrace. "No. Not at all."

Her lips pressed against his inexpertly, all awkward enthusiasm, and it was his turn to moan. It would be so much fun to train her. Making love to her wouldn't be the same as making love to a whore. She wouldn't be doing it for money. Her cooperation wouldn't be guaranteed and that wildness in her, depending on how well he handled it, would either work for him or against him. The challenge titillated his senses, the possibilities, his desire, the potential, his need. He wanted to consume her from the inside out, own her, mark her, love her. The last drew him up short.

He broke off the kiss, realizing with a start he was breathing as hard as she was, felt as drugged as she looked, and that just rattled him more. He never lost control. And the last place he should be losing it was here. With this woman.

Liar. His heart screamed. He caught her chin again, holding her gaze to his. She should have looked shattered. She just looked fucking beautiful, confident and, damn it all, determined.

"It's time for you to go, Pet."

She raised her eyebrows at him. Looked around and said, "This is my house."

"Not from here. From Simple."

"I don't have the money."

"I'll give it to you."

He expected her to argue. Instead, she asked, "What about the Providence?"

"I'll take care of it."

"It's not your responsibility."

"I'm making it mine."

She opened her mouth again, and he put his hand over it, silencing her, keeping her pressed between his hand in her hair and his hand over her mouth, controlling her. And she liked it. The realization just sent his blood spiking higher. Damn it, so did he.

She didn't struggle like a lesser woman would. She didn't look afraid; she just watched him like prey watched a predator, except there was a bit of predator in her, too, and that, he realized, was what he liked about her, her strength. She didn't back down. She didn't give up. She just changed direction when necessary.

"You're leaving. This…between us." He shook his head. "I don't want it."

Holding her as he was, he couldn't miss her flinch. He expected tears. He got resistance. She made a muffled sound behind his hand, and her brows came down.

"I'm not saying that to spark your interest." She needed to understand that. "It's the flat-out truth. You've said all along I'm no good. You were right. You're right about other things about me, too. There are a lot of things I've done in this life that I'm not proud of, but I've never destroyed a woman's innocence, and I'm not going to start with yours. So in two days when that stage comes through, you're going to have a ticket and you're going to get on it. Understand?"

"Oh, I understand." Sliding off his lap, she yanked her dress down and glared at him. "Your needs, your wants, it's all about you."

He stood. She didn't back off or down, she just folded her arms across her and gave him back glare for glare. He admired that. Wanted that. Fuck.

"It takes two to tango, my pet, and I'm not dancing."

"I'll take the ticket, then, but you needn't look so smug about it," she snapped. The words came at him in a steady pelting, like raindrops in a sudden storm, fat and hard, striking all his vulnerable places.

"I'm taking it because I deserve better, and I won't be that woman who has no value to the man toying with her. When I give myself to someone it's going to be with my heart and soul and I'm going to know that the gift is cherished."

"You should save it for your husband."

She rolled her eyes. "I don't demand marriage, but I do demand decency and that, Ace Parker, leaves you out."

That stung. "Awful high-and-mighty for a woman who was just squirming on my lap."

Folding her arms across her chest she said, "And you're being awful high-and-mighty for a man who's pretending nobility when he's really just a chicken shit. But thank you for the lesson." She walked to the door and held it open. "Merry Christmas, Ace. You're free."

Ace slammed his hat down on his head. Cursing himself, fate and that damned spirit that made him want to snatch her up, even now with his good intentions screaming, he walked out. Doing the right thing sucked.

CHAPTER TEN

ACE WAS AS good as his word. When the stage pulled up in front of the mercantile two days later, little plumes of dust kicking up from the stop, Petunia was there, the ticket he'd bought her to California in hand, all the bittersweet goodbyes said, feeling more despondent than she had when she'd landed in this little town. She looked over her shoulder, half expecting to see Ace coming down the walk, but all she saw was Luke. Her stomach sank. She knew what that meant. Ace and Luke were like peas in a pod. Where there was one, the other usually wasn't far behind, but if he wasn't, it was for a reason. She'd been bouncing between hope and dread about seeing Ace again after their time together. He made her hunger. He made her worry. He made her want to see how far he could take her. She was all but starved for his attention, and he wasn't even going to see her off. Damn him.

She forced a smile when Luke got close. As always he was dressed impeccably. Today he had on a red-and-gold-paisley vest under a perfectly cut black suit. She wondered if the tailor had to make allowances for his guns. "Good morning, Luke."

He tipped his hat and smiled, revealing perfectly even teeth. Why couldn't she have fallen for him? "Morning, Miss Wayfield."

She sighed. "Surely we know each other well enough for you to use my first name."

"Probably, but such familiarity invariably leads to speculation when dealing with a man with my reputation."

"Oh."

It was his turn to sigh. "That was a joke, Petunia. It was supposed to make you smile."

It was hard to smile when she felt awkward and silly, the way she always did when she was fighting tears. "I'm sorry. Did you come to see me off?"

"Yes. I figured someone should handle the formalities." He glanced at the bags at her feet. There were a lot of them. When she'd left Massachusetts it wasn't with the intent of returning. "All packed up?"

She nodded.

Sunlight glinted off his cuff links as he tested the weight of the biggest. He really did have a sense of style. She felt dowdy by comparison in her brown plaid traveling suit.

"We might need a bigger coach."

She forced a smile she didn't think would fool anyone. "I packed on the theory that smaller bags were easier to manage than a large trunk."

The driver got down from the stage. This was the first stop of the morning. The horses were chomping at their bits, kicking up clouds of dust as they stomped their feet. She waved the drift away from her face. They so needed rain.

The driver grabbed a bucket off the railing, scooped water out of the trough and brought it to the lead horse. He was a lean, bent, grizzled man with a countenance as battered as the stage and clothes as ragged as her emotions. Not at all what she'd expected. Somehow, she'd imagined her departure populated with grander moments as fitting the launch of a dream. With a nod he acknowledged her waiting. "Be with you in a minute, miss."

"Thank you."

Instead it was…deflating.

"Howdy, Luke." He tipped his hat to Luke.

"Howdy, Gil."

"It will be a little bit before Gillian's ready to go," Luke said. "If you wanted to grab something to eat, I'd love the company."

The last thing she wanted was food. The swaying of the coach often made her nauseous. Petunia shook her head. "Thank you, but Maddie handled that for me."

"Made you up some cinnamon rolls, did she?"

Her smile faltered. Tears threatened. "I'm going to miss her."

Luke shook his head and reached into his pocket, shaking out a handkerchief before offering it to her. She had no doubt it was clean.

"You don't have to go, you know," Luke said. "You could always stay and make your place here. You've got the school started up and folk riled enough something might actually get done."

She glanced up the street. She'd been reminding herself for two days this wasn't the school she wanted to start—it was too small, its scope too limited—but just looking at the big house with its faded whitewash and neglected yard tugged at her heartstrings. There was so much still to do… "With Luisa and Antonio volunteering to help, Hester can handle the school."

"Hester's a competent woman, but that's not the same as a teacher."

"Then they'll pressure the town to provide one."

"They'll have to." Luke named the woman whose position Petunia had taken. "Rumor is Mrs. Arbuckle is with child."

She couldn't avoid another pang.

"That frown tells me you care."

"Of course I care."

"Then stay."

She couldn't hold a smile anymore. "I think when a man buys a woman a ticket out of town, it's a pretty good indicator that she needs to move on."

The handkerchief fluttered as Luke offered it again. "One man does not the universe make."

This time she took it. "He's your friend."

Luke shrugged. "Doesn't mean he can't be wrong."

It didn't mean she was right, either. She'd been so naive. In her inexperience she'd thought he'd been as caught up in their passion as she was, but she'd been wrong. Grossly, humiliatingly, abjectly wrong. The reality had been driven home when Jenkins had knocked on the door with the ticket in hand. Ace hadn't even bothered to include a note in the envelope with the ticket. He apparently felt he'd said it all. She crumpled the handkerchief in her hand. "It was never my plan to stay."

She couldn't resist taking another look down the street toward the saloon where Ace no doubt was lounging. Hope just wouldn't die.

"He's not coming," Luke said softly.

She flushed. "Am I that obvious?"

"Yes."

"Who's not coming?" Gillian interrupted. "I was only expecting one. We got a passenger not on the manifest?"

Petunia let Luke handle the responding. "Miss Wayfield was referring to Ace. He'd been called away."

She just bet he had.

"Ace Parker?" Gil asked, patting the near horse on the shoulder.

"Yeah."

"Good man, that one. Right handy in a fight." The driver shook his head and scooped more water and brought it over to the second horse. "Shame he's not riding along. Heard tell of Indian trouble between here and San Antonio."

Luke frowned. "Sure it's Indian? The Comanche haven't been bothering folk for a long while. Heard there was trouble down Wild Gulch way but I thought it was wranglers who fessed up."

The driver shrugged. "Don't know about that." With an exaggerated flex of his right leg, he added, "But I do know my knee's been acting up and that's a surefire sign of trouble."

The thought of an Indian attack terrified Petunia. She'd grown up reading about the Indian raids of old in both the paper and the lurid dime novels sold in the stores and street corners. The news might be highly sensationalized, but common sense said being abducted by a band of men wearing not much more than a loincloth bent on revenge couldn't go well for a woman.

The coach that had looked so solid pulling up now looked ridiculously flimsy. She licked her lips. "They wouldn't attack the stage, would they?"

Gil was no comfort. "Been known to happen. I got a couple riders I'm picking up here." Using the dirty handkerchief around his neck he wiped the sweat from his face, adding a smear of cleanliness amidst the coating of dust. "We should be fine."

The one thing Petunia'd learned about the West was that one was never completely safe. "Pick good riders, please. I want to get to California safe and sound."

"California? That's a long trip for a pretty thing like you to be taking alone, ma'am."

She didn't feel pretty right now; she felt ragged and worn and, she admitted, discarded. "Thank you for your concern, but I'll be fine."

"That's what a lot of folk tell me." He watered the last horse. "We're going to be leaving in a bit, ma'am."

"A bit? But the schedule says ten o'clock." It was quarter past now.

"Yup, it does, but I got a late start, and I'm hungry so it's going to be a bit."

And that was that. The headache that had been threatening bloomed. Rubbing her forehead, she sighed, and resigned herself to the delay. "What will I do with my bags?"

Luke grabbed them and tossed two up on the back of the stage before reaching for the third. The driver grunted, watching as he wedged them in.

"Not traveling too light are you?"

"The ticket said I could carry two bags and a trunk."

"Yeah, well, that'd be more like normal-size bags, and that second one is pushing trunk size."

"I am within the rules, am I not?"

Another grunt and a glare was the response. She didn't care. She might not be leaving with the experience she wanted, but she was leaving with her darn luggage.

Luke shook his head and lashed the bags down. "Funny how you fight for your luggage."

"Somethings are just better left alone," she shot back, folding her arms across her chest.

"Uh-huh." He hopped down. Dust poofed around his feet. Sweat dribbled uncomfortably between Petunia's breasts. Even the weather was against her. Who needed a heat wave in December?

The horses stomped their feet and snorted with impatience. She knew just how they felt. A bit Gil had said... She'd steeled herself to make it through the last ten minutes, and now she had to wait an undefined *bit*. She wanted to grind her teeth. She wanted to swat someone.

"I'll be in the mercantile," she told the driver, who merely grunted in reply. She did not want to go through another round of tearful goodbyes. She didn't think she could stand it. It'd been harder than she expected to leave the school and the budding orphanage, her budding friendships. She took her anger out on Gil in a hard stare. "Do not leave without me."

Gil waved his hand at her as she stepped up onto the walk. Didn't even look back as he snapped, "Don't be late."

How could she be late to *a bit* or so? She rolled her eyes. Contrary man.

Luke came up beside her. "He's just doing his job."

The driver wasn't heading to the restaurant; he was heading to the saloon.

"Is he going to drive this stage drunk?"

"Doubtful, but I think he aims to drive it guarded, and the saloon's the most likely place where he'll find his hired guns."

"Guns?"

"The Comanche aren't to be taken lightly."

"But you said they have been peaceable for years."

"I said they haven't stirred up anything for years, but you can only push anyone so far and they're going to kick up their heels."

"What does that mean?"

"You'll be safe, Petunia."

She hoped so. "Why'd you come by, Luke?"

"To wish you a safe journey."

"That's all?"

"Well, that and to see if you were going to be sensible."

"I'm always sensible."

"So I was let to believe." He tipped his hat and headed back across the street, to the saloon, she realized.

Did all men ever do was get drunk? She shook her head and turned back and headed toward the mercantile. A sarsaparilla would go down good right now.

The spook the driver had given her about Indians just wouldn't shake. She opened the mercantile door. The little bell chimed. She went to the counter and sat down on the stool by the window. When Glenda, the shopkeeper's wife, came out of the back, straightening her apron, Petunia forced a smile.

"Could I have a sarsaparilla please?"

The woman put the bottle on the counter.

"Thank you." Petunia sighed and worked the cork loose. Why couldn't everything be so straightforward? Ask and receive. No fuss. No muss. No hurt. No regrets. Not like this mess. Taking a sip of the beverage, she concentrated on enjoying the fizzy sweetness, pushing aside the nagging regret. She had a feeling between surviving Ace and the Indians, the Comanche would be easier.

"ARE YOU REALLY going to be this stupid?"

Over the years, Luke had asked Ace that question with varying degrees of impatience. Today was the first time he'd said it with genuine anger. Ace looked up from the cards he was shuffling. "Do you really want to come at me with that question when I'm just settling in for a good drunk?"

Luke pulled out the chair opposite. It slid across the floor with a grate. "Apparently, since you're sitting here playing solitaire after letting your woman board the stage this morning."

"Then, yes. I intend to be this stupid."

Ace placed a red king on the black ace.

"Just tell me why."

The queen he needed was covered by the ace of spades.

"Because she's destined for better things."

"And you're destined for what?" Luke waved expressively with his hand, indicating the saloon and the few seedy inhabitants that clung to the escape they found here: a man in the corner draped over a table snoring, two whores drinking coffee, the bartender wiping lazily at the counter. "This?"

"It suits me."

"The hell it does. You're Hell's Eight."

"Hell's Eight is changing."

"What Hell's Eight *does* might have changed, mellowed a bit, I'll grant you, but we're still the same men who scraped and clawed to survive. We're still the same men that protect what's ours."

Ace flipped the cards over. The king was free; the queen stayed buried. "I know who I am." And *what* he was.

Ace laid out a new layer of cards.

"That two will go up on top," Luke pointed out.

Ace shook his head. "You never could keep your nose out of another man's game."

Luke tilted the chair back, balancing it on two legs. "Some people need the help."

The urge to send him the rest of the way over was high. "Try."

"It's not entirely impossible there's Indian trouble. You know the army's been pulling it's cavalry out, moving them back East with that conflict brewing."

Ace shook his head. "It's not going to be pretty if this country comes to war."

"It's not going to be pretty if Petunia's stage gets attacked."

Ace flipped the cards. This time he had a move and then another. It freed the queen, but now the king was covered.

"If anything happens to her you'll never forgive yourself," Luke added unnecessarily.

"Nothing's going to happen to her." He looked at the cards. No matter what he did there was no move that put the king and queen together.

Bringing his chair back down on four legs, Luke pushed his hat back "You're a fool, Ace Parker. If I had a woman like that fancying me, I'd do whatever it took to bring her into my life."

"I'm not afraid of being alone."

"Well, I sure as shit am. What's more, I'm tired of it. Tired of waking up in the morning and having nothing to look at but an empty pillow on the other side of the bed. I'm tired of cooking meals and sitting down and having only myself to talk to. I'm tired of looking into the future and seeing nothing but more of the same. I want a legacy."

"I don't."

"Yeah, you do." Luke swept his hand across the table scattering the cards. "And all your fancy tricks can't hide that from me. I grew up with you. Fought with you. Survived with you. I know you. Petunia is what you need, so stop being such a goddamn chicken shit and go after her."

That was the second time this week someone he'd loved had called him a chicken shit. He might be going soft in his old age. "I'm not afraid of loving."

"Then what are you afraid of?"

"Destroying it."

There was a long pause. It was too much to hope Luke was going to let it go. "She's not as fragile as you think she is."

"She's not as strong, either."

"You don't have to succumb to those urges."

Which just went to show that even though Luke knew about his preferences, he didn't understand them. "It would be impossible not to with her."

"Then have someone on the side."

"No." He wouldn't do that to Pet. It would destroy her.

"So you're just going to let her go?"

"You don't see her staying, do you?"

"What I see is for the first time in her life, that woman's got her world rattled, and she doesn't know what to do about it, so she's running, and you're letting her."

"For a reason."

"Even with the threat of Indians?"

Ace sighed. "Every time Gillian comes through here, he talks about seeing Indian signs. He remembers the old days when the Comanche terrorized this area. Those days are gone." Like his opportunity with Petunia. "It's only forty miles to the next stage stop. He's got two men as outriders, and Gillian's no slouch with that repeater."

"But you're not worried," Luke challenged.

Ace worried whenever Petunia was out of his sight, but he couldn't succumb this time. He'd stolen her idealism. He wouldn't get in the way of her dream. "The stage has made that run a hundred times."

But it still bothered him that she was on it. Alone. Out of the reach of his protection. Something Luke knew damn well and good.

Luke sighed. "You're a fool."

Rose came sidling over. Her hand was on Luke's shoulder, but her eyes were on Ace and full of hunger. He knew why. The marks from their last session were probably fading.

"You want a little company?" she asked.

Yeah, he did. He scooted back his chair and she sauntered over and dropped in his lap, but for once he didn't appreciate the softness of her curves, the weight of her body. She was too heavy, too soft, too perfumed, too wrong.

Luke must've read his expression. "She feels that way, too."

There was no doubt who *she* was. The wall around Ace's longing cracked just as Luke intended.

Gathering up the cards he'd scattered, Luke sorted them and then set them very neatly, very precised in a stack in front of Ace. "Gillian said his knee's hurting him."

Everything in Ace went cold. He pushed Rose off his lap.

"Hey!"

The black ace covering his queen.

"What did you say?"

"You heard me."

"Why the hell didn't you lead with that?"

"Because I'm not superstitious, like you."

Ace stood and grabbed his hat. Gillian's knee was never wrong.

"Where you going?" Luke asked, standing also.

"Where the hell do you think?"

He was getting his queen back.

THE STAGE ROCKED back and forth, back and forth, up and down, side to side. Petunia grabbed at the strap above her and held on as tightly to that as she did to her stomach. She hated riding the stage on the best of days, but this driver—Gillian—seemed absolutely compelled to hit every bump, sway and dip in the road. Her bones felt shaken; her teeth hurt from snapping together, and any minute now she was going to lose her breakfast. Yet none of that made her as miserable as the "what-ifs" plaguing her with every turn of the wheels.

What if she'd stayed? What if she'd let Ace do what he wanted to do? What if she'd stepped out of her safe little place and demanded her place in his world? What if she was leaving the only man she was every going to feel this way about? She wanted to tell the driver to turn around but it wouldn't do any good. Gillian wouldn't stop until he got to the next post. And there wasn't anything of substance waiting for her back there.

What if she swallowed her pride and telegraphed her father for money? He'd yell, say he told her so, start arranging parties full of men in stiff-collared suits and give her a timeline within which to marry. Her father loved her, but he had very strict ideas of what his daughter's perfect future should be. She sometimes thought he believed the tightness of his plans were a talisman against the fate that had befallen her mother. As if wrapping her in a cocoon of conformity warded off all illness and misfortune. The only problem was, she couldn't breathe in a cage, no matter how gilded.

The coach lurched as it hit a rock or a tree or whatever the hell the driver was aiming for. It sent her flying across the compartment. Thank goodness there weren't any other passengers. She didn't have to worry about landing in an undignified heap in a stranger's lap. She banged on the side of the coach.

"Be careful, can't you?" she called up to the driver.

The only response was a "Hyah!" and the sound of reins slapping the horses' backs. Of course, requesting he be careful set him to driving like a maniac. Was everyone out here contrary? Scrambling back into her seat, she braced her feet against the bench opposite and straightened her jacket. She knew darn well her hat was askew, but every time she reached up she lost her balance. She was afraid if she tried to fix it she'd end up snatching herself bald.

"Hang on tight, miss."

"What is the rush?" she hollered above all the clamor.

No answer. The coach picked up speed. Another bump sent her flying across the bench. She hit her head hard enough to see stars. She wasn't worried about her hat anymore. She was worried about coming out of this alive. She had at least ten bruises already. She slammed her hand on the side of the door again.

"Slow down or it's not going to be a stagecoach, but a hearse!"

Gillian's voice took on an edge as he continued to yell at the horses while the carriage pitched and hawed.

She heard a gunshot.

Then another. And another. Then from Gillian, "Hold on to your bloomers, miss!"

As if she could do anything else.

"What is it?"

"Comanche."

The one word guaranteed to strike terror into her heart. She hadn't been raised in the West. She hadn't been here for the raids twenty years previous, but she knew about them. The first war cry rose in a terrifying trill. It was followed by another and another.

It was foolish. It was dangerous. She had to look. She pulled the curtain away from the small rear window and immediately wished she hadn't. There was safety in that little bubble of wood that constituted the chassis and the ignorance that came from not knowing. But looking out that window she felt all hope die. Indians. Wild men with painted faces and guns and knives riding wild running ponies. Of their outriders there was no sign. Petunia forced herself to calmly count.

Fourteen. There were fourteen Comanche and only two of them and one of them was driving the coach.

"Dear God."

This time after she rapped on the wall, she leaned out the window.

"Give me a gun."

The sounds and smells were so much stronger.

"Women can't shoot."

Really? "Then think of me as a man, but give me a damn gun."

Gil took a rifle, held it down. It took three grabs before she could get it.

"Don't drop these. They're all we've got." He tossed her the box of bullets.

She barely caught them with the carriage careening on the path. The Indians closed in, their screams louder. She shoved a shell into the chamber and leaned out the window again. Gunshots peppered the air. There was a plink as one hit the wood above her head. This was real. She was amazingly calm. One of the riders had a bright red feather in his hair. She took aim on him.

"Don't be wasting those bullets," she heard from above.

"Keep the damn coach straight for a minute, and I won't."

She took aim and fired. Red feather toppled from the horse. She jacked another bullet into the chamber. One down, thirteen to go.

CHAPTER ELEVEN

ACE AND LUKE caught up with the coach far earlier than they'd expected. It tipped on its side in the middle of a clearing, wheels bent and broken, doors open. A wooden carcass stripped of all of its essentials. The horses were nowhere in sight. Ace wasn't surprised. There was nothing more valuable to a Comanche than a good horse, and Gillian prided himself on his team. Overhead, a vulture circled.

"Shit," Luke said, pulling up.

Ace didn't have room in him for words. His heart had been in his throat since they'd found Gillian's outriders shot dead two miles back. All the signs pointed to Comanche, from the unshod hoofprints to the sweep out of cover flanking attack. Along those two miles, someone had done some fancy shooting. It wasn't easy to hit the broadside of a barn from a moving coach, let alone a man on a horse. At least four Comanche were dead or dying. But the odds had never been with the coach. And the end was inevitable.

Sliding off Crusher, Ace approached the carriage. All around the ground was churned up from the stomp of horses' hooves and the trample of raiders feet. Later, he'd figure out how many, but right now there was only one thing he wanted to know. Step by step he approached the carriage, one step, two step, his breath caught in his lungs, a solid ache of dread. His heart beat sluggishly as he approached the door.

Luke was right behind him. He caught his arm. "Wait up, Ace."

Ace shrugged him off. He wasn't waiting for anything. He had to know. Feeling as if he were fighting a headwind in a slow-moving world, he opened the door. For one heartbeat he couldn't look. Couldn't know. In the next, he saw it all. His breath exploded outward on a curse.

"She there?"

"Fuck." He shook his head, holding on to the coach to steady himself. There was nothing in the carriage. No body. No bags. No blood. "Looks like they took her."

"Thank God."

Most folk considered a woman's fate at the hands of the Comanche a fate worse than death. He wasn't one of them. Only death was final. Everything before that was possibility. He'd forgotten that for a bit. He wouldn't ever forget it again. "She probably doesn't feel that way."

Luke looked up from where he knelt at the back, studying the prints in the dirt. "The important thing is that she's still alive to feel anything at all."

Ace nodded. Whatever had happened, whatever *was* happening to Petunia didn't matter. Whatever the repercussions he'd fix it, make it right. "I should have ridden with them."

"There was no reason to think there was need. Gil's been seeing the vengeance signs for twenty years. Just luck this time that he was right."

"His knee hurt."

"He was sixty years old. Probably every joint in his body hurt."

Luke wanted to absolve him of guilt. It was a point-less endeavor. Ace would go to his grave with the weight of his choices this day on his soul. Pet was his woman. Hell's Eight by default. He owed her better than he'd given.

Moving to the front of the carriage, he saw Gil's crumpled body. No bloody pool seeped out from beneath. The thirsty earth had drained it all, leaving him a too-pale husk of the tough-as-nails son of a bitch he used to be. Ace turned him over. His head lolled unnaturally. From the look of things he'd been alive when the coach had overturned. Shot but alive. It was a blessing the fall had broken his neck. The Comanche weren't kind to their enemies.

"He dead?"

Goodbye, old man.

Ace stood and dusted off his hands. "Yeah."

Luke took off his hat. "Shit. He was a tough old coot."

Ace nodded. "He was."

"What do you want to do? Go after them or wait for a posse?"

Ace picked up the reins of his horse. "What do you think?"

They'd ridden together so long they were almost an extension of each other. Luke was swinging up into the saddle before he got the words out.

"We ride." Ace checked his rifle in the scabbard, his eyes on the horizon, his mind already on the battle ahead. "And then we make them pay."

For every moment of fear Pet suffered, for every bruise on her lovely skin, for every shadow they put on her soul, they'd pay. In blood and suffering. He swung up on his horse. They had no right to touch what was his.

Crusher pawed the ground. Ace stilled him with pressure from his knees.

Luke's horse Buddy tossed his head and hopped in a circle. Even the horses could feel what was coming.

"There's at least eight in the party," Luke said.

"Including the dead?"

"No."

It didn't matter how many there were. However many there were, they were going to die. Screaming.

"Tough odds."

Luke tugged his hat down. "We've faced tougher."

Not in Ace's memory, but Luke was Luke. Deadly and loyal. They'd been to hell and back together. His brother in spirit. His best friend. The one man Ace trusted above all others. The only one he'd always joked with whom he'd want to ride into hell. And now they were. There was only one thing to say.

"Thank you."

Luke smiled that perfect smile of his. "You can owe me."

THE COMANCHE RAIDERS were moving fast. They weren't taking time to cover their tracks. Either they weren't expecting pursuit or they had enough numbers waiting up ahead they didn't fear it. Shit.

Ace and Luke rode harder.

It was a long six hours before they caught up with the raiders. The trail led straight to a small cutback canyon.

Ace's first instinct was to charge right in. Luke grabbed his horse's reins. One word was all it took to snap him back.

"Think."

He couldn't. Not then. Pet was there, within reach,

suffering. The knowledge tore at his reasoning. Luke didn't let go of the reins. His gaze was stone-cold as the muzzle he pressed into Ace's thigh.

"Get your head right, Ace. Or get home."

"You'd shoot me?"

"Without batting an eye."

Ace would do the same if the situations were reversed.

The gun stayed pressed to his thigh. "Petunia doesn't need your emotion, she needs your skills."

"Fuck." Luke was right. He knew it.

"So what's it going to be?"

Ace wasn't a rash man in or out of battle. He was methodical and thought things through. He closed his eyes and reached deep, pushing aside his worst fears, finding his balance. When he opened his eyes, he was who he needed to be. "You can let go of the reins."

Luke did, slowly. "I realize what she means to you, but riding straight into a bullet isn't going to do her much good."

"I know." The familiar chill of prebattle encased his nerves.

"I doubt they've seen us, so we've got surprise to our advantage plus it's going to be darker than a hole in a pocket tonight."

Ace agreed. "If we take out the guard, we should be able to slip in unnoticed. I doubt they're expecting so few so soon."

"I know they're not expecting Hell's Eight."

Over the years a mutual respect for each other's fighting skills had developed between the Comanche and the members of Hell's Eight.

"I'll take all the advantages I can get."

"It'll be dark in a few hours."

It was those few hours that gnawed on Ace. A man could do a lot to a woman in a few hours. Eight hard-ass Comanche, an unbelievable amount.

As if reading his thoughts, Luke muttered, "Don't think on that, Ace."

"I'm not thinking anything."

Luke dismounted and ground-tied Buddy farther behind the bluff shielding their position. "You're thinking the same thing I am, but if we do this right, there'll be a point to that thinking later."

Staying low, Luke started climbing the bluff.

Because if they did this right, Petunia would be alive. Ace fondled the butt of his revolver. Usually Ace was the calm one of the two, but tonight Luke could be the voice of reason. He'd settle for being the hand of justice. Dismounting, he followed Luke.

"You with me still?" Luke asked as he hunkered beside him near the lip of the bluff.

"You worry too much."

Luke pushed his hat back, took a sip from his canteen and passed it to Ace. "Must be because I've never seen you in love before."

Ace took a long pull. The water was warm and brackish but it did the job. "And you're not likely going to see it again."

"What's it feel like?"

He couldn't explain the mix of fear, excitement and perfection. "Like sitting with your legs dangling over the edge of the highest cliff you've ever seen."

"That bad?"

Ace handed the canteen back, studying the canyon wall. "That good."

"Shit."

"Yeah."

Ace pointed to the craggy right side of the wall. "I figure the most likely place to have sentries is that ledge right there. It's close enough to get a shot off at anyone past this bluff but still provide some cover. Visibility is clear on all sides. With a man stationed there, you would only need one sentry."

Luke pointed to the left. "That spot over there would be my second choice."

"Cover's not as good, and that outcropping blocks the view to the west," Ace countered.

"Yeah. That's why I'm betting that is where they're going to have the sentry. Which only leaves one question—"

Ace didn't need him to finish. "You can take the sentry."

For a long moment, Luke just studied him. Then he nodded.

"All right. I figure it's going to take me a good five minutes to get down off the wall. Think you can curb your impatience that long before rushing in?"

"When you take him out, I'm going in."

"The plan is you wait."

Ace nodded and drew his knife, checking the edge.

Luke shook his head. "Why do I get the impression I'd better grow wings?"

"No clue."

Sliding down until the angle of the bluff served as his pillow, Luke settled his hat over his eyes. "If I'm going to be running down mountains like a goat, I'll need my rest."

"I'll stand watch."

Luke smiled. "That was my plan."

The hours passed slowly. The silence was only broken

by birdcalls and the relentless chime of his conscience. At the top of each hour, Ace scanned the canyon walls, looking for anything he might have missed, anything that might have changed, any potential threat Luke hadn't seen, any eventuality Ace hadn't predicted. The hours passed with no change except the gradual dip of the sun below the horizon. When the sliver of moon began its rise, Luke woke, checked his revolvers and picked up his rifle.

"It's time."

Ace nodded and patted his rifle. "I've got you covered."

Luke turned. Stopped. Turned back, held up his hand, fingers spread. "Remember, five minutes."

Ace nodded. "I heard you."

A few steps farther, and Luke blended into the shadows. Ace crawled up to the ledge and balanced his rifle on a rock. It was too dark to see much, but he didn't need more than a rifle flash to pick off the sentry. After that they probably had five minutes before Comanche came spilling out of the canyon. Luke had better get that damn sentry.

The minutes ground by with excruciating slowness. It took every bit of discipline Ace had not to rush that canyon. He wasn't foolish, but Pet made him feel that way sometimes. He was a fool for thinking he could take on twelve Comanche alone. A fool for thinking a woman like her would be happy with a man like him. A fool for thinking he could even be happy. He shook his head. He wasn't a man destined for joy. He was destined to be what he was, a gambler, a gunfighter, Hell's Eight. He tightened his grip on the rifle. Justice.

There was a scuff of a boot on dirt behind him. He

spun around, knife ready. Just before he struck, Luke cautioned, "Easy."

He stopped the thrust midway. "Son of a bitch, I almost gutted you," he whispered under his breath. "Why in the hell didn't you give me the call?"

Luke squatted down beside him in their meager cover and studied the canyon. "Something's wrong."

"How wrong?"

"There's no sentry."

"There?"

He shook his head. "From up there, I can see all around. There's no sentry anywhere."

Fuck, they'd wasted all this time. Ace sheathed his knife. Cold, clammy dread settled in his stomach. "They didn't stop."

"They stopped. I can hear the horses."

"What the hell?"

"I don't know. I don't like the feel of this."

Neither did Ace. "It could be a trap."

Luke nodded. "Maybe. But even that doesn't make sense. It's not like Comanche to waste time with the odds so high in their favor. They could have attacked hours ago."

It didn't make any sense at all. Ace scooted back down the bluff. "Guess there's only one way to find out."

Luke was right behind him. "Yup."

THE STRETCH FROM the canyon to the Indian campsite was the longest of Ace's life. It wasn't the first time, second time, third time or even the hundredth time that he'd crept up on an enemy, but it was the first time he'd felt like he'd aged a hundred years in the process. He wasn't worried how he'd find Pet. It was likely she'd been tortured. Raped. He was braced for that. What he didn't want to find was that she'd been murdered.

The closer they got to the camp, the stranger the whole situation got. The only sounds breaking the night were crickets, the occasional hoot of an owl, the stomp of a horse's hoof and the sound of men snoring. Why hadn't they posted a sentry?

Ace shook his head. It made no sense. He'd taken the path around the left perimeter; Luke had taken the right, watching for the sentry or guard. There was none. As he got closer, the faint red glow that had been the Comanche fire reduced into a pile of glowing embers.

Another shiver went down his spine. Comanche wouldn't make a fire on the way back from a raid. They were warriors through and through, as tough as this country. One of the fiercest enemies he'd ever faced. He might not share their philosophies, but he respected them as warriors and enemies.

From across the way Luke gave him a signal. The soft hoot of an owl cut short followed by two calls, four warbles each. Luke had reached the far perimeter. And he counted eight men.

The sliver of moon didn't give out much light, but Ace was careful, very careful, not to step on a stick, not to break a branch. The only rustle marking his progress was the rise of the breeze.

He wanted to charge in, find Petunia, snatch her close, keep her safe, apologize, tell her it didn't matter. But it did. He knew it did. For all her bravado, she was a good woman, and tonight was going to change her life but he would fix it. He was good at fixing things. Card games, claim disputes at the assayer's office, just subtly working in the background moving things around, playing the odds until they came out right. And he'd make it right for Petunia. He'd do what he had to now to get her out of this mess, and when he got her home, he'd convince her nothing that had happened today mattered. Because it didn't. Not now. Not to him. Not ever.

Another snore permeated the dark. The wind changed direction, and a sour smell blended with the clean night air. Every boy over the age of ten was familiar with that smell. Hooch. Gil had been carrying hooch on that coach, which might explain the unnatural stillness of the camp.

Ace sent an answering signal back to Luke. He slid his knife between his teeth and pulled out his revolver, waiting for the little hairs on the back of his neck to stand on end, but while every nerve ending was snapping with attention, the warning tingle was absent. There was danger here but not an imminent threat. Normally, he would have just gone with that but ordinarily, Petunia wasn't in the line of fire. He couldn't afford a mistake. He crouched down and inched forward. A twig snapped beneath his knee. He swore internally and froze. No one stirred in the camp.

Up ahead there was another snore. This close it was easy to pinpoint the person's position. Asleep or not, it shouldn't have been as easy as it was to creep up on the sentry sitting braced against a tree, but it was a cakewalk. Grabbing the man from behind with a hand over his mouth, Ace cut his throat, left to right, so fast the raider didn't even tense up at the mortal wound. Along with the smell of blood came the sour stench of alcohol. There must have been a lot of hooch on that coach.

Ace gave the signal. One down. From across the way came Luke's return signal. Two sentries down, six men to go. He eased the body to the ground, knowing the Comanche way, wondering if he'd had a turn on Petunia. The thought made Ace want to kill him all over again with that thought but slower, piece by piece, looking into his eyes while he understood retribution had come. Ace wiped the knife on the man's pants, put it back between his teeth and crept forward. Drunk or not, six-to-two odds were barely even.

Creeping deeper into the camp, he found a second warrior, a shadow on the ground framing the edge of the fire just beyond what would have been its light, had it been tended. He died as easily as the first. It gave Ace no satisfaction. Across the way he knew Luke was doing the same. He shook his head as the stench of vomit and alcohol and stale sweat surrounded him. There was a time when he would have shaken his head at how low a drink could bring the mighty Comanche, but right now, as he went from bundle to bundle, all he could think of was the hell they must have put Pet through before they'd passed out. And be grateful God had evened up the odds.

He knew Petunia would be toward the back, tossed like so much debris to be used as they saw fit. God, he hated the thought of them with Petunia. She deserved flowers and tender touches and a man who guarded his nature as well as he guarded her. It hadn't been fucking him.

One of the Comanche rolled over and fumbled to his feet. He stood and swayed, clearly still intoxicated. Ace snarled, drawing his attention. The man spun around, instincts far sharper than his reflexes. Ace didn't wait for him to find him in the shadows. As the raider reached for his knife, Ace grabbed his wrist, stepping in close, grabbing him by the back of the neck. This close he could see the darker marks of scratches on his face. With another snarl he turned the Indian's blade and shoved it forward, gutting him on his own knife. The raider's eyes flew wide, the whites gleaming. A harsh gurgling sound erupted from his throat.

"For Pet, you son of a bitch."

Ace jerked the knife up, feeling his blood seep through his clothes, knowing he'd killed him. It wasn't enough. The beast in him growled and writhed. The implications of those scratches stuck in his mind. He wanted to tear the world down. With a silent snarl, he pushed the disemboweled man off the knife.

Three more feet he could make out the darker shadow of another body. Too big to be Petunia. He took a step; as he did his foot brushed something hard. Feeling with his foot, he found a short stake and a length of rope. There was only one thing the Comanche would tie up. Pet.

Carefully, ever so carefully, Ace reached for the man's face noticing even as he did that this shadow was different. A quick study revealed he was curled on his side. Adjusting his stance, Ace slipped his hand over the man's mouth and slit his throat with the same efficiency as before, cutting him off midsnore. Blood spurted over his hands. A gasp snapped his gaze up. Even in the pale light he could make out the soft shine of Petunia's eyes looking back at him from under the raider's corpse.

She was alive.

Thank you, God.

Signaling to Luke that he'd found her, Ace dragged the body of the dead Comanche aside. He reached for Pet's shoulder. Instead, he found her naked armpit, then her ribs, then her torso. No material blocked his touch but thanks to him, she was covered in the Indian's blood. The bastard had been sleeping wrapped around her. He put a bloody hand over her mouth and softly intoned, "Shhh."

He prayed like hell she recognized his voice. Slowly he removed his hand. She didn't scream. That was something. He skimmed his hands quickly over her body, checking for any obvious broken bones. When he got to her hips she started fighting. Again he put his hand over her mouth. Tapping her cheek with his finger, he brought her gaze back to him. He doubted she could see his face backlit as he was by the only source of light, but he knew she would see the shake of his head.

Sliding his free hand up her arm, he found the ropes pinning her to the ground. He cut the left and the right, repeating the procedure on the ones binding her feet. Against his hand her head jerked. Damn, he couldn't even afford to let her cry. He leaned down until he covered her body, feeling her tense, blocking her blows, whispering in her ear, "Quiet, Pet."

She only fought harder, and damn the woman was strong. He pinned her legs with his knees and her arms with his elbows, keeping his hand over her mouth and leaning in again, he breathed the words in her ear. "Unless you want another go with these Comanche, you'll hold still."

Fear did what his presence couldn't. Pet went stiff as a board. Her chest rose and fell in rapid pants beneath his. Her breath hit his palm in soft, silent protests he couldn't let her voice. Not yet. Above his hand, her eyes accused. Below, her body protested.

"Don't move. Don't make a sound until I tell you. Understood?"

It took a second, and she stopped breathing all together first, but then she nodded.

Still keeping his whisper as light as the creeping moonlight he asked, "Can you do that if I let you go?"

The nod didn't come immediately.

"I need to cover Luke."

He didn't know if she was nodding "yes" she couldn't stay still without him, or that she understood what he was saying. He stroked his thumb across her cheek.

"They won't ever touch you again, I promise. Even if I step away, know that. They'll never touch you again."

He could feel her fear fighting with that relief. She needed something to hold on to. He gave it to her.

"I'm not asking you, Pet, I'm telling you. I'm giving you an order and for once in your goddamn life, you're going to follow it." He gave her a little shake. "Because I'm the one giving it. You're going to lie there as still as a mouse as if you're still tied. You're not going to move, you're not going to cry out. You're just going to lie there and wait for me to come back."

She shook her head. Grabbing her chin, he stopped the denial.

"I *will* come back. That's what you believe in and hold on to, all right?"

He took his hand from her mouth, kissed her briefly, delicately, mindful of the injuries he couldn't see, just a short touch of his lips to hers that he needed. "You're mine, Pet, and you're safe."

With that, he got up, not looking back. Leaving her with the expectation that she'd obey, hoping like hell she would.

CHAPTER TWELVE

ACE SLIPPED THROUGH the dark, rage pulsing in his blood, the need for revenge a coppery taste on his tongue. They'd touched her, hurt her. He was going to enjoy making them pay.

He found another Comanche passed out on the ground and turned him over. The warrior's eyes snapped opened, a faint glimmer of white in the dark of the night. Surprise muddled in his gaze longer than it should for a seasoned warrior. Ace pressed his knife against his throat and waited until through the befuddlement came knowledge.

"You shouldn't have touched her." He drew his knife across his throat quick and clean, cleaner than he wanted. Blood sprayed. There was a gurgle of sound, and then it was over.

He moved on, wanting there to be a next one, but there wasn't. All he found was Luke standing over another body leaving Ace standing there with the scent of blood clinging to him and no place to go with the rage consuming him.

"That the last?"

"Yup." Luke wiped his knife on the dead man's shirt and sheathed it. "How is she?"

Haunted, scared and broken. A far cry from the bold-as-brass woman who'd called him chicken shit just the other day. "About as good as you'd expect."

"They rape her?"

Probably. "I don't know."

"Shit." Luke sighed. "Sometimes it doesn't pay for you to play God."

Ace looked up, startled.

"We been riding together for more years than I could count, Ace. You don't think I don't know when you're cutting off your nose to spite your face?"

"I put her on that stage to protect her."

"Never thought I'd say this," Luke said, looking at him out of the corner of his eye, "but I'm beginning to think you don't know shit about women in general." Grabbing up a canteen and blanket from one of the bedrolls, he handed it to Ace. "You might want to clean up before you go back to her."

"Why?"

"You go to her with your face like that, she's liable to start screaming."

Ace touched his fingers to his face. They came away wet.

"You're covered in blood."

Dousing the blanket in water, Ace scrubbed hard and fast. "Better?"

"A little."

It was as good as it was going to get.

Luke tossed him another blanket. It reeked of horse and smoke. The man was ever resourceful.

Petunia lay right where he'd left her. She hadn't moved. As he'd ordered. That in itself told Ace the level of damage that'd been done. The woman he'd known would have been scrambling for some weapon, escape, something. She wouldn't have just lain there like a broken doll, body quiet, eyes screaming. He knelt beside her and drew the back of his fingers down her cheek. Her skin felt wonderful against his. Soft. Warm. Alive.

"You ready to go home, Pet?" he asked, draping the blanket over her.

Her eyes darted around as if looking for enemies to be springing out of nowhere.

"There's no one here that's going to hurt you. Just Luke and I, and you already know you've got both of us wrapped around your little finger."

Slipping his hand down her cheek on the next pass, he opened his hand, curling his fingers around the nape of her neck. "Are you hurt anywhere serious?"

She shook her head. He didn't believe her.

"Any of your bones broken? Any bad bruises?" Luke asked.

Her gaze didn't leave his. Her dry lips worked, struggling for words. She shook her head again, the "No" an aborted attempt.

Ace forced a smile. "Then I'm going to lift you up but if anything hurts you let me know. Fast."

He just didn't like the way she was lying there. Sometimes a body in shock wasn't aware of how much damage had been done. He pulled her up gently, supporting her with his hand, slipping the second around her shoulders as he got her a bit off the ground. Drawing her up and over, she leaned against his chest, her face tucked into the hollow of his neck as if it belonged there. She smelled of dirt, sweat and the faintest scent of perfume. She shuddered and let out a sigh.

Stroking her hair, he whispered, "You gave me quite a scare, woman."

She nodded then took another shuddering breath. Her

fingers crept up his vest digging in at the shoulder, asking permission.

He kissed the top of her head. "Put your arms around my neck, please."

Luke made a rough sound in his throat. Petunia's arms slowly encircled his neck. There came another broken breath. She was trying not to cry, he realized. He stopped immediately.

"Are you hurting?"

Another shake of her head. Slipping his hands under her knees and his arm all the way around back, he lifted her up into his lap and just held her for a minute. As long as she was alive, he could make it up to her.

There was another sound from the vicinity of his chest. He looked down. Her hair brushed his cheek, tickling his nose. He didn't move it aside. "What'd you say?"

The sound came again, raspy on her dry lips. This time he could make out the words. "Thank you."

Son of a bitch! She was thanking him. He looked up to find Luke looking down. The other man just shook his head.

"Trust me, my Pet, it was my pleasure."

Ace made a rough sound in his throat at the endearment, then, "We'd better be going."

They traveled back in silence to the horses. Halfway there, the back of his shoulders were burning, and his thighs were shaking.

Luke looked back. "I can take her for a bit."

Pet's fingers tightened around his neck, his arms tightened back. He'd almost fucking lost her. "Not yet."

By the time they reached the camp, Ace's breath was soughing in and out of his lungs and he had to sit down.

Luke reached the horses first. They nickered a soft greeting. He came back with a blanket and a bundle.

"What's that?" Ace asked.

"I picked up some of her clothes that were strewn around while we were back at the stagecoach."

He unrolled the blanket to reveal shirt, skirt, camisole and shoes. All matching.

Ace just shook his head.

Luke smiled. "Bet you won't begrudge my preference for the necessity of a good wardrobe in the future, huh?"

"Never again."

Petunia would feel better in her own things.

"I'll go water the horses while you get her settled."

"Don't take too long. That canyon had the look of a permanent stopping-off point."

"I noticed."

Luke led the horses away. As Ace peeled off the blanket, he touched his lips to Pet's hair. "It's going to be all right. I promise you."

She didn't say a word. He didn't suppose she had to.

PETUNIA WANTED TO stay in her cloud forever. That soft, fluffy place where sound was muted, sensation was blurred and time drifted. Just like the white clouds in a summer sky. There was peace in the cloud. She didn't have to face anything in the cloud. The cloud was her haven. And while, on some levels, she knew things were happening outside it, they didn't really touch her. Not the voices. Not the hands. Nothing. She just drifted.

She was aware of a soft murmur of new voices, the jostling of being moved. Hands undressing her caused a hiccup in her peace. She started to fight, but then she heard *his* voice again. Ace had a wonderful voice, deep and melodic. Commanding. He'd told her she was safe, and as long as she could hear his voice, she was. She cuddled into the next words, not even sure what they were, just listening to his deep drawl, letting it soothe her. Ace always felt soul-deep good.

She whispered, "Thank you." Or she thought she did. There was a breathy little sound, a vibration in her throat.

"Why is she moaning?"

"I imagine because the bed feels good." Hester's voice was an unwelcome intrusion, too brusque and too matter-of-fact when she wanted that masculine touch of safety.

"Do you think she really hears us?"

"Yes, she can hear us," Hester said.

"Then why isn't she talking? The woman talks nonstop. She could talk a fly off a pile of shit given the inclination."

That was not a flattering analogy and not even entirely accurate. She didn't talk all the time.

"I imagine because she doesn't want to think."

Yes. Hester understood.

"Maybe she won't remember."

There was a sensation on her forehead. Comforting, awkward but comforting, as if the person wasn't sure quite what to do, and she could understand that. Clouds were a delicate business. One had to be careful. She liked that he was careful. She liked a lot about Ace. She focused on his smile, the way his lips stretched back revealing those even teeth and the chip in the left canine. It was an imperfection, just a slight one; not much but she liked it. It gave him a sense of vulnerability. She liked the thought of him being vulnerable to her.

"When is she gonna wake up?"

"When she's ready."

"When will that be?"

Hester snorted. "You said yourself, she's a stubborn woman. Might not be for a spell."

"I don't like this. She should be up."

"And screaming?" Hester asked. "And ranting and raving? Leave her alone, Ace. She'll deal with what happened when she's ready."

"I don't want her screaming."

The covers lifted up over her shoulder.

Petunia was glad he didn't want her screaming because she had no intention of screaming ever, of giving in, of breaking. She was a strong woman, and no one moment would define her unless she chose the moment. The thought, just saying that, opened a crack in her defenses. Memories crept through like fingers of a nightmare tickling her consciousness, tugging at her cloud, darkening her moment. She turned away, closing that door, pushing it back. This was her cloud, and she didn't want it dirty.

The hand stroked across her forehead again, cupped her cheek as natural as the next breath she took.

"What did Doc say?"

She knew it was Ace's thumb that stroked her lips and slid along them, bringing back the memory of his kiss. Oh, my, that man's kiss. It made her a stranger to herself. A wild, wanton, entirely happy stranger. She wanted to melt into him, give to him, be for him, just from the touch of his lips. Her breath caught but not in a bad way.

"That she'd be fine so there's plenty of time for you to get yourself cleaned up," Hester said.

"I'm staying," Ace said.

Yes, stay with your thumb on my lips and your kiss in my memory. Stay.

"She's going to need you when she wakes. A woman

of Petunia's courage and determination won't hide long. When she does, she's going to need her friends, but right now you're just in the way."

"I could use a bath," he admitted.

"And then some."

"Shit." Ace's hand left her; the bed rocked. His presence left her, and she was alone on her cloud holding tight to its fragile softness while the nightmare fingers pried at its edges.

"Come back when you're clean and rested. Not a minute before. A shadow of a man won't do her any good."

No, she didn't need any more shadows.

"I'll be back," Ace said.

Pet clung to that. There was more talk. She didn't care. Ace was coming back. It would be all right. He'd promised.

A KNOCK AT the door jostled her cloud.

"You needed me, Hester?"

Petunia recognized Luke's voice. The fingers pried the crack open a little wider as she was fighting them back.

"I need you to help me get her into the tub."

"But she's dressed. You want to put her in the tub dressed?"

"Her clothes need washing anyway, and she's not ready to part with them just yet."

Petunia fought the hands that lifted her, fought the nightmare reaching in, struggled as she was lowered down, no, not down.

Soothing heat wrapped around her. Stinging at first, but then soothing her aches. The crack in her safe place sealed shut as pleasure enveloped her. She moaned.

"Shit, am I hurting her?"

"I'm thinking for the first time in a couple days, she's feeling good."

"You sure?"

There was a snort. "When you soak in that tub in the bathhouse, how much pain do *you* feel?"

"I guess she's not hurting."

"Of course, I imagine you have some sweet young thing running her hands over you…"

Luke's hands left her. "That's quite the imagination you've got there, Hester."

"I know men."

There was a pause.

"You don't know me, but you might want to start."

"Why? You are who you are, and I am who I am, and there's never a time those two can meet."

"I don't know where you get your notions from, Hester." The floorboards creaked. "But you've got the wrong end of the cat."

"I don't even like cats."

He snorted. "So you keep telling me."

There was a click as the door shut and another snort from Hester. "Like I'm fool enough to take that man serious."

More water poured into the tub. The warmth spread out around her. Petunia sank into it. She drifted in the tub the way one drifted on the cloud, buoyed by the water.

"Lean back, honey."

A hand behind her neck tilted her head back. Water poured in a gentle stream over her hair, once, twice, many times. It felt so good, like summer rain on a brutally hot day. She focused on the sensation, and the rip in the seam mended again but the stitches were there. Big, awkward and weak but at least they were there.

"I can imagine what happened to you, honey, and it's happened to many women before."

She wished Hester would just pour the water and not talk.

"It's a shameful thing but it's not your shame. The shame is on the men, but I don't imagine you're thinking that right now. But down the road you remember, all right?"

The scent of rosemary wrapped around her as Hester's fingers massaged her hair.

"Those boys went to town, didn't they?"

She didn't know what she meant. More water poured over her head. A cloth wiped at her face.

"We'll get this all off you, and you'll feel better."

She felt better already.

"You're lucky you have the man you do. Not many men would have gone after you. Not many men could have brought you back, but Ace did."

Yes, he had.

But that was all later, and right now she just wanted to stay in this tub, floating in the water, floating on her cloud until she floated away like nothing had ever happened. That's all she wanted.

Time passed. She didn't know how much. Hester chatted. Petunia didn't know about what, but when Hester tried to get her out of the tub, she knew one thing. She wasn't going anywhere.

WHEN ACE KNOCKED on the door an hour and a half later, he expected to be greeted by Pet's anger, at the very least a sharp "go away." He would have preferred either to the way he'd left her lying there like a ghost of her former self, pale and listless like the spirit had already left her, and she was just waiting for the body to follow. He would never let that happen.

He knocked again. A hard tap of heels across the floor preceded the door being thrown open. Hester stood there, the front of her gown wet, locks of hair falling free of her bun in tight curls. Her eyes were as red as her face.

"You do something with her!" she said, stepping back and flinging her hand at the tub.

Ace took a second to take in the scene. The problem was evident. Pet sat in the tub, her lips slightly blue, looking amazingly content.

"What the hell?"

"She's gonna catch her death," Hester said. "I can't add any more water to that tub without overflowing, and I refuse to throw another bucket out that window to drain it out."

"She been like this since I left?"

Hester nodded. "She won't get out of that damn tub. You try to take her out of that tub, she goes for your face, tooth and nail."

That explained Hester's battered appearance.

"Are you hurt?"

"Hell, a little thing like her couldn't hurt me."

Ace looked at her again. For all Hester's talk she really wasn't that big. She was a curvy, kindhearted woman who'd had a tough turn at life, but she wasn't a giant.

He walked over to the tub. He could see the gooseflesh on Petunia's white shoulders where her chemise pulled away. He could see the slight rise of her breasts beneath the water, the pucker of her nipples against the now transparent cotton shirt, feel the utter desolation of her spirit.

Hester came up behind him. "The only joy of my

evening was when one of those buckets of water landed smack-dab on Brian Winter."

"Has he given you any trouble?"

"Well, not before I dumped that bucket on his head. But he did say afterward he was going to see the sheriff."

Ace nodded. "Do me a favor, go fetch Luke."

"Why would I want to fetch that man?"

"Because I want to talk to him, and he needs to talk to the sheriff."

"You don't need to talk to him for that."

He cast her another knowing look. "Do you think he hasn't noticed the way you've been avoiding him of late?"

"It's not of late. I've been avoiding him from the get-go."

"Agreed. You want me to talk to him, or do you want to talk to him?"

"If you talk to him—" with a jerk of her chin she indicated Pet "—do I have to deal with her?"

"Somebody has to."

"Then I'll talk to him." She waved her hand toward the tub and headed for the door. "That is yours alone."

Through the whole conversation, Petunia hadn't moved. She just kept skimming her fingers slowly across the top of the water, humming some song. He wasn't even sure it was a song. It was just noise under her breath, even and slow, in rhythm with her breathing. Kneeling by the tub, he caught her hand.

"Hey." No response.

If it was any other woman after any other event, he'd force her to look at him, but Petunia had been through enough, more than he'd probably ever know, more than he ever wanted to know. And no doubt in the way of women, she felt somehow it changed her, but it didn't. Not in his eyes.

"Hester says you don't want to get out of this tub. Any particular reason you're sitting there freezing your tits off?"

The words were chosen deliberately. He wanted to shock her. Not even by a ripple did he see any sign of it. She was well and truly entrenched in wherever she had gone. Taking the passive way out when his Pet was a fighter.

"You get her out of there yet?" Hester hollered up from the street.

He went over to the window, not because he necessarily wanted to answer Hester but because he didn't want to stand there anymore and look at what he'd caused to happen. Leaning out the window he saw Hester standing with Luke. Neither one looked happy, but he could tell from the set of Luke's shoulders that the woman had his whole attention, and it dawned on him that the reason there was always those sparks between Hester and Luke might just be because there was something else between them, too. Damn, that would be complicated.

Luke always had a perfect image of his perfect woman in his perfect world. Hester didn't fall anywhere near that, but the woman had a heart of gold. Maybe Luke couldn't see that, or maybe the whole problem was that he did. Ace stored the information for later.

"No!" he called down. "She's just lying there like a potato popped out of the field."

"She stays in that water much longer, she's going to catch cold."

"Well, what do you suggest I do to get her out that you haven't already tried?"

Luke looked at Hester then up at Ace. He said, "I always find that getting the woman riled tends to move them out of a stuck spot."

"You want me to piss her off?" He looked over his shoulder. He didn't think even Brian White could piss her off in her current condition.

"I don't know. What do you usually do with women who aren't doing what you want?"

Find their weakness. Find their security. Play one off the other until the friction was the only thing in their world, the heat the only thing they could think of and him the only thing they could cling to.

He looked over his shoulder again. And smiled. "Good idea."

Hester gasped. "Ace, she's not one of your saloon girls, don't you go…"

Luke grabbed her arm and shoved her down the street. "Hush, woman. The man has an idea," he heard Luke say as they moved down the street.

"Where you taking me?"

"You wanted to go see the sheriff."

There were more words back and forth, but he couldn't hear them anymore. The film of dirt on the upper half of the window blurred his reflection, softening the angles of his face. He and dirt got along fine. It was the whole proper whitewashed civilized world that he had an issue with.

He returned to the tub. But maybe in this instant Petunia didn't need a civilized man spouting civilized nonsense. Maybe she just needed someone to make her understand, to tell her who she was, to show her how she mattered. He took his hat and hung it on the top of the poster. That he could do.

Taking the empty bucket off the floor, he carefully siphoned some of the water out of the tub. It was cold, colder than the lake. He dumped it out the window without even looking. He guessed he didn't hit anybody from the lack of shouts below.

"Figures you'd have to have a front-facing bedroom," he said. "A room in the back would have been much more convenient."

Two more trips and the water level was depleted enough that he could go downstairs and get some hot water off the fire. It was heavy work lugging it up the stairs, which explained all the wet marks on the stairs. Through it all, Pet sat there, her fingers making small circles in the remaining water. Little by little, he added hot water to the tub. He tested it; it was still cool. The second bucket brought the water up to her waist and the heat to acceptable. He set the buckets on the floor and reached up to the top button of his shirt.

"You understand," he said as he unbuttoned his shirt, "that if I do this there is no going back?"

Still no response.

"If I bring you into my world, you won't be satisfied with any other man."

That wasn't technically true, but he intended to make it so.

"I fought this for a long time, but you tempted me too long and once I make you mine, that's it."

That might have been a twitch in her fingers. Cooler air hit his chest as he tugged his shirt free of his pants and tossed it onto the bed a few feet away. His undershirt came off next. She didn't move as he kicked off one boot then the other, just stayed in that place that he hated, and as each article of clothing hit the floor, his anger grew. And so did his determination. When he stood naked by the edge of the tub, his own words came back to haunt him.

There's no going back.

"I hope to hell you know what you're doing."

He wasn't sure who he said it to, her or himself, but in the end, it didn't matter. The line had been crossed. The decision made. With his hand on the middle of her back, he pushed her forward. She went easily with no resistance. He took it as agreement.

"On your head be it, my Pet."

The double entendre didn't hit him as wrong, which should have been a warning sign but he was pretty much past warning. He'd always been the type to go for what he wanted, to play the odds, to take the chance. He might not have ever played for stakes this high, a woman's sanity was a hell of a thing to risk, but his instincts had never steered him wrong, and right now every single instinct directed that he lift Pet up and slide in behind her.

Water sloshed as he sat down. Her breath expelled in a slight gasp as he brought her down on top of him. There was no way she could miss his erection, but it shouldn't shock her. He'd wanted her since the day he saw her. His own personal wild card. He'd always thought it was a mistake to pull for the wild card. But in this case…

Pushing her hair aside, Ace wrapped his arms around her just under her breasts and pulled her back against him. She was warm, the water cool. In a moment that should have been full of pain and agony, there was just peace. He looked up.

It wasn't often he spoke to God. It wasn't like they weren't on speaking terms, it was just he never felt the need to reach out too often. Today was a reaching day. "You picked a hell of a way to make your point."

Petunia sat in his arms, stiffer than before, and her hands weren't making those restless movements but they did kind of drift about as if she didn't know what to do with them. He leaned against the high back of the tub. He wished it were bigger. His knees poking out looked silly as hell.

"You can put your hands on my knees if you want."

She didn't move.

"It's a pretty unthreatening place to touch a man, in case you didn't know."

It was a lie. Anywhere she touched him was going to burn like fire but well, if this was the lie he was going to hell for, God just didn't have a heart. He needed her cooperation before he could build her trust. And he only knew one way to do that. Working from the bottom up.

Taking her left hand, he pressed a kiss into the palm before settling it on his left knee. The little catch in her breathing gave him pause. But when she left her hand there, it gave him hope.

"See? That's how we'll do it. Nice and easy."

He gave her a moment to protest. When she didn't, he scooped up her right hand and repeated the procedure. The test came when he took away his support. She left her hands where they were. When he leaned back, she followed. Soft, sweet and trusting.

He sighed, releasing the breath he didn't know he'd been holding. "One step at a time."

CHAPTER THIRTEEN

ONE STEP AT A TIME.

Her battle cry reflected back to her in this moment of peace. Petunia sat in the warm water, feeling the soothing rhythm of Ace's steady breath, and the persistent pressure of his arousal, and wavered between calm and panic. Peace and turmoil. Ace summed up in one poignant moment. Frowning softly to herself, she drew her middle finger up his hand. He had to be exhausted—she knew she was—but instead of curling up with one of his lady friends in the saloon, he was here with her, coaxing her to where she didn't want to go with the same sleight of hand he manipulated the cards with.

A woman had to admire a man like that. Probably as much as she should be scandalized by her own behavior at being with him so, but after the past twenty-four hours, she truly had nothing to lose. Her reputation was forever ruined. At least here where it was known. She could run naked through the streets and all it would do was refer people back to the bigger scandal of her abduction. For the rest of her days, she'd be the schoolteacher with whom the Comanche had had their way. Nothing she could ever do on her own would top that.

Ace hummed in his throat and turned his hand. She stroked her finger over his palm as she mulled that reality over. It was oddly…freeing.

Ace's grip shifted. "What are you thinking?"

"That I'm forever ruined now."

His growl was rich in her ear. "The hell you are."

She added two more fingers to her stroking. "However do you manage to be so successful in gambling when your emotions are so easily provoked?"

He snugged her up a little tighter. "The rest of the world doesn't provoke me."

She sighed and accepted the truth no one else likely would. "It's all right, you know. I don't mind."

"Damn it, woman."

She twisted and leaned back just far enough so she could see his expression. It was tight and about as stubborn as she felt inside. "I don't. Having nothing to protect means I also have nothing to lose."

With a slight shake of his head, he asked, "Is that what you've been…quiet about all night?"

"A little."

The hiss of his breath tickled her ear. "You need to stew some more if that's the fool notion you came to."

"There were other things."

His hand moved against hers, and when they aligned, he wove his fingers through hers, anchoring her. "Like what?"

She thought she'd known all there was to know about the violence in the world, seen all there was to see, prepared herself for the increased frequency in the West, but she hadn't realized there was no preparing oneself for the raw reality. It was scary, terrifying, actually, to know that you could be plucked from your life at any random moment into a world where you had no control and then just as quickly plucked out of the evil and dropped back into your life as if that transition hadn't happened.

The past twenty-four hours felt like a nightmare she'd dreamed, and if she just opened her eyes, she'd be in her bed with all her possessions and she'd know nothing had changed. But she knew if she opened her eyes that wasn't going to be the case. She'd be stuck in that nightmare she was calling a dream. And it would become truth. But dreams were flexible. They could be anything the person dreaming them wanted. The thought lingered, settled into the rhythm of their breathing, oddly in sync and yet different.

She studied the pattern because it gave her something to focus on rather than the reality that was getting stronger and stronger. Ace's breaths were deeper than hers so he started first, then her, then him, then her. Him, her, him, her, in a slow, even rhythm. Safe.

"Hey, you still down there?"

"Yes."

"Want to share?"

"No."

His chest puffed out in what could be a chuckle. Or exasperation. Without seeing his face or hearing his voice she couldn't be sure. His fingers opened on her abdomen, moving in lazy, small circles. She liked where she was, surrounded by his arms, surrounded by warmth with the sounds from the street muted. It made it easy to believe there was nothing more in the world than this moment, this time with this man.

"You realize, my Pet, this water is going to cool soon, and I'm not so fond of procrastination that I'm going to stay in it until my balls turn blue."

He was preparing her for the intrusion of reality. "I understand."

She felt the featherlight brush of his lips across her hair.

"I know you don't want to think," Ace continued in that low, tender drawl she could listen to forever. "I know you want to run away. But you can't stay stuck. You've got to take things one step at a time, and the first step you're going to take is when I say it's time, you're going to stand up and you're going to get out of this tub, brush out your hair, get in your nightgown. And then you'll lie down and get some sleep."

"All that's going to happen just because you decree it?"

This time she felt his smile. "Yup."

She knew he could. He might not be able to make his words true, but he could make her leave her dream. And when she stood, the nightmare was all going to be there, screaming in her face. She so didn't want that. She was still in that dream world where anything was possible, and if anything was possible then anything could be changed. This was her dream. She could make it what she wanted.

The thought lingered, lazying around the quiet, making its presence known with an occasional poke. She pondered it harder, wondered longer, and a little kernel of determination started to blossom.

This was her dream; she could control it.

Opening her hands over his knee—he had bony knees—one by one she stretched her fingers, testing her emotional balance. The world didn't tilt, and the howling stayed muted. She tested further, grazing her hands back down his thighs just a little distance, just to see.

His breath sucked in. "Pet?"

"I'm just seeing something."

He relaxed his grip; she started to float. When she

grabbed his knees, he snugged her up safe. And she realized, as long as he held her, she had balance.

She controlled the dream.

And if she controlled the dream, the dream could end
the way she wanted. Such a tantalizing deception to play
upon herself, to take this moment in history and rewrite
it. How many times had people wished they could do
that very thing, and now she had this opportunity to
take something ugly and finish it beautiful? All she had
to do was dare? That had been the catch her whole life,
daring. People thought she was so bold because she did
so many things that no one believed should be done but
the truth was, it took a lot of anxiety and debate before
she steeled herself to do anything. Did she dare?

It had taken her four years to decide to strike out from
her home. To put aside her family money and prestige,
the safety of her culture, and go out in the world, determined to make a difference. It was one thing to be the
protected, pampered daughter of a wealthy man and do
good within those circles. Safe little protests where her
father showed up for her in ten minutes to pull her out
of jail, or paid off those upset. No real consequences
beyond his exasperation and threats of forced marriage
and the safety of knowing he loved her. It had been safe
but it hadn't been enough. So she'd left her little feath-
ered nest and had gone into the world knowing that if
things got bad, she could always contact her father, not
understanding things could go bad with no recourse, and
when she could place that telegraph or write that letter, it
would all be over, and she'd just be picking up the pieces.
He'd told her she didn't understand the real world, and
she hadn't. Now she did, and she needed to decide what
she wanted to do about it.

"You all right?"

He kept asking her that. She didn't have an answer. She needed to find a way to have an answer. Rubbing her thumbs on the insides of his knees, she debated her options. She could feel his cock pressing into her back, feel that subtle hum of tension under his skin.

She was old enough and experienced enough to know what that pressure meant. He wanted her, but he wasn't doing anything about it, which just went to show he had to suspect the worst. Lord knows, she would.

"Ace?" Her voice was barely a sound. She was surprised when he responded.

"Yeah?"

She didn't know how to put what she wanted into words. His hands left her stomach and floated on the water, touched the outsides of her arms, sending little chills up her skin. There was always such a sense of possession in his touch as if he knew something she didn't, but that wasn't true. She knew as much as he did, she was just fighting it harder. Not the sexual attraction but the other, the emotional. She didn't want to be tied down to a man, subject to his rule with no life of her own. She'd seen how that happened. How her suffragette friends started out all full of vigor and conviction and then they married and suddenly became the pillars of community, who couldn't say boo to a ghost, who tried to push away from the ideas they'd once said were so valued. She didn't want to be that person, but she didn't want to be who she was now, either. Somewhere there had to be a middle ground.

"What is it, Pet?"

She shook her head; she didn't have the words for what she wanted and honestly, she thought as his fingers curled around her upper arms and slid upward to her shoulders, maybe it just wasn't one of those times when words would suit. Maybe it was just one of those times when a woman had to act.

Water sloshed as she sat up.

"Ready to get out?"

She shook her head again and kept her hands on his knees pushing up, trying to turn without too much intimacy, which was stupid considering what she wanted. After a few seconds of fumbling, she came to the conclusion there was no graceful way to do what she wanted to do so she just did it. With a grunt, she turned on her side, feeling the seductive slide of his flesh against hers, the prickle of hair and the culmination of his skin against hers as his cock pressed into her stomach in silent demand. At least he still wanted her. That would make everything so much easier.

His big hands settled in the hollow of her back, warm and calloused, imbued with that sense of possession she relished. This was Ace. He was…safe.

His eyebrows rose right along with her hands as she slid them up his hard, muscled chest. He had hair there, too, and it tickled her palms.

"Why the smile?"

"The hair on your chest tickles."

"It can tickle other places, too."

She just smiled, wincing as the cut on her lip stung. He frowned. Touching her fingertips to the furrow between his brow, she smoothed it out. He was such a sexy man, handsome in a harsh sort of way. The only softness on him was the emotion revealed in his eyes right now. He was a maverick, a force to be reckoned with. But so was she. It gave them common ground.

It was awkward in the tight confines of the tub to move. Her knee jerked up into something soft, and he grimaced and his breath expelled a harsh, "Careful!"

The seduction wasn't going so well. Meeting his gaze with hers, she touched her thumb to the corner of his mouth the way he did her, the way that always centered her attention and made her feel special. She surrendered to the inevitable.

"Help me."

His fingers slid down her arm around her elbow and up to her wrist. Holding her hand he pressed a kiss into the palm.

"You ready to get out of the tub?"

She shook her head.

"I don't think I understand what you're asking for."

"Help me forget." Forget the loss of control, the loss of self, the terror, the pain.

His eyes narrowed. The flickering glow of the lamp-light sent shadows dancing across his face. "I think it's probably a bit too soon for that. We need to get you cleaned up. You'll feel better in the morning."

He was turning her down because he thought he knew what was better for her, but he didn't know. Nobody knew. They didn't know how she felt inside, and she didn't know how to explain. She just knew that if she wanted to rewrite the nightmare, she had to do it now.

"I don't want to go to bed."

He looked at her, his gaze steady, his eyes assessing. It felt like he was looking through to her soul. She hoped so because she didn't think she could put into words that anybody would understand what she wanted right now.

"You said there's no going back," she reminded him.

He nodded.

"Then I only have two choices left. I can stay here, or I can go forward."

She wasn't surprised when he didn't ask for clarification. Ace seemed to understand her at a level that went beyond the simplicity of words.

"You're not thinking straight."

But she was. She really was.

"I know what I'm doing."

She rose to her knees and started to unbutton her shirt. She expected him to reach out and stop her, but he didn't. He just kept watching her with that steady assessment as she fought with the wet fabric. He wasn't looking at her body, or her breasts, which she knew showed clearly through the material. He just kept staring into her eyes, into her soul. Her fingers fumbled on the second button, and her breath caught in her lungs. This wasn't going to work.

"Touch me. Please."

Reaching over her shoulders, he lifted the wet rope of her hair, fanned it out over his hands, let the silky mass fall over shoulders. The strands tangled on his fingers. "Tell me why."

"What's happened to me the past day or so might very well be the most life-changing thing I'll ever endure. I'll have to live with it the rest of my life. I don't have a choice in that. But if I have to remember it, then I don't want it to be because of a bad thing."

"You want me to make love with you."

It was a statement. "I want you to make me feel good."

"It's been a long time, my Pet, since I've simply made love to a woman like you're talking."

Did he think he could scare her more than fourteen screaming Comanche? "Does that mean you can't?"

This time it was his hand that touched her face and his fingers that stroked and his thumb that centered her.

"It's just been a long time."

She had the defeating urge to ask him if she was pretty enough. Water lapped against the side of the tub making little metallic sloshes. "I want this, Ace."

"I know, but you're not thinking straight and come morning, you're probably going to have a whole different take on this situation, and I don't want to be the man who took advantage of you."

"You're sitting naked in a tub with me!"

His lips quirked in a smile. "I'd have gotten in dressed but Luke's been harping on me about taking better care of my clothes."

He wanted to make her laugh. That was sweet. The chuckle was painful, rasping out of her disquiet. His thumb stroked across her lips from middle to side. His finger kept that subtle pressure on the nape of her neck. Maybe she should have been scared; it was the touch of a conqueror, but she'd never feared Ace. Not that way.

"Can't you make it beautiful?"

With the honesty that he always gave her he said, "I can make it intense, but beautiful…" He brushed her hair out of her face. "Beautiful hasn't been in my repertoire for a very long time."

But it was. When he kissed her in the street that day it had been wild and crazy and scary and wonderful and very, very beautiful.

And when he touched her the next time feeling his hands come around her it had been like coming home. And there wasn't anything more beautiful than that. She realized that now more than ever. Many people had touched her in her life; very few of them had felt like home. "Maybe we have different definitions of beautiful."

He was back to studying her. She didn't even try to hide. What was the point? He saw through it anyway. "Would it be less stressful for you if I settled for you making it good?"

His laugh jostled them both. Water sloshed, caressing the sides of her breasts. "You're killing me, my Pet. You're just flat out killing me."

He was weakening. She went back to work on her blouse. "In a good way, I hope."

He shook his head. She wished she dared ask if he were answering her question or expressing what he felt. "There are a lot of things I've done in my life that I'm not proud of, but the one thing I don't want to stand up in front of God and defend, is betraying you."

"It's not a betrayal."

"Did they rape you?"

She got the third and fourth button free. "They raped my soul."

"And you want it back."

Absolutely. "I want it back."

His smile was a challenge and a promise all in one. "So you've come to the devil to claim it?"

She smiled. "You're not the devil."

"There are those who say I am."

"And there are those that say you're a savior. I want you to save me, Ace. I want you to kiss me and touch me all over. I want you to put your hands where they put theirs. I want you to put your mouth where they put theirs and then I want you to take it further, and I want you to make beautiful what they tried to make ugly."

His big body shuddered under hers. "And what do you think that will do for you?"

"It will make me whole."

"It could just add to the damage."

She shook her head at him. "You're such a stubborn man."

He snorted. "You put the definition in the dictionary."

The last of the buttons gave way. She tried to shrug the wet shirt off her shoulders but it wouldn't go. "Then we should be fine as there's nothing two stubborn people can't accomplish."

"Or destroy."

Giving up on the shirt, she cupped his face in her hands and leaned forward. "Would you just hush and kiss me?"

It wasn't the most romantic proposition Ace had ever heard, and it surely wasn't the most passionate but it was the most heartfelt. Pulling her closer he leaned in, stopping just short of contact, teasing her with the anticipation. Her lips parted. His cock jerked. Damn, the woman was pure enticement. "Ask me nicely."

Without hesitation she whispered, "Please," teasing him right back.

This close it was hard to see much beyond the paleness of her skin and the contrast of the darker bruises.

"They hit you."

"I fought."

Very gently he touched his lips to her swollen ones. "I killed them."

She blinked. "Thank you."

He kissed her again. Once. Twice. Taking her gasp on the third one for what it was. Desire. "You're welcome."

He watched curiosity narrow her eyes, felt a smile smooth her lips. "More," she whispered.

The woman did like to give orders. "Ask me nicely."

"Please."

He happily gave her what she wanted. It was what he wanted, too. Letting his mouth linger, he rubbed his lips ever so lightly over hers, wanting more, too aware of her delicate state to demand it. It was her tongue that came out to touch his. Her desire that tempted him to let loose. He'd give her what she needed, but not more.

There was a strange logic to her thinking that he approved of. A body couldn't help what happened to them, but they could determine how it defined them. When his town had been wiped out, the Hell's Eight had all had the option to curl into a ball and cry. Instead, they'd leaned on each other and become strong. Making that moment in time into the one that'd shaped Hell's Eight into the force they'd become.

And now Pet was coming to him, seeking his guidance, asking for his strength to take the horror and make it a base for something good. The satisfaction sank deep. It was a big task she laid at his feet. Turning something ugly into something beautiful. Creating one single memory strong enough to overcome a dozen more. Giving him her trust. As she should. Her fingers dug into his shoulders, sending desire rippling through him. This was right. His woman. His responsibility.

He pushed the paleness of her hair off the flush of her cheek. "I don't want to hurt you."

"You won't."

Such confidence she had in him. Such trust. There was nothing more arousing than a woman's trust to a man like him. Nothing more inspiring.

"There's nothing you can do to me that would hurt me like them." Her forehead dropped to his. That was probably the saddest thing he'd ever heard a woman say, and it brought out every protective instinct in him. Pet wasn't the first woman he'd rescued who'd been abused by a man. Many of them fell into apathy, but not his Pet. She was coming out swinging. She was fighting the only way she knew how. He respected that.

He cupped her in his hand, just holding her, giving her that balance she needed. "You do know how to put a man on the spot."

"I'm putting a lot of stock in your reputation."

It was a weak joke. The smile that backed it even weaker, but she was determined. He had no doubt she'd back out or panic before things got too far, but it wouldn't hurt him to indulge her need. A fighter sometimes just needed to fight with whatever tools they had. And right now he was hers. He could give her a kiss, a caress, all the softness he could find inside him.

"Put your arms around my neck."

She obeyed immediately with a seductive eagerness that threatened to undermine his good intentions. He tugged her up so her breasts were against his chest and her lips were against his. His cock settled naturally into the crease of her pussy. If he hadn't been holding her so close, he wouldn't have felt her start.

"Come here."

She blinked and sucked in a slow breath. He liked how she didn't panic. Just held her ground. "How much more here can I get?"

She was about to find out. "A hell of a lot closer."

Again she obeyed with that rare naturalness. Stretching up, she fitted her curves better to him. He threaded his fingers through her hair. Instinct demanded he tighten his grip and position her for his kiss. His muscles tensed. At the last moment he reined in the impulse. This was Pet. She didn't need that side of him. But he could push her with words.

"Tilt your head back."

She did, looking at him expectantly.

"A little more to the right…"

She did, straining to hold the uncomfortable position, simply because he asked her to. Fuck, she was killing his good intentions with that instinctive compliance. Lust surged. She had no idea how seductive that was. If she hadn't been going to get her wish before, she was definitely going to get it now.

"Good girl."

She smiled a little. "This isn't very comfortable."

"I know."

Releasing his hand in her hair he made a cradle of his palm, cupping her skull in his hand. Giving her support.

"Now kiss me." He brought his mouth to hers.

Her lips were sweet and soft. He wanted to ravish, to push, to take, to claim. Instead, he was gentle, kissing her lightly, trying to give her sweet, gradually increasing the pressure, running his tongue over her lips in a silent request. She parted hers immediately, toying a little bit more with his control. Did she have no idea what that instant compliance did to a man of his nature?

He seduced her gently until her mouth moved against his, her tongue touched his, lightning shot through him. It'd been a long time since he kissed a woman this innocently, if ever, but he liked it. The water cooled but their bodies heated. He lifted her just a little, just enough. Stroked his cock on her pussy and slid her back down, notching it carefully. Her eyes grew wide as her clit rubbed against the thick tip. He broke off the kiss to nibble her cheek, her neck, the hollow of her throat. Her head fell back naturally into his hand. Her breasts rose up naturally into his mouth. In the gentlest of caresses, he brushed his mouth across one nipple. It was soft and pouty, not hard and demanding. In definite need of attention.

She moaned and arched her back a little bit more.

"That's right, give it to me," he whispered against her skin.

She gasped, "I'm trying."

He wanted her response, not what she thought he wanted. "Don't think. Don't worry. Just follow my lead."

He had to be satisfied with her nod.

Sprinkling a path of kisses, he moved his mouth to the other breast, feeling the nipple harden against his tongue almost immediately. Her hips rocked on his cock in a subconscious plea, teasing them both, and he smiled. Whatever had happened to her, it hadn't ruined her. If a man went slow and easy, she could work through it. Lust speared deep, settling like a certainty in his gut. He was going to be that man.

He released her nipple with a little pop, and she jumped. They weren't soft now. They were hard and red and demanding more. The only thing keeping her upright was him. He wouldn't let her fall, and she knew it. He liked that. Trust mattered.

"Steady now."

Catching her hips in his hands, he started rocking her harder and faster on his cock, watching her face. Looking for the little telltale signs, listening to her breath, waiting for that special catch that told him he'd found the right spot, the right rhythm. They came in the next second. She caught his rhythm and set a bit of her own. Normally, he wouldn't allow it but this was Pet and this was what she needed. He'd always give her what she needed.

If he could hold on long enough. Christ, he hoped he could hold on long enough. The slick little glide of her pussy, the catch of her clit riding up and down his cock was driving him crazy.

Her nails dug in. Her thighs clutched at his. Her breathing fragmented on the whisper of his name. His own breath was just as ragged. "Like that," he groaned. "Just like that, Pet. Take what you need."

She rose up and his cock, rock hard, slipped back, wedging naturally into the well of her vagina. This time her gasp was louder. This time her eyes opened, and he was the one that groaned when their gazes met. So much passion, so much desire, and he couldn't do a goddamn thing about it except give her this. He lifted up, just a little, his hips spreading her thighs, his cock spreading her pussy. She was tight, much tighter than he'd expected.

Her nails dug deeper into his chest, dragging down, making little furrows. As she pressed back he wanted to grab her hips, pull her down, push up, claim her in a long, blissful "mine." But this was Pet, and she needed gentle, and if it killed him he was going to give her gentle.

He rocked his hips in little pulses. She moaned and pressed down.

No turning back.

He caught her slender hips in his hands, loving the delicacy that housed such passion. She was all fire under that pale, cool exterior.

"No," she said, "don't stop."

She thought he was stopping? "I don't think I could stop if I wanted to."

Not with her tight pussy milking the sensitive head of his cock in the same rhythm of his pulses. Not with her gaze clinging to his, revealing everything she felt. Every bit of wonder. Every dart of pleasure. She pressed down, her nails digging deeper. The sting blended with the pleasure. He groaned and gritted his teeth, feeling those delicate muscles part. Feeling the heat waiting beyond. It went completely against his nature to be passive, but if it killed him, goddamn it, he'd give her what she needed.

The thought lasted for two seconds and then he felt it. That thin layer of skin that changed everything. A virgin; she was a virgin. Thoughts raced faster than reason. How the hell had they not raped her? Thank God they hadn't raped her.

Lust burned like fire. His. She was so close to being his. Only his. His hands trembled. Fucking actually trembled. "Pet…"

Her gaze was unfocused, her expression impatient. "What?"

Damn, she was beautiful.

"I can give you pleasure without taking your virginity."

Her nails scraped across his already scratched skin. She growled in her throat, "No going back."

He growled right back. "I'm trying to be the gentleman."

And it was killing him.

"I don't want a gentleman," she moaned. "I want you."

A man could take that many ways. He chose to take it as an invitation.

Reaching between them, he grazed his fingers down

her stomach. She didn't make it easy, pressing against him, wanting to rub her nipples against his skin but he had another place he wanted to rub. She was hot for sure, but he wanted her wild.

"You feel so good in me."

And he wanted her quiet, he added. Many more words like that and he was going to turn into the animal he was trying not to be.

"I know something that's going to feel even better."

"What?"

His thumb slipped between her pussy lips, working between the thick folds, finding the smoother center, finding that hard nub.

"Spread you legs."

"I can't…"

"Spread them."

He rubbed and she did. Bracing herself against him, rocking her hips on his cock, taking more as the pleasure built. He wanted her to come. He wanted her to know that little death. He needed her to know that first time was with him. All her firsts belonged to him. All her seconds. Her lasts.

Her eyes closed, and her head fell back. A flush spread down her chest; her nipples peaked; her whole body went stiff. He rubbed harder, faster. She shook and tightened. Her pussy grabbed at his cock, milking it with little internal flexes that drove him crazy. He gritted his teeth and groaned right along with her.

"That's it. That's what I want. Open your eyes."

She did.

"Good girl."

Her gaze focused. He increased the pressure, lifting his hips. His cock slid deeper. He was big and she was little, and he worried but she was so lost in the pleasure she didn't notice the pain, becoming one with it. His pain, her pain and the pleasure, just so much pleasure. She was close. So close. So was he.

"Come for me, Pet."

She looked at him, not understanding, and he caught himself. Had he ever had a virgin before?

"Just let go," he murmured. "Let the pleasure take you. Don't fight it."

"I don't know…"

He cut off her protest with a light drag of his nail against her swollen clit, brought her to the edge with a series of circling caresses. She moaned and clutched. His balls drew up tight.

"Right there?"

She nodded, relaxing totally into him, gasped when he did it again. And again. Her muscles pulled taut and a fine quiver started deep.

"That's it." He rubbed harder, holding her gaze, gauging her pleasure,

"Come for me." With a fast, hard rub, he sent her over the edge. "Now."

Her orgasm took her in a shuddering convulsion. He watched it start in her eyes, felt it spread outward, body shuddering, eyes closing, nails grabbing and digging in a rhythm that matched the clenching of her pussy. Hard and fast she milked his cock. Demanding even as she took. Impossible to resist.

"Goddamn." Fisting his hands in the silk of her hair, he arched her back, inching deeper into the hot, slick perfection of her pussy. Feeling that hard pulsing start in his balls, holding her put as he jerked within her. As she came that first time. For him. With him. His. Fucking his. No one else's. Ever. She was his.

"Ace!"

"No one else," he groaned, forcing the words past the hard knot of desire. The woman was going to burn him up.

Closer. He needed to be closer. Deeper. So deep he'd always be a part of her. She moaned. With every jerk of his cock she clenched. It was good. The most innocent lovemaking in which he'd ever indulged, and it was so damn good.

"Come here."

He needed her closer. Taking her with him, he collapsed back against the tub, his breath soughing in and out of his lungs. Damn, he might never take a full breath again. Pet collapsed against him. So sweet and delicate. So passionate. Her arms came around his neck. His went around her back. Her cheek found his shoulder. She sighed and shivered. Her hug summed up everything he felt.

Home. He finally understood what it meant. He was home. Kissing Pet's forehead, her cheek, pulling her hair out of her face, seeing the stunned wonder on her face. He couldn't help a chuckle. He felt good, inside and out, in a way he never had. At peace. Right.

Rubbing the base of her spine, he kissed her temple. His fingers naturally cupped her ass. "Come morning we'll find the preacher and get married."

CHAPTER FOURTEEN

THE SALOON DOORS slammed open, the late-morning sun temporarily chasing away the interior shadows. For a moment, a familiar silhouette stood in the doorway, Caden Miller. And right behind him, Luke.

Ace swore. His day only needed this.

Caden strode into the near-empty saloon like he owned it, a shotgun cradled in his arm. Luke followed right on his heels. Not many came through the doors on a Tuesday. Ace shuffled the cards through his fingers, sliding them one over the other. Didn't take a genius to know why they were here. The shotgun was a good clue. When he was in a killing mood, Caden favored his revolvers. Ace took a sip of his whiskey and laid out the first tier of his solitaire game. The shotgun meant Caden was annoyed. Luke tagging along meant he was bored. Or annoyed. Shit again. He hoped Luke was annoyed. Luke bored was too creative by half.

"Preacher's set up and waiting," Caden said without preamble when he reached the table.

Ace spared him a glance. "Yeah?"

The muzzle of the gun slipped toward him.

"Yeah."

Chairs scraped as a couple of patrons noticed the confrontation.

"I'm a bit underdressed for such an occasion."

Luke pushed his hat back. "He's got a point, Caden. A man can't get wedded up in denims and a torn shirt."

"He can change."

Ace shook his head and dealt the first row of his solitaire game. "No."

Luke grunted. "Doubtful he's got anything in his saddlebags to do the lady proud."

More chairs scraped. A couple creaked as the patrons perked up to the potential excitement. Shit.

Caden wasn't deterred. "He can borrow yours."

Ace made a couple of moves with the cards. He could already tell the game wasn't going well. Laying out another row of cards he said, "You two are making a spectacle of yourselves."

Caden panned with the shotgun to include the greater world beyond the saloon. "I'd have to go a bit to make a bigger one than you did last night."

If he and Pet hadn't tipped over the tub getting out, they might not have made a scene at all, but things were what they were. With a jerk of his chin, Ace indicated the audience. "I'm not the one making a spectacle of the woman's name in a saloon."

To his surprise, Luke backed him. "Another good point."

Caden growled under his breath. Ace kicked out an empty chair with his foot. "Take a seat before you give anyone any more gossip to gnaw on."

Caden grabbed the chair and cut him a glare. "Just so you know, if I'm not happy with the conclusion to this talk we're about to have, I'm going to blow your toe off."

"Boots won't fit right without a toe," Luke observed, pulling out a chair for himself.

The bartender looked over. Ace nodded and motioned. "I'll bear that in mind."

Silence reigned for a minute. The new barkeep put two glasses on the table. Ace had to think to remember his name. "Thanks, Tim."

Uncorking the bottle, Ace poured whiskey into each and then pushed them over.

Caden looked at his. "A little early to be drinking, isn't it?"

Luke took his and lifted it in a silent toast. "I'm thinking not."

Ace followed suit. Caden's gaze jumped between the two of them. On a curse he threw his back, too. It was too much to hope a single shot would be much of a distraction. Caden's glass hit the table.

"So spill it."

Ace refilled the glasses. "This may shock you, gentlemen, but you've got the shotgun pointed at the wrong party."

Luke choked on his drink. Caden slowly narrowed his eyes, the way he did when he was absorbing something.

"We're going to need another bottle for this." Luke motioned to Tim, who brought it over immediately. "What the hell happened?"

Ace poured the last of the bottle with not too steady a hand. "The lady turned me down."

Luke cocked an eyebrow at him as the bottle rapped on the lip of his glass. "How many of these bottles have you had?"

"None of your business."

Luke glanced to the barkeep. Tim held up one finger. Caden snagged the second bottle before Ace could.

"Then you're done."

"The hell I am," Ace snarled. To Tim he said, "You're not long for this saloon."

"I'm sorry, Mr. Parker. Mr. Miller's—"

Caden cut him off. "Don't worry about it, Tim."

Very deliberately, Ace moved the black two on the red three. "Fuck you, Caden."

"You need a sober head to deal with women problems."

"Who said I have problems?"

Luke huffed. "The fact that your lady love needs a shotgun turned on her to see the sense in accepting you? Just a thought."

"That's not doing Hell's Eight's reputation a lick of good," Caden added, leaning back in his chair.

Ace scooped up the cards. "Not much left of that reputation after your wife not only rejected you but threw you out of her house."

Caden leaned back in his chair, a smug smile on his face. "Only until she saw the light. But you'll note, in the end, she *did* become my wife."

"Maddie's different."

Caden shook his head. "True. Maddie had a need to know who she was. There's no lack of self-knowing in Petunia."

That was the truth. "I'm beginning to think that lady knows herself too well."

"Meaning?" Caden asked, pulling the cork from the second bottle and pouring a shot into two glasses.

"I thought you said we were done?"

Caden took one glass, Luke the other.

Caden smiled. "I said *you* were done."

Ace grabbed the bottle back. "Uh-huh."

He poured a glass. Luke confiscated it.

"Son of a bitch. Why don't you two worry about your own women?"

"I don't have one." Luke grinned.

"Maddie said you've been around Hester quite a bit lately," Caden offered.

It was Luke's turn to frown. "Maddie needs a new hobby."

That was news to Ace. He cocked a brow at Luke. "You're interested in Hester?"

"We're not talking about me."

"*I'm* talking about Hester." He'd much rather have the conversation focused on Luke. "Pass me the shotgun, Caden."

Caden didn't pass the gun but he did sit back in his chair and study both of them. "Now, I can understand Hester wanting to stay man-free, but Petunia's been goggle-eyed over you, Ace, since you ran her over at the bakery."

"Now, there's an image." He poured another whiskey. This time no one took it from him.

"So what happened last night?" Luke asked.

The liquor shone a dull amber in the glass, sitting as it was far from the sunlight, struggling to make it through the saloon's dirty windows. "I don't think Petunia is fond of the institution of marriage."

Luke poured another glass. "Can't say that I blame her. She's used to doing what she wants, when she wants, and you would definitely hamper that."

"Like hell."

Caden snorted. "Have you met yourself? You couldn't help it. You been lusting after that woman the way a dog lusts after a bone, and it's not in you to be halfway with a woman. You'd want all of her. In all ways."

Intensity. Totality. Yes, he wanted that. "There's plenty of women here in town would tell you differently."

Luke scoffed. "We're not talking about dalliances. We're talking about that rare woman who can hold her own with you."

"And still be giving," Caden added with emphasis on the *giving*.

He hadn't realized they understood him so well. "Ya'll been studying me?"

"You've been the topic of conversation a time or two."

"Even placed a bet a time or two."

"On what?"

Luke shrugged. "Hard to pick just one thing."

"So who won on this one?"

Caden sighed, took Luke's glass and tipped the contents into Ace's. "No one, it appears."

"What is she going to do?" Luke asked. "Head on out to California?"

"I imagine."

"You don't know?"

"The conversation ended when she said no."

"And you left it there?" Caden asked.

"No place to take it."

Ace picked up his glass. Nothing had ever taken him aback as much as that no. He'd been holding marriage as his ace in the hole. And it'd been nothing against the wild card of her independence.

Luke swore. "Damn."

Ace put his glass down, the liquor untouched. He'd started the morning with the plan of getting stinking drunk, but the drunker he got, the less appeal he was finding in the idea. He was too damn old to be waking up hungover.

Lucas filled his glass again. "Short of hog-tying, how do you plan on keeping her here?"

Now, there was an image to fire a man's blood.

"More than that, what makes you think you have the right?" Caden asked too casually.

"She could be carrying my baby."

Caden reached for the shotgun and whistled under his breath. "That's a hell of a lot of right."

Ace nodded to the shotgun. "If you point that at her, I'm going to be unhappy."

Caden shrugged. "It might scare her into being reasonable."

"Have you met Petunia?"

With a sigh, Caden put the gun back. "You've got a point."

Luke swirled the whiskey in his glass. "So even after the trauma with the Comanche, she let you touch her?"

She hadn't just let him, she'd begged him. It had been the hottest yet sweetest lovemaking he could ever remember having. And he wasn't a man who thought he valued sweet.

"She had her reasons."

Caden whistled again. "That's one tough woman."

"Worth holding on to," Luke added.

Yes, she was. Ace took his shot glass and poured the contents into Caden's. "Yup."

Caden looked at it before leaning back in his chair. "I heard Rose was in here draped all over you the other day when she came in. Women tend to frown on that."

"Proud women even more," Luke tacked on.

Caden spun the glass between his fingers. "It's never good for a woman to know about a man's past dalliances."

No, it wasn't. And Petunia knew all about his. The foreign sense of helpless frustration swelled. "Shit."

A couple of cowboys burst through the door, their hooting and hollering too raucous for his mood. Ace considered shooting them.

Luke shook his head. "Don't."

Ace paused, hand on his gun. "Why the hell not?"

"'Cause we're the ones that would have to clean up the mess."

It was a good point.

"Still doesn't mean I'm not going to shoot *you*," Caden said, adjusting the shotgun against the extra chair.

"What the hell for?"

Caden sipped the whiskey Ace had just poured him and met his gaze squarely. "There's the little issue of you two taking off after Comanche without me."

"Oh, shit."

"Did you think I wouldn't know?"

Luke shrugged. "You're married."

"Married or not, I'm still Hell's Eight."

Those were fighting words for Caden. Ace pinched his nose between his thumb and forefinger and pushed the liquor away.

It really wasn't his day.

It really wasn't her day. Last night had been the most tumultuous of Petunia's life. There was nothing she wanted more right now than the time and privacy to sort out how she felt about what had happened. Instead, she had a room full of friends wanting to make her feel better about the kidnapping, about Ace, about everything. But mostly they wanted to fix what they saw as a pressing problem. Her compromised state.

"In my day such things did not go on," Luisa repeated for the third time in her thick Italian accent from where she stood by the window.

"It's not what it seemed," Petunia hedged, sitting on the side of the bed rubbing her forehead.

Hester, over by the wardrobe, huffed and folded her arms across her chest. "What else could it mean when a man stays in a woman's room?"

"You're not helping, Hester."

Hester snapped back, "I'm not trying to."

"I wasn't myself." In the beginning, at least. But in the end... In the end, Ace had given her back herself. Petunia owed him for that.

"Hester is right," Maddie said, pushing her hair off her face. "There's only one way that will look."

Luisa fussed with the curtains. "For a man to stay in a woman's room all night, this is serious."

"I think we all know Ace well enough to know he's always serious," Hester said.

Petunia cut her another glare. Hester smiled sweetly back.

Maddie licked her lips, fussed with her skirt, grabbed the post at the foot of the bed as if she needed the balance and then took the bull by the horns. "He needs to be serious about you, Petunia."

"As in proposing?"

"Yes!"

"I don't want to be married."

Maddie waved her hand as if her wishes were nothing. "But marriage will solve everything."

For everyone else. "What everything?"

"The rumors and gossip..." She looked away and didn't finish.

Luisa crossed herself. "A woman's reputation, this is a fragile thing."

"Mine's tough as nails," Petunia said.

Maddie shook her head. "You say that because you haven't left this room yet."

"Already, there is talk," Luisa whispered, looking out the window nervously as if she expected those talking to be gathering at the door.

"What talk?"

"About what was done to you."

Part of her cared. How could she not? But this town wasn't her home, and she'd soon be leaving. When she did, she'd leave the talk behind. "They're going to speculate one way or the other. Marriage won't stop that."

But marriage would stop her.

"Neither will leaving. Because that's your plan, isn't it?" Hester asked. "Just to leave us all here to cope as best we can while you run off to a shiny new life?"

"The world is not so big that this won't follow you," Maddie cautioned. "Being kidnapped makes you... notorious."

"Spending the night with Ace makes him notorious."

"For a man this doesn't matter," Luisa said.

"It matters to some," Hester protested.

Finally, Petunia could get a word in edgewise. "I'm sure his reputation will survive."

"He's a good man," Hester said. "And he's Hell's Eight. A Texas Ranger and proud. What makes you think he wants to be thought of as a low-down despoiler of women?"

Luisa and Maddie looked at Hester askance. Petunia sagged in exasperation. Damn it. Why did Hester have to make sense? Why did she have to keep hammering this point? Why did Petunia have to care? About Ace. About honor. About any of this. Smoothing her hair back, she asked, "Is there a lot of talk?"

"Enough."

"There might have been sympathy before about the Comanche, but once Ace spent the night…" Maddie sighed.

"You are the teacher of the children. People worry for the little ones."

"That's ridiculous! I'm a Wayfield, for heaven's sake."

"Your family name means nothing here."

No, she realized, it didn't. Along with leaving behind the protection of her family's money, she'd left behind the protection of their reputation. "No, I don't suppose it does."

"Caden isn't happy," Maddie confessed.

Petunia pinched the bridge of her nose, trying to stop the encroaching headache. She was tired. She just wanted to take a nap, not sit here having a pointless debate. "Don't tell me you talked to him about it."

Maddie's "It's not right, Petunia" wasn't any more encouraging than her "Ace may do what he wants with the women over in the saloon but with a good woman, there are limits."

"I think we should call the preacher," Luisa said, arms folded across her chest. "Then there will be no more of this nonsense. Ace will be a man and make the proposal." Letting the curtain drop, she nodded emphatically. "I will speak to Antonio about it."

Petunia could feel the walls closing in. "The situation doesn't need a preacher. It just needs to be left alone."

Luisa and Maddie exchanged a guilty glance. The one Hester shot Petunia was a knowing one. Damn her, she just smiled that knowing smile. She'd told Petunia she couldn't contain this and leave it to feed on itself. That it was unfair to Ace. Petunia hadn't believed her then, but now, seeing that shared look between Maddie and Luisa, she had a sinking feeling Hester had been right.

"Maddie, what did you do?"

"I was upset…" she began.

"About what?" Petunia pressed.

"About what happened to you. About Ace. The way he treated you."

"He treated me like a gentleman. You had no reason to think otherwise."

Maddie wouldn't look at her. "Sometimes I can't separate what's me and what's others. I was crying."

Oh, God.

"Caden saw…"

Oh, my God. Maddie's tears would make everything more critical to Caden.

"He grabbed the shotgun."

"Good!" Luisa exclaimed. She reached over and patted Petunia's leg. "Caden, he's a good man. He will set this to right."

Petunia didn't need it to be set right. She didn't need Ace pinned down by the business end of a shotgun and forced to marry her. She'd wanted to be made love to. She'd wanted to feel like a woman not a victim. She'd wanted a lover, not a lifetime. How could she explain that to these women? That Ace had offered marriage, and she'd refused? Maddie and Luisa wouldn't understand and to Hester it would be a slap in the face.

"In my day, men did not play fast and loose with a woman's reputation," Luisa continued.

"I agree."

How could Maddie agree? "Maddie, you *lived* with Caden before you married him."

"We were discreet."

Petunia dropped her hand to her side. "Your fights were legendary. There was a whole betting board set up in the saloon."

"But there was never any doubt in anyone's mind but mine that we were getting married. Caden had 'mine' written all over anything pertaining to us."

"Uh-huh. And Ace doesn't when it comes to Petunia?" With a shake of her head, Hester picked up her breakfast tray. "I can't listen to any more of this foolishness. I'm going to see what the children are up to."

"I never thought I'd say this, but I am ashamed of Ace Parker," Luisa said as the door closed behind Hester. Through the wood came the sound of Hester's disgusted huff.

Maddie sighed. "I never expected such behavior from him. It goes against everything Hell's Eight stands for."

Petunia sighed. She couldn't let this continue. "You can stop fretting. Ace is all you thought. He asked me to marry him last night."

Like a struck match, Maddie's expression brightened. "He did?"

She nodded. "He did."

Luisa jerked her apron down. "I knew he was an honorable man."

Petunia held up her hands. "Don't get all excited. I said no."

Both women just stared at her. Maddie found her voice first. "But why?"

Petunia didn't know how to say it so they'd understand. She settled for "Because as much as I needed to feel whole again, I don't want to be married."

Luisa folded her arms across her ample bosom and glared at Petunia. With a jerk of her chin, she motioned Maddie toward the door. "You, you go fetch the gun from your husband. I will get the preacher."

"The preacher isn't going to change my mind."

"Why not?" Luisa snapped.

"What happened to me was beyond my or anyone's control. I will not pay the rest of my life for something over which I had no control."

Luisa pursed her lips. Her arms didn't unfold. Maddie plucked at her sleeve.

She might as well hear it now. "What?"

Shrugging, Maddie said, "You didn't say anything about Ace spending the night with you. You had control over that."

"I'm a grown woman. He's a grown man. What we choose to do is between us."

"There could be consequences." That was from Maddie.

Petunia blinked.

"Bambinos," Luisa clarified unnecessarily.

Petunia didn't need to speak Italian to know what that meant. A baby?

"Unless you know how to protect yourself from getting with child?" Maddie offered.

"There are ways to stop such a thing?" She hadn't even thought about pregnancy.

"Well—" Maddie sighed "—that answers that."

Still standing there, arms crossed like a guard at a prison, Luisa huffed, "The best way to stop *such things* is not to lie down with a man."

Maddie rolled her eyes. "That horse has long since bolted from the barn, Luisa. You can't keep harping on it. It's done."

"This harping could keep it from happening again."

She could be pregnant. The idea kept circling Petunia's mind. "It was only one time."

"One time is all that's needed."

"With any man," Luisa added.

It took Petunia a moment to realize what Luisa implied. "The Comanche didn't rape me. They tried but they'd had too much to drink by the time they remembered I was there."

Maddie nodded. "Nothing gives a man more inspiration and less wherewithal than liquor."

"Thank the *buon Dio*."

Sadness tinged Maddie's smile. "There've been times in my life when I was grateful for that particular combination of alcohol and ability, too."

A baby. Petunia couldn't get the thought out of her mind.

"How does a woman—" she waved with her hand filling in all the unmentionables "—know?"

"That she is *incinta*?"

"If that means with child, yes."

It was Maddie that answered. "Missing your menses is a sure sign if you're regular."

She'd just had hers the week before, but she wasn't always regular.

"Another will be you get sick for no reason."

"I don't have any of those signs." Though she was feeling a bit queasy at the thought of a baby. Queasy and then a little excited. As the years had passed, she'd accepted she'd never have a child. "Aren't I too old?"

"Who told you that?"

She shrugged. "I just assumed."

Luisa snorted. "This is such nonsense. *Dio* blesses women of all ages."

Again, that inner falter between hope and horror.

Maddie cocked her head to the side. "What will you do if you are with child? Would you have it?"

"Maddie!" Luisa looked horrified. "Such talk is sin."

Petunia hadn't even known there was an option. For a modern woman, she was amazingly uninformed in the basics.

Maddie shrugged. "Such talk is truthful."

"I imagine I would go home."

Luisa nodded her approval and came and sat beside her on the bed. "Family is important."

"If they'll accept you and a baby," Maddie added, taking a seat on her other side.

Both women waited. She didn't know what to say. Petunia hoped her father would accept an illegitimate child, but she didn't know. He valued his reputation and standing in the community. It would probably be easier if it were a boy. He desperately wanted a son to carry on the Wayfield name. Either way he could afford to buy some acceptance within the community. But his willingness to do so? She truly didn't know. Her stomach churned.

"*Will* they accept you?" Luisa asked gently.

"I don't know."

Patting her thigh, Luisa said, "You will always have a place with us."

Doing what? She couldn't teach school as an unwed mother. Wouldn't be able to work in any decent establishment. She'd be like Hester, trapped between a rock and a hard place. How would she support her child? Luisa was right. A reputation was a valuable but fragile thing.

It was Maddie who surprised her. Standing abruptly, she smiled encouragingly. "These things have a way of working out."

Luisa looked at her askance. "But we came to talk sense to her."

"I know, but I've decided we don't need to."

"Why do we not?"

Maddie straightened her skirts. "Because I have dough to prepare, you have a lunch shift to run, but mostly because Petunia knows what she's doing."

She'd thought she did. Luisa looked as skeptical as Petunia felt. Maddie, on the other hand, glowed with optimism.

Luisa stood. "She did not even know one time could make a child."

Petunia continued to sit, feeling queasy, torn and a bit foolish.

Maddie smiled. "But Ace did."

Luisa *pshawed*. "That one. He is a gambler."

"Ace gambles with money, but never with anything that matters."

And a child would matter to Ace.

Luisa said, "Still, I will send Antonio by to check on her. A woman alone cannot be too careful."

Behind Luisa's back, Maddie made a face. Petunia wanted to make it back, but she didn't. Luisa was a good woman, and she was looking out for her. They were at the door before Petunia remembered.

"Wait a minute. With all the excitement, I forgot to ask."

"What?"

"I want to get the children together later."

"For what?" Hester appeared in the doorway, flipping through some envelopes in her hand. "The mail came."

"After lunch, I want to take the children out on an excursion."

"Where to?" Luisa asked.

"It's almost Christmas."

Hester nodded and looked up. "And?"

"I want to get a Christmas tree."

Hester blinked. "A what?"

"A Christmas tree. We'll put it in the parlor and decorate it. It will be our project."

"I've heard of that," Maddie piped in. "There's a picture of one in the catalog. They sell ornaments for it. You set it up in the house and decorate it. I could bake cookies!"

"A tree in the house?" Hester parroted.

"We always had one back home." That wasn't exactly true. They'd only started a few years ago, but she loved the idea and the sense of continuity it gave her. Every year finding different ornaments. Learning to make new ones. It gave her a connection to the past and to the future. It was a gift she wanted to pass on. "The children need a distraction, and frankly so do I."

Hester didn't have an argument for that, though she still seemed doubtful. "Are you sure you're up to it?"

Beyond the ache of a few bruises, she was fine. She was a very lucky woman. If Ace and Luke hadn't have come along when they did… She didn't like to think of that. "Yes, I'm sure."

"I'm not sure it's safe," Hester interjected.

"I will ask Ace to escort us," Maddie countered.

It was hardly the enthusiastic response she was looking for. Clearly nobody around here had heard of a Christmas tree. But it was a lovely, fun tradition, and it would catch on here as it had back East. And even if it didn't, the tree made her think of peace and harmony and celebrating and all the good things that had been missing in her life for the past year. All the good things she thought she'd never experience again when the Comanche had carried her away. In the wake of her abduction, she was finding tradition important to her. And today, she needed to build forward.

"But right now I need some sleep." She tugged back covers, wincing at the pull on her muscles. She was exhausted. "I was thinking after lunch."

Hester shook her head. "I don't know what Ace is going to think, cutting down a perfectly good tree and putting it in the house."

Neither did she. He might think she was crazy. He might think it was charming. He might not care anyway at all. But she wanted to know. And darn it, she wanted him to approve.

"I guess we'll all see if he shows up."

CHAPTER FIFTEEN

THEY WERE ALL waiting for her downstairs after lunch. A more skeptical crowd she'd never seen. Phillip, Brenda, Terrance, Hester and Ace. The last made her heart skip a beat. He'd come.

A shiver went down her spine as her gaze met his. The squeaky stair groaned under her foot. As she grabbed the rail, he took a step forward. The tenderness between her thighs took on erotic significance. Her breath caught. She gave him a tentative smile. He raised an eyebrow. A shiver went down her spine.

"Luisa couldn't make it?" she asked, a little breathlessly.

"Antonio needed her."

She figured that would be the case. There were a couple other restaurants in town, but they weren't the quality of Antonio's, and business was steadily growing. "And Maddie?"

So that just left Hester and Ace as the adults along. Almost like a date. She arched her brow at Hester when she handed her her coat. The smile she got back could have meant anything.

It was Ace that answered. "Caden needed her."

There was something in the way he drawled that that brought a flush to her cheeks.

"Well, then," she said to the children cheerfully, "we'll have to have enough fun for them, too, won't we?"

Terrance looked at her as though he wanted to say something, but bit his tongue. Phillip rolled his eyes. Brenda, being younger, nodded eagerly. Clearly, no one thought Christmas-tree hunting would be fun. Including Ace. Her lips felt stiff when she smiled at him. Her hand touched her stomach, and she couldn't stop the wonder, would a child between them have his eyes?

"Well, I'm glad you could join us."

"I wouldn't miss it for the world. It isn't often someone cuts down a perfectly good tree and drags it into the house."

"Are you looking for boasting rights?"

"Absolutely." He held out his hand. "When I tell the story, I'll be able to end it with, 'And I was there.'"

Placing her hand in his, she let him help her down the last step. Awareness crackled between them.

Her "Is that the only reason?" was a bit breathless.

The wicked edge to his smile as he slowly grazed his fingers along hers and stepped back did nothing to steady her breathing.

"That, and I could use the fresh air."

That would be true if he was a pasty-faced gambler, but Ace brought the feel of the outside with him everywhere. His skin was tanned and vibrant, his eyes snapping with life and his mouth… She licked her lips. She did like his mouth, especially the way the right side quirked just a little bit higher than the left.

She forced more cheerfulness into her tone than she actually felt. "Is everybody ready for our first Christmas-tree hunt?"

"Is it like an Easter-egg hunt?" Terrance asked.

She'd told the children stories of holidays from her youth. Terrance had been fascinated with the concept.

"No, it's much more specific."

Phillip cocked his head. "How?"

She pulled her gloves out of her pocket. "Because it can't be just any tree. It has to be one that can hold our hopes for our loved ones and the New Year."

The children's eyes widened.

"That's a tall order," Ace said.

She nodded. "Of course. That's why it's a hunt."

"And you think we're going to find it around here?" Hester asked.

She nodded. "I do, because Christmas is a magic time. And magic is everywhere."

"Better not let the preacher hear you say that," Ace warned so no one else could hear.

"Better not tattle, then," she warned just as softly.

He laughed and leaned back and spoke loud enough so the others could hear. "I do like the way you think, Miss Wayfield."

Hester snorted. The children giggled. And that fast the mood lightened.

"And so we're going to find a tree to put in the living room and then," she continued, "we are going to have a whole bunch of fun decorating it. We can bake cookies. We'll cut out special decorations. We will—" she paused dramatically "—do Christmas proud."

Whether she felt like it or not.

The children's eyes lit up, whether at the thought of cookies or the activities, she couldn't tell, but they were enthusiastic, and that was good. "Now, go get your coats and we'll go."

The children raced to the back door where their coats

hung, feet pounding on the wood floor, giggles and challenges floating behind.

"And what do you do with this magical tree when Christmas is over?" Hester asked, tugging on her own gloves.

With a wrinkle of her nose, Petunia confessed, "Use it for firewood."

Ace opened the door. The chill of the outside air hit her hard, and she froze. She remembered lying there on the dank ground, shivering in fear and dread waiting for the rapes that, thankfully, never came.

"You all right?" Hester asked.

Tugging on her gloves, she nodded. She hadn't been raped. She had nothing to cry about. "Of course. It is beginning to feel like winter, though."

"We could always wait for a warmer day."

She raised her eyebrows at Hester. "It's a Christmas tree. It's supposed to be cold."

"I could wait for warm and pretend it's cold."

"What happened to the legend of the tough Western women I read about back East?"

"She froze to death and sensible took her place," Hester retorted.

Ace laughed and grabbed up an ax and his rifle where they were propped against the side of the building. Petunia tugged up her collar and grinned. "I can't argue with sensible."

"But we're still going out in the cold?"

"We're still going out in the cold."

The children came charging back down the hallway, shrugging on their coats. She made note of the material and the newness. Hester had been busy. Ace held the door open and they shot through. The adventure had begun.

The kids stuck close on the way out of town, carrying the conversation in a barrage of questions and speculation, but as soon as they hit the outskirts and the options expanded, they were off like a shot, running ahead.

"There go your buffers," Ace said.

She couldn't tell if he was teasing or serious. "I've still got Hester."

Hester smiled and walked a little faster, putting some distance between them, and the notion that Maddie's and Luisa's absence was deliberate strengthened.

"Traitor," she called after her. Hester waved and kept on walking.

"She just wants what's best for you," Ace offered in that steady drawl of his.

She looked at him out of the corner of her eye. "And marrying you would be it?"

"You could do worse."

That was true. "Maybe."

"Which way we going?" he asked, interrupting her thoughts.

She paused for a minute, looking around. There was a copse of pine trees over to the right that looked possible. "That way."

He nodded and whistled through his teeth. The children perked up. He pointed, and they were off like a shot running in that direction.

"They've got a lot of energy.

"I could use some of it today."

"Tired?"

"A little."

The wind kicked up, nipping at her cheeks. She shivered and hunkered down into her coat. She couldn't believe it had been just two days ago that she'd been complaining about the heat.

"It's a good tradition," she said, defending her plan.

"I believe you."

"The kids will enjoy it."

"I'm not arguing."

Stopping, she turned to face him. "Ace, why are you here?"

He patted the rifle slung over his shoulder. "Protection."

"This close to town it's doubtful we're in danger."

But underneath the bravado, her conviction wavered.

"There is another reason."

"And that would be...?"

"Somebody's got to carry the tree home."

She hadn't thought of that. She said so.

"There are a lot of things you haven't thought of, like the advantages of being married to me."

She should have known she couldn't prevent this. "It's not that I don't appreciate the gallantry that brought about your change of heart, but the one advantage to being well and truly on the shelf is I'm not worried about being proper."

That got her a look.

She shrugged. "A woman worries about being proper to safeguard her reputation so she'll be seen as marriageable."

"You don't see yourself as desirable?"

She shrugged and trudged on. "There was a time when I wanted a family and home but I adjusted to my circumstances. A woman's life can be rich in many ways outside of a husband and children."

"You make it sound like you're ancient."

"For marriage, I am."

He cut her a glance and fell into step beside her. "That was no crone in my bed last night."

She could feel the blush start in her toes. "For heaven's sake!"

His smile was pure devil. "No angel, either."

"Oh, my God." Stopping, she pressed her hands to her cheeks. He swung around in front of her. Protecting her, she realized, from the others' view. "You are outrageous."

"I prefer to think of it as honest."

"I don't see the need for that much honesty!"

"I'm sure, which brings us around to the point I wanted to make."

"And what would that be?"

His gaze never wavered from hers. "There may be more reasons than your reputation for us to marry."

Oh, heck. Had everyone but her thought of that? "It's only been a day."

"A day. A month. Pregnant is pregnant."

She increased her pace and once again he caught her arm, pulling her back.

"Running away isn't going to resolve anything."

"I never run away," she snapped back. "Walking fast helps me think."

"What is there to think about?"

"The possibilities, remedies, the resolution."

"The only resolution for you being with child is we get married."

She wanted to stomp her feet and say no but the truth was, she wasn't sure she had it in her to raise a child alone. She'd have to go back home in disgrace. And after all she'd said and done, she truly wasn't sure how her father would handle that.

"I'm sure I'm not pregnant. It was only one time."

He looked at her. "You realize it's usually the man that usually makes that claim."

"Well, it's true. I've known women that have been trying for years to get with child."

"And I've known foolhardy virgins that got pregnant their first time."

"So how many of these foolhardy virgins are with your child?" she fired back.

He shook his head.

His silence just goaded her. "I've seen how you are with women."

"You've seen me play with women who know the score. You have no idea how I am with *my woman*."

His woman. She remembered that first kiss, the passion, the aggression. It made her nervous. It excited her. Oh, yes, she did know how he was. He was possessive and demanding. Not the type of man to let his wife have her projects.

"Well, I'm sure I'm not pregnant so—" she brushed her hands down her skirt "—there's nothing to worry about."

"I hope you are."

She stumbled again, and he caught her. She didn't know what annoyed her most, that he caught her off guard or that he was always there to catch her.

"Will you stop doing that?"

He didn't do innocent well. "Stop doing what?"

"Stop saying things to shock me just to keep me off balance."

Ahead of them, the children reached the trees. Hester was right behind them. They turned back. Even from here, their impatience was palpable.

She called out, "Start looking for the right one."

"You're going to have to be more specific than that," Ace said.

"Why?"

"Because they're children. They're going to look for the biggest. And the biggest one isn't going to fit in your house."

"We'll just have to do some trimming."

"Uh-huh."

Darn it. He was right again. "Do you always have to be right?"

"Yup."

She gave him a hard glare before calling out, "Make sure that it's one that will fit in the house."

His chuckle just irritated her more. Which made no sense. His fingers slid down her arm, threaded through hers. Squeezed. And the irritation vanished.

"You're safe, Pet."

She didn't think she'd ever feel safe again. "Thank you."

With a tug he brought her around to face him again. She wanted to hide. His finger under her chin wouldn't let her. "You could pretend to believe me."

"What's the point of starting to lie now?"

The squeeze on her hand coincided with the glide of his thumb across her lips, her shiver with his smile. "None at all." Subtle pressure and her lips parted. His thumb entered, just the smallest bit. All the events of the previous night came flooding back. Her nipples tingled, and her knees weakened. "I won't tolerate dishonesty from you."

"Won't tolerate?"

"You can scream, shout, curse and take a swing at

me, but you—" he leaned in and kissed her "—won't
lie to me. Ever."

She caught his wrist in her hand, her lips clinging to
his even as she tried to pull his fingers away. "And what
about you?"

His smile felt good against hers. "I'll lie my ass off."

"That's not fair," she laughed, not believing him at all.

"No, it isn't."

She took a step back. He allowed the distance but
didn't let her go. There was something comforting in that.

She tugged at her hand. "You are a very presump-
tive man."

"But a good one to have around."

His confidence was unparalleled.

"No comment."

"I'm working on a lie."

That got her a chuckle. He turned them toward the
copse. She tugged harder at her hand. "Let go."

"Why?"

She jerked her chin to Hester and the children. "They'll
get the wrong idea."

"Ask me nicely."

"Please."

To her surprise, he released her.

"Thank you."

"You're welcome."

With a tip of his hat he headed toward Hester and
the children.

And she just stood there and watched him go, rubbing her tingling fingers against her thigh. She did not
understand that man. With a shake of her head, she followed. Ace Parker was a puzzle, for sure.

"I LIKE THIS ONE," Brenda said in her high-pitched little-girl voice, blue eyes smiling, ringlets bouncing. The tree she was standing in front of would fit in the parlor if they bent it double and hacked the branches in half, something Phillip was quick to point out and Brenda didn't appreciate. The bickering that followed was normal. Brenda and Phillip were blossoming since coming to Providence. Terrance was another story.

Petunia sighed. She didn't know what she was going to do with that boy. He brought serious with him everywhere. While the other children were running from tree to tree, touching their hands at the base, trying to come up with a formal decision, he just stood there at the edge of the copse, hands in his pockets, expression solemn, weighing them from afar.

Arms crossed over her chest, she walked up to him. "They won't bite, you know."

"I know." His shoulders seemed to hunch inside themselves.

"Then why don't you go join the others?"

He shook his head.

"Why not?"

Terrance didn't raise his eyes. "'Cause I already made up my mind."

"Just like that? From here?" Petunia asked.

He nodded. "Which one is it?"

He just shrugged again.

Phillip called her over.

"I'll be right back."

He was standing with Hester and Brenda, pointing to another big tree. If she took out the second floor of the house, it would fit. Hester rolled her eyes.

"Now we'll see," Phillip said to his mother.

"See what?" Hester asked.

"It has to be a grand tree," Brenda insisted. "This is a grand tree."

Phillip backed her. "It is a fine tree."

"I don't think it will fit in the house. It's very tall."

"It'll fit." His jaw set. "It will fit just fine."

"No, it won't." Terrance had followed Petunia. "It's bigger than two houses."

A fight was clearly brewing between the boys.

"It's not too big!"

"It is, too, dummy," Terrance said.

"Shut up!"

"You shut up!"

And all that energy that had been feeding on tree hunting all of a sudden broke down into a fistfight. It was Terrance that threw the first punch, Phillip who landed it. The scuffle turned violent so quickly that Petunia could only gasp.

"Hey, there!" Hester said. "Break it up!"

Ace set the ax down and in one smooth move grabbed each boy by the back of their coats, pulling them apart. "Cut it out."

They kept swinging. He knocked their heads together. They stopped swinging.

Petunia could only watch in awe. "I need to learn how to do that."

Ace dropped the boys to their feet. Hester shook her head, grabbed each boy by the collar and shoved them. "Let's go look over there."

Brenda went skipping along, clearly more happy with the choosing process than she was on settling on a choice.

"Don't forget to grab some pinecones," Petunia called after them. "We can use them for decorating."

"You're dead set on this?" Ace asked, picking up his ax. "You're going to take a pine tree, living outside in the woods, happy in its own little world, already sprouting pinecones, already thriving, cut it down, get up dead pinecones from other trees, bring them all into the house, hang them on the tree and call it a holiday?"

"For a gambler you lack imagination."

"Is that what you plan on doing?"

"Yes, that's what I'm planning on doing."

"Why?"

"I told you. It's a good tradition and it's all the rage."

"Are you that bored?"

"No, but it occurred to me that building a tradition would make Terrance feel part of something, and maybe he wouldn't miss his dad so much and he'd begin to think of here as home."

Ace shook his head. "You're not going to be *here* next year, remember?"

"I'll leave instructions for the next teacher."

"The next teacher isn't going to worry about imagination. The next teacher's going to plunk her butt in that chair and collect her paycheck between shoving some ABCs down the kids' throats."

Not with her students, she wouldn't. "That would be a waste of time. There are some very bright and inquisitive minds in this town."

"And nobody's going to give a shit about them after you leave."

He had to keep pounding on that sore spot. "I couldn't make a change anymore anyway."

"You could if you married me."

Nor that one. "The school I plan to build in San Francisco will help a lot of people."

"You're already helping a lot of people."

"I'll help a lot more people."

"Which matters more, the scale of the help or the scale of the need? Because I guarantee you nobody needs you more than this little town right here."

And you, she wanted to ask, *do you need me?* She bit her tongue, holding it back.

Hester called her over. This time the four of them were standing by a tree more suited to the size of the room. The only problem was it was a sorry little tree. It didn't have many branches, and the ones it had grew at awkward angles. It was clearly being choked out by the bigger trees.

When she got close, Terrance stuck out his chin. The spot on his cheek where Phillip had struck him glowed red in the pale of his face. His face looked tighter and more angular, almost a little more adult, and she realized he was clenching his teeth.

"I like this one."

"I don't," Phillip said.

"I don't, either," Brenda said.

Hester kept her opinion to herself. Ace didn't say a word, just looked at her.

Petunia asked the only thing she could think of. "Why don't you like it, Phillip?"

"It's ugly."

"I know," Terrance said, "that's why it's perfect."

With everybody watching him, Terrance got more quiet. He shoved his fists into his pockets. If a hole opened up in front of him, Petunia bet he'd jump right in it.

Ace walked up beside him and put his hand on his shoulder. The boy flinched, and then he relaxed.

"Why do you like it, son?"

"Because…" He paused then tried again, his voice a hush of sound. "Because Christmas is all about loving people no matter what, not just because they're beautiful or perfect."

"Still an ugly tree," Phillip muttered.

Terrance nodded. "I know and nobody would ever want it, but I do. If we leave it here the bigger trees will just ignore it until one day it'll lose its needles, and its branches will break off. But if we take it home and make it pretty, it will be something."

"It will be dead," Phillip said.

He nodded. "But it will be something before it dies."

"We're taking this one." Surprisingly, it was Hester who spoke up.

"Terrance is right," Petunia agreed, "Christmas is about charity and good feelings and doing the right thing. I think choosing this tree represents all of that."

"Everything should be wanted," Terrance added, touching the little pine needles on a spindly branch. "Even an ugly tree."

There was silence, then Phillip nodded. "This is our tree."

Hester was trying not to cry but Petunia felt a tear leaking down her own cheek. Ace glanced over.

"You're mush," he told her.

"So are you."

"What makes you think that?" He hefted the ax. "I'm the one going to murder it."

"You're sending it to glory. That's not the same thing."

He swung the ax. "Tell it to the tree."

LATER THAT DAY, she and Ace were sitting in the kitchen sipping coffee. The tree had been set into a bucket of earth and plunked optimistically in the parlor. The children had had their hot chocolate, a special treat, indeed, and Hester had taken them upstairs claiming she was going to bed herself. Some chaperone she turned out to be.

"What were you thinking about when Terrance said everything deserved to be wanted?"

"What made you think I was thinking about anything?"

She rolled her eyes. "All of us thought of something. Terrance thought of his dad. Hester thought of her husband. Her children thought of their father. I thought of, well, it's pretty obvious what I thought of, and it occurs to me you must have thought of something, too."

"I'm Hell's Eight. I belong. I've always belonged."

"You live in a saloon. You date women with whom you'll never have a future, and you're about as far away from Hell's Eight as you can get. You thought of something."

He shrugged. "Some things just don't need putting into words."

"I disagree."

Ace took a sip of his coffee. "Lucky for me, you don't tell me what to do."

"You seem to feel you can tell me what to do."

"That's because of who I am and who you are."

"What does that even mean?"

"It means I like to give orders, and you like to follow them."

She almost choked on her coffee. "Whatever gave you that idea?"

"Are you saying you don't?"

"I'm saying I can bring you out a line of witnesses a mile long that would dispute that claim."

"Uh-huh." The look he cut her from beneath his lashes slid over her senses with the smooth decadence of warm melted chocolate. "Spread your legs, Pet."

"You're outrageous."

"You're aroused." He took a sip of his coffee.

It wasn't a question.

He was right. She didn't know whether to be angrier that she'd responded or that he knew about it.

"That doesn't mean anything."

"It means a hell of a lot to me."

She played with her coffee cup because she didn't have anything else to do with her hands.

He sighed and placed his hand over her cup, putting an end to her fidgeting. "Didn't your mother tell you anything about passion?"

"My mother died when I was young."

"So did mine."

"Mine died of pneumonia."

He nodded. "Mine at the hands of Mexican soldiers."

She'd heard the stories. "It's a sad thing to have in common."

"We got by all right."

"*We* meaning Hell's Eight?"

He nodded. "We were a scraggly lot back then."

"You were young."

"Young and mad as hell. I had this happy life, and one day there was no more happy, and there wasn't anything I could do about it."

She knew how that felt. "It doesn't feel good to be out of control like that."

Or to have the ones around you so lost in grief they

forgot you existed. Like her father had for a few years after her mother's death, losing himself in work and drink while she, well, she'd found comfort where she could. In her books.

"No, it doesn't."

He was clearly uncomfortable with the conversation, but he was still sitting there, and he was still sharing with her. It was more than she'd expected.

"You like it when you're out of control with me."

The heat started in her toes. It took everything she had to get out, "That was a surprise."

His brows rose on that. "What were you expecting to have with a husband?"

"Setting aside my acceptance that I wouldn't have a husband?"

His "Yeah, setting that aside" was a bit dry.

"I assumed it'd be warm. It'd be comfortable. It'd be soothing."

"Damn!" He shook his head and cut her another skeptical glance. "Really?"

He didn't have to make it sound so ridiculous. "Yes. Really."

"You'd be bored in a minute."

"There's a lid for every pot."

He smiled. "You realize you're not helping your case?"

"Just because I like what you do to me in bed—"

"And in the tub and in the alley…"

She glanced toward the door. "Hush! You have no shame."

"It's the truth."

It was too much. "Then start lying!" she snapped.

He laughed outright. She couldn't even blame him. "Ace, just because I like *that* with you, doesn't mean I want everything else. You want to possess a woman, Ace. With you, a woman wouldn't have room to breathe."

He didn't deny it, and the part of her that always was hopeful gave a little whimper.

He took another sip of his coffee. "Some women want to be possessed, need that totality."

"I'm not one of them." *Liar*, the little voice said.

Ace pushed his cup aside, his chair back and came around the table. He towered over her. Her heart gave a little lurch as he caught her chin in his hand and lifted her face to his. His eyes were dark with emotion, but his voice was calm, his tone casual.

"There's a reason you haven't married, Pet."

Her gaze locked on his lips, she found enough voice to ask, "What's that?"

She watched his lips caress the words. Inhaled his intoxicating scent. Remembered how those lips had touched hers intimately, how he'd filled her mind, her senses. Inside, the flames flickered and surged. He had a fabulous mouth. "You're not on the shelf, my Pet. You've simply been waiting for the one man who can make you burn."

CHAPTER SIXTEEN

THE ONE THING she didn't need, Petunia decided a week later, was another place to burn, because apparently, according to the attitude of the townspeople, she was already slated to burn in hell. She shivered as the wind cut right through her cloak. Not that she'd mind a few stray flames from that pit right now. The heat spell was long gone, and winter was settling in with a vengeance. Pulling her cloak more snugly around her, she hurried down the street.

She was used to her modern ways of thinking, setting her outside of traditional expectations. But losing her good reputation in a small town where nothing much happened had left her as the only grist for a very hungry rumor mill, and it was a completely new experience. Ace's sudden disappearance hadn't helped, either. She didn't know where he'd gone, just that he had left the morning after his statement about making her burn. And the pressure of the town's censure combined with the worry over his disappearance and the reasons behind it was telling on her. She couldn't sleep, and she was as jumpy as a cat on a hot tin roof.

Two women approached from the mercantile. Before her unfortunate experience, as she'd come to call it, they would've nodded a greeting and had a nice cordial exchange. She would have even looked forward to the chats.

But today, just approaching a stranger put butterflies in her stomach. She had no way of knowing if they'd nod, or if they'd pull their skirts away instead. As if what had happened to her were contagious.

She'd helped other women fight this attitude her whole life. How many times had she advised them to ignore the snubs and dirty looks and remember that they were more than what had happened to them? But she hadn't truly understood. She'd advised without really understanding the sheer unrelenting, demeaning process of being socially snubbed. On some level, she had thought those women weak, but with the weight of social ostracization now pressing down upon her, she couldn't believe how brave they'd really been. Or how naive and arrogant she had been in her righteous pursuit of equality. Turning, she pretended an interest in the display in the millinery window. When the women passed by, she resumed walking. She didn't recognize this cowardly part of herself.

Luisa, Hester and Maddie were her only friends. And she'd seen how that friendship was costing all of them. No one would go in Maddie's bakery if she was there. When she ate at Antonio and Luisa's restaurant, patrons often left or demanded a table farther away from hers. Although Maddie and Luisa had both told her to not worry about such petty people, that she was as welcome as ever, business was business and money was money, and Petunia cared about both of them too much to take them up on that offer.

She was a social pariah. It was what it was, and her life had become what it had become, but it would go back to normal as soon as she left this town. Discreetly touching her hand to her stomach, she stepped off the walk and crossed to the other side of the street. All around her signs of Christmas abounded, fliers for church services were posted. Store windows were stocked with little trinkets and gifts, hoping to attract buyers. Maddie had put up a sample cake in case anyone might have a big party. Antonio and Luisa were serving a Christmas buffet. School was closed. And the one place that shouldn't be doing a booming business this time of year, the saloon, was packed.

She shook her head. A line of horses waited patiently for their owners out front. The stench of manure drifted with the breeze from the area. Jenkins had hired a boy to clean up after the horses, but he hadn't been as careful as he should've been around the animals, and he'd gotten kicked. The result was a broken arm and no one to clean up. She wondered, ruefully, if she'd be considered good enough for that job now. With a wistful glance at the schoolhouse, she kept on. She did miss the children, and couldn't help worrying about them. She could petition the board to be reinstated, but since the board was comprised of the same people that were snubbing her daily, she didn't have much hope of getting her job back. Hopefully, the fill-in new teacher was keeping on top of Buster, and spending time with Milly on her letters. That child had the worst time keeping them straight.

With a sigh and a last glance at the schoolhouse, she stepped up on the walk. Touching a hand into her stomach again, she felt a tickle of worry. It was a bold statement to say she'd go home with her baby, but while she could run away from this town and her reputation, there'd be no running away from a child, no hiding its illegitimacy. Her father's money could provide her comfort, but it wouldn't be able to shield her from the talk. Worse yet, it wouldn't be able to shield her child.

No child of mine would grow up not knowing his father.

Ace wanted a child. She slid her fingers to her hip. *This* child, that might not even exist. He was willing to marry her. She bit her lip, feeling the walls closing in and her choices narrowing. Ace was not an easy man. On the surface his needs were simple, but she'd seen below the facade, and she hadn't been speaking lightly when she said he would possess a woman totally. He would. From the inside out. With no secrets and nothing withheld. His woman would belong to him completely. And he was man enough to make her enjoy it. Part of her quivered in breathless anticipation at the thought. A sense of "at last" flowed through her.

Some women want to be possessed, need that totality.

Even not knowing what all that meant, she had a feeling she was one of them. But she didn't want to be or maybe she was just afraid to be who she was. Before Ace, she'd seen herself as a strong, independent woman. But now she was beginning to see herself as a strong, independent woman who wanted a choice.

But was it really a choice or just a trap? Was this how all women lost themselves? Emotions turning their thoughts to need? And when they acted on that need, succumbed to the temptation of a man's persuasion, when there was no going back, did they regret the choice? If she gave in to her inner urgings, would she end up just one more woman littering the trail of Ace's path through life?

She bit her lip as the wind blew again. This time when a couple approached, she forced herself to keep walking with her chin up and her shoulders back. The man nodded. The woman avoided her gaze. She counted the man's nod as a victory. And felt a bit more herself, but her mind wouldn't quiet, because there was one thing that would tip the balance.

If she was with child, did any of her doubts even matter? She'd chosen to lie down with a man. She'd foolishly disregarded the possible consequences. Did she have a right to foist those consequences upon an innocent child? Then again, was it truly a blessing for a child to be born to parents who were unhappy with each other?

Who said they had to be unhappy?

Oh, why did these thoughts persist?

She didn't know what to make of any of it. Her mind was chaos. Her soul was aching. And all she wanted was Ace. She hadn't seen him since the day they'd put up the Christmas tree—the tree that was supposed to represent all that hope, yet hers had just come to a screeching halt. She wasn't even sure who to blame for that. Ace, because she'd wanted him to pursue her despite her rejection or herself because she wanted what she shouldn't have. The man had made his intentions clear. She'd turned him down. For anyone that would be the end of it. It was only in her mixed-up mind that it should be a beginning.

Rubbing her forehead, she only knew one thing that could help calm her nerves. She needed a cinnamon roll.

She was across the street before she saw who was coming up the walk toward her. Wonderful. Her day only needed this. Brian Winter. Instinct said *run.* Pride said *no way in heck.* No matter how unpleasant this encounter, she wasn't running from it. As he got a little closer, she could see the smirk on his face. This wasn't going to be pleasant.

He hated her, and she had a hefty dislike for him. He'd gotten brave since her kidnapping. Even trying to come around and see Terrance. Hester had greeted him with the shotgun. It'd dissuaded him somewhat. But he'd turned his frustration onto her. Hester told her to tell Ace, but Petunia couldn't go running to the man every time she had a problem. She had to learn to make her own way. Which didn't mean she was foolish. She'd accepted a gun from Hester. She kept it in her pocket next to the letter she'd written to her father asking for help but wouldn't allow herself to send. The gun wasn't big, but it would do the job. Patting it through the material, she forced a smile. She'd shoot the bastard if she had to.

But she wasn't of a mind to shoot anyone today, and she really didn't want to hear any of his venom. The mercantile stood between them. She quickened her pace, hoping to get to the door first. If she ducked inside he'd move on, and she'd be spared his comments for another day. But his legs were longer and he got there ahead of her. Leaning up against the doorjamb, he waited. For one heartbeat, she considered turning back, but his arrogant, know-it-all grin ticked her off. She'd be damned if she'd run from the likes of him.

Lifting her chin, she kept calmly walking, daring him with every step to say something. It was a mistake. Her father used to tell her *Never dare a fool*. And Brian Winter was a huge fool on his best day. Today was no different. As soon as she got close enough for her destination to be clear, he shifted his position so she wouldn't be able to get through the mercantile door without brushing up against him indecently.

"Well, well, well. Look what we have here."

With no other choice, she was forced to stand there clutching her reticule. "Excuse me."

That smirk of his broadened. "The way I hear it, there's a whole lotta people whose pardon you should be begging." He hitched up his pants. "Acting all high-and-mighty, like butter wouldn't melt in your mouth, but you're nothing more than a Comanche whore."

She hadn't expected nice, but she hadn't expected such an open insult. In a chilling rush, the blood drained from her face, leaving her cheeks cold and her hands shaking. She'd suffered a lot of slights over the past week, but no one had dared confront her. But she had dared a fool, and there was a price to pay for that.

Counting to three, she steadied her breath and said in the calmest voice she could muster, "You really are lacking in common decency, aren't you?"

"Why? Because I call a spade a spade?"

"Because you don't have the sense God gave a gnat."

He leaned in. "I've got enough sense to see through you."

His breath hit her like a blow. "I wish you had the sense to brush your teeth." She waved her hand in front of her face. "You stink of liquor."

"And you stink of Comanche."

"If that offends you, then maybe you'd do well to stay away."

"Or maybe you need to spend some time with someone else." He leered suggestively.

"I presume you mean yourself?"

He leaned a little closer. The stench of stale sweat joined the stench of liquor. "Why not?"

Because you're an idiot. A drunk and a brute. It wouldn't be wise to say that, but she wanted to. Oh, dear heavens, she wanted to. Gritting her back teeth on the impulse, she made to duck under his arm. Before she could complete the move, he slammed his hand across the doorjamb, blocking her way. It was a bold move. It was a public move. It said more than anything else that he had no fear of repercussions. She should have been afraid. She slipped her hand in her pocket.

"Move your arm."

"Give me a kiss."

She eyed the fourth button down on his pants. If he pushed her, that's where she was aiming her gun. She doubted it would be a lethal shot, but she bet it would be memorable. "We're standing in the middle of the street."

His eyebrows went up. Excitement tightened his voice. He truly was disgusting. "Are you saying you'd give me one if it were private?"

"I'm saying you're an obnoxious boor to proposition a good woman in the middle of the street."

His tone deepened. "But you're not a good woman, are you? How many was it?" He was so close she could see the food particles stuck in his crooked lower teeth. "I heard tell it was upward of twenty."

She changed her mind. She was shooting him right in his filthy mouth. She said in her best schoolmarm voice, the one that always worked before, "It wouldn't matter if I had willingly and eagerly laid down for an entire battalion, your behavior right now is unacceptable."

A bluff backed by years of social respect. Brian didn't even bat an eyelash. A glance down the street showed many onlookers, but no one willing to help her. She was clearly on her own.

"As I said, you're not one to be preaching about proper behavior."

She couldn't take his stench much longer without losing her breakfast.

"It makes me sick to think about my poor little boy stuck over at the house with you," he went on. "No tell-

ing what shenanigans you get up to at night. What he's
been forced to see." He paused and then added, "Maybe
even forced to do."

That was it. She was done. "You are a disgusting toad,
and next time Ace or Luke gets a notion to shoot you,
I'm going to cheer them on."

"The hell you will."

The hell she wouldn't. Shoving against his arm, she
tried to force her way by. He defeated her with the simple downward movement of his arm. It took everything
in her to suppress a gasp. She wasn't used to this level
of disrespect. Harder still to realize no one was going to
come to her aid. She took a step backward, closing her
hand around the butt of the derringer. When Hester had
given it to her, it'd felt like a hefty piece of weaponry,
but now it felt woefully inadequate. Common sense said
at this range a bullet was a bullet, but emotion wasn't
logical. And right now one of those big old buffalo guns
would suit her just fine. The man wasn't just stupid, he
was dangerous in a rabid animal sort of way. One had
to move carefully around a rabid animal. They couldn't
be trusted.

Reluctantly letting go of the derringer, she slowly took
her hand out of her pocket. With the same deliberate con-
centration, she rubbed her hands together in front of her,
gathering her strength. Then, before Brian knew what
she was doing, she punched the heel of her hand into the
inside of his elbow. His hand dropped.

"What the—"

Before he could complete the sentence, she pushed
hard against his chest. In the second he was off balance,
she shoved past him and into the relative safety of the
store. Blinking against sun blindness, she felt for the

corner counter that defined the center aisle. Through a combination of touch and squint, she followed it straight back until the haberdashery counter gave her no option but to stop. Heart pounding, she leaned against the glass display. Around her, bright ribbons, shiny buttons and colorful threads filled the space with a cheery presence. Pretending an interest in ribbons she didn't really have, she watched out of the corner of her eye to see if Brian would follow her inside. Her heart stuck in her throat as he put both hands on the doorjamb and leaned, in trying to see through the dimness. He slammed the jamb in frustration.

"This isn't over, teacher," he threatened, before taking a step back. "I want my boy back."

He could want until the cows came home. As long as there was fight left in her, Terrance was staying safe. After another futile glare around the store, Brian left. It wasn't until she couldn't hear his boot steps anymore that she turned and leaned back against the counter. Closing her eyes, she let the fear drain.

Fumbling beneath her cape, she took her hankie out and dabbed at her cheeks. She would never let that brute have access to Terrance. He could come bearing court orders with a judge in tow, and she wasn't going to let it happen. Terrance was just a child. If Brian scared her, what must he do to a boy helpless under his care? How many times had Terrance hidden in a dark corner like she'd hidden in the mercantile, hoping and praying his father wouldn't find him? How many times had those prayers failed? How many times would they fail again?

She licked her dry lips. It was too easy to imagine exactly how he'd felt, because she was feeling it now. And it had her legs shaking and her breath soughing in and out of her lungs. A movement out of the corner of her eye caught her attention. If she trusted her legs, she would have walked over. As it was, she settled for turning her head. Mr. Orvis, the shopkeeper, was behind the grocery-laden counter, one of his hands out of sight. Two smartly yet plainly dressed women stood before him.

"You all right, Miss Wayfield?" he asked, catching her eye.

Picking up a red velvet ribbon, she pretended to study its quality. "I'm fine, thank you."

It wasn't a complete lie. She would be in a moment.

After a glance at the door, he brought both hands up to the counter and started packing the groceries into a box. The women, ranchers' wives she saw in town infrequently, looked between Mr. Orvis and her, then at each other. "We'll be back later for our purchases, Mr. Orvis, when you get things—" another look at Petunia "—cleaned up in here."

It was an insult pure and simple, and as the women swished out, spines straight, it stung. Petunia knew it shouldn't—she knew the truth—but it did.

"I'm sorry about that, Miss Wayfield," Michael said with a sigh, continuing to pack the groceries. "Some people have more money than manners."

She forced a smile and put the ribbon back on the spindle. "I hope I'm not driving away customers by frequenting your establishment."

Mr. Orvis smiled and put a pack of sugar into the box. "Not a chance of that. There isn't another mercantile around for fifty miles. If their tail gets too much into a twist, they can order from the catalog, but—" his smile took on a conspiratorial edge "—they'd still have to place that order through me."

Because he was also the post office. "I still appreciate the support."

"You taught my Milly her letters after the last teacher said it was impossible. I'll not be forgetting that."

"Nothing is impossible."

"That's a good motto to live by."

Yes. It was. "All the same, thank you."

She wandered away from the haberdashery, no clear direction in mind. Still too nervous to leave.

"Do you need help with something?"

The letter in her pocket rustled. Did she want to send it?

There would be no turning back if she did. Her father would come for her or send someone. They would sweep her up and carry her off just like a princess in the fairy tale and install her back in her tower. Her father would pull the drawbridge, summon the Prince Charming of his dreams and for the rest of her life, she would plod down the path he laid out.

She rubbed her fingertips over the envelope in her pocket. She had to make a choice. Brian Winter was gone for now, but he'd be back. Ace was gone, but he'd be back. But for right now, everything was calm.

"No, I don't think so."

He motioned with his chin. "I can give you some of that ribbon for two cents a yard."

"That's very generous." But without her teacher's salary, her money was very tight. Another worry to add to the pile. She smiled politely. "Maybe another time."

"All right, then, another time." He moved the box aside. "Anything else?"

With the box gone, the jars filled with sweets took prominence. She thought of Terrance, Brenda and Phil lip and the start she'd wanted to give them. Guilt stabbed deep. "I could use three sticks of that maple sugar candy you got in."

Her funds might be low, but she could afford that.

"Always thinking of the children, aren't you?"

"I try."

He tore off some paper in which to wrap the candy. "For what it's worth, Miss Wayfield, I don't think it's right you can't get your job back. This town was darn lucky the day you were robbed and had to stay in Simple, if you don't mind my saying. It's not easy getting a teacher in here at all, let alone one who cares more about the children than finding a husband."

"I'm sure your next teacher will care."

"Well, until we find one it's old maid Chester who's filling in again."

"Oh, dear."

"Exactly. She's the one who told me my Milly was too stupid to learn her letters."

"Milly's not stupid."

In two folds he had the candy secure. "I know it, but she had Milly and every kid in town believing it."

Oh, she was well aware of that! Petunia didn't know what was wrong with Milly's mind. Things got confused from the page to her brain, but she wasn't stupid. She clutched the candy.

"I contacted a very learned man in Boston about her situation. I had hoped to have a response by now, but…" She sighed. "The mail is so uncertain."

"What will my Milly do now that you're gone?"

"You'll just have to work with her yourself."

"I'm not a teacher, ma'am." He handed over the candy. "I wouldn't even know where to start."

She took the package from him. "At the beginning."

"She was so proud when she learned to write the letter *A*."

"It was a big day." She smiled, remembering that moment. The child had practiced laboriously for a week to get that letter right.

He spat. "She won't even go in that building now."

This was news to Petunia. "But she must! She's come so far."

Mr. Orvis shook his head. "She won't, and I can't see where there's a point with prune face Chester riding roughshod over that class."

She clutched the candy. "You can't let her give up."

Both of his hands flattened on the counter. "You have."

"I certainly have not. My situation changed."

"I understand the difficulties, but bottom line, ma'am, when you tucked your tail between your legs and gave up without even a fight, you left a lot of children holding the bag."

Including his daughter. "It was never my intention to stay."

"We all know you intend to go to California and help a bunch of children you don't know."

Taking her coin out of her reticule, she held it out. "Then I don't understand the problem."

He waved away her money. "We kind of hoped you'd come to the conclusion our children mattered just as much."

Petunia didn't know what to say to that. It was all a moot point. "Whether I wanted to stay or not is neither here nor there now, is it? A woman with my sullied reputation won't be allowed around the children. The school board was quite clear on that in the letter they sent me refusing my request for reinstatement."

He huffed. "As if those who come out here from the East don't have a skeleton in the closet."

"What makes you think that?"

"Why else would they choose the hardship of Texas over the ease of living back East?"

He had a point. She could only shrug. "It's easier to ignore a skeleton you haven't had a peek at than the one that jumped right out and yelled, 'Boo.'"

He frowned. "Yeah, but it's still not right."

No it wasn't. Neither was it fair for him to taunt her with the impossible. "Thank you for the candy." She held up the package. "The children will enjoy it."

With a sigh he nodded. "You're welcome. And Miss Wayfield?"

"Yes?"

"Don't be a stranger."

FOUR LITTLE WORDS, but they echoed in Petunia's mind, lingered down in her spirit, and lifted her mood. More so than any cinnamon roll ever could.

Don't be a stranger.

As she headed back home, Petunia wondered if Mr. Orvis knew how much those four words meant to her. How much his praise meant and his continued faith in her shored up her faltering courage. Ever since she'd landed in Simple, the convictions of her lifetime had been shifting. Her abduction had rattled them around good, shattering a few and straining some others. But in the middle of that hell, she'd also found the parts of her that mattered. She'd grabbed a piece of victory from chaos. She'd come out of the flames of hell stronger and more determined.

But not alone. The little voice inside insisted on being heard. *You didn't come out alone.*

No, she hadn't. Ace and Luke had saved her. Ace had balanced her. Hester and Maddie had given her acceptance. Luisa had given her comfort. She'd thought that was the end of it, but now Mr. Orvis had offered a hand, too. And well, she shook her head, wrestling with the potential of that. Did that mean everyone in town didn't condemn her? Was that even possible?

Stepping down off the walk, she crossed the alley. It was amazing how much difference one offer of friendship during bad times made in a person's outlook. It was a hard-earned lesson, and one she wouldn't soon be forgetting.

Hefting up her skirt hem, she attempted to climb up the other side. An effort that would be easier if the town would settle on one height for these sidewalks rather than experimenting with different ones. But that was just part of the charm and growth of Simple. Everyone had an opinion. Every decision spurred an argument. And every argument resulted in the process of solving it being recorded. It was, when she thought about it, a unique way of reserving one's spot in history.

The scent of tobacco drifted over. With one foot on the sidewalk, the other firmly planted in the dirt, she looked down the alley. There, halfway down, Brian stood, hat pushed back, leaning against the building, one knee bent with his foot braced against the wall. He could have been doing anything, but as he smiled around the smoke clenched in his teeth, she knew he'd been waiting. For her.

Again that cold, sick gathering of fear in her gut, only this time it wasn't so easy to push it aside. *Rabid-skunk crazy*—her father's phrase for the cleverly insane—jumped into her head. The man was rabid-skunk crazy. She couldn't look away from his eyes, his smile or the threat contained in both.

"Are you going to stand there all day, or are you going to take my hand?"

She'd know that calm, even drawl anywhere. *Ace.* He was back and standing on the walk before her. A big broad-shouldered, lean-hipped silhouette backlit by the sun. Calm. Strength. Safety. Ace.

Petunia not only took his hand, she practically jumped into his arms, too.

CHAPTER SEVENTEEN

ACE CAUGHT HER EASILY, his arms closing around her back. He smelled faintly of wool, coffee and just, well, him. His heavy coat cushioned her landing. Her cape swirled about her legs. She took another breath, inhaling him as best she could, blatantly cleansing her sensory palate. Sunshine and earthy potential. That was Ace. Balance and peace simmering with dark excitement.

His voice rumbled by her ear. "I would have helped you, if you'd let me."

She shook her head, clinging to him and the illusion of safety he presented a second longer. After the confusion of her thoughts the past hour... "I couldn't wait."

Nothing could have been more true.

His finger under her chin lifted her face to his gaze. Beneath the brim of his hat, his eyes narrowed. "We'll have to work on your impatience."

"Or we could just let this time slide."

His brow lowered. "Any particular reason this time is special?"

She leaned against him, shamelessly extending this moment where the world was balanced. "None that matter now."

Hopefully, her smile didn't look as forced as it felt. The last thing she needed was for Ace to see Brian and jump to conclusions. She wasn't up for a fight right now.

She was too aware of how it could look, Brian being in the alley and her lingering in the entrance. Either way would set Ace off and right now she just wanted…she took another breath…this.

Over Ace's shoulder, she saw Luke's familiar gray eyes and easy smile. She'd been so wrapped up in Ace, she hadn't even seen his friend standing there. The way he touched the brim of his hat in an informal salute was a warning. Her breathing deepened as he walked around her and Ace. It caught as he leaned back to look down the alley. Breathing stopped altogether when his brow cocked up. Was Brian still there? Had Ace seen him? His expression was deadpan in response to her frown. She bit her lip. He pushed his hat off his forehead and leaned back against the wall. But he didn't say a word. She let her breath out in uneasy relief.

"I stopped by the house," Ace said. "Hester said you were off in search of cinnamon buns."

"You stopped by the house?"

He shrugged. "The school. Providence. Whatever you want to call it."

"It is a school. And a house." She stepped back, everything in her protesting the distance. Propriety gave her no choice. "You're correct with either."

He let her go in gradual increments. Shoulder, arm, hand and then the starkness of freedom. His smile didn't fool her probably any more than hers fooled him. He was studying her. She kept her smile steady. "It's looking good with that new paint."

They'd been dressing up the place one room at a time. The colors were far bolder than she would have chosen. She shifted her stance, renewing her balance. "I thought the colors were a bit bright, but Maddie said the house lacked a smile."

"Nothing a child needs more than a smile," Luke interjected from where he lounged.

Who could argue with that? But she still missed the soothing tones of her home. Bright yellow in the parlor was just jarring. But there was no denying the children's pleasure in the choosing and the results. "Yes. And with all that color it should be a very big one."

Luke smiled. He had a nice smile with just the slightest unevenness that gave him a charming boyish appeal, totally ruined when one's gaze dropped to his gun belt and the weapons attached there. "I heard Brenda has a bright pink in mind for her room."

She sighed. "I'm afraid it's a done deal as soon as Mr. Orvis finds the paint color."

Her campaign for soothing tones was definitely dead.

Ace chuckled. "She'll change her mind in a few years."

"I somehow doubt the color choices will get better."

"You don't like them?"

She straightened her cape. If only it was that easy to straighten her composure. "I prefer something more… soothing."

"And elegant?"

She avoided his gaze. "Liking harmony isn't reprehensible."

"No, it isn't." His grip switched to her elbow. "Did you get that cinnamon roll yet?"

"I got distracted." Out of the corner of her eye, she could see Luke's eyebrow raise. The urge to shake her head at him to keep quiet was strong.

"I heard tell Maddie just pulled a fresh batch out of the oven," Ace murmured, his fingers stroking so lightly on the inside of her elbow, she couldn't think of anything else.

"You're trying to entice me."

His head cocked to the side, and the corner of his mouth kicked up in the slightest of smiles. "I'm doing my best."

Her mouth watered. He'd smiled at her just like that while they'd been making love. A teasing, purely masculine smile that slipped beneath her defenses and found everything feminine within her and sparked a response.

"Did she really make them this late in the day?"

"Yup."

The pressure of his fingers through her sleeve was light. But with every second that passed she became more aware of each individual digit of the pressure of the imagined heat. She looked up at him, liking the way the sun warmed his eyes. "You wouldn't have anything to do with that, would you?"

"Or maybe Maddie just took a notion to make a fresh batch of rolls."

It was possible. It was also possible that Maddie had made the rolls especially for her. Ever since her attack, her friends seemed to think food should be her solace. To the point her dresses were getting too tight, and her curves a bit more amplified. She wished it were possible to touch that curve of his lips. To steal that smile for herself, to keep it and the feelings it inspired within her forever. "Anything is possible."

Ace glanced up. "You coming, Luke?"

Luke smiled that easy smile of his. "Not right now. I've got something to do."

"Need any help with that?" Ace asked too enigmatically for Petunia's peace of mind.

"Nah." Luke tugged his hat down. "Just going to spread a little Christmas cheer."

Ace's grip on her elbow tightened imperceptibly. Petunia got that sinking feeling in her gut. She'd seen how men were when it came to women with a sullied reputation. Things that before were unthinkable in regard to a woman suddenly became plausible. She found it hard to believe that anyone would believe that she would meet Brian in the alley, but there were very few options open to a tarnished woman for employment. Most of them relied upon the generosity of a man. Now, common sense would say Brian didn't have a pot to spit in, but she'd found through her experience in life and work that where speculation flourished, common sense often held no place.

He paused, looked at Luke. Then at her. Before she knew what he was doing, he glanced down the alley. His breath drew in. His brows snapped down when he studied her face.

Her smile faltered.

"Son of a bitch."

She would have fallen if Luke hadn't caught her, so strong was her fear.

Ace propped her against the wall with a "Stay put" before turning back to Luke. "Why do I get the feeling you were going to spread that cheer without me?"

"My gift to you."

"Uh-huh."

"Ace, it's not—"

"I know exactly what it is." He stepped down off the walk, stopped and turned back. "Did he touch you?"

She shook her head. "Just blocked my way and said—"

"I can guess what he said."

"But—"

She started to follow to do what she didn't know. Stop Brian from spewing his filth, stop Ace from hearing it…

"Don't." Luke caught her arm. "It's his right."

Brian, the fool, didn't even have the sense to run. The fight was short. Bloody and vicious. Brian landed one blow before Ace flattened him with a right to the face.

"That cost him some teeth," Luke observed, not sharing her disquiet at all.

Her stomach heaved when Ace dodged Brian's kick and grabbed his arm. Dropping to his knee he bent the appendage over his thigh.

"He's not going to…"

In the next breath there was a crack, and Brian screamed. Ace had broken his arm.

"I'm going to be sick."

Luke put an arm around her waist and guided her over the edge of the walk. "The bastard knew what he was inviting when he touched what belongs to Ace."

Her stomach heaved but wouldn't empty. "He's a fool," she gasped.

"A fool who won't be insulting you again."

She wiggled out of Luke's grasp. "All done being queasy?"

"I hope so."

"Me, too. Puke's a bitch to get out of leather."

"You were worried about your boots?"

With the slightest of smiles, he nodded. "Yup. Look lively now, here comes Ace."

She tried, but from the look on Ace's face, she didn't succeed.

"You all right?" he asked, stepping up on the walk beside her.

He wasn't even winded. "Yes."

"If he bothers you again, you tell me immediately."

There wasn't anything else to say but "All right."

"You two go on and get that sweet roll." Luke tipped his head in the direction of the alley. "I'll clean up this mess."

Luke's casual tone put a chill down Petunia's spine. Ace tucked her hand into the crook of his elbow. "He's not going to kill him."

Luke smiled and tipped his hat. "I have a rule against murder before dark."

Was she supposed to believe that? "I would hope so."

With subtle pressure on her arm, Ace guided her down the walk.

Guided, Petunia realized. Not forced. Protected. Not exposed. It was an oddly sheltered feeling to have for a woman who'd grown up under the umbrella of her father's money and influence. But this was different. This was personal in a way that went beyond her experience. And landed straight in her long-denied expectations, she admitted. Every woman wanted a man who could hold her safe. Every woman felt they had to behave a certain way to make that happen. For her that had always been impossible. But with Ace… She sighed to herself. With Ace she got to be someone else. She simply got to be herself.

His grip tightened subtly in a warning when they approached a rough part of the walk. She always liked that about Ace. He had a way of controlling any moment in a way that allowed her to relax. Like she was now. For no reason. The man with whom she was feeling so safe was also the man who'd disappeared for the past week without a word.

Using the next gust of wind as an excuse, she freed herself from his grip to smooth her hand over her hair. She looked up at him. She wanted to ask where he'd been. She wanted to not have it matter.

"Why this sudden urge for my company?"

His brow cocked up. "What makes you think I was ever without it?"

She hated how he answered a question with a question. "I haven't seen you for a week."

A very long week in which his parting words had teased and titillated her desire and festered in her insecurity.

You've simply been waiting for the one man who can make you burn.

Who said that to a woman and then just ran off for a week? A week in which she'd found herself watching the door and then the street out the window, looking for him. Waiting for him to act upon that ever so subtle threat. The letter in her pocket rustled. She should have mailed it a week ago when the school board turned down her request for reinstatement. But standing here in the street and looking at Ace she knew why she hadn't. She'd been hoping for just this moment. For him to notice she still existed. For him to see her standing on her own against the tide. For him to see her again as strong. Lord, she was becoming pathetic.

"Then you'd be leaping to assumptions."

He caught her elbow again.

"I got a telegram from Caine relating to some activity around a claim that was filed recently," Ace explained. "Luke and I had to check it out."

"Assayers check out claims?"

"This one does."

She didn't know whether to believe him or not. "I see."

It didn't explain why he hadn't said goodbye.

He shook his head. "Sometimes I wonder what you *do* see."

The bakery was only half a block away. There were a few people out and about. Petunia could feel the stares like weights on her feet, imagined the speculation. She kept her gaze straight ahead. "I see a man who doesn't feel he owes me an explanation."

"It came up sudden."

Ace shortened his steps to match hers. Their boot steps fell in tandem, the sound blending together. It was a seductive way to look at them. A silly way. Ace was who he was. A gambler. A lawman. A womanizer. She remembered him pinning her hands above her head, kissing her as his hard body pressed against her, holding her where he wanted her, as he wanted her… And mostly, she remembered the thrilling joy that reveled deep inside when he did.

She pushed the envelope deeper in her pocket. "Well, I'm happy that something occupied your time beyond loose women and gambling, but I'm not a toy you can pick up and put down on a whim. Nor am I a child to be appeased by a sweet treat."

He brought her hand to his lips. "Never thought you were."

It was a bold move. It was an Ace move. And she couldn't find it within herself to resent it. "Uh-huh."

"It really bothered you I left, huh?"

"Only for a minute, so you can stop your smiling."

They reached the bakery. The sweet scent wrapped around them. "That minute's got me fair optimistic."

"Oh, please."

With a chuckle, he reached around and opened the door. The little bell jangled. Maddie appeared from the back room. The polite smile of greeting on her face widened when she saw them together.

Before she could get the wrong idea, Petunia shook her head. "It's not what you think."

"It's everything you think," Ace countered.

Maddie tilted her head to the side. From the sparkle in her eyes, it was already too late for a protest to take hold.

Petunia blew out an exasperated breath. "I will not be with a man out of guilt."

"Good," Ace retorted, "because I wouldn't want a woman for anything less than passion."

"I don't—"

It was Maddie who interrupted. "No sense finishing that sentence. There's no one in this room that will believe it."

"You don't even know what I was going to say."

Maddie shook her head and put a cinnamon bun in a piece of brown paper and pushed it across the counter. "I know it was going to be something stupid."

"What makes you so sure?"

With a jerk of her chin that sent the curls escaping her braid bobbing around her face, Maddie indicated Ace. "That knowing smile of his."

Petunia turned, and Ace was indeed still smiling. It did funny things to her insides. "Stop it."

His thumb slid across the back of her hand. "You don't give me orders."

The tingles started immediately, blending with the warmth of his touch.

She tugged at her hand. "You need to go away."

He turned back, roll in hand, fragrant and rich. Dangling temptation just a few inches away. "I already did, and it wasn't to your liking."

"I could develop a taste for it…"

It was his turn to say, "Uh-huh."

Maddie wrapped up another roll. "You want one, Ace?"

"No, thank you, Maddie. We'll share."

Oh, no, they wouldn't. "I don't share my cinnamon buns."

He shook his head. "Always so quick with the no and so lacking in the trust."

"I do not lack trust."

His "mmm-hmm" made her want to smack him. "Hold out your hand."

If it had been anything other than a cinnamon roll, anyone other than *him*, she wouldn't have obeyed. But it was him and it was a cinnamon roll, so… She grudgingly stuck out her hand.

He placed the roll in it with an air of satisfaction that should have annoyed, but didn't. "Good girl."

A shiver went down her spine. "You are a most impossible man."

"I prefer to think of myself as a most *possible* man."

He was that. She eyed him from head to toe, taking in the breadth of his shoulders, the narrowness of his hips, the scuffed toes of his boots. Gamblers were supposed to be smooth and fashionable. Ace was rugged and hard. Compelling. Openly sexual. She remembered that night. Infinitely satisfying.

Breaking off a piece of the roll, he held it up to her lips, brushing the treat against the soft surface. Desire whipped through her as lightning shot from his fingertips. Within her the storm built. She was always such flotsam to his desire.

"Open your mouth." She did, hopelessly, helplessly, willingly. Sweetness and desire flowed over her tongue.

His fingers lingered then withdrew. Slowly. Pleasure filled her. Cinnamon. And man. The flavors mingled. And then there was the sweet aftermath of the glaze. Her knees quivered. She couldn't look away. She was in so much trouble.

"I'll wrap a few of these for you to take back," Maddie said.

"Thank you, Maddie."

Petunia glanced up, only to find him watching her with a gaze so hot her toes curled in her ever so proper shoes. Her appreciation was a barely audible, "Yes, thank you."

"You're both very welcome."

The curtains rustled as Maddie left the room. They were alone. Catching her hand, Ace pulled her close. Hip to hip, chest to chest. The clothing that should have been protection was an annoying barrier. His arms came around her. A haven within the chaos of emotion she didn't know how to handle. She stood there awkwardly, holding the cinnamon roll to the side.

Ace didn't seem to expect her to do anything with the energy pulsing between them. He just held her there in that shop, for that moment, the only privacy provided by the time of day and the half curtains covering the window. And just…held her while her fretting turned to wonder and wonder to confusion.

Resting her forehead against his chest, she whispered, "I don't know what you want from me."

It was another one of those betrayals she couldn't contain.

His lips brushed her cheek. The shadow cast by his hat provided an illusion of cover. "I want you, exactly as you are. All of you—mind, body and soul."

His voice was low. His touch gentle as he tipped her chin up. The emotion in his eyes surrounded her in a hug she wanted to believe. "I want your surrender."

Another shiver and another realization. He terrified her on a level that went past the physical right to her core. She opened her mouth to say—she didn't know what. His thumb straddled her lips, stealing the impulse. When his hand slid between the frogs on her cloak and cupped her breast, she flinched. She had so little to offer in that department.

"You are a very beautiful woman, Pet." The softness of his tone pulled her gaze up.

"Everything about you is shaped to please."

His hand didn't move; he didn't move. It was as if she realized studying his expression, he, too, needed that connection.

"What do you want from me, Ace?"

He took the roll from her hand, allowing her arms to relax. "Everything you've got to give."

"What if that's too much?"

It was her deepest fear.

"I'd never ask you for more than you had to give."

She believed him. It felt so natural to put her arms around his waist. To cling to him. To breathe deeply of his scent. The heady aroma wafted all around, cocooning her in its comforting embrace, offering as much support as his arms around her back and his heart beating beneath her ear. She shouldn't feel so safe here with the threat of *him* lingering. Because it was a threat. A threat to everything she'd created to believe in. She snuggled tighter against him.

His lips brushed her temple. "Did you truly think I wasn't coming back?"

She shrugged. "You'd had what you wanted."

She felt the shake of his head. "You have no idea what I want."

That was probably true. "Then why don't you tell me?"

"I already have. You're just not listening."

It was another of those explanations that wasn't an explanation.

She shook her head. "I don't understand you."

"Try harder, then."

"I am." As much as she could without actually having to. He stepped away, depriving her of his warmth. His hand lingered on her breast, his thumb pressing against the hard nipple. He smiled and stroked the tight bud. She couldn't suppress her gasp. His smile broadened. "I like that."

"That's just the sin of lust."

"Because between us the only sin is not giving in to the passion."

He said that so persuasively. She found the strength to take a step of her own back. From where she didn't know. The man might be a gambler, but he was also part sorcerer, and whatever spell he'd cast over her bound her will tighter than chains ever could. "That goes against everything I've ever been taught."

She flinched when he reached out. He paused, eyes narrowing. And then slowly took her left hand and put the cinnamon roll in it.

"And what I'm doing goes against all I believe."

"What does?" She tugged her coat closed, that niggling sense of not good enough rising fast. He made her feel like a bug under a magnifying glass.

"Claiming you."

He wanted to claim her? "Why?" Was she too old, too plain, too flat-chested?

"Because you deserve better."

Maybe she did, maybe she didn't. But he was what she wanted.

The thought sent her forward a step. He stood there with all his usual confidence. And yet, somehow, so alone. This time she put her right hand on his chest, over his heart, feeling it beat. Solid and steady. She spread her fingers wide. "Maybe you do, too."

His head tilted to the side; his smile was slow coming, slow finishing. But sincere. "I know what I want. And who."

What was she supposed to do with such honesty?

Nothing, apparently. Ace nodded to the pastry she was still holding. "Ready to share?"

"I'm not sure."

His stomach rumbled. He pulled a pathetic face.

She sighed and shook her head. He wasn't that good with pathetic. "You have no conscience when it comes to getting your way, do you?"

"Not a bit."

She couldn't help it. She chuckled. "Well, just so you know, looking sad isn't your best ploy."

He cocked his head. He did do endearing well. "Does that mean you're not going to share?"

She pretended to consider it hard. "It's a cinnamon roll."

"I saved your life."

She looked up at him under her lashes. "But it's a cinnamon roll."

"I've still got scars." He showed her the darkened scars on his knuckles. She wanted to kiss every one. The ones he got from saving her and the ones he got from saving everyone else. He could have the whole roll if he wanted.

She went to hand it to him. He shook his head. "Tit for tat."

She knew what he wanted. She broke off a piece. Her hand trembled as she held it to his mouth. His lips parted, but his gaze didn't waver. Slipping the pastry between his lips, she gasped as they tickled her fingertips. His tongue came out and rubbed against the sensitive pads. She shivered again and leaned against him. He was just going to have to support them both.

Ace had no problem supporting them, standing steady when she came up on her tiptoes. His breath caressed her fingers. His eyes caressed her face. His chest expanded against hers. She wished she wasn't wearing the heavy cape. Biting her lip, she fed him the next piece, suppressing a moan as he nibbled at her fingers.

His "good girl" drifted through the energy swirling around them, binding them together.

She wanted to be his girl, plain and simple. She wanted to be anything he wanted. She wanted his hand on her breast. She wanted his kiss.

The roll hit the floor with a splat as she asked for it. First with her eyes, then with her hands and lastly with her voice. "Ace?"

"What?"

"Stop fooling around and kiss me."

His smile was pure sex, pure promise. Pure Ace. "Ask me nicely."

"Please."

"That's my girl."

He bent down; she stretched up. His hand cupped her head, pulling her closer, holding her steady. She expected passion, possession, but what she got instead was…tenderness. Sweet, sweet tenderness. And it was so much better than the passion she'd thought she'd needed. But this, this was the balm for which her soul was crying. How had he known? How could he know what she hadn't known herself?

The question formed against his lips. His answer was a low growl and a string of kisses over her cheek, down her neck. "I've got you."

He did. And all she'd asked for was a kiss. He held her for a couple more minutes before murmuring, "Time to go."

"Uh-huh." The little bell jangled as he opened the door. His hand in the small of her back was possessive. It was just pure bad luck that the biggest gossip in town, Matilda Hex, chose just that moment to walk by the shop. In one quick glance she took it all in. Petunia's flushed cheeks, mussed hair, Ace's proprietary manner. Her disapproving frown spoke volumes.

Ace nodded. "Good afternoon, Mrs. Hex."

The sanctimonious biddy huffed and stuck her nose in the air. The snub cut deep. Petunia ducked her head. Ace squeezed her shoulders. It was enough to remind her who she was.

Mrs. Hex made it two steps before Ace drawled softly, "Matilda?"

She turned, her expression stiff and disapproving. "Yes?"

"It would be a mistake to offend Hell's Eight."

Matilda's "I have no idea what you mean," faltered.

"Then let's rectify that." The words were quiet, calm, but they held the intensity of truth. "If one rumor gets back to me about Miss Wayfield, you and yours are going to be on the wrong side of Hell's Eight."

She swallowed hard. "But…"

"No buts." There was steel in his tone. "Miss Wayfield is Hell's Eight." As Matilda looked them up and down he pulled her close, and clarified. "Mine."

It was a threat and an announcement.

Petunia blinked. Matilda retreated on a hasty "Of course."

"You made her run."

"No one hurts what's mine."

"I've never seen Matilda retreat." She watched her hurry away so fast her skirts swirled about her ankles. It was an amazing feat. "I think half the town will be sorry they missed that phenomenon." His grunt brought her back to the present. And to what he'd said. It was her turn to frown. "And I never said I wanted to be yours."

The kiss he pressed on her brow was sympathetic, sweet and comforting. And hotly possessive. Not at all what she expected from Ace.

He squeezed her shoulders. "Pet?"

"Yes?"

"There's something you need to understand."

"What?"

Resting his forehead against hers, he ran his finger down her cheek and smiled. "It's about what I want now. And I'm claiming you."

CHAPTER EIGHTEEN

WELL, MERRY CHRISTMAS to her. Petunia stood on the back porch of Providence, braced against the chill of the wind and Ace's lingering impact on her senses. She could still feel the heat of his body, the pressure of his fingers, the soft caress of his breath. Lord, that man was as addictive as laudanum. He made her want and crave. And run. Lord, he made her run. Leaning against the door, she shook her head. She'd bolted, plain and simple when Ace said he was claiming her. And he'd let her. Why he'd let her go, she didn't know. Why she'd run, that was easier to discern. She felt raw and vulnerable, stripped of her defenses. Open for him to see. To judge. She didn't like being judged.

The scandal of her abduction would never go away completely, but it could get pushed to the back of the gossip stove. As long as nothing new occurred. Ace thought he could accomplish it with glowers and threats, but she knew better. Shredding reputations was a woman's weapon. And women played by their own rules. The Matilda Hexes of the world might murmur sympathetic words to her face, but behind her back, they'd be whispering "Did you knows" and make sure with every spare moment they had that the fire got fed. She was just that kind of person. And that made her a threat. Petunia should care about that. Her future might depend on it.

It's about what I want now. And I'm claiming you.

As insidious as the lingering whisper of his touch, as dangerous as Matilda's proclivity for gossip, Ace's words slipped through her mind. Something else she should care about. His apparent indecision about wanting her. She'd spent years after her mother's death fighting for her father's attention, trying to matter. To finally find her place, ironically only finding it when she pulled away and went her own way. As a child needing him, her father couldn't love her. But as an independent woman marching to her own drum, she'd earned his respect. Now Ace was putting her in that same can't-win place. And she didn't like it. Because she deserved better, had always wanted more. She wanted stability in her life. She wanted love. She wanted children. She wanted to make a difference. None of those things could she have with a gambler. All of those things she could have with Ace. But at a price she already knew she couldn't afford to pay. She'd die inside a little each day giving all to a man who didn't want it. Until one day she'd wake up and there wouldn't be a Petunia anymore. She'd come too far, made herself too strong to go back to that lost place. But she could enjoy what she and Ace had. She just had to convince him to do it on her level.

Shaking her head, she sighed and put her hand on the knob. How had her life become so complicated? Opening the door, she could smell dinner simmering. Stew. She wrinkled her nose. Again. Hester claimed stew was nutritious but Petunia was beginning to believe Hester didn't make it for that reason so much as for the fact it was easy to cook. All it took was tossing the ingredients together, letting them simmer, then thickening the gravy and it was done. Petunia couldn't really complain. She didn't like to cook and besides, Hester made some of the best biscuits to accompany the stew. She really needed to get Hester's recipe before she left.

Stepping into the kitchen Petunia paused and leaned back against the door frame. It felt good to be home. Beyond this room there likely was chaos, but in here, everything was in order. The dishes were put away, and the floor was clean. She felt a trill of satisfaction. The children had done their chores. Such a little thing that happened every day in every home in town. And it was happening here now, too. The children were settling in, finding their place.

Beneath the scent of stew she could smell the aroma of pine. It was a festive, comforting aroma that subtly lifted her mood. The Christmas tree had been a good idea. It gave them all something to focus on besides their worries. Shrugging off her cape, she hung it on a hook by the door and walked through to the parlor. Hester was sitting in the chair by the fire, knitting. Brenda, Terrance and Phillip were playing a game with a spinning top that involved a lot of laughter and cries of foul. Clearly, the rules were being made up as they went, but they weren't fighting. Another Christmas miracle. Hester looked up as she came into the room. "How was your walk?"

"More eventful than I wanted."

"Oh?"

The children looked up.

Petunia smiled at them. "What game are you playing?"

Terrance eyed her in that cautious way of his. "We haven't decided yet."

"I see."

Movement under the wing chair caught her eye. "I thought we agreed Lancelot should stay outside."

"It's cold outside." That was from Brenda.

"He's being good," Terrance chimed in.

"He chews the furniture," she countered.

"I put vinegar on the legs."

Hester, too? "Does that work?"

Hester shrugged. "We're finding out."

The chewing issue solved or not, there was another issue with Lancelot's transformation to house bunny. "That doesn't stop him from—" she waved her hand "—relieving himself everywhere."

"We made him a box."

She looked at Terrance. "Does he know it's for him?"

Terrance scooped up his rabbit that was showing definite signs of plumping up. "He's very smart."

Lancelot wiggled his nose at her and dropped an ear. A piece of greenery dangled from his mouth. She didn't know about smart, but he was cute. She sighed and sat in the other wingback chair next to the fireplace. The heat from the fire swirled around her ankles as she arranged her skirts. "I hope so."

"He can stay?" Phillip asked.

It was the first time Phillip had shown signs of being interested in anything.

Three pairs of eyes focused on her. The needles stopped clacking. The fourth set weighed heaviest. A log in the fire popped. Petunia sighed. She knew when she was beaten.

"Of course he can stay. He's family."

The only one who didn't whoop or smile was Phillip. He stroked Lancelot's head with a quiet intensity that was a relief to see. Until he spoke.

"Yes, he's our family. We have to keep him safe."

Terrance nodded. Brenda frowned, doubled up her fists and jumped to her feet. "I'll sock anyone who tries to hurt him."

She punched the air. Petunia caught her hand, pulling her around. "Has someone threatened Lancelot?" She thought of Brian and couldn't help asking, "Or any of you?"

As one, the children shook their heads no.

"If anyone ever does, you come to me immediately, you hear?" Hester ordered.

All three nodded. Lancelot continued to chew his bit of greenery.

"You hear?" Hester repeated.

"I hear," Phillip said.

Terrance plopped the rabbit in his lap. "It's your turn, Phillip."

And that fast they were back to play. Petunia wished she had that ability to drop her cares so easily.

Hester caught her eye. "Were we ever that carefree?"

"I hope so." She motioned to the brown-and-red scarf. "How's the project coming?"

"I've dropped a stitch or two, but I'm finding the rhythm again." She smiled. "It's been a long time since I knitted."

"It looks beautiful to me." It did. The yarn was a rich earth brown. Hester was working in strands of a deep red giving it depth. It was clearly a scarf meant for a man. "Who is it for?"

"I haven't decided."

A scarf so specifically designed had to have a recipient in mind. "Really?" She took a stab in the dark. "That shade of brown would look good on Luke."

The needles faltered. "I hadn't much thought about it."

Petunia was wise to Hester's ways. "But you have thought *some* on it."

She got a glare for her audacity. "So what happened on your walk?"

Petunia sighed. A quick glance at the kids showed they were more interested in the bag of popcorn waiting to be strung for the tree than they were the adult conversation. Still... "This really isn't the place to discuss it."

"I was thinking a cup of tea would be nice."

Petunia was thinking staying just where she was at was even better. Hester bent on getting information was a force of which the Spanish Inquisition would be proud. Hester gathered up her knitting and set the needles into the thick ball of yarn. Light caught on the wide strip of material.

"That truly is a beautiful pattern."

It wasn't a lie. From what she could see developing, it was a work of art. "Whomever it's for is going to be a happy man."

Hester didn't take the bait. Her kitting settled, Hester headed for the kitchen, calling over her shoulder, "It could be for Ace."

She followed. "If it were, that'd be a waste. I doubt the man leaves the saloon in winter."

Hester poured water into the teapot and set it on the left side of the stove. Grabbing a piece of kindling, she opened the door beneath and slid it in. "You have a strange opinion of that man."

Petunia sighed and got the delicate teacups out of the cupboard. The special porcelain cups were dainty and more fragile than the more traditional mugs. Using them made her feel more feminine. The same way being in

Ace's arms did. She huffed the thought away. Making a big to-do over nothing was not going to help her stay on her course. The man probably flirted with everyone like that.

"So what has he done to upset you today?"

Teased her with his scent, his breath, his kiss. The man made her knees buckle with just the touch of his finger under her chin. And when he started whispering intimate orders… "He likes to make me feel weak."

Hester shook her head and set the tea can on the counter with a thump. "Have you ever been courted by a man?"

"Of course."

"Are we talking a few sad examples back East that squeaked in a hello between your social causes and charity meetings?"

That was too close to the truth for comfort. "It's not a sin to have a higher purpose."

"It's a sin to deny you're a woman. Or worse, run away from it."

Petunia snorted. "Says the woman hiding out here."

"I'm not hiding." Hester took a seat. "I'm here in Simple ruining my reputation in plain sight."

"Why?"

She sighed. "One, because I have nowhere else to go, but also, I think there's a part of me that hopes Dougall will wake up and realize that while he doesn't have to be a husband, he can still be a father." She pulled one of the cups and saucers closer. "My children need their father."

"Even if he's a no-account?"

"The man I married wasn't." She shook her head and frowned. "Somewhere along the way between home and here, that person got lost."

"And you hope he'll come back to you?"

"No. Not that. There's no erasing what either of us have done, but I hope Dougall will come back to his children. They're his blood, his legacy. They're worth whatever amount of forgiveness we both have to find to make their lives good."

The one thing a Wayfield understood was a legacy. "So you stay here."

Hester nodded. "And hope."

Petunia understood that, too. "I admit I had my qualms when you applied for this job, but your being here has been a blessing. You're a very capable woman."

"Thank you. It makes it easier living with my…" A wave of her hand encompassed her past and brought it forward.

It irritated Petunia that she felt the need to apologize. "You've done nothing to be ashamed of."

Hester looked at her like she'd lost her mind. "I married a man that abandoned me, divorced me and then I became a whore. That's not a lot to be proud of."

"The law and your husband gave you no choice."

"There's always a choice. Didn't I hear you say that before?"

Why was everyone making her eat her words today? "When the choice is either to watch your children starve or sell your body, there's really not a choice." She pulled open the tea lid and measured the tea into the metal ball infuser. "But there should be."

"It would have been easier if Dougall had wanted his children."

"But he didn't."

Hester shook her head. "It would have ruined everything he'd built here. His lies hog-tied him."

"And that's why Phillip and Brenda don't ask about him and play along?"

Hester sighed. The kettle rattled on the stove. "They hope, too."

It was an impossible situation. "I can't imagine how they feel."

"Neither can I, but I know I thank God for you getting stuck here."

"God had less to do with that than a skilled pickpocket and my own carelessness."

Hester pushed her chair back. "God works in mysterious ways."

Petunia hated that quote. "I for one would appreciate more efficacy and less mystery."

Hester shook her head and picked up the kettle. "That's blasphemy."

Maybe. "It's the truth." Dropping the tea ball into the brightly painted pot, she pushed it toward Hester's side of the table. "I've been fighting for years and nothing's changed."

Hester turned. "I find that hard to believe."

"Believe it. Women don't have the vote. They can't own squat and even their dreams float on a man's whim."

And she was so frustrated by that she could just spit.

Hester poured the boiling water into the pot. "But progress has been made."

"Where? I'm almost thirty, Christmas is a week away and I don't have the money for even the smallest of gifts thanks to an event I couldn't control. A week after that it'll be 1861 and everything will be the same as it was in 1860."

Just another year and another unmet dream.

Hester dropped the lid on the pot with an angry clink.

"Not for Terrance. Not for Ace. Not for me or my children. For all of us, 1861 is looking pretty damn good."

But it didn't for her. "I had such plans." Petunia shoved her hair back from her face. "I shouldn't even be here. I should be in San Francisco."

"Maybe you should and maybe you shouldn't." The kettle landed on the table with a solid *thunk*. "Or maybe you're just so stuck on making a citizen of the year difference." At her surprised look, Hester nodded. "Oh, yes, I know all about those dinners where all the highfalutin folk get their pats on the backs. I was wait service at a few. I wasn't always trash, you know."

"I never said you were."

"No, you just assumed." Her voice was carefully hushed. "You do that a heck of a lot. Like you do with Ace, and me and people in general. You might have a ton of book learning but what you need is people learning. Maybe if you had that you'd stop being so damn blind and see what you've accomplished here in Simple."

"I—"

Hester cut her off with a wave of her hand. "This may be a backwater town and we might be backwater people of little note in the society pages, but damn it, we matter. You're the only reason we matter to all the narrow-minded folk in this town. And in some ways to ourselves. But you take that kind of knowing for granted." She stabbed her finger at her. "And now you're going to up and leave, move on to more important folk, letting all that's started here crumble."

"I'm not—"

Again she was cut off. Face flushed and eyes narrowed, Hester continued, "Don't give me that hogwash about how you've set it up to go on. Without you here to keep this moving and people motivated, Providence will just fall apart. But that's all right. You won't be here to see it, and once you get on that stagecoach, we won't matter."

To Petunia's horror, the ever so strong Hester, the woman who always did what was necessary with gruff efficiency, the one who'd taken on Brian Winter without a quibble, broke down in a sob. Covering her mouth quickly as if to snatch the sound back, Hester turned away.

Left staring at her back, Petunia didn't know what to do. She'd never seen Hester flustered, let alone crying. She wanted to reach out, touch her. Apologize. Explain... something. "I don't know what to say."

Hester didn't turn around. She just squared her shoulders.

"There's nothing to say. You are who you are."

Anger bit into Petunia's shock. Hester made it sound as if she'd done something wrong. "And what's that?"

"Someone who should be ashamed."

PETUNIA SAT AT the table a good fifteen minutes after Hester left. Part of her expected the other woman to come back and apologize. Her attack had been unwarranted. Petunia hadn't done anything but take care of everyone here. Doing what she could in the time she'd had available to fix things, but not once had she lied. It'd never been her intent to stay. It'd never been her intent to actually set up the school, but once here, she couldn't ignore the need. What had Hester wanted her to do? Leave Terrance to his father's beatings? Pretend Hester's own situation hadn't been in need of repair? She'd seen this all her life, over and over, town to town, time after time.

Women trapped in impossible situations, locked in by the
law and society's inequities. Children, victims of their
parents' frustrations, beaten and abused, left in ignorance. It was a huge problem affecting every single person in this nation. The letter to her father pressed into
her leg as she shifted positions. Taking it out, she set it on
the table. Her father's address stared back at her boldly.
Anyone who hadn't grown up in the East wouldn't recognize the name. Here he was just nothing. Just as she
was. Here she wasn't hampered by his expectations, nor
by men pretending to understand her cause in an effort
to gain access to her father's fortune. She couldn't expect
Hester to understand that freedom, though. For all that
Hester had grown up back East, she still thought small.

Petunia didn't want to think small. Didn't want to
work small. She wanted to smash through that wall of
oppression. She wanted to make a dent in women's rights.
She wanted women like Hester to have options other
than selling their bodies. She wanted kids like Terrance
to have a voice somewhere through someone. She didn't
fool herself. If Ace and Luke hadn't gone out to Terrance's house, he'd still be trapped—beaten daily, humili-
ated, denied the right of every child to learn, to laugh,
to hope. She wanted women like herself who, through
no fault of their own, suffered fates that wounded reputations, to still have a future. Not just rich women like
her, but all women.

Her father once told her that everything didn't happen
at once, but from what she could see, it wasn't happening at all. And she couldn't stand that. She'd grown up
watching him move mountains in business every day by
putting the right pieces in the right place. He never accepted little gains. He always went big. She tapped her

finger on his name. Why didn't he, or anyone else for that matter, understand that when it came to what mattered to her, she had to go big, too?

"My mom is crying."

Brenda's scared, high-pitched voice flicked across Petunia's conscience with the bite of a whip. Rubbing her fingers across her forehead she took a breath and turned. Brenda stood in the doorway, fingers clutched in front of her, her big blue eyes wide. Phillip stood behind her. No fear lurked in his gaze, but a whole lot of belligerence glared out at her.

"What did you do to her?"

She was still trying to figure that out. "I don't know."

"My mom never cries."

Terrance approached a lot more slowly. The dread in his expression about broke her heart.

You won't be here to see it, and once you get on that stagecoach, we won't matter.

Hester couldn't be more wrong. She mattered. Children mattered. Everything Petunia had done here had mattered. The people she touched here were more than names. What she'd done here was bigger than the collecting money and organizing she'd done in the past. What she'd done here had touched her life, too. Hester was right. She really hadn't understood. "Phillip?"

"What?" he said gruffly. Clearly, he expected bad news to fall upon them, and why wouldn't he? Nothing in his life had been permanent. He knew she was leaving. And now his mother was crying. How could he interpret that as anything else but bad news? "Could you go to the well and bring me some cold water?"

"Why?"

She pushed her chair back and stood. "Because your mom is going to want to wash up."

"Why bother if you're just going to make her cry again?"

She ignored the belligerence but she couldn't ignore the disrespect. "Phillip?"

"What?"

"You're still a child, and I'm still the adult."

"What'll you do? Give me a whooping?"

The sneer in his voice made it very clear he didn't think she was capable of any such thing.

"She might not, but I will."

Petunia blinked. She'd rarely seen Terrance be the aggressor. She placed her hand on Phillip's shoulder, ignoring his attempt to shrug it off. As he continued to glare at her, she clarified, "Nobody's going to give anybody a whipping. You're going to do it, Phillip, because I asked you to and because it's for your ma. And you, Terrance, are going to help him, because Phillip is your friend, and friends help each other that way."

"And me?" Brenda asked, wanting to be part of everything as usual.

Petunia gave her a smile. "You, sweetie, are going to go get me one of those nice facecloths we keep for guests."

Their tasks assigned, the children disappeared in a heartbeat but were back just as fast. She didn't know what they worried she might get up to in the short amount of time it took to perform their tasks, but they were in a hurry to get back. Phillip and Terrance stood just inside the back door frowning at her. Clearly they'd been talking outside.

Phillip shoved the bucket at her. Terrance elbowed

him in the side. With a shuffle of his feet, Phillip said, "I'm sorry."

She took the half-full bucket. "Thank you."

Brenda handed her the washcloth. Pouring the water into a pitcher and draping the towel over her forearm, Petunia added, "And children?"

As one they looked at her. She felt the weight of their stares keenly, understanding with every passing second what Hester meant. She wasn't a catalyst here. She was part of this. She held these children's lives and futures in her hand. The responsibility made her tremble deep inside. But in a good way. A new way. This was what directly making the difference felt like. "None of you have to worry. Everything's going to be all right."

THE STAIRS CREAKED a reprimand as Petunia climbed them. She felt small and ashamed by the time she reached the landing. She should've known Hester was worried. She should've known what she was doing by leaving. Her only defense was she'd never truly been in the trenches before. She'd raised money, given lectures, listened to stories, but she'd never before been the one that actually did the work. She'd never been the one people depended on. She'd never been the linchpin in the plan.

Hester's door was closed. Petunia wasn't surprised. She knocked and wasn't shocked when Hester told her to go away. She hadn't come this far in life, however, by being easily dissuaded. She tested the handle. The door was unlocked. She walked right in. Hester pushed up from where she lay on the bed. Above her narrowed eyes, random tight curls stuck up and out like bits of red flame. That more than anything else told Petunia how upset Hester was. Hester was ruthless in containing the willful nature of her hair.

"What do you want?" Hester demanded, wiping her wet cheeks.

Petunia walked over to the bedside table and poured water into the basin. She dipped the towel in the cold water and handed it to Hester. "I think the children are going to mutiny."

Hester took the cloth and wiped her swollen, blotchy face. "They've never seen me cry."

All she'd been through and they'd never seen her cry? "Not even once?"

"No. I was all they had."

And Petunia understood. "I'm sorry."

Hester pulled the cloth away from her eyes. "For what?"

"For being selfish."

At that Hester lowered the cloth. "I don't understand."

How did she say this? Petunia motioned to the side of the bed. "Do you mind if I sit down?"

Dipping the cloth in the cool water, Hester muttered, "Go ahead" before placing the cloth back over her eyes.

Clearly, she wasn't going to make this easy. "I've never built something like this before. Never been on my own before. I don't tell anybody, but my family, my father, actually has a lot of money. And as such, he wields a lot of influence."

"No fooling."

"You don't look shocked."

Lifting the cloth, Hester gave her a wry smile. "I told you I wasn't a hayseed. Only the wealthy have the belief that nothing can get in their way."

"Why didn't you say something?"

"It wasn't my place to say anything and besides," she said, shrugging, "your crusades worked in my favor."

That was blunt speaking. "I suppose they did."

"So what do we do now that you're done crusading here?"

She wasn't done. She didn't know what she was, but done wasn't it. "Well, first, I think we need to talk to the children downstairs."

"And tell them what?"

Petunia fussed with her skirt. "That they're safe?" It was her turn to shrug. "Honestly, I don't know."

"We can start with safe."

Petunia was the first to break the silence that followed. "You were right when you said I didn't understand. I've always done this from afar."

"It wasn't very satisfying, was it?"

"I don't know about that." Bracing her hands on the mattress, she shifted backward. "There were challenges."

Hester carefully folded the cloth in half. And then just as carefully, in half again. "For someone who doesn't know much about what makes her happy, you're sure doing a lot of running away."

That stung. "I think of it more like I'm running to something."

Hester snorted. And then sniffed. And finally rubbed her nose. Her face was red and blotchy from crying. Her eyes swollen. None of it diminished the force of her disapproval. "The only thing waiting for you in San Francisco is a half-baked plan shored up by a whole lot of dreaming."

"And what do I have here? I can't even stay at the school with the damage to my reputation. Soon enough, the good people of this town are going to demand that I stop living here so the children aren't corrupted by my presence or by the unsavory element 'my type' brings around."

From the arch of Hester's eyebrows she might have revealed a bit too much. "Just how disturbing was that walk of yours?"

Petunia didn't know how much to tell.

"I'm hardly in a position to judge," Hester reminded her.

"You're my friend. Your opinion matters."

"Then if I'm your friend, tell me so I can help."

"I saw Brian."

"Well, I can see where that would put you off your mood."

The joke fell flat. Petunia licked her lips. "He propositioned me."

"He thinks you're desperate."

"I am."

Hester snorted. "Not that desperate. What did Ace say?"

She smoothed her hair. "I didn't tell him."

Hester took a slow breath. "Why not?"

"We were in the alley and—"

"And what? And why were you and Brian in the alley?"

"I wasn't in the alley when I met him. I was in the store and he kind of cornered me, but when I met Ace it could've looked like I was meeting Brian in the alley." She sighed. "Luke saw."

"If Luke saw then Ace knows."

"Ace knows. He beat Brian up."

"Good."

"I know, but I don't want them to think...to believe...

when he has time to reflect on things…" She couldn't bring herself to say it.

Hester had no such trouble. "You don't want them to think you're that desperate."

"No." She didn't. "Not even for an instant."

"Ace isn't the type of man to tolerate secrets between you."

What he would and wouldn't tolerate both scared and aroused her. "That's going to make surprising him at Christmas a challenge."

The joke fell flat. "You're planning on surprising him with something?"

"I'm not sure of anything anymore."

"Except leaving. Providence won't survive without you."

"I think you underestimate your abilities, Hester. You could keep this school going with one hand tied behind your back."

"I never underestimate myself in any situation, but I don't have your skills."

"Well, I don't have—"

A knock on the door downstairs interrupted her. Petunia jumped. Hester dropped the washcloth. They looked at each other.

"Where's the gun?" Petunia asked in a harsh whisper. If Brian was out there, they needed a weapon.

"In the parlor."

"Darn it. Ace's going to be ticked."

"Not only ticked, he's going to tan your butt."

Petunia shook her head and stood, moving quickly to the door. "He can't be ticked about what he doesn't know."

Hester was right on her heels. "You've got a point there."

They made it to the bottom of the stairs in record time, both of them skipping the creaky stair. There was no sign of the children. Hester and Petunia exchanged a worried glance. Hester eased the curtain away from the side window. Petunia slipped into the parlor.

"What are you doing?" Hester asked.

"I'm not going to cower in here like a mouse." She grabbed the gun and pointed the barrel at the door. With a jerk of her chin, Petunia indicated the other woman open it.

"You're crazy."

"No, I'm just ticked. Open the door."

With a short nod, Hester did. The only thing that charged in was sunshine and a blast of cold air. There wasn't anyone at the door.

"Damn." Relief nearly buckled Petunia's knees. From the expression on Hester's face she was feeling the same.

"You don't suppose the children are playing games?" she whispered as a thought hit her.

"I'll skin them alive if they are," Hester growled.

The knock came again.

"They're at the back door."

Hester closed the front door. Petunia stepped forward and locked it. Everything in her said it wasn't the children who were knocking.

"Are you ready?" asked Hester.

"You're getting pretty feisty for a city girl."

"I blame Ace."

"I'm fine with that."

They started down the hall.

Hester stopped dead just inside the kitchen. Petunia bumped right into her. "What's wrong?"

"I thought I heard something."

In the next second, Petunia heard it, too. A thin mewling cry. Oh, damn. Handing Hester the gun, she opened the back door. On the narrow stoop balanced a round basket piled high with what looked to be a blanket. The cry came again. Petunia looked around. There was no one in sight. The blankets wiggled and the mewling cry became a banshee wail of displeasure.

She pulled the blanket back revealing clenched fists and a scrunched-up red face. A baby. Someone had left a baby on their doorstep. No doubt someone who wanted him or her to have the better life she'd promised Providence would offer. Looking up at the sky, she asked, "Really?"

Wasn't she under pressure enough?

"Who are you talking to," Hester asked from behind her.

"God."

Hester looked over her shoulder at the screaming baby in the basket. "Is He listening?"

She picked up the basket. "Not to me."

CHAPTER NINETEEN

TWO HOURS LATER there was another knock at the back door. This time, there was no doubt who was demanding entrance.

"Open the door, Pet."

Only one man gave orders in that calm yet commanding way. Upstairs in Petunia's bedroom, Petunia looked at Hester; Hester looked right back at her. "He's your man. Did you really think he wouldn't come?"

She tightened the tie on her wrapper and glanced at the window. The only thing she could see beyond the building across the street was the dust hazing the bright stream of the late-afternoon sun. "I was hoping for more time. Were you expecting him?"

Hester raised her eyebrows. "Yes." Snapping out the petticoat she'd pulled out of the drawer, she continued, "Frankly, I'm surprised it took him this long."

Petunia sighed and placed the scissors she'd been ready to use to cut up petticoats into diapers on the bed stand. "He doesn't sound happy."

"No reason he should be what with you flip-flopping about like a landed fish." Hester tossed her another petticoat. "That should do for the diapers."

She caught it just as the knock came again.

"Damn it, Pet. I'm not going to tell you again."

That didn't sound good. Petunia glanced warily at the door. "He wants so much."

Hester shook her head and picked up the baby girl. "An all-or-nothing man isn't a bad thing."

Hester grabbed the blanket out of the basket and used it to swaddle the baby. Alarm shot through Petunia.

"Where are you going?"

The back door creaked as it opened. They'd forgotten to lock it after the shock of seeing the baby on the doorstep. Darn it.

Hester settled the baby on her shoulder. "I'm taking this innocent out of the line of fire."

And leaving her to face Ace alone? "Traitor."

Staccato boot steps sounded in the lower hallway.

"I'm just leaving you to talk."

"Uh-huh." Those footsteps didn't sound conversational. "You could at least leave the baby."

The loose stair creaked.

Hester smiled. "I'm going to do one better," she stated as calmly as if Ace wasn't about to burst through that door any second. "I'm going to find the children and take them over to Antonio and Luisa's for dinner."

Leaving her alone in the house with just Ace and her complete lack of defense to his appeal.

Balling up the petticoat, she put it with the scissors. "That's not fair."

Hester headed for the door. "You don't need fair. You need to stop running from things."

She wanted to scream. She was not a coward. She was just…cautious. "I could hunt up that gun."

"It's downstairs in the kitchen."

Where they'd left it when they'd found the baby. She

sighed as Ace's footsteps came down the hall. A promise and a threat. "Wonderful."

Another thing for which Ace would take her to task.

Hester shook her head. "There are some things you just can't run from, Petunia. Being a woman is one of them."

Before she could answer, Ace did. "And I'm another."

Dark and rich, that low drawl rolled across her nerves in a smooth coat of honey. A slight turn of her body was all it took to see Ace standing in the doorway, his broad shoulders filling the space, his presence filling the room. With his hat pulled down low and his sensual mouth set in a straight line, it was clear he was here with an attitude, but it wasn't fear that had her licking her lips or had her remembering how his lips felt against the delicacy of hers. Relishing the utter mastery with which they parted hers. How completely he took possession when he stepped in.

I'm claiming you.

She caught her moan before it could fully escape, reducing it to an awkward hiccup that had everyone looking at her.

Hester just shook her head and patted the baby on the back. "Afternoon, Ace."

As if the greeting were an invitation, Ace entered the room. He touched his finger to the brim of his Stetson. "Afternoon, Hester. Heading out?"

"I thought I'd treat the kids to dinner at Antonio's." She cut Petunia yet another glance over her shoulder as she headed to the door with the baby. "Between dinner and Luisa cooing over this sweetie—" she pulled the blanket back showing Ace the little one's face as she drew even "—I don't expect we'll make it back much before seven."

Seven was two hours away.

"And who is this?" Ace asked, moving the blanket back farther with his finger. The set of his mouth softened as he took in the infant. He liked children, Petunia realized, a bit belatedly considering all he'd done for Terrance.

"A foundling," Hester said at the same time Petunia found her voice.

"We haven't named her yet."

She longed to snatch the shaky words back. She wanted Ace to see her as strong in these negotiations. Not needy.

I'm claiming you.

Lord help her, everything feminine and sure inside her wanted to be claimed, while everything independent and insecure said run. The man had her at war with herself.

"She was a bit of a surprise this afternoon," Hester elaborated when Petunia didn't say more.

Ace met Petunia's gaze. The impact made her toes curl in slow-drawn pleasure. She became vividly aware of the thinness of her robe and nightgown. Completely enthralled with the implication of standing in her bedroom with him while so dressed. Hester slipped out of the room. Petunia smoothed her robe. Her pinkie caught on the edge of a pocket. She left it there, letting the tension balance her.

"Someone left her?" His knowing smile let her know he knew what she was doing. "So your plan is working out. The children are coming to you."

One syllable was all she could muster. "Yes."

Her tongue eased over her lips. His gaze dropped. Her

lower lip trembled, remembering the nip of his teeth, the press of his mouth, the sweeping possession of his kiss...

"Good."

Ace smiled, and Petunia's heart joined the game, skipping a beat while her lungs gave up functioning completely. A schoolgirl had more maturity around this man than she did, but she couldn't help it. There was just something about Ace that made her want to surrender. Mind, body and soul.

As if he heard the secret she wanted hidden, Ace murmured, "All or nothing, my Pet. Everything you are."

It was eerie how well this man understood the need that no one had even sensed before.

"Stop."

"Stop what?"

Stop knowing what she was thinking, stop affecting her senses like this... Stop walking toward her. She placed her hand in the middle of his chest, measuring his heartbeat beneath her palm. Steady and strong. Like him. "Stop." She tested the solid muscle with firm pressure. Summing up everything crazy she felt inside she whispered, "This."

His fingertips grazed up her side. His answer was simple and to the point. "No."

"That's not fair."

"I don't care."

She didn't even know where to go with that. Not because she couldn't find the words but because she couldn't find the impetus. She liked the way Ace took charge of things between them, wiping out the confusion and the conflict she hid within herself. Centering her focus with a simple touch of his thumb on the side of her jaw, bringing everything that mattered to the fore with an equally simple, "Why not?"

It was a leading question. She followed as always. "Because."

His thumb stroked over her lips catching on the dry surface as his gaze continued to probe hers. The hat shadowed his eyes, letting her see only some of what he was thinking when she needed to see it all.

"Because isn't an answer."

Swallowing hard, she tried again. "It's all I have."

His smile preceded the touch of his lips. Warm, hot and masculine, they teased hers before lifting on a whisper. "That's a lie. There is so much more to you."

He saw her so differently than she saw herself. She touched her tongue to his kiss. "Like what?"

"Like strength, loyalty, purpose, devotion."

"You make me sound like a dog."

He smiled. He touched his thumb to the dampness left by her tongue. "I see your strengths, Pet, but I also see your need, and that's my concern."

He saw too much. "What need?"

It was a bluff pure and simple. She wasn't surprised when he called her on it.

"For clarity and direction. Right now you're leaning away from me, but your tongue is tickling my thumb in the sweetest of invitations."

He was right. She tucked her tongue back into her mouth, savoring the faint hint of his flavor. His smile was almost tender. "So tell me, which message do you want me to hear?"

She didn't know. "The right one?"

"Are you asking me or telling me?"

He offered her no quarter and part of her was glad.

She was so tired of men who couldn't match her strength. But that didn't help her find the answer he wanted. To be vulnerable this way. "Ace..."

"You know what I want." Working his finger between her lips, he ordered, "Give it to me."

"I can't."

There was a pause. His thumb pressed and then slowly relaxed. For a soul-dropping moment she thought he was going to walk away.

"I want your surrender."

She wished she could. Too much of what she'd convinced herself up to this point in her life was a "must" lingered.

"I'm an independent woman." Even if she didn't sound it.

With a shake of his head Ace brushed aside her claim. "You're mine. Always have been. Always will be."

"Not unless I agree."

His smile was softly dangerous. Knowing. His hand swept down from her shoulder to her hips resting on her buttock. The thinness of her gown offered no protection when he pressed his fingers into the crease between. Neither did her conscience. This was Ace. Her protector. Her friend. Her...lover.

"You already have."

It was only then that she realized she was completely relaxed against him. Her resistance had been so pathetic, even she hadn't noticed its departure. "That's just physical."

This time his thumb pressed and parted her lips, sliding into the moist heat beyond. "Lie like that to me again and I'll put you over my knee."

Her shiver was involuntary. His smile faded. "And not in a good way."

Lust hit her so hard her knees buckled. She would've stumbled if not for the pressure of his hand in the small of her back. She could see it so easily, feel it so clearly, being held down across his lap, helpless and vulnerable. His.

"I've got you."

He always had, she realized. From the moment she'd landed in this town he'd been an invisible force in her life. Shaping it, guiding her, protecting her. She never realized how much until just now.

Reaching up, she grasped his wrist, needing something to hang on to. "You made sure I got the teaching position, didn't you?"

"You're qualified."

"And you sent Hester over here, didn't you?"

"It worked out for both of you."

She looked up into his eyes, seeing that flash of something she'd seen so many times before. That something she hadn't understood but she did now. "That's not why you sent Hester."

"Is that a statement or question?"

She cocked her head and tested the thread of certainty within, tracing its spread through their history from incident to incident connecting them in this subtle band of knowledge. Nothing that happened since she'd arrived in Simple with the exception of her kidnapping had been happenstance. The luck she'd been so grateful for all along had been because of this man who watched over her, and took care of her and gave her what she wanted. She remembered that day at the station when she'd waited for him to come and stop her. He hadn't because she'd chosen to leave. Her choice.

Some of her panic left. She still felt like she was standing on the edge of a cliff, but she wasn't so worried about stepping off anymore. "It's a statement. But I do have a question."

His head tilted to the side. His hand slid around the back of her neck. "Maybe I don't feel like answering it."

"But you will."

His right eyebrow flicked up, disappearing into the fall of his hair. The shadows of his hat blended with the shadows in his eyes. She could only shake her head at herself. How could she have looked at this man and only seen the facade that he flashed the world? Why had she chosen to ignore her instincts? She'd prayed her whole life for a man like him. One who could see her and accept her. Someone for whom she had value on all levels. One who was strong enough to hold her safe. One to whom she could surrender the control she'd clung to for so long because she'd never found someone she could trust to give it to.

"What makes you so sure?" he asked as if he were discussing the weather.

It was a test. She wasn't worried.

"Because I need to know, and you always give me what I need."

His eyes narrowed, hiding the shadows within. "I won't always give you everything."

The warning didn't worry her, either. She was finally figuring it out. "I trust you."

Like she'd shot him, his breath caught. Against her hip, his cock twitched. On a growl, Ace took a step forward. She didn't have any choice but to take one back.

And then he took another. And another. Every time the outside of his thigh brushed the inside of hers, excitement slid up, pooling in a hot ache in her pussy. He came to a stop. The folds of her wrap swirled around his ankles, binding them together in a subtle promise.

"Ask your question," he growled.

He thought he was taking her down a path he shouldn't. Such foolishness. As clearly as he saw her, she was beginning to see him. And he might not be perfect, but he was strong, loyal, passionate about everything in his world. Protective and caring. Even the women he "used" for his needs saw him as someone upon whom to rely. But she was the one he held. And that mattered.

Hugging that knowledge tight, she breathed deeply, keeping her hand over his heart, counting the beats, knowing that exact moment when he realized the shift in her thinking, smiling inside when that rhythm sped up. For her. She did like the way he responded to her. Almost as much as she liked this pulsing sexual tension between them. So vivid it demanded to be cherished and nourished. To be brought to fruition. She had all she needed under her hand.

"It doesn't matter anymore." It didn't matter with what he struggled. They both had their battles. If she controlled this, they could only both win. She just had to control it.

The next step was hers. Initiated by her. Wanted by her. The backs of her legs hit the bed. The smile hit her lips. Curling her fingers in Ace's shirt, she tugged slightly, dragging him with her. The mattress gave as she landed, bounced again as he came over her. His hat tumbled off and hit the floor, and then there was nothing hiding the emotion in his eyes. Nothing protecting her from the raw passion in his gaze. Nothing saving her from the enormity of what she was doing. But she didn't care.

"Do you know what you're doing?" he asked, bracing himself above her.

She reached for the buttons of his shirt and started undoing them. "Yes."

She was taking what she could accept.

"Look at me."

She did, not stopping in her undressing of him. The man was a dream come true, and she wanted to feel him against her, around her, in her. A shiver shook her from head to toe.

His knee nudged her thighs. She parted them willingly. He didn't come between them. That more than the repetition of her name had her looking up.

"What?"

He just shook his head. Where before there had been passion, now there was resistance. "There'll be no going back, Pet."

She loved how he said Pet. All the tenderness and possession a woman could want haunted that one syllable.

"I know."

"Do you?"

She loved him more for the concern now that he was getting what he wanted. Dear heavens, she loved him. The realization flowed over her, spilling out from behind the walls she'd built. With everything in her. That's why she was so susceptible to him. That's why he rattled her, why she pushed him away. She loved him. Almost as much as she hated the insecurity she saw in his eyes. Did he truly doubt she could want what he had to offer?

Holding his gaze, she reached down and tugged at

her wrap and gown, hiking it up over her knees until she could bend her legs up and out. "Yes. Do you need me to prove it?"

His breath soughed in and out of his lungs. His right hand gripped her left ankle, pinning it to the bed. Desire shot through her so hard, her pussy clenched. His "Yes" was as harsh as the need grinding in her.

Her smile spread wider, feeding on the growing realization inside. Cupping his face in her hands, she kissed him softly. The resistance from her position only increased her lust. He had her. If she had her way, he always would. Lowering herself just as slowly back to the bed, she let her hands fall above her head.

"Shit."

Placing the back of her left hand into the palm of the right, she said, "I love you, Ace."

His free hand caught her wrists in his, pinning them to the bed. He held her with his hands, his weight, his passion. "Be sure, Pet. Because after this—" he growled, pushing her thighs as wide as the material would allow "—there'll be no more secrets, no more resistance. You'll be where I want you, as I want you. Whenever I want you."

"Yes."

He blinked. Had he expected resistance? She was to him as he was to her. The other half of his whole.

"Just yes?"

She nodded.

"There will be days I'll want you waiting on your knees."

She couldn't hide her shiver any more than he could hide his.

"Others when I'll want you bent over and waiting. I'll take you hard, soft or quick with or without preamble."

"But you'll take me?"

His hand slid up her calf and then down her thigh until he found the swollen heat of her pussy. His touch streaked through her like lightning. "There won't be any-place I won't know you." Wet with her juices, his fingers slid lower, brushing the tight bud of her ass. Lightning streaked again. "Anyplace you won't know me."

"I'm not afraid." Nervous yes, but not afraid.

"You should be."

"I trust you."

Again, his breath hissed in, and his body jerked. His finger pressed intimately. She couldn't decide whether to lift up or press down. He took the decision from her, pulling her hips up. Three tugs and her gown was over her waist. Before she could lift her torso, his hands were on the front. In a single wrench, her nightgown tore. Pushing the robe and the material aside, he cupped her breasts in his hands. His palms rough as they slid over her nipples. She braced herself for aggression even as she savored the sensation.

"No." He shook his head. "Relax. I won't hurt you."

Damn, he hoped he wouldn't hurt her. Ace gritted his teeth, reaching for the control he'd always had, feeling how tenuous it was with this woman who meant so much.

I love you.

He couldn't believe she'd said that to him. She de-served someone better. Someone cultured and soft. Couldn't believe she was lying before him with those delicate white breasts exposed. The tips pouted for at-tention, her white flesh pinking beneath his grip. Fuck, he wanted to own her.

As if hearing his thoughts, she whispered, "Please."

He pinched her nipple gently, watching her eyes, looking for that line where pleasure became pain. Something flickered in her gaze. "Be sure, Pet."

"I love you." There it was again. That surrender manifested in words. The acceptance in the arc of her back, thrusting herself into his touch, following where he led, taking what he gave her, the pleasure and that first hint of pain. Her level of trust humbled him. Her acceptance seared through his defenses. He squeezed a bit harder, pushing her. She took more than he'd expected. He held the pressure, watching uncertainty and passion blend in confusion. His cock throbbed as she took the slightest bit more. Surrendering to him, giving with that whole-hearted way she did everything. Body and soul. So beautiful. So perfect. He expected her to flinch away, protest. And if she had, he might, just might have been able to get up and walk away, leaving her to the life of which she'd dreamed, but she didn't. And he didn't. And when she smiled at him, he knew he never would.

Petunia had burrowed under his skin. She was part of him now. She'd given him her virginity, her trust and her love. He'd give her security, comfort and challenge. Leaning down, he replaced his hand with his mouth, running his tongue over the hard nipple, soothing it, prodding it, stimulating it, making it harder. His cock twitched as her gasp whispered over his head.

And love.

She arched up, offering him more. Fuck, he'd love her, protect her, challenge her, take that "serious" she kept falling into and fill it with laughter. She wasn't safe with him, but he wasn't safe with her, either. They were a gamble. Pure and simple. Anticipation blended with pas-

sion. He whispered her name against her breast, stroking her with his tongue and his desire, loving her with
his mouth, his body, with everything in him. She was
his and after today, they'd both know it.

"That's it, my Pet. Give me everything."

He nipped her breast and she moaned. "Ace…"

"Right here."

Her fingers slid through his hair, tugging him closer.
He should have reprimanded her for the disobedience,
but the wonder of her touch slid through him with the
same bliss of her whisper. He'd been touched with anger,
with passion, with greed. He couldn't remember a time
since his parents died being touched with love.

She arched, thrusting her breasts up. Her mouth
brushed his neck, his ear. When he shivered, she lingered. "Make love to me, Ace."

She was fire in his arms, burning him with her innocent caresses. Teasing him. He wanted more.

Catching her chin in his hand, he turned her eyes to
his. The flare of excitement at the possession caught the
edge of his lust, honing it to a fine edge. Fuck, he wanted
her. Beneath him in bed, kneeling at his feet, standing at
his side. Building, fighting, loving for how many years
he could wrangle from a future he'd never considered
particularly likely. Quite frankly, he'd grown bored with
life. Petunia had given him his purpose back.

Kissing her deeply, he pulled his mouth the slightest
bit from hers, giving her his breath. Taking hers. "Stay
just like this."

Her hand dropped from his chest as he stood.

"What are you doing?"

"Don't question."

She frowned. "It was just a question."

He traced the pleat between her brows with his fore-finger and smiled. Such a combination of submission and will. She would take a lifetime to tame. He smiled wider. Or more.

"Wait."

He stood. She stayed. Not as he wanted, she'd propped herself up on her elbows, but she was still on the bed. Crossing to the wardrobe he pulled a scarf from the drawer. Her eyes widened as he drew it through his fingers.

"Second thoughts?" he asked, retracing his steps.

She licked her lips. He could see the nervousness in her expression. Watched her form the lie she thought would make him happy.

"No."

She had a lot to learn. "Rule number one..."

"I don't tell you no?" she hazarded.

"That, too." The mattress sagged as he knelt beside her. "But first and foremost, you don't lie to me." Her eyes widened. "Especially about the way you're feeling." He dragged the scarf across her wrists as he leaned in and nipped her lower lip before soothing it with his tongue. "I'll push you, Pet, make you nervous a time or two, but it's never my intention to hurt you on the way to the edge."

She licked her lips but didn't flinch away. Damn, she was something. The softness of her "What about when you get there?" revealed her fears and her insecurities. Both of which he would do his best to soothe into nothingness. He wanted to add to her life, be her rock, not destroy the foundation she'd built for herself. He wanted her bold and confident.

"I will never allow myself a loss of control at any point where that loss could endanger you."

Her gaze searched his. "You promise?"

"I promise."

"A Hell's Eight promise?"

"Hell's Eight, Parker, you can take either to the bank."

Her smile was only a little shaky as she visibly relaxed. "Then do your worst."

He couldn't help a chuckle. Another new thing. Laughter amidst the intensity of passion. Looping the scarf around her right wrist, he shook his head. Who would have thought it would be as hot as the soft glide of skin on skin? "Not worried I'll take advantage?"

She held up her other wrist. "I trust you, and we've got to start somewhere."

He tied off the bond. Only a blind man could miss her shiver of arousal. And her attempt at controlling him. "And in bed is as good a place as any?"

The shyness left her smile. She gave the knot a tug. "I'm thinking it might be the most fun."

"Oh, it definitely is. And yes," he said as she almost slipped her hand out of the right loop, "you can get free if you want to."

She frowned. "Doesn't that defeat the…purpose?"

He pressed a slow, hot kiss into the center of her palm, touching the sensitive flesh with his tongue before closing her fingers around it. "I'm not interested in just fucking you, my Pet." He'd had too many of those go-nowhere encounters that left him empty and frustrated in the aftermath. "I want to build a life with you, for however long we have, in and out of bed, and the first step is trust."

"I said—"

He cut her off with a shake of his head.

"I heard you. And now you'll trust that I know what I'm doing." Too often women expected their fantasies to be reality, but being helpless was a scary thing. Take a woman to complete helplessness too fast, and she could panic. A bound, panicked woman was always a tricky business.

"I'm not fragile."

He wanted to kiss the pout from her lips. Instead, he secured her left wrist and tied the end of the scarf to the left side spindle headboard. She was more fragile than she knew. "Good to know."

She tugged on the bonds. He stood and finished unbuttoning his shirt.

"You can test those bonds all you want, but it would be a mistake to test my temper by questioning my judgment."

Her mouth opened on an immediate retort. Another shake of his head had her closing it just as fast. He shrugged his shirt off. Her gaze dropped to his torso. "Good girl."

It snapped right back up, a question in the depths. "You showed restraint. I approve. You showed lust." He holstered his grin and kicked off his right boot. "Of that, I approve more."

"I did not!"

He paused midtug on the left. "You don't get wet looking at me?"

Pink crept up her cheeks. "Sometimes."

The boot plunked on the floor.

Stepping between her thighs, he shoved down his denims. "Now, that's a darn shame, because just thinking about you makes me hard and looking at you—" he stepped out of his pants, and cupped his aching cock in his hand "—makes me hungry. Every time."

Her eyes followed the slow stroke of his hand along his shaft. Up and down, his fingers circling the head with each pass. Rubbing his thumb in the moisture gathering on the tip, he asked, "Do you see how hungry you make me?"

She nodded. He smacked the side of her thigh more to startle than to sting. If he'd wanted it to sting, he would have aimed for the inside or just below the buttock.

She jumped and jerked on the bonds. They held, and her eyes widened. It was dawning on her just how much power she was surrendering.

"Exciting, isn't it?" he asked. "Giving up control. Trusting me to push you to the edge, wanting me to, but worried that I will?"

From where he stood he had a clear view of her pussy. Deeply pink, temptingly moist, with the lips just beginning to unfurl. She was submissive, and she wanted him. And this, all of this, excited her. Sliding his finger between her folds, he wanted to moan himself as her juices coated his fingers and her hips arched up. Teasing him. Tempting him. She was going to burn him alive.

She nodded in response to his question. His response was immediate. This smack landed lightly on her labia, this time giving her a bit of sting. Again, she jumped and jerked at the bonds.

Her cry was one part resentment and seven parts eager curiosity. The woman did enjoy a bit of persuasion. And it was as much hell on his self-control as the deepening flush of her skin.

"Words, Pet. I want the words."

He wanted more than that. He wanted her, physically,

emotionally and mentally naked before him. Ready to follow him wherever he led. He wanted her sweet, open and giving, on all levels, trusting him to care for her. To give her pleasure. Damn, he wanted to give her so much pleasure.

This time when he slipped his fingers between the now-wet petals, he found her clit and stroked it lightly. "It excites you to be bound, doesn't it?"

The blush deepened, but she gave him what he asked for. Honesty in a "yes" but then "I won't want it all the time, though."

Did she really think she could surrender and still maintain control?

Gathering her juices, he rubbed the silky moisture onto her swelling clit. He wondered if she'd come when he spanked her there. How much she'd need, how hard she could take it, how long she could tease them both before she came. His cock jerked. Pre-come beaded the smooth tip. Circling a little faster, he ignored her and asked, "Yes, what?"

"Yes," she groaned. "It excites me to be bound."

"By anyone?"

She shook her head before biting her lip. She was getting wetter. He was getting harder. He slapped her again. A little harder. Before she could catch her breath he did it again high up so the sensation vibrated through her clit. She jerked and shuddered.

"Ohhhhhh!"

"Words, please."

She fell back on the mattress, her thighs spread wide, the remains of her torn gown spread about her body. Eyes bright above the flush on her cheeks. When she licked her lips, leaving them wet and glistening, his breath hissed out.

"I've only wanted this with you."

Holding her gaze, he brought his fingers to his lips and licked them clean. "Good girl."

He didn't want her to doubt how good she tasted to him. Ever. It was a short trip from the foot of the bed to the side. As naturally as breathing, she turned her head toward him not even pulling back when those full, pouting lips were just inches from his aching cock. This time the "good girl" wasn't calculated.

"Do you want me, Pet?" He had to ask. Had to hear it.

"Yes." The answer blew across the sensitive head, sending lust and something more shivering up his spine.

"Then open your mouth and show me."

She hesitated but her eyes didn't leave his cock, and her tongue swept over her lips the exact way he wanted it to caress his cock. She was unsure, but eager. She just needed help getting past the fear of failing. His Pet had a canyon-size dislike of failing at anything.

Still holding the base of his thick cock with one hand, he fisted his other in her hair. The shudder that went through her as he pulled her to him bound them more securely than the scarf.

Trading cupping his cock for cupping her pussy he watched as his darker finger slid between the delicate folds, disappearing into the heat and dampness beyond. So sweet. He eased his fingers deeper, finding the well of her vagina, hearing the catch in her breath. She was so hot and sweet. So fucking feminine. So wet.

"Open your mouth," he coaxed. "Show me with your body what I see in your eyes. Give it to me."

The slide of her lips over the head of his cock tore a

moan from his soul. His Pet was so generous with her passion. Her time. Her love. Without will or thought, his grip turned caressing. "Yes. Like that. Just like that."

The glide of her hot little tongue burned through his control, bringing it to a searing need.

He tried to hold back. She struggled to take more. Her tongue whipped around the large head while her lips and throat worked with an enthusiasm he couldn't withstand long. She cried out as he tugged on her hair, sucking harder rather than lighter. Goddamn, she was so naturally passionate, so completely, so perfectly— he stroked his fingers down the nape of her neck—his. Her teeth grazed the rim. His knees damn near buckled. Where had she learned that? As fast as the thought came, it left. What did it matter as long as she was doing it to *him*. Drawing the backs of his fingers delicately down her cheek, he pulled her gaze to his.

"You're perfect, do you know that?"

She shook her head and then stopped to answer.

His "no" was too quick, too rough. It was a struggle to soften his tone when everything inside him was reeling. "No. Right now we don't need words."

Her chuckle was another unique sensation, rippling along his nerve endings, catching on the pleasure in his core, his soul, bringing light to all the darkest places, piercing his senses, lightening his spirit even as she brought forth his most base desires. He blinked. Had he been hiding so well he'd actually forgotten how truly good *good* felt?

With the next pass of her tongue, he knew it was true. He had. And his light was right here, looking up at him with doe-soft eyes and a smiling heart.

He couldn't help it. Didn't care if she saw it. Not anymore. It was what it was. "Goddamn, I love you, my Pet."

Her eyes widened. He knew exactly how she felt. She couldn't be any more surprised than he was by the realization that that effervescent, possessive, happy, damn-the-world, all-encompassing emotion that plagued him was love. With everything vital inside him, he loved this woman. Cradling her head in his palm, he held her to him, limiting her movement. She tugged at her bonds and twisted. Her hair splayed around her flushed face, her mouth stretched around his cock. Her eyes crinkled at the corners with the same smile he felt inside. Tilting his hips forward, he deepened the connection between them, giving her as much as she could take, or he could take, because she had him so close to coming, and he didn't want to. Not like this. Not without her. Never without her.

"Easy now," he murmured. "Just be easy and let me show you how you make me feel every day. Inside."

She blinked up at him. In answer to the question in her eyes he stroked her clit, lightly, steadily, easing her focus to where he wanted it. On her pleasure. When her breath took an uneven cadence, he pressed harder, circled faster, monitoring her passion through her eyes, her breathing, gritting his teeth in an effort not to come, wanting it for her first, wanting her to feel that smile that didn't end. Just wanting. As he always had. Even as he knew every run of luck had an end. But his wasn't ending now. This was their beginning. For however long. He wanted to be her strength. Her reason to smile. Her life.

She stiffened, straining against her bonds, gasping around his cock. Her back arched. Caught between his desire and his will. So close. She was so close.

"Come for me, Pet." He stroked faster, harder. She

twisted and moaned. His balls pulled tight. He gritted his teeth against the need. "Come for me. Come." With a delicate slap, he brought her to the edge. With another, he sent her over. "Now."

"Ace!"

She lurched and strained and bucked on the bed. Catching her jaw in his hand, he kept her from biting down. Replacing his cock with his mouth, he pushed her higher, kissing her deeply, passionately, wildly, feeling her pussy pulse, her heart race, taking her desperate gasps of his name into his lungs, his heart. His. She was his. So fucking perfectly his.

"Ace."

Kissing her hard, cradling her close, he untied the scarf from the headboard. He lifted her still-bound arms. Moaning, she twisted and draped them over his head, burrowing closer when he wrapped his arm around her waist and rolled onto his back. She couldn't get close enough for him.

He smacked her ass, chuckling when she jumped, smiling when the sting turned to heat and she quivered and squeezed his still-hard cock between his thighs.

"Are we done?" she whispered from the vicinity of his neck, her voice a combination of wonder and hope.

Rubbing the spot he'd just spanked. "Do you want to be?"

She tried to sit up. Her bindings prohibited the freedom. Her grunt made him smile.

"No."

"Good." Bracing his arm under her hips, he lifted her as he worked himself upright against the headboard. When he was done, she was flush-faced and straddling his thighs.

Sliding her hips up his cock, she wiggled on the tip. "Now, this has promise."

"You think?"

Her nails dug into his shoulder as her body opened that little bit. "Yes."

Fisting his hand in her hair, he drew her head back, stretching her spine with a subtle tension. "Why don't you show me how much."

Her eyes narrowed. Her tongue peeked out.

"Right now?"

He leaned back and smiled. Bound as she was, she had no choice but to go with it. She couldn't look away from his face. His fingers tugged at her wrists, sending the scarf floating to the floor. Ace's smile sent fresh shivers down her spine. "Then I'd say there's no time like the present to press your luck."

CHAPTER TWENTY

TEMPTATION. THAT'S ALL Petunia could think of with Ace's sexy smile before her and his hard body beneath her. His cock pressed against her clit, sending up prickles of sensation, out and amok. He was her world. He was her strength. He was her center. And he was consuming her resolve. Everything within her wanted to just let go, just trust. But she couldn't. She had to remember that distance. Had to be careful. But then his hand was between them, too, stroking and rubbing her clit, sending that fire ripping along her nerve endings, making her hips arch and logical thought fly away. So much sensation. She soared on it, fed on it, gloried in it. Only Ace could match her like this, give this to her. And when his thick cock parted her folds and stretched her that first delicious time, she cried out. He felt so good. So strong. So complete.

Yes, she sighed as he slid in, making a place for himself. Ace made her complete. The wild and reckless in her was welcome with him. Contained, guided, given a place. She dug her nails into his chest, holding on to him with everything she had. With a growl he anchored her hips as he withdrew with excruciating slowness, dragging the ridge of his cock along the sensitive inner tissue, sending frissons of sensation streaking inward. The feeling caught on invisible wires inside, vibrating along

their length, sending goose bumps racing down her arms
and across her chest. Her nipples pulled tight, and her
breasts swelled until it felt impossible to take a breath.
Everything inside felt swollen and aching and needing.
But it wasn't enough. She needed more. So much more.
Digging her nails into his back, she pulled closer. Hard
muscle bunched under her touch, stretched and flexed.
Power. Strength. It was her turn to growl when his grip
tightened, preventing her from moving. But even the latter was exciting.

He held her there, poised on the brink of bliss. His
gaze dropped. Hers followed. His cock, thick and shiny
within her. "Do you want me, Pet?"

Such a silly question. Her hips rocked, and her pulse
pounded. The answer rolled off her tongue in a sibilant
exultation. "Yes."

"How much?"

She blinked as thought tried to pierce the drugging
passion. He pushed his cock a little deeper, stretching
her more. The seductive burn had her moaning and rolling her hips.

"How much are you willing to gamble on us, Petunia?"

Petunia, not my Pet. Panic nipped at her passion. She
much preferred the passion.

"I don't understand."

"How much are you willing to give me?" His thumbs
dipped between her legs, teasing her clit with the promise
of sensation. "Are you willing to give me your body?"
He skimmed his fingertips up her stomach over the un-
derside of her breast, flicking the hard nipple before centering the hard tip in his palm in blatant claiming. Heat

infused her breath. And longing filled her soul. His gaze never left hers as he asked, "Your heart?"

"I already told you I loved you."

He frowned. Before she could say more, his touch moved on, skimming her shoulder. Chills chased up her arm as his fingers locked around her wrist, tucking it behind the small of her back, arching her slightly. The subtle tension honed everything she was feeling to a fine edge.

"Everything you are?"

Including the indecision. She didn't want him to see the indecision. She didn't know if she could give him the all he wanted. With an arch of her back and a slow circle of her hips, she opted for distraction. "Can't we talk about this later?"

His fingers tightened. His cock flexed. "I asked you a question."

His tone was as hard as his cock, but not as pleasing. She wanted pleasing. For once, just pleasing. Taking control, she circled her hips again, teasing them both, she ordered, "Later."

A different sort of tension invaded his body. His eyes narrowed.

"What did I say about giving me orders?"

"You don't like it, but—"

"No buts. All or nothing, my Pet."

His cock grazed her clit. Her pussy ached; her nipples burned. She didn't want to talk about this. Not now. "Later. We'll talk about it later, but right now…" With a hard push she took that first bit, feeling him entering, stretching, feeling that unique pleasure pain. On a gasp she finished, "Right now I want you to make love to me."

His grasp switched to her waist. She braced her hands on his chest. "Then later it will be."

Just that fast all that heat and promise was taken away, and she was plopped unceremoniously on the mattress.

"What?"

Hitching her leg up, she shifted her position so she could see him. She expected the worst, and she found it. Ace lay against the pillows looking at her, his cock hard and jutting, and his expression stern and forbidding. Her pussy throbbed with frustrated desire, but her pulse slowed with dread. She had the irrational impulse to touch the flat plane of his stomach. In apology, she realized. Curling her fingers into a fist, she resisted the urge.

"What's wrong?"

"I asked you a question."

"At a bad time."

Surely he could see that. The time to talk was not when her senses were scattered to the four directions.

He propped another pillow behind his head. She wanted to yank the sheet over his cock. How could he be so calm when everything in her was in chaos?

"You can't control me, Pet."

She wanted to lean over and take that hard shaft in her mouth, feel it slide over her tongue again. She wanted to make him moan, make him mindless. She wanted him to want her more than he wanted to control things. Or maybe not. Right now she just wanted the mockery of her nakedness covered. Grabbing the sheet, she tugged. To no avail. It was stuck in a tangle beneath them. Grinding her teeth, she dragged the comforter from the foot of the bed across her breasts, breaking his view. He didn't say a word. That set the indecision into a surge.

Pulling her leg up, she tackled it head-on. "Who said I wanted to?"

"You want to surrender to a point."

She couldn't dispute it, but that didn't mean she had to like the way it made her feel. He felt so distant. She could see his desire. Feel his tension but the two weren't related anymore. Inside her the indecision that had been a kernel swelled. Her stomach knotted.

"This is new."

"That's an excuse."

"You're mad because I didn't want to talk when you did?"

He swung his legs off the bed and sat up, shaking his head. "You continue to think that you can control me."

"You felt good. I didn't want to stop." She threw up her hand. "What's wrong with that?"

Grabbing his shirt off the back of the chair, he shrugged it on before reaching for his pants. She didn't know what to do. How to fix it. She licked her suddenly dry lips, tasting him. "You're not leaving now, are you?"

He stepped into his pants. The belt buckle jingled as he pulled them up. He looked at her evenly as he buttoned them. "There's no reason for me to stay."

Petunia debated letting the comforter drop, but she couldn't. Not when he was dressing to leave. Of course, he noticed her aborted movement.

"Do you think if you cover your breasts I don't remember how they look? How they feel?"

He reached out and stroked her cheek. The caress was surprisingly tender. With a tap under her chin, he brought her gaze to his. What she saw there scared her so. He was holding nothing back, letting her see him as he was. She couldn't breathe. Couldn't move. Couldn't go there. Because if she did, there'd be no going back. Not for her. She wasn't made like others. She couldn't keep her distance.

"That's a damn shame because the only way I want you is naked." His thumb pressed against her lips. "Defenseless." Parted them. "Vulnerable."

While she was still coping with the storm of emotion, he slid his thumb inside, stopping just short of contact with her tongue.

The denial of contact hurt. She needed more than that. She needed him to hold her. To tell her it was all right. He always saw that before. Why couldn't he see that now?

His hand dropped to his side.

Hurt coiled, lashed out. "You want a doll."

"I want you."

His counter lacked her heat. "Defenseless."

"Yes."

His calm drew her in. Her fear pushed her away. "I've never been that way."

"I won't accept any less."

"So you're going to leave me again?"

"I've never left you."

She hiked the comforter around her, hating the feel of it against her skin. Hating she felt like she needed it. She didn't want to be guarded with Ace. But she needed to be safe. Why couldn't he accept her as she was? She didn't know how to be any way else. With anyone. "You couldn't prove it by me."

That got her a mocking cock of his eyebrow. "I've been your protector, your confidant and your savior. I've asked you to be my woman. How is any of that leaving?"

Yanking the sheet from under her hip, she rose up on

her knees. Maybe that wasn't but there was an important detail in his wording. "You rank woman over wife?"

Ace just shook his head, unruffled by the challenge, and buttoned his shirt. "Anyone can be a wife."

"Meaning not anyone can be your woman?"

He kissed her lightly. Almost soothingly. "No."

Instead of calming her, that sent that panic expanding more, pushing out the last bits of desire. This was serious. That kiss felt too much like goodbye. The emotion welling inside her felt too much like failure. All that earned her was another shake of his head.

"I told you, no shame. Just surrender."

His saying such things didn't help. "What if it's not in me?" The fear escaped on a whisper. She'd been fighting so long. What if she'd forgotten how to relax?

Tucking his hand behind her neck, Ace leaned in. Her lids drifted down. Instead of focusing on the panic, she focused on the slight rasp of his calloused fingers over her nape, the strength of his touch, the calm that always surrounded him. This kiss was just as soothing. This kiss lingered. But when she opened her eyes, nothing in Ace's attitude had changed. He was serious about this.

"I'd never ask for more than you can give." The next kiss landed on her temple. "That's all you need to remember, my Pet. Nothing else."

Grabbing his boots and socks, he headed for the door, and heaven help her she couldn't find her voice to call him back. But inside she was screaming.

As if hearing her silent cry, he stopped at the door. Looking impossibly handsome and completely remote, he turned back. "When you understand that, come find me."

The door closed softly behind him. She sat back on the bed, staring at the dark wood. Touching her tongue to her lips, she remembered the other kisses. How he'd positioned her. How he'd held her. Her pulse kicked up. As it always did. She wanted to give him what he desired. As she always did. And yet she couldn't. As she never could.

Damn it! Grabbing the pillow, she threw it at the door. Damn it. It was happening all over again. Someone asking and her not being able to deliver. The pillow hit with a dull plop before falling harmlessly to the floor. She stared at it for the longest time, too aware of the similarity between its effectiveness and hers.

I'd never ask for more than you can give.

Tears burned her eyes, and once again she was the little girl staring at her drunken father, doing her best to appease his grief at her mother's death, being pushed away, hearing again those words when she tried to make him smile. Tried to make him see her.

Go away. You're not her. You'll never be her.

The pain of that rejection was as fresh as it had been twenty-three years ago. And she knew, just knew, she couldn't be the wrong thing for the right reasons again. She didn't have it in her to fail like that again. Why couldn't Ace see? Why couldn't he want…less? Why did she want him to? Downstairs the front door slammed shut. The panic burgeoned.

I'd never ask for more than you can give.

She pulled the comforter up over her head and fell back on the bed, whispering, "Maybe you just did."

HESTER BREEZED INTO the kitchen two hours later, her smile annoyingly bright. "Evening."

In Petunia's current mood the cheeriness in her voice

wasn't much less annoying than her smile. Petunia took a sip of her now-cold coffee. "Hi."

"That is not the happy face of the woman I left enjoying the attentions of a handsome suitor," Hester said, hanging her coat on a peg by the back door.

Petunia sighed. "I don't think he's a suitor anymore."

"Uh-oh." Hester grabbed the coffeepot and a mug and poured herself a cup. "What happened?"

Petunia pushed her cold cup away. She could hear the children laughing outside, the glow of the sunset streaming in the window. Smell the homey scent of pine from the Christmas tree. See the spices lined up on the counter. They were supposed to bake cookies tonight.

"He wants too much."

Hester plunked down in her seat. This close Petunia couldn't miss the swollen fullness of her lips. The slight pinking of the skin around her mouth told the rest of the story. Even her blue eyes had an extra sparkle.

"Hester, have you been out sparking?"

Hester lifted the cup to her lips. "Maybe."

"With whom?"

"A lady doesn't kiss and tell."

Since when? "I thought a lady didn't kiss at all."

That brought the cup down and Hester's eyebrows up. "In what world?"

Out back, the pump clanked as the children washed up. "In this one."

"I must have missed that sermon."

"Or forgotten it."

"Could be. There's a reason the preacher warns so heavily against the sins of the flesh. Once you get a taste…"

Petunia sighed. "You always want more."

"Amen."

Hester fell silent. Petunia wondered if she were thinking of her husband. Or of the man she'd been out with. She hoped it was the latter. Hester deserved happiness. Even if it were a sin. Though how it could be when that husband had remarried, she wasn't sure. Petunia sighed. "I need to go to church more."

Hester's cup settled on the table with a little thump. "Either that, or make an honest man out of Ace."

"Like you intend to make an honest man of Luke?"

It was a shot in the dark. Hester could have been out with anyone. Except that was Luke's deep drawl she heard over the children's laughter.

Hester glanced toward the back door. "Luke and I have an understanding. He doesn't ask for more than I can give, and I indulge his whimsy."

"Luke has whimsy?" Petunia considered herself an educated woman with an active imagination, but even she couldn't get her mind around a whimsical Luke. The man was too darned…male.

"Either that or he's plum out of his mind." Hester shrugged. "Since I'm not kissing on some crazy man, he's got whimsy."

And that was that. "All right, then. Whimsy it is."

"So what has Ace got that has you so down in the mouth?"

Petunia glanced toward the door again. She didn't want the children to hear.

"Don't worry about them," Hester said. "Luke promised to play stickball with them before it got too dark. We've got a spell, unless someone tags someone out too enthusiastically."

She blinked. Luke was playing with the children. "Luke?"

Hester shrugged and while admitting to kissing didn't make her blush, admitting to this did. "The man has some hidden sides."

Petunia eyed that blush and all it could mean. Was Hester falling for Luke? "So I see. About Luke…"

Hester cut her off. "You're not going to warn me about men, are you? Because that would be truly ridiculous." She shook her head with a wry smile. "The schoolteacher warning the whore."

"I'm not a schoolteacher anymore. And you're not a whore."

"Honey, you'll always be schoolmarm proper and I'll always be a whore."

Would she? Would Hester? Were they just doomed by forced choices to never be more?

"I don't believe that."

"Then that would make you very unrealistic. You might be stubborn, but you're not unrealistic."

"I prefer to think of myself as determined."

"I imagine you do." Hester picked up her cup. The children's excited cries from outside blended with the crackle of the stove fire.

"So how did that determination fail you with Ace?"

Petunia considered busying her hands with her own coffee, but it was cold. She settled for twirling the cup. "He wants too much."

Instead of looking surprised, Hester merely nodded. "Ah. I wondered when you'd hit that wall."

"You knew?"

"I know his tastes."

"And?"

With a shrug, Hester said, "And with some men it's all or nothing. Ace is one of those men."

How could she argue when he'd said roughly the same thing to her?

She gave the cup a push. "I'm not that kind of woman."

"Aren't you?"

The way Hester said that irked her. She knew who she was. And wasn't. "What does that mean?"

"There's some reason you've never married, Petunia. A pretty, wealthy woman like you has to run damn hard to escape the marriage trap."

She hadn't thought of it like that, but amidst the parties, and fund-raising and planning, maybe she had been running. And maybe not. "There was always so much to do."

"I'm sure."

"There was!"

"And nothing strong enough to distract you away from it."

No, nothing had distracted her. That was true enough. She gave the cup another spin.

"Until now," Hester added pointedly.

Petunia stopped spinning the cup. "I don't think I want to talk about this."

"An all-or-nothing man like Ace is a rare thing."

"I know."

"It can be scary when a man demands everything of you."

It was downright terrifying. "And impossible."

Hester smiled. "Impossible is for those that don't understand determination."

Why did people feel compelled to throw her own words back at her?

"I don't think I can…trust him to the level he wants."

"That's the beauty of loving a man like Ace, honey. You don't have to do anything. Just take his hand and let him show you just how easy it is."

That wasn't easy. That scared her to death.

"And by the way, the children mailed that letter for you that you left this afternoon."

She clutched the table edge. "What letter?"

"The one you left on the table."

She grabbed for her pocket. The letter to her father. Oh, damn!

"They said they were just in time. They said they caught the coach."

Of course they had. The letter she'd written but never intended to send. Her admission of failure in all its glory had made the coach. She wanted to bang her head against the wall. Her day only needed this. Instead, she just said, "Thank you."

JUST TAKE HIS hand and let him show you just how easy it is.

Just.

Why did everyone think everything boiled down to a just? Hours later, Petunia leaned against the wall in her bedroom and stared out the window, seeing her reflection in the dark glass and the night beyond. Lamplight spilled out of the occasional window, bathing the streets in a homey glow. Christmas decorations cast shadows on the walks. Such a peaceful scene. So soothing. Yet it did nothing to alleviate the restlessness inside.

Just.

Running her hands up and down her arms, she fought for calm. So many times in her life she'd stood like this,

staring into the night, looking for answers, feeling the
walls closing in. And as she had so many times before,
she gave up and grabbed the quilt off the bed, wrapped
it around her and sneaked down the stairs. Thoughts of
Brian gave her pause on the landing, but it wasn't enough
to keep her put. She needed space. Air. Something to
clear her thoughts. Pausing only to grab the rifle from the
kitchen, she slipped out the front door. The chill of the
night met her first. Then the distant hum of the saloon.
She took a breath and then another. She didn't want to
think about Ace. She couldn't help thinking about Ace.

A slight breeze caressed her cheeks. Leaves rustled
gently. She set the rifle against the house and sat in the
rocker on the wide porch with a weary sigh, leaning back
and taking in the peace. Clouds whipped across the sky
backlit by the light from the half-moon. The calm settled
over her without the usual settling of her thoughts. She
tucked the quilt against her.

*Just try. Just be. Just don't fall to pieces when that
trying to be what's wanted—what Ace wanted—and failing, crushes you into the ground.*

It figured she'd fall in love with a man who demanded
the one thing she couldn't give.

"Why did it have to be Ace?" she muttered. She hadn't
expected an answer. She about jumped out of her skin
when she got one.

"It's a bad sign when a pretty woman sits alone in the
dark talking to herself."

She paused midlunge. Luke. That was Luke. She
closed her eyes briefly and took a steadying breath. As
soon as her heart started beating again, she was going
to smack him. Hard. Now that her eyes were adjusted,
she could see him sitting in the corner of the porch, a

darker shadow among the shadows. She tapped the gun butt on the floor. "It's a dangerous habit to lurk in the dark outside a nervous woman's home."

There was the sound of sulfur being struck and then the hiss of the flame catching. A faint light started low and rose along with his arm. "You're nervous?"

She could just make out the amused tilt of his mouth. "Don't I have reason to be? What with Brian lurking about?"

"Winter won't touch you or Terrance."

The barrel was cold in her hand. She took a metaphorical shot in the dark. "And Hester?"

The match blew out. The scent of sulfur drifted over. Luke's voice went darker than the night. "No one will touch Hester."

A shiver went down her spine. "Brian is unpredictable."

"Brian is under control."

"Is that why you're out here on my porch standing guard?"

"I wasn't standing, I was sitting. And I wasn't guarding, I was waiting."

"For what?"

"For you."

Something in the way he said that raised the hairs on the back of her neck. "You might've had a long wait."

Another scrape and another flare of light. In the glow of the flame, she saw Luke's expression. The corners of his eyes were crinkled as if something were amusing. It better not be her. She wasn't in the mood for his jokes.

"The one thing you are, Petunia Wayfield, is predictable."

No one ever said that about her before. She didn't like him saying it about her now. "Excuse me?"

Shaking out the match, he said, "It's not my pardon you need to be begging. You let Ace down."

"Whether I did or not is none of your business."

"Ordinarily, you'd be right." As he stood, his shadow stretched out before him, encroaching into her space. He took a step toward her. "But Ace and I go way back."

She'd forgotten how tall he was. A little bit bigger than Ace. Maybe she'd just never noticed because whenever Ace was around she couldn't see anybody else. Or maybe Luke was just better at blending into his smile. He took another step. She stood, that trickle of warning expanding.

His smile glimmered in the dark. "Thank you."

"For what?"

"Making this easy."

By the time she realized what he was up to it was too late. With seemingly effortless ease, he grabbed her hand and pulled her forward. The quilt that had been keeping her warm became a muffling prison, trapping her arms and blocking her view as he heaved her over his shoulder and her world turned upside down. A swat on her butt cut off her scream. Even through the quilt she could feel the warning.

"Stop struggling. You want this."

This. He kept mentioning *this*. She wiggled harder. What was *this*? "Put me down."

"In a minute."

"Now!"

His chuckle jostled her out of sync with his steps. "In case you haven't figured it out by now, Petunia, I'm not a man to take orders."

"Ace will kill you."

"Maybe."

There was no *maybe* about it. Her "He will" lost its impact as he stepped down. She had no idea of where he was heading. She opened her mouth to scream. It came out as an "Uff" as he stepped up. She grabbed as she started to slip, finding nothing but material to hold on to.

"If you don't stop, you're going to get us both killed."

She couldn't see his face. She didn't know if he was joking. Erring on the side of caution, she held still. It made more sense to conserve her strength. At some point he had to unwrap her, and when he did, she was going to kill him. In the meantime, she'd try reason.

"What are you up to?"

He knocked on a door. "Settling a debt."

He ignored her "To whom?" The door creaked and they were in motion again. His footsteps were hollow markers. Wherever they were, it was empty. Maybe even deserted. The sound of the door closing echoed behind them. The acrid taste of fear filled her mouth.

Ace!

She wished he could hear her. She wished he were here. She wished she'd never balked when he'd asked for her trust. Because that was what it had all been about, she realized, whether from all the blood rushing to her head or just all the time she'd spent mulling on it, what Ace had wanted was her trust displayed in obedience.

"I'm coming up," Luke called out. She pushed up against his back. With a grunt he bounced her back down. "Just a warning," he called out to whomever was in the house. "You get trigger happy, and you will regret it."

That got a response but beyond recognizing the muffled voice was male, she had nothing. Her fingers tight-

ened around the quilt. She was alone in a vacant house
with at least two men. Concentrating, she forced her
breathing to slow and worked on bringing it to even. She
was going to need her wits about her when Luke got to
wherever he was going.

"I brought you a present." Luke's grip on her shifted.

In the next minute the world tilted, and she was set
on her feet. Instinct obliterated her calm. She stumbled
into a bolt, tripped and fell. There was cursing, all of it
familiar, another off-balancing tug on the quilt and then
strong hands caught her and pulled her close.

"Goddamn it, Luke, what were you thinking carrying
her like that? Did you forget she might be pregnant?"

"Shit."

The quilt was pulled away from her face. Through
the hair covering her face, Petunia glared at Luke. She
wasn't ready for this.

"You're a miserable kidnapper."

Her glare bounced off the amused twist of his lips.
"But a hell of a best man."

Best man?

Ace brushed the hair from her cheek. She didn't let
her eyes turn his way. She wasn't ready.

"This is none of your business, Luke," Ace growled.

Luke took a step toward the door. "Obviously, I disagree."

"We don't even know yet if I'm with child," she said.
Someone had to point out the obvious.

Ace's grip tightened but Luke was the one who shook
his head. "You still think that has any bearing on anything?"

Yes. No. Maybe. She made the mistake of looking
at Ace. For in that brief instant, everything she felt she

could see in him she did. The longing. The wanting. The "maybe" fell by the wayside, followed quickly by the "no." Ace needed her the same as she needed him. Why had she never seen that? Touching the stubble on his cheek, she acknowledged the truth. Because she hadn't allowed herself to. Because she'd been afraid. "I'm sorry."

Ace's eyes narrowed. "Nothing's changed. I am as I always was."

Yes, he was. A gambler. A Ranger. Hell's Eight. A man. And beneath the seemingly precariousness of his lifestyle, Ace was a rock of stability. She cupped his cheek in her palm. She was the one who, for all her outward stability, was uncertain. "I know."

His gaze heated. "I don't play, Pet."

No, he didn't. And his intensity gave her pause. But only for a moment. Because this was Ace. And he fit her. And she him. "I know."

He didn't smile. She didn't care.

Without breaking eye contact with her he called, "Luke?"

"What?"

"Get out of here."

"My pleasure."

CHAPTER TWENTY-ONE

PET HELD IT together for ten seconds after the door closed. It was longer than Ace had expected. She was submissive but lost. Somewhere along the way, she'd learned giving in meant failure, and fight meant survival. He stroked his fingers through her hair, untangling a snarl. But she was here, determined to give him what he needed. Even if she did think he needed it all at once.

"Look at me, Pet."

She did, albeit slowly. Suspiciously. The nervousness in her gaze didn't upset him. It was to be expected. This was the beginning. She had a lot to learn about him. He had a lot to learn about her. The only difference was he was looking forward to the experience, whereas she was worried about what it would be. His proud independent I'll-believe-it-when-I-see-it woman was taking him on faith. He stroked his thumb over her plump lower lip. He'd never been given a more precious gift.

"I'm not going to turn into a monster, you know."

She licked her lips, leaving them a shining temptation. "I know."

He couldn't resist. On a murmured "Do you?" he took a kiss. Just a small one to carry him through the conversation. Her lips were soft and sweet. The tiny gasp tempting. Later he'd push her, test her, stretch her boundaries, but right now, this time, the first time, he just wanted to cherish her. Let her see what she meant to him. What it meant to be his woman on the most elemental of levels.

"I've waited a long time for you, Petunia Wayfield. Not anyone else. Not someone else. Or you as everyone else." He kissed her again a bit longer this time, relishing the flutter of her response. "You. As you are." He touched the pad of his thumb to her lip, feeling her focus in her sudden stillness. "Never doubt that."

She blinked the way she did when she was absorbing something. Grazing her cheek with his lips, he whispered against the lobe of her ear. "I know who you are, my Pet. Beneath everything, I see you."

He drew back. Panic flashed in her gaze.

He shook his head and pressed. "And I like what I see."

She sighed instead of blinking this time. Her breath wafted over his hand in a moist caress. "Why won't you just tell me what you want from me?"

"Because I don't know yet."

She actually tried to take a step back. He stopped her with the slightest of pressure against her nape. "No."

She halted at the order. That, he liked. "This isn't the end, Pet. It's our beginning."

Leaning back, she cocked her head. A little of the tension left her expression, and some of the impossible, lovable, tilting-at-windmills adventurer returned. "So you're gambling on us?"

"I'm making a very calculated bet."

"But still gambling."

So maybe he was. He lifted her chin with his thumb. "I don't give a shit." He'd prepared his whole life for this moment.

"Because you think you always win?"

It was his turn to smile. "Because I always win."

Her lips compressed wryly. "That wasn't what I said."

"It's what I heard."

She huffed. The amusement spread inside like rays of sunshine. "Is this what it's going to be like?"

He turned her slightly to the right. "Maybe."

She resisted. "Maybe?"

"A gambler doesn't tip his hand as easily as he tips his hat."

"You're not a gambler."

He turned her a bit more. "Of course I am."

"You're bored and frustrated, and the gambling alleviates that somewhat, but I suspect keeping you amused is not its main purpose."

"You do, huh?"

"I do."

He took a step forward, inching her back toward the bed. And she went, smooth as silk, that busy mind of hers consumed with reasoning rather than observing. He might have to work on her focus in the future. Then again, he decided as she mindlessly followed his lead, maybe not, because he could see that distraction being as useful in the future as it was now. The soft press of her thigh against the inside of his had his cock jerking in his pants, and the pull of the nightgown across her breast had it throbbing. Just the thought of her sprawled on that bed, thighs open and eager accepting, his for the taking—that had his heart pounding.

"Explain." He wanted her distracted just a little bit longer. Two steps to be exact.

"I've been thinking."

"Nothing new on that."

"About you."

"Should I be hurt, or I should be flattered?"

"Neither." Her pale amber brows pleated in a slight frown. "You should be looking smug, because I'm feeling a little bit embarrassed that I didn't see this earlier."

One step down. One more to go. "Oh?"

"Your whole life everyone thought you were good, and then all of a sudden you just become dissolute…?"

The backs of her legs hit the foot of the bed. "Oh!"

"Pet, I was and am a coldhearted son of a bitch."

"I don't agree."

"Figures." As he slid his hand across her cheek, the silk of her hair tangled around his fingers. He made a fist, anchoring them both. Him to her. Her to him. "And what did you deduce?"

He pulled her head back just a little, giving her that subtle tension that made her breath catch. Her lips parted. A soft little sigh escaped her control. He liked that and all the other telltale signs that said while her brain was working on one level, the rest of her was vividly aware of him. Woman to his man. Heart to his heart. Her nipples peaked beneath the thin muslin of her gown, tenting the fabric in greeting. If he turned her, he'd see their shadow through the light material. But he didn't need to turn her. His imagination was enough. He could see the pale pink of her rising for his mouth. Hardening at his breath. Inside, those rays of sunlight changed to fissions of lightning, recklessly flashing, arcing from him to her and then back again. Her breath caught. So did his. Lust blended with power. Desire with want. Strength with strength. Her gaze locked with his.

"Well?" he prompted.

She blinked. Her eyes dropped to his mouth. "It's an act. A way to get information."

"I'm a damn good gambler." He touched the inside of her leg with his outer thigh. They instinctively separated, making a place for him. He smiled. He did like her instincts.

"That just makes things easier," she finished on an airy squeak.

He hummed a noncommittal agreement.

Her breath was coming harder, pushing her breasts against the fabric. Small round mounds topped with hard peaks silky to the touch, warm. He wanted to see them. "Untie your nightdress."

She swallowed delicately. Her fingers came up to the ribbons. He liked that she began unlacing them immediately without quibbling, doing what he wanted with sensual obedience.

"Thank you."

She smiled. "I'm right, aren't I?"

She was still on the other. "You're many things. Smart, sexy, intelligent—" He lost his voice the second she pushed the gown off her shoulder letting the material slide down her soft white skin until it caught on her pert little nipples. He waited her for her to push it the rest of the way, but apparently, she'd learned a thing or two because instead of pushing, she let her fingers linger as she glanced at him from under her lashes. A siren all too willing to lure him to his downfall. And he was all too willing to go, but not to his death. They both knew this wasn't death. This was life, a gift he never thought to receive. With a jerk of his chin he indicated the precariously clinging fabric. "You stopped a little soon there."

"Did I?"

It was a challenge. An invitation. His cock went rock

hard. He did like her like this. "You angling for a spanking?"

He didn't miss the widening of her eyes. "Nope, though I think I probably wouldn't object to one if you gave it to me."

"So what are you angling for?"

Her smile turned sultry. "For you to do it yourself."

He'd be more than happy to, but first, "Ask me nicely."

"Please."

"Good girl."

His finger teased the edge of the material, tracing over her arm. Goose bumps sprang up immediately and so did his lust. The muslin quivered with the next breath. And his breath caught in the next as she shivered, but that fabric stubbornly refused to fall. Damn it. "You, my Pet, are too smart for your own good. And yes, you're right." That fabric had to give soon. "What tipped you off that I might not be all gambler?"

"The assayer job. It makes no sense for a gambler to take a job as an assayer. But it makes complete sense for an officer of the law to keep an eye on the claims around here."

He retraced his path up over her collarbone, coming to rest on the pulse. "I'm Hell's Eight."

"What does that mean?"

He thought back to those days. "I fought with Hell's Eight. I buried my family with Hell's Eight. I learned with Hell's Eight. I prospered with Hell's Eight. I owe them everything."

"They're your priority."

He shook his head. "They're my family." She had a lot to learn. "You're my priority."

He leaned in just a little farther, just enough to send

her off balance. She tumbled back, catching her weight on her hands. The mattress dipped. Her breasts pushed up, and he couldn't have asked for a more perfect invitation. "Now, that I like."

She frowned at his murmur. He knew she wanted to pursue the discussion, but he didn't. Everything he wanted was right before him. Sweet, willing woman, ripe with passion, the delicate lines of her body displayed to perfection, her legs spread for his pleasure. Running his nail over one taut peak, he chuckled as she jerked. If he hadn't caught her with a hand in the small of her back, she would have collapsed.

But again, no complaints. Draped over his arm she was elegant temptation. "Stay just like that."

"I don't know if I can."

"But you will."

Her "What makes you so sure" came out as a breathy challenge. So different from before. This was play, not resistance.

"Because it makes me happy."

She didn't have anything to say to that but a huff, which he ignored. They both knew she wanted him happy. It was her nature and pleasure. His blessing. The fine muslin between her legs caught on her mound. He could make out the lips of her vulva. He wanted to kneel between and taste her. Hell, he wanted to start at the top and just work his way down, tasting the cream of her orgasms and the salt of her pleasure and then when he'd had his fill, work his way back up again. He couldn't get enough of her, probably never would. She challenged his mind and his senses. She was ecstasy in female form. She was a…gift. A moment of divine intervention. She was…his Pet.

Grabbing the front of her gown, he tore it open. Her cry filled his ears as the pure lissome beauty of her form sent a growl to his throat. "Don't move." Grabbing the material lower down, he tore it again, revealing her dainty pussy and the trembling in her thighs.

Cupping the plump inside curve of the right one, he asked, "You're trembling. Scared?"

He had to be sure.

"I'm excited."

Her voice trembled as much as her legs. "Good."

"Easy for you to say."

That prompted a chuckle. "Yeah, it is. Spread your legs farther." She did but it wasn't wide enough. He wanted her fully open, completely accessible. Vulnerable. He knelt. "More."

Down the length of her body, she glared at him. "That's as far as they go."

Testing the tension along the inside he guessed it was. "We'll work on that."

"We will?"

Giving her thigh a light smack and a push, he nodded. "We will."

She didn't have much to say to that but it could have been because his lips were where his hand had been, and she went still. Very still. Her scent teased him. Womanly. Spicy. He needed to know how she tasted. It was his right.

She shifted her feet.

This time he tapped the outside of her thigh. "Did I tell you to move?"

"No."

He waited.

Her "For heaven's sake" made him smile. The play of muscles in her thighs as she returned her feet back to their original position made him moan. She was exquisitely made. Delightfully tuned to his senses. As he set his teeth against the soft flex, another "For heaven's sake" burst out. What the exclamation lacked in heat it made up for in anticipation. The woman might be nervous but she was more fire than trepidation. And it was that fire that drew him. In and out of bed.

Turning his head, he kissed the inside of the thigh, taking the soft flesh and sucking it gently. Her nails scratched against the quilt.

"I can't stay like this if you're going to do that."

He was going to do a hell of a lot more than that. He could see the first beads of moisture in the fine pale hair between her legs. She was aroused. So was he. Parting the puffy outer lips with his finger he found more of that thick cream. With slow circles that mimicked the rhythm of his tongue he spread it outward, covering the pink flesh until she glistened from the inside out. Her thighs trembled. The stress of her position was taking its toll, but more so than that was the anticipation of his touch and the knowing that he was looking at her. Nothing made a woman more emotionally vulnerable, more physically sensitive than knowing all her secrets were exposed. "You'll stay, what's more, you will enjoy it."

The quilt pulled up as she gathered it in her fists. "It? What's it?"

Slipping another finger in with the first, he parted her, revealing the flange of flesh concealing the prize he sought. He leaned in and with the utmost delicacy licked that spot once. Twice. The third time, he let his tongue linger. He took her moan as his cue to apply more pressure, circling and lapping, bringing forth more of what he craved.

"Ace!"

"Right here."

He would always be there for her.

Her body tensed. Her thighs quivered. She tasted of the sweetest nectar. She tasted of future promise, of growth, of dreams coming true. He couldn't get enough. He licked faster, driving her higher. Her body shook. He couldn't get close enough, deep enough. With a growl he lifted her legs over his shoulder, holding her up for his pleasure with a hand under her hips. The other he used to spread her wider before pulling the protective skin back from her clit. This time when he wiggled his tongue, her scream echoed in his ears. Her fingers grabbed at his hair.

"My God, stop, I mean…"

He didn't care what she meant. He wasn't stopping now, not until she screamed his name and the world exploded, and the only thing that existed was him and her and the surrender she couldn't help. He was hers, and she was his. After this they would both know it. After this, there would be no going back. Her taste filled his mouth. Her scent his nostrils. She was fucking his. He drove her higher; she fought harder. He could feel her starting to fight.

"No!" With a nip at her clit, he centered her.

"Ace!"

"Take it," he growled against her pussy. "Take what I'm giving you."

"I don't know—"

He cut her off. "I do." Another nip on her clit followed by a fast circle. "Trust me."

Her reaction was immediate. Her hands fisted his hair, opening and closing with the silent battle she fought. Taking full advantage of the little movement he allowed her, she drilled her shoulders into the bed, shaking her head in denial even as her body raced for what he offered. Too fast. She was going too fast.

"Not yet."

Her heels tattooed his back in a frustrated protest. "Yes."

"No." He wanted a little bit more. To savor this first little bit longer. She'd never surrender to him again the way she did tonight, with nothing but trust to guide her. He didn't want it rushed.

"I can't."

His cock throbbed painfully in his pants, adding its protest to hers. "You will."

"I can't, Ace. Not when you do that." She bucked against him. "I can't. I can't. I can't. I can't. I can't."

But she was. Clinging to him as if her sanity depended on it, but holding back, because he asked for it. And then he was the one that couldn't wait. He wanted to see her orgasm, taste it. Revel in it. "Come for me."

Slipping his finger inside her snug little vagina, he tested her slick heat. She was tight, but not too tight. He added another, sliding them in and out as he sucked on that turgid nub of flesh where all that sensation blossomed.

"Please!"

The *please* put him over the edge.

"Now," he ground out, pushing his fingers deep, searching for that certain spot. Covering his teeth with his lips before biting down, giving her a bit of pain to push her over that edge.

And she went. On a scream of his name, she went.

Body jerking, pussy pulsing, her nails ripping across his neck. Adding her own brand to his skin.

Yes!

He wanted the pain, the mark. The passion. He wanted everything she had to give. By morning she'd bear marks of her own. Savoring the burn, he gave her a moment to settle, suckling gently, easing her back to a simmering calm. Letting her legs slide down his arms, he stood and lowered her to the bed. He didn't follow her immediately. Instead, he just looked at her, from the tousled blond silk of her hair to the slender elegance of her feet. She was beautiful. So very beautiful. She took a shuddering breath. He placed his palm over her mound, centering her focus. Her gaze snapped to his.

"Good girl."

He saw the flash of resentment in her gaze, followed just as quickly by pride. She took another breath. And another. With a dip of his finger, he destroyed her grab for composure. He wanted her off balance. Her vagina clutched at him. She gasped again when he pumped it in tiny pulses, stroking the ultrasensitive inner tissue. Her breasts quivered with every breath, the normally creamy white skin flushed with residual passion. Atop each a berry-red nipple begged for attention. Coming down over her, on his way up to her kiss, he nibbled each. With a gasp, she grabbed his face and pulled his mouth to hers.

"I love you," she whispered into his mouth between frantic kisses.

The declaration sank all the way to his soul. This was his Pet. She didn't do anything by half measures. Sliding his arms around her, he rolled to his back, cuddling her above him. And she went easily, ending in a complacent, slack-thighed heap atop his chest. She wiggled and

scooted until they were hip to hip, chest to chest. Heartbeat to heartbeat. Stroking his hand down her hair, he
said the only thing that mattered, "Mine."

Her teeth brushed his shoulders. She bit delicately.
When he looked down she was looking up at him, a smile
on her lips. "You do like to drive me crazy."

He pushed her hair off her face. Some things needed
complete understanding. "No, I *love* to drive you crazy."

"My mistake."

She shifted her position, straddling him as she had
this afternoon. He allowed it, holding her steady. There
would be time later to teach her the finer points of what
it meant to be his woman, but right now he wanted to feel
her love pouring over him, filling all the empty spaces,
bringing the light out of the dark, bringing him home.
And she did, unbuckling his belt, then his pants, pushing them down when he lifted his hips. In an endearingly
awkward move that had him gritting his teeth, she took
that first inch.

Home. The word echoed in his mind as his cock entered her heat. He was home. The thought wouldn't leave
his head. When he should be thinking of thrusting, he
was consumed with thoughts of Pet. Pet waiting for him
at the door; Pet cooking dinner. Pet on her knees welcoming him with a warm mouth and a happy smile, in
his bed, spread across his thighs. Pet big with his child.

Placing his hands on her slender hips, he stilled her
descent. He wanted, no, needed, to see her. Really see
her. His woman.

"What?"

"I want to look at you."

It was a bald statement that produced the predictable
hesitation. She was beautiful with the light from the

lamps reflected off the golden strands of her hair. Her skin glowed with a sheen of passion. Her hard-tipped breasts begged for his mouth. She was beautiful. So fucking beautiful. His gaze dropped to where they joined. His hands were dark against the pale skin of her hips. His cock appeared impossibly huge between her thighs. So close to paradise.

His.

Inside. Outside. Now and into the future. This wasn't for this week. Next month. Or next year. This was… forever. Pet was his ace in the hole. The wild card tossed in his forever mix. The game he'd never played. Because he'd been afraid, he realized. Afraid he'd never find a woman with his commitment, with his strength.

"You're marrying me, Pet."

She fell forward, bracing her weight on his chest. Her hair tumbled about his face, partially blocking the light so he saw her expression in bits of color as she flipped her hair back. The white of her teeth, the blue of her eye, the red of her lip. Part, when he wanted it all. The sting of her nails blended with the burn of lust.

Gathering her hair at her nape he tipped her head back, and then he had what he wanted. All her love. Her passion. Her humor. It shone down on him right along with her happiness.

"We don't even know if I'm pregnant."

"I don't care."

She wiggled her hips. A creamy drop of fluid dripped down his cock. He licked his lips, remembering her sweet taste. Damn, he wanted her. His cock jerked impatiently.

Her smile slipped. "Do you promise to love me even on those days I forget to trust?"

"I will love you always." Tears misted her eyes. He

couldn't stand to see her cry. He pulled her in for another kiss. "But that doesn't mean I won't spank you when it's called for."

He slapped her sexy ass for emphasis. Then, because she tightened and squealed so delightfully, he did it again, shivering as those hot, silky muscles clenched around him and another drop of fluid followed the first, bathing them both in desire. "But just to be clear, this is how it's going to be between us," he managed to grind out through the haze of lust. "First you're going to fuck me, then we're going over to drag the judge out of bed and then—"

She worked down on him. Taking a quarter, a half, and it wasn't enough. It was never going to be enough.

He thrust. She gasped as she took him all, her nails digging into his chest. "And then?"

"And then," he gritted out, tilting her head back farther. "You're going to stand in front of him, still wet with my seed, and you're going to make an honest man out of me."

"I am?"

"You are."

On a soft, pleasure-filled sigh, she sealed their fate.

It DIDN'T GO the way Ace had planned. The judge wouldn't get up. By the time he did answer the door, Hester was awake. As soon as the word *wedding* was mentioned, all control slipped out of Ace's hands and into the women's. His access to Petùnia had been cut off, and even his time with her had become limited because of all the plans that somehow "had to happen" in addition to the holidays. Now a month later, Christmas had come and gone, and he was standing at the altar, the bluest balls a man ever had tucked inside his pants, family and friends filling the pews, waiting for Pet to formally give herself to him.

He folded his hands in front of him and immediately changed his mind when his ribs protested. Beside him, Luke chuckled.

"Petunia's dad weighed in a bit heavily on his daughter's pregnancy?"

He wasn't happy. But Ace was. In a soul-deep way he'd never expected to feel.

He touched his tender rib. He'd have been happier if Petunia's dad wasn't a big Swede with fists like sledgehammers and an uncompromising attitude. "The son of a bitch wouldn't approve the marriage without tossing an opinion."

Cocking his eyebrow, Luke asked quietly, "How many of those opinions did he land?"

"Three or four?" Truthfully, the first had left him so befuddled, he'd lost track. Been a long time since a man had been able to do that to Ace. Jarl Wayfield was a man to be reckoned with. The grudging respect irritated him even more.

"Shit, didn't you fight back at all?"

But not as much as that comment. It was Ace's turn to cock a brow. "He's going to be my father-in-law. What do you think?"

"I think you should have forgotten he's going to be your father-in-law. That man has fists as big as a summer ham."

Ace pressed that tender spot again. "No shit."

Another clearing of his throat from the reverend.

"Oh, give it a rest, padre."

"We are in the Lord's house."

"Can't be disrespecting the Lord now, Ace," Tucker

offered helpfully from where he sat with his wife, Sallie Mae. Even sitting he towered over everyone.

"Especially when you're skating on thin ice with His good graces as it is," Caine added.

The front four pews were filled with the men of Hell's Eight and their women. Only Sam and his Bella couldn't make it. Center front was Tia and her husband, Ed. He wanted to pitch every smirking one of them out the brand-spanking-new stained-glass windows. The men anyway. "Why don't you send out a telegraph, all of you?"

So far no one outside the family knew for sure of Petunia's pregnancy.

"We considered it," Tracker tossed out.

"Even had my horse saddled up," Tracker's twin, Shadow, said too casually in that quiet, powder-keg way he had.

"What stopped you?"

It was Caden who answered. "Her father stepped off the stage."

"Those boys sending that letter saved me a heap of trouble."

Ace glared at Shadow. "If you wanted a fight so much where were you when he was kicking my ass?"

"Close enough to interfere if necessary."

That Ace didn't doubt. "You want a thanks for *almost* stepping in."

Shadow bared his teeth in that cold smile of his. "Wouldn't hurt."

Luke covered a laugh in a cough.

"It's not more than he deserved, taking advantage of Petunia like that," Maddie muttered loud enough for the whole congregation to hear.

"Damn it, Maddie. I asked her to marry me."

"Doesn't make it right."

"Actually—" The preacher began.

"It doesn't!" Maddie snapped.

Ace sighed. No, it didn't. "I'm sorry, Maddie. I know she's your friend." Too much of Maddie's past haunted her for her to be relaxed when it came to the people she loved.

Caden took Maddie's hand and tucked it under his arm. "Petunia is marrying the man she loves. Focus on that, Maddie. She loves him."

Ace rubbed his bruised jaw. Another gift from Petunia's father. With a name like Wayfield, he'd been expecting someone small and...businesslike. Not a bruiser like Jarl. Not even Tucker hit that hard. "No shit."

The preacher frowned at him. Frustration had Ace snapping, "The good Lord bore up under worse than a cussword in his day."

"Easy, Ace."

"I'm not some damned horse pitching a fit at the sight of a bridle, Luke."

"Didn't say you were, but you are jittery."

"Hell." Ever since last night's confrontation with his soon-to-be father-in-law, Ace had been possessed of an odd emotion. This morning he'd finally identified it. Fear. He was afraid Petunia wouldn't walk down that aisle today. Jarl Wayfield had made it very clear he had enough money and influence to buy his daughter out of anything, including the scandal of being an unwed mother.

A door hinge creaked at the back of the church. A squeak from the stool in front of the organ as Hester checked the disturbance. Turning back, she caught his eye as she flexed her fingers. "It's that time. If you're going to bolt, best do it now."

"I'm where I want to be."

"Let's hope Petunia feels the same," Luke hissed out of the corner of his mouth.

"Shut up, Luke." He didn't need his fears made real by speech.

Luke patted his coat pocket. "Just in case, I brought a flask."

Ace's response to that would have had him thrown out of the church if just then the organ hadn't wailed with one long, discordant note.

"Oops. Sorry about that," Hester apologized. "It's been a while."

She started again. The notes flowed. Ace clenched his fist. The door opened. For a heartbeat, nothing filled it. Something was shoved into his hand. Inside, a growl started. Where was Petunia? There'd be hell to pay if she thought she'd get out of this. If he had to, he'd follow her all the way to Massachusetts and drag her ass back. Let her daddy buy her out of that scandal. He started for the back of the church. Luke grabbed his arm. "Hold on. She's coming."

And so she was. Dressed in a pale blue dress with a fitted bodice and a voluminous skirt, a white veil covering the pale blond of her hair in a shimmering cloud, she walked beside her father, head high. Around her neck she wore his wedding gift. To others it looked like a gold necklace with an intricate clasp. Only they knew the significance of the collar. Only they needed to.

Luke elbowed him in the side. "Smile before you send her packing with all that glowering."

Ace didn't feel like smiling. He felt like…fetching his

bride. Shoving the flask back at Luke, he did just that. Ignoring the murmur of the crowd, he met her halfway. Jarl frowned. Petunia smiled wider.

"Hi."

The gold of the collar glowed through the mesh. "Hello, my Pet."

"I detest that nickname," Jarl snapped, his blue eyes so like his daughter's flaring beneath the thick head of graying blond hair.

Ace didn't spare Jarl a glance. "Then I won't call you it."

The man said something in his native tongue. Pews creaked as Tucker stepped free. Sallie Mae caught his arm. "Tucker!"

Ignoring the commotion with her usual calm, Petunia stood on tiptoe and tugged her father down so she could kiss his cheek. "Daddy?"

"What?"

She turned and faced Ace. Beneath the veil her fingers touched the choker. Love and confidence lit her smile as she said loud enough for everyone to hear. "This is my choice."

Four words he hadn't even known he needed to hear. Four words that shredded fear and replaced it with a bone-deep joy. With a crook of his finger he motioned her closer. With a cheeky smile, she took a small step. Terrance and Phillip alternately cheered and groaned. Hester just beamed.

He shook his head and pointed to the spot directly in front of him. Two more steps and she was there.

"Lift the veil."

She did. She was so beautiful, her eyes bright and shining, her skin flushed and glowing. She was radiant.

His wife. His lover. The soon-to-be mother of his child. His other half.

"Now, kiss me."

"Right here?"

He nodded. "Right here. Before God, our family and friends. Pledge yourself to me, Petunia Wayfield."

Her hands slid up the wool of his suit. Her legs pressed against his through the layers of clothing. The bliss of contact.

"Here, now?" the reverend protested. "But I haven't performed the ceremony yet."

"Looks like they're doing their own," Caine observed.

And they were. Hands linked behind his neck, Petunia tugged him down, breathing into his kiss as his mouth met hers. "I give myself to you, Ace Parker. All I am, all I ever will be, I give in to your care. You are my choice. For this lifetime and for all the ones to come, I'm yours."

He inhaled the vow, taking it deep, feeling it sink into that hollow core that had only known wildness for so long. Feeling it expand, filling all the nooks and crannies until certainty ruled. The words when they came, came from there. Her gift magnified and reflected back. Slipping his hand under the bun at the nape of her neck, tilting her head back just a little more, he felt that quiver of pleasure that always went through her when he took control. And it was his turn to smile. The only time he'd bet on the wild card. And he'd won. Grabbing her around the waist, he spun her a quarter turn.

"I goddamn love you, Petunia Parker. With everything in me, I love you and always will."

He kissed her then, hard and deep, letting his love, his passion, his everything, pile into that kiss. Stealing her balance and her breath in one smooth dip. It was hot.

It was torrid. It was scandalous. He couldn't imagine it ending. Fifty years from now he'd be kissing her just like this and she'd be taking it, begging for more, just like this, because she was who she was and he was who he was and together they were...*this*. Heat. Magic. Balance. Perfect. Around them he heard cheering, shocked exclamations, protests. He didn't fucking care. He had his Pet. The world was right.

His smile faded. Seeing the question in her eyes, it was his turn to whisper. He only had one word. One word to convey his love. His guidance. His loyalty. His protection. His forever.

His thumb pressed the delicate gold collar against her throat. "Mine."

All question disappeared.

It was enough.

* * * * *

JULIE PLEC

From the creator of *The Originals*, the hit spin-off television show of *The Vampire Diaries*, come three never-before-released prequel stories featuring the Original vampire family, set in 18th century New Orleans.

Available now!   Coming March 31!   Coming May 26!

Family is power. The Original vampire family swore it to each other a thousand years ago. They pledged to remain together always and forever. But even when you're immortal, promises are hard to keep.

Pick up your copies and visit
www.TheOriginalsBooks.com
to discover more!

HQN™

www.HQNBooks.com

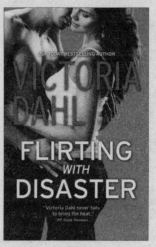

REQUEST YOUR
FREE BOOKS!

2 FREE NOVELS
FROM THE ROMANCE COLLECTION
PLUS 2 FREE GIFTS!

YES! Please send me 2 FREE novels from the Romance Collection and my 2 FREE gifts (gifts are worth about $10). After receiving them, if I don't wish to receive any more books, I can return the shipping statement marked "cancel." If I don't cancel, I will receive 4 brand-new novels every month and be billed just $6.24 per book in the U.S. or $6.74 per book in Canada. That's a savings of at least 22% off the cover price. It's quite a bargain! Shipping and handling is just 50¢ per book in the U.S. and 75¢ per book in Canada.* I understand that accepting the 2 free books and gifts places me under no obligation to buy anything. I can always return a shipment and cancel at any time. Even if I never buy another book, the two free books and gifts are mine to keep forever.

194/394 MDN F4XY

Name	(PLEASE PRINT)	

Address		Apt. #

City	State/Prov.	Zip/Postal Code

Signature (if under 18, a parent or guardian must sign)

Mail to the Harlequin® Reader Service:
IN U.S.A.: P.O. Box 1867, Buffalo, NY 14240-1867
IN CANADA: P.O. Box 609, Fort Erie, Ontario L2A 5X3

Want to try two free books from another line?
Call 1-800-873-8635 or visit www.ReaderService.com.

* Terms and prices subject to change without notice. Prices do not include applicable taxes. Sales tax applicable in N.Y. Canadian residents will be charged applicable taxes. Offer not valid in Quebec. This offer is limited to one order per household. Not valid for current subscribers to the Romance Collection or the Romance/Suspense Collection. All orders subject to credit approval. Credit or debit balances in a customer's account(s) may be offset by any other outstanding balance owed by or to the customer. Please allow 4 to 6 weeks for delivery. Offer available while quantities last.

Your Privacy—The Harlequin® Reader Service is committed to protecting your privacy. Our Privacy Policy is available online at www.ReaderService.com or upon request from the Harlequin Reader Service.

We make a portion of our mailing list available to reputable third parties that offer products we believe may interest you. If you prefer that we not exchange your name with third parties, or if you wish to clarify or modify your communication preferences, please visit us at www.ReaderService.com/consumerchoice or write to us at Harlequin Reader Service Preference Service, P.O. Box 9062, Buffalo, NY 14269. Include your complete name and address.

ROM13R

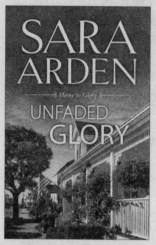

SARAH
McCARTY

77705	SHADOW'S STAND	___ $7.99 U.S.	___ $9.99 CAN.
77699	CADEN'S VOW	___ $7.99 U.S.	___ $9.99 CAN.
77653	TRACKER'S SIN	___ $7.99 U.S.	___ $9.99 CAN.
77627	TUCKER'S CLAIM	___ $7.99 U.S.	___ $9.99 CAN.
77626	SAM'S CREED	___ $7.99 U.S.	___ $9.99 CAN.
77625	CAINE'S RECKONING	___ $7.99 U.S.	___ $9.99 CAN.

(limited quantities available)

TOTAL AMOUNT	$ _____
POSTAGE & HANDLING	$ _____
($1.00 FOR 1 BOOK, 50¢ for each additional)	
APPLICABLE TAXES*	$ _____
TOTAL PAYABLE	$ _____

(check or money order—please do not send cash)

To order, complete this form and send it, along with a check or money order for the total above, payable to HQN Books, to: **In the U.S.:** 3010 Walden Avenue, P.O. Box 9077, Buffalo, NY 14269-9077; **In Canada:** P.O. Box 636, Fort Erie, Ontario, L2A 5X3.

Name: _____

Address: _____ City: _____

State/Prov.: _____ Zip/Postal Code: _____

Account Number (if applicable): _____

075 CSAS

*New York residents remit applicable sales taxes.
*Canadian residents remit applicable GST and provincial taxes.

HQN™
www.HQNBooks.com

PHSMC0215BL